Daughter of the Mob

ILANA QUINN

This book is dedicated to my parents, who inspired my love of literature and history.

Table of Contents:

CHAPTER 1

New York City, Upper East Side, October 1954

Pamela Anne Kelly watched the flame of the candle before her as it flickered, casting mottled streaks of indigo and crimson upon the foggy windowpane. Serpentine threads of smoke overpowered the comfort of the soft golden light and warmth slithering into her lungs, making her cough.

Sitting across from her date for the evening—Ivy League law graduate Timothy Atwell, she tried to ignore the dark lipstick stain on the side of his cheek that had not been from her.

She watched in silence as her date sliced his steak, carefully carving up the hulk of meat with the measured precision of a Venetian sculptor. His silver wristwatch gleamed in the golden glow of candlelight, and he smacked his thin lips in a churlish manner.

She looked down at her own dainty plate of peas, carrots, and salmon. Her food was practically untouched except for a slight scrambling of the peas and a crescent-shaped slice gone from the scaly neck of the fish.

She hated eating fish—or any kind of creature. She loved animals and detested the idea of consuming their pitiful carcasses, though Timothy taunted her endlessly about that sensibility.

"You're not hungry." Timothy's chewing muffled his baritone voice, letters slurred together and nearly indistinguishable. Clearly, his indulgence in gin and sherry belied his usual care for table etiquette. Just the other night, he had scolded her for chewing her bubblegum too loudly.

It wasn't until he raised his blue eyes to Pamela that she realized he was waiting for her reply.

"Not very," she dabbed the corners of her mouth with her napkin, subconsciously pushing the legs of her chair with her ankles sideways so it angled her away from him.

"You don't like this place? Your mother told me it was your favorite." He leaned forward. "Honestly, Pamela, before I know it, you'll be a beatnik just like your commie brother. You've been reading that rubbish Kerouac, haven't you?"

A male server minced over to the table, granting some much-needed relief from the exceedingly terse exchange. "Is everything satisfactory, sir and madame?"

While Pamela nodded, Timothy shook his head. "Absolutely *nothing* was satisfactory. You can tell your chef that the steak was too dry, and not the rare one I had requested."

"I am very sorry, sir. I will inform him of your displeasure immediately." The server bowed before scurrying back to the kitchen like a tailed lizard.

Pamela was tongue-tied. She was embarrassed to be seen out with such a rude man, especially when people assumed the pair to be a married couple. She had been out with Timothy Atwell many times over the past year and it seemed with every new outing, he only became less agreeable and more mean-spirited.

"Pamela, I have something to ask you." Timothy ignored her intensifying discomfort—or else he was too busy savoring his last bite of steak to notice. His Adam's apple bulged as he swallowed the final piece. "We've been going steady for a year now. How would you feel if we got hitched?"

The question was so abrupt that Pamela had to believe he was joking.

He had brought her out to dinner only to humiliate her by ogling their pretty blonde server, then disappearing for half an hour without saying where he was going. When he returned, the evidence of his mischief had been written across his lipstick-smeared face.

It was already unbearable, hearing whispers of Timothy's unfaithfulness among her mother's social circle. But having him betray her at their first-anniversary dinner was far worse than any rumor. Pamela was often told that men were prone to dalliances and liaisons—that it was only natural for them to act so recklessly. Apparently, in Europe, it was common for men to keep mistresses with their wives' knowledge. But such a thing did not sit well with Pamela.

Pamela ran her hand through her thick blonde hair, her polished finger snagging a curl. "I don't understand why you're asking me this *now*."

"What?" Timothy demanded, irritated by her resistance. "What is there to think about? Our mothers practically arranged our union when we were kids. Your father and mine do business together, and our folks are some of the wealthiest people in New York. Can't you see *everyone* expects us to end up together? You'd be selfish enough to disappoint them?"

Pamela hated the cold logic that ran through his words. Perhaps it was his law degree or his family's old money, but he always seemed to speak as he knew better than her.

"What kind of man proposes marriage moments after..." She wasn't even sure how to phrase what Timothy had done with the waitress, so she let her voice ebb into silence before voicing the thing.

But Timothy wasn't listening. Yet again, his attention was ensnared by a brunette woman striding into the restaurant, a fox fur scarf hugging her slender neck. She was likely in her thirties, walking with the relaxed poise of an elegant woman and matching the definition of a *Camellia beauty*. Perhaps she would be his second conquest of the night.

The thought sent Pamela out of her chair.

"Where are you off to?" Timothy demanded, hardly extracting his gaze from the brunette.

"Home." She removed her eyes from Timothy's stolid profile and swung her coat about her slender shoulders, wanting to disappear within the heavy tweed fabric. "I am quite through with this evening. If you haven't noticed my discomfort, you are quite blockheaded."

"Before giving me an answer?" Timothy rose after Pamela, baring his teeth in a manner that reminded her of some brutish beast. "I'm only kidding, Pam. Let me walk you outside. You can hear me out. Okay?"

Pamela was incredulous, but after Timothy paid their bill and buttoned up his overcoat, she accompanied him out onto the street.

New York City was a lovely place at night.

Though the moon and stars were hardly visible against the backdrop of twinkling city lights, the sapphire of the sky acted as a pleasant replacement—neon signs shivering against the thick night. Men and women brandished their sports jackets and swing dresses as if in a celebratory parade, going to and from various dinner clubs, parties, motion pictures, concerts, and restaurants.

The scents of gasoline, horse manure left by the carriages in Central Park and women's flowery perfume combined to form a puzzling aroma.

Under different circumstances, Pamela would have enjoyed the scenery.

Timothy grabbed Pamela's hand, his skin cool and clammy. He pulled her over to the side of an Italian restaurant, where a leaning oak tree granted them some privacy. "Now tell me why you don't want to marry me. Be reasonable about this, Pam."

Pamela surveyed her suitor's pursed lips, the creased brow beneath his close-cropped brown hair, and his liquid blue eyes.

Misinterpreting her earnest self-reflection for devotion, Timothy leaned forward. He hooked his fingers around her face, aiming his steak-saturated lips at her mouth.

Before his lips could make contact, Pamela jolted back. "Timothy! Please! You just kissed another woman with that mouth, and now you want to kiss me?"

"What I do is none of your business!" Timothy growled, releasing her. "Besides, if you weren't such a square, perhaps I wouldn't have to seek amusement elsewhere."

Rage surging through her, Pamela wrenched herself away from him, meeting his surprised blue eyes with a glare. "We're through, Timothy Atwell. Don't bother calling. Ever again."

Pamela stood outside the door of her family's Fifth Avenue apartment. She bit the inside of her lip as she waited for a moment, hoping to collect every fragment of courage within her person to confront her mother.

Running the doorbell, she heard the ominous march of feet echo down the hallway, then saw the door crack open to reveal her mother's concerned face.

"Mother," Pamela said the name as though uttering a curse.

Letting the door open, Pamela followed her mother through the winding corridor to the parlor, where they wordlessly slumped into the velvet upholstery of the sofa together. Pamela removed her flatties—her mother said she was too tall to wear pumps like other girls—and began massaging her aching feet.

Though the heat of the fireplace blanketed her in a comforting physical warmth, goosebumps still speckled the flesh on Pamela's pale arms. Leaning forward in her seat, she pinned her attention to the red and orange flames gorging pieces of wood. Soon, she knew she would metaphorically be among them.

"Barbara called," Caroline Kelly released the words as a sigh, dipping her chin so that Pamela was forced to stare into the endless frosty blue of her eyes.

"Mrs. Barbara Atwell?" Pamela asked, fear cresting in her throat.

"Yes, my dearest friend, Mrs. Barbara Atwell. Frankly, I'm not sure we know any other. *She is* your beau's mother, after all." Caroline sighed heavily, the harsh lines between her eyebrows marring her rigid face. "She informed me you rejected her son's proposal."

Pamela let the information hang between them. She had resolved not to speak unless she needed to. Between Timothy's outrageous display and her mother's apparent ire, she had little energy left.

Caroline cleared her throat, fixing the strand of white pearls around her swan-like neck with manicured hands. She had always boasted about her flawless hands. "I assume this rejection was some kind of misunderstanding?"

"It wasn't a misunderstanding."

"I beg your pardon?"

"I declined his offer. I do not love him, Mother, and he doesn't love me. He is a terrible oaf."

"*Love* you? Of course not. How could he love you, when you have not yet married?" Caroline rose to exhibit her skeletal frame—almost unnatural for a middle-aged mother of three grown children—and began a walking survey of the impressive room. Her stiletto high heels crashed against the linoleum floor like the slamming of keys across a pianoforte.

It was only natural for Caroline Kelly to be concerned. After all, Pamela was not prone to irregularity. She was a wholesome American girl, from a wholesome American family, with wholesome American dreams. What kind of obedient daughter would reject the hand of such an accomplished young lawyer, from one of the best types of folk on the Upper East Side?

The only thing that exempted the Kelly family from being considered a flawless clan was the much-discussed heritage of the patriarch, Patrick Stuart Kelly, Caroline's husband and Pamela's father.

Disapproving neighbors had whispered that Patrick, who had been going by the name Stuart, was, in fact, a bog-trotter: an Irish immigrant from Dublin. He had fled Ireland with his parents in childhood, desperate to taste the sweet nectar of the American Dream.

Patrick, or Stuart, depending on who you asked, began his career as a janitor, and eventually founded his own construction company: Stuart Kelly & Sons. Though he had been the president of one of the wealthiest construction companies in New York City when Caroline met him, her family had shunned her for her decision to marry new money, and Catholic money at that. Eventually, they overcame their uneasiness, and Caroline, one of the most eligible girls in Upper State, New York, married a self-made Irish millionaire.

"You are a foolish child, Pamela." Caroline scolded, glaring down at her daughter.

"Mother, I can't marry him. He is an absolute pig! You must know how I feel. You and Father married against your parents' wishes. Don't I deserve to marry someone for the same reasons?"

The pair stared at each other.

Pamela had never spoken so much to her mother at one time. She was the quiet, composed daughter who respected her parents' wishes and did as she was told. She had always been.

"I married your father because he provided for me."

It had not exactly been a love match, and if it had, it had been one-sided. Stuart wanted a dutiful trophy wife to affirm his power, and Caroline, being fifteen years younger than him, fancied herself in love, smitten with the idea that an older gentleman desired her hand in marriage. Yes, other men had pursued her, but she had always enjoyed a challenge. She was the most beautiful girl at finishing school, the winner of 1924 Miss New York, and a proper beauty queen through and through.

And then she met the enigmatic businessman.

Stuart had been introduced to Caroline during the prohibition when they had crossed paths at a New York speakeasy in the middle of a blizzard. Stuart had asked her to dance, and dance they did, galloping to the Fox-Trot and the Charleston and consuming glass after glass of illegal alcohol.

Eventually, any trace of love dwindled and died.

Predictably, Stuart was the breadwinner. He was often absent. When his busy schedule freed up, he would claim the time for his friends at the country club, or spend hours on the phone with a potential business partner. Family dinners were often sat behind the television screen, and the conversation was limited to a cordial greeting or parting word.

In the early years, Caroline and Stuart had enjoyed a relatively affectionate relationship. However, after the successive births of three healthy children, Stuart had vanished from anything outside of his role as a publicly formidable spouse and conversation piece.

Stuart Kelly was a philanderer, but he knew how to excuse his behavior and diminish any suspicion in his wife's mind. A mysterious woman's glove found on the floor of Stuart's automobile, balmy with Moonlight Mist by Gourielli, could be pardoned as the property of a business associate or secretary. Stuart could gift a lace chemise in the guest bedroom as a present for Mrs. Kelly at the last minute, though he would never see her wear it.

Caroline had resigned herself to the life of a European wife: hearing everything but saying nothing. Calls from Southern belles and cocktail girls became ingrained into her routine, but she attempted to convince herself that they were irrelevant.

She would answer their questions with a voice as saccharine-sweet as synthetic honey. "Yes," she always said, "my husband is absent at the moment."

Caroline took tremendous satisfaction in reminding the anonymous girls that she was married to Stuart and they were not. The women were shadowy phantoms of another world: one she would and could never cross. They were harlots, simpletons, and would secure nothing from her husband other than his ever-fleeting affection. Then, they would be forgotten from Stuart's life, like once glorious candle flames snuffed out and faltering in smoke.

Caroline was the matriarch of one of the most powerful families on Seventh Avenue. She was content to enjoy the perks of her social status, both financial and social.

"I don't want to marry a man simply because he can provide for me." Pamela choked out, her eyes watering with tears.

She wasn't blind. She had seen the tension between her parents, and she had always promised herself that she would be different. She would find a man who would tolerate her: love her even. Her children would see them laugh together and never doubt for a moment that they loved deeply.

"You are being horrifically stupid, Pamela." Caroline spoke, her blue eyes narrowed with seething rage, "You haven't considered my feelings, now, have you? Barbara is one of my dearest friends, and she'll never forgive me if you turn her beloved Timothy down. And what will your father make of this disobedience?"

Pamela's stomach tightened with guilt. She hated disappointing her parents, especially her father. The reason she had gone out with Timothy had been to please him.

Pamela would have much preferred to further pursue her education than be courted by a man she didn't care for. She had always wanted to follow the rest of her female classmates off to college, even if the reason they went was only to get an M.R.S. degree, while she wanted to study literature, Art History and romantic languages.

She was one of the best pupils in her graduating year, receiving high-class honors and many awards. All of her teachers had recommended that she attend a women's college. But Caroline Kelly did not believe in the merits of education for young women like Pamela. She believed that the integrity of America required strict adherence to the nuclear family order—with women tending the household and men earning prestigious degrees and money.

Pamela did not let her mother's expectations damper her dreams.

She wanted to travel someday, and set off into the world like an explorer in her childhood books. She wanted a splendid adventure, like the ones described in novels such as *Around the World in 80 Days*, or *Swiss Family Robinson*. She didn't know how or where, but she knew that if she remained on Seventh Avenue for an indefinite amount of time, she would surely wallow in self-pity for the rest of her life.

"I'm sorry Mother. I—I..." Pamela had run out of reasons for rejecting Timothy Atwell. But wasn't one enough?

"I understand, my dear Pamela. You acted out of impulsivity, and nothing more. You did not mean it. I will call Barbara and tell her and dear Timothy to meet us at the Biltmore for lunch," Caroline sighed, striding over to the telephone to make the ill-fated call.

CHAPTER 2

"*What did you say?*" Barbara Atwell leaned forward on her pale elbows, the crimson-red tablecloth beneath her crinkling to match the confused expression on her face.

Light poured from the glittering chandeliers hanging from the Biltmore Hotel ceiling where the group was having brunch, illuminating the society lady's soft features and chestnut-brown bob.

In contrast to her mother, Pamela had always found Barbara to be rather amiable.

She had known the woman since childhood when she would visit the Atwell's grand Victorian mansion on Carnegie Hill to play dress-up with the sumptuous damask dresses and feathered, ostrich-plume hats. Barbara had been quite accommodating with the children who visited her husband's inherited property, allowing them to roam the manicured lawns without chaperones and sneak pastries from the kitchen without consequence.

But on that rainy afternoon, something in Barbara Atwell's polished demeanor had shifted. Anger boiled just beneath the surface of her booming voice, like a volcano about to erupt.

"I am sorry, Mrs. Atwell, but I said that I cannot marry your son. I know I told my mother I would reconsider, but his continued unfaithfulness prevents me from accepting a proposal." Pamela let her eyes wander over toward her mother, who was simmering over her untouched plate of toast, marmalade, and assorted berry jams.

"*Unfaithfulness*?" Barbara's mouth hung open. "What are you accusing my Timothy of?"

Pamela felt Timothy squirm beside her. His cologne tangled with Barbara's perfume, making her throat itch. She hadn't wanted the server to seat them together, but her mother had insisted, as though his nearness might make her change her mind.

Timothy's cheeks flushed. The expression could have been endearing if placed within a different context. He glared at Pamela. "I don't know what she's talking about, mother. I've been nothing but good to her. Frankly, I suspect *she's* been going around with other fellows. Everyone at the club says it."

He was referring to the gentlemen's club on Sixth Avenue he often frequented to play pool and discuss the stock market with other young lawyers and aged businessmen.

The accusation was preposterous. They both knew Pamela had never been the most popular girl. Men had rarely approached her, perhaps because of her reserved nature and affinity of reading books instead of going on dates. Besides, between attending an all-girls school and never venturing off to college, she had met few eligible bachelors outside of her mother's unpleasant social circle, and most of them were already courting the daughters of society ladies.

At that moment, Pamela desperately wanted to spill some of her ketchup onto Timothy's crisp white cardigan. Or slap him across the face—like an outraged heroine in one of her favorite motion pictures.

"You *know* he's being ridiculous." Pamela snapped, overcome by the anger pulsing through her.

What was Timothy trying to do? Coerce her into a marriage where neither of them would be happy? Force their future children to endure their shared unhappiness? Surely he could find a more agreeable girl who was willing to ignore his bad habits—though she hoped it would not come to that.

"How *dare* you say something so vile!" Barbara's eyes flashed with anger. Turning to Pamela's mother, she straightened her shoulders. "Caroline, dear, I'm no longer sure that Pamela is well-suited for my Timothy. I thought she was quiet and well-mannered, but she seems to share more in common with your beatnik son than your daughter."

"Pamela's rudeness is only because of her wedding day jitters. Every soon-to-be bride is nervous when expecting her marriage," Caroline laughed apologetically, though her eyes were pale with terror.

Pamela couldn't take it anymore.

She stood up, her hands flying over the broad skirt of her lavender satin gown. "I'm feeling faint."

She grabbed her purse and flew through the hotel lobby, passing walls of beautiful paintings she would have enjoyed under different circumstances.

As she slipped through the glass hotel doors, the cool air of the city caressed her bare neck and face. She could feel the footsteps of her mother pound after her, but she refused to look back. She was treated like a disobedient child long enough. Even as a child, she had been berated and insulted—like she was an unwelcome visitor or an unwanted piece of furniture without feelings or thoughts of her own.

She gulped back tears, hearing Lorna's soft words drumming through the back of her mind. "You're not like them. You're special. That's why they treat you badly."

"If I was truly as good as you say I am, then why would they hate me so much?" Pamela had trembled, letting herself slump onto Lorna's soft shoulder as they rode the bus back from Central Park. It was springtime, so flowers were growing from the trees and spilling over the wooden garden planters that were suspended from apartment windows.

Lorna's dark eyes had glistened with tears and the recognition of something that Pamela could not quite see herself. "Because you're different, Pamela Anne. The kinda different that makes the world a better place. And some people don't *like* different."

Pamela leaned her back against the side of the brick hotel wall, staring into the river of people that rushed continuously up and down the street. If she stepped into the rhythm of the city, she would be lost forever. She would become someone else, with a new job, new friends, and perhaps even an education. Her mother could never find her.

"Pamela!"

Pamela twisted her head around to glimpse her mother crashing through the hotel exit, her eyes wide with rage.

She glanced back at the swarm of people.

For the first time in her life, she joined them.

Pamela did not waste time in returning to her apartment and collecting some things. She purchased a ticket at the Grand Central Railway Station that headed directly to Greenwich Village. If she was going to deny her mother's wishes, she decided it would be best to stay with her elder brother, Sean, the black sheep of the family.

She had only seen her brother once since he had moved out, but she remembered the day it had happened, as clear as glass.

He had graduated from college and told her parents that he wanted to become a writer. He was disillusioned with conventional society, exhausted with the idea of inheriting a construction company he cared little about, and working under a father he found impossible to impress.

The day after he revealed his dissatisfaction, they sent him packing with nothing but a handful of loose change, and the Kelly patriarch accusing him of being a communist.

The two younger children, Pamela and Cecelia, were forbidden from visiting their eldest sibling, but in her sophomore year, Pamela looked up his address in a phonebook and bought a ticket to go see him.

Pamela knew that if she confided in her sister Cecelia: the suburban housewife and probably the inspiration for every homemaker magazine, she would be chastised and sent off to marry Timothy within the month.

After twenty-odd minutes, she pushed her recollections aside and found herself at Sean's apartment door. Unlatching the lock, her brother's whiskered but recognizable face emerged in the candlelit darkness.

"Pam?" He stared at her in disbelief, wiping bread crumbs from his scraggly beard and tossing his napkin to the floor as he gaped at her with awe.

"Sean." Pamela breathed a sigh of relief. She found it strange, saying his name after so long. It almost felt like she was speaking in a foreign language.

"What are you doing here? Well... I guess I should tell you to come in. I have some... company over. But of course, my kid sister is welcome here anytime!" He stammered, thrusting the door open shakily.

Pamela wasn't sure if she should take her heels off or not, but for the sake of her aching feet, she did.

Her brother was much changed. He no longer bore resemblance to the gawky playmate of her youth, and rather stood tall and relaxed. To her shock, he appeared almost gaunt, with vague hollows painting the areas around his cheeks and below his eyes. He wore paint-smeared slacks, a black turtleneck shirt, and a vest missing over one of its buttons.

"Goodness Sean," Pamela chastised familiarly, "you look so thin!"

She tried her best to conceal the worry in her voice with her jesting, but Sean cast her a knowing look. "I'm fine Pam. When I get published, money will be less tight. For now, I have enough canned soup to feed the whole Soviet army!"

Pamela laughed awkwardly, remembering how fervently her father had tried to convince them that Sean was some sort of communist himself. But then again, Stuart Kelly had accused everyone from his barber to the mailman of being a Soviet spy.

From the living room emerged a petite woman with the same lazy type of dress as Sean. She too wore button-down slacks, a striped shirt and a male vest, accentuating her slender, boyish form. Her hair was short and jet black, falling around her head in awkward chunks. Positioned haphazardly on the top of her head was a felt green beret. She didn't appear to be the type of girl that used cosmetics, but she walked with the kind of comfortable confidence that earned both envy and admiration.

"Howdy." She tilted her head up as if to get a better view of Pamela, squinting her copper-brown eyes and tugging on her emerald beret.

"Karen," Sean beamed through a veil of discomfort, "this is Pamela, my kid sister."

Sean then turned back to Pamela, making a formal introduction as their mother had taught him. "Pam, this is Karen, my girl."

"Nice to meet you." Pamela opened her mouth in a forced smile. What if Sean and this girlfriend of his turned her away? Where would she go then? Would they force her to wander the streets in search of a job, or beg a stranger to take her in?

"I wanted to ask if you could help me..." Pamela dismissed her fears and spoke. "I want to get a job for myself and gain some measure of independence. I saw a posting in the paper, and I'm going to apply."

"What kind of dough do you think I have?" Sean laughed. "I'm working as a pearl diver in a greasy spoon down the block."

"I thought Lorna said you had gone back to school." Pamela refuted. Lorna was the housekeeper who had been devoted to the Kelly children since their childhood and still remained in close contact with Sean, even after the Kelly patriarch had disowned him.

"I did..." Sean leaned his back against the counter, running his hands through the bush of hair on his chin.

"They expelled him," Karen rolled her enormous eyes. "Apparently, academic institutions do not take well to senior students writing obscene statements in their term papers."

"Focus your audio. If I hadn't taken your suggestion to use profanity in my poems, I would still be enrolled." Sean snapped, glaring down at his girlfriend.

"You misunderstood." Karen bit. "I told you to violate convention in your poetry, but not in your term paper. But like usual, you refuse to think before you write! Don't you know Al got published with my help?"

"Al, your jilted lover?" Sean rolled his eyes dramatically. "What I wouldn't give to be in his place."

"At least he knew how to get his stuff published!"

After the duo spent a few wasted minutes quarreling, Pamela retired to the couch for the evening as a livid Karen stormed out of the pale gray tenement, vowing never to return.

When Karen left, Sean resolved himself to his bedroom, where he said he was going to write and wasn't to be disturbed under any circumstance.

Pamela had never felt like more of an unwelcome visitor. She missed Sean deeply, and she was saddened by the distance that had grown between them. Unsure of how to bridge the chasm between them, she used the solitude to spend the rest of the evening completing job applications and praying that someone would hire her.

A mere two days later, one business sent a reply.

Pamela was cleaning the apartment when she saw a thin white envelope tucked under the front door. Glancing at it, she felt her eyes squint so that she could be sure she wasn't imagining the words on the page.

Dear Miss Pamela Anne Kelly,

I am pleased to announce you may join us as a saleswoman. You will be provided room and board and are to share a flat above Albright Trimmings & Co. with two other girls who work at the store. I hope you will accept my invitation by joining us, October 7, Tuesday.

Sincerely,

Mr. Clyde Friedenberg

She twirled around the living room in a clumsy pirouette, almost knocking one of Sean's glasses from the coffee table.

"What gives?" Sean sighed in confusion, his eyes lazily spilling over the cover of his new paperback book *The Town and the City* by Jack Kerouac.

"I got the job!"

CHAPTER 3

Pamela was jittery as a jive dancer as she dragged her suitcase along the concrete road off Fifth Avenue. Her darkened blonde hair bobbed in the wind, her lips parted in concentration as she attempted to heave her luggage onto the curb.

She hoisted the bag up onto the sidewalk with some help from a courteous street vendor.

Thanking him, she rounded a corner and stared up at the Altman building: one of the oldest buildings in the city, if the newspaper articles she frequently read were correct. The contractors had constructed it as an elegant department store, encouraging other businesses to set up shop uptown and attracting wealthy clients to the once barren block.

Shiny display cases lined the streets—each the stage of an idealistic world where middle-class women cleaned and cooked in frocks and stage makeup and men lounged about the backyard in Hawaiian camp shirts and shorts, grilling steaks on the barbecue and throwing balls for the family dog.

In the caricatures, Pamela saw her elder sister Cecelia and the image of everything a good American girl ought to become: a subservient wife and mother without her own ambitions or plans. Everything Caroline Kelly desired for her daughters. Everything Pamela wasn't.

Fifth Avenue, or the 'Ave' as her mother had affectionately dubbed it, was a two-way street within the stomach of Manhattan, with traffic swarming each way and cars honking incessantly like two opposing battalions readying themselves for war.

The thoroughfare boasted bands of ornate mansions and established museums, though it wasn't as posh or snobbish as some places on the Upper East Side. The Ave was one of the unique places in New York where the privileged and the poor, the young and the old, the black and the white crossed paths: an intersection for thoughts and people and ideas.

Pamela sank into a throng of straw hats.

Nervousness ignited her senses and the noise buzzing about her became magnified: the crude whistling of working people and the cackling laughter of women, the hum of automobiles as they waited, and the roar of engines as the stoplight flashed from green to red. Teenage greasers cruising around in their fords, whistling at girls and looking for something to do.

Pamela straightened her shoulders as she approached her destination, totally unaware that she looked as though she had stepped out of one of the five-cent magazines advertised on the shelves of the convenience store.

She was dressed in a pretty pastel rose circle dress, complete with a cinched-in waist and a sweetheart neckline, her lips coated in a red shimmer, and her eyelashes thick with jet black mascara.

When she reached Albright Trimmings & Co: a simple shop with velvet drapes hanging in the windows, she rushed inside.

A strong gust of wind swept into the place followed by a booming voice. "Well, if it isn't the notorious Pamela Anne Kelly!"

Her new boss, Mr. Friedenberg, revealed a yellowed smile. He pulled the coat off her shoulders without asking, hanging it on the coat rack near the door.

"Hello, Mr. Friedenberg!" Pamela braved a smile.

"I presume you had a decent trip?" Clyde Friedenberg squared his back so that he was eye-level with Pamela. He was perhaps as old as her father, with a polished head losing silvery hair that appeared to have once been red. He wasn't handsome, but his grin was jovial, and his smile spread from his mouth to his slanted brown eyes.

"Yes. Thank you."

"Hey! Caterina! Come on and help the new girl carry her things upstairs, why don'cha?" A woman with black cat-eye glasses barked.

Pamela took a moment to observe her surroundings.

Everything was pastel pink or baby blue, from the carpeted floors to the argyle striped wallpaper. Rolls of fabric adorned the shelves, ranging from bright red to salmon pink to midnight blue, with tiny stars etched into the design.

The lights were unnecessarily bright, considering that the two massive store-front windows already let in plenty of the sky.

"Whaddya think?" Mr. Friedenberg winked, gesturing to his business proudly.

"It's lovely."

"You aren't from Brooklyn," Mr. Friedenberg joked. "It'll be nice to have an educated, fancy talkin' sales girl for a change. We don't get many uptown ladies around here."

The woman with cat eyes glasses folded her arms across her chest defensively and jutted out her lip in a pout.

"Take it easy, sweetheart." Mr. Friedenberg shouted, raising his voice a few levels as if everyone except for him were hard of hearing. "Jealousy gets you nowhere."

"When shall I begin work?" Pamela asked suddenly, redirecting the conversation.

Mr. Friedenberg rubbed his shiny head in contemplation. "Don't worry about starting yet, sweetheart. I have some business to take care of."

Pamela found it strange that he had disclosed no information regarding the start of her work or her hourly wage. Wasn't it standard for an employee to be aware of their pay and work hours?

Another sales assistant named Caterina strolled out from behind the cash register and propped her elbows on the counter, her chin resting on the sides of her palms. Her lashes were long and black, curled to create little shadows along her eyelids.

"Whaddya you think you're doin' back there? Get over here and help the poor girl with her junk!" The cat-eyed woman pressed her plum-coloured lips together as she sneered at Caterina.

"Yeah, yeah." Caterina snorted under her breath, succumbing to the orders and lugging Pamela's bags up the stairs without looking behind her to see if Pamela was coming along.

Once the storefront disappeared from view, nothing remained to show they were in the same building she had entered. The stairs were dirty, and the walls were grimy, a mouse hole burrowed into one of the lean plans of wood. The floorboards cried and groaned every time she stepped on them.

As the two girls reached the top of the rickety stairway, Caterina nodded for Pamela to follow her.

"I care little about cleanliness," Caterina shrugged as she unbarred the door to the apartment. "You can keep your heels on as I show you around. Whatever you want."

Caterina had a thick Italian Brooklyn accent, one Pamela had only ever heard in passing on the street or fashioned by the occasional housemaid her mother had hired to come clean for them on Sunday mornings when Lorna had gone to church.

The apartment was cramped, with two small bedrooms next to one another and established only by a thin plank of wood that snagged a hook in the ceiling. The kitchen was separated from the rest of the residential quarters, sealed off by a wooden door that lacked any sort of doorknob. Inside, the fumes of burnt toast and spoiled scrambled eggs wafted to reach Pamela's flaring nostrils.

She wanted to clean everything up, but she didn't know where to start. She had helped Lorna do the chores when she was a kid, but never really got her hands dirty, being given the menial tasks of stacking the plates or polishing the china and silverware following her mother's direction.

"A girl of her age should learn how to host a society party, not doing the work of the help," her mother had scolded Lorna one night while Pamela had listened from behind the door.

"With all due respect, Mrs. Kelly, she should learn these things so that when she marries, she will know how to care for her own." Lorna had insisted.

Pamela always suspected that Lorna had secretly wanted to rescue her from her mother's ire. She didn't mind; she had loved listening to Lorna's gospel songs, her animated stories about life in prohibition-era Chicago, and enjoying her Southern delicacies.

Caterina's off-tune humming drew Pamela back to the grimy apartment.

The remembrance of Lorna's maternal embrace was far preferable to the mired scene before her.

A half-open can of Campbell's soup sat haphazardly on the stained countertop. Cigarette butts were strewn everywhere, and there was a puddle of acrid water leaking through the ceiling, dropping into a silver bucket. Garments of clothing were flung about every room—hanging off doors, strewn across the sofa, and even tucked into the refrigerator.

Pamela gasped at the sight of a cobweb and fat spider in the room's corner, above the sink where food was supposed to be prepared.

"We don't gotta cleanin' lady. And I'm not around much to look after things." Caterina shrugged, justifying the mess.

"I understand. Perhaps I can help you out with some cleaning since I'm here now," Pamela suggested, pushing a stray cobweb out of her eyes.

Caterina scrunched up her nose, seemingly skeptical of her new roommate's offer.

"We'll be startin' work sometime, but don't ask when. Mr. Friedenberg's got business to take care of before he can open up shop." Caterina explained.

What type of business could be so important that the entire company should be indefinitely closed? Pamela wondered.

"Well, I guess I'll leave ya to it." Caterina flipped her dark curls over one shoulder. "I've gotta date tonight."

That night, Pamela washed the dishes and scrubbed the floorboards as best as she could, using a pair of cotton mitts to scrub more efficiently and some polishing wax to remove stains, like she had seen Lorna do in the past.

When she was done, she unpacked her things and laid them out on the stained bedspread, feeling the city talk and move although darkness had already consumed the glittering streets.

She felt strange being away from home. From the moment she was born, she had lived in the same apartment on Fifth Avenue, only leaving for brief vacations and school trips. Though she was excited, she also felt a thread of dread winding its way through her stomach.

She wasn't used to the loud jumping sound that pounded against the walls of her new apartment. It was so loud and full of life, and yet it felt like nobody would hear her once the city swallowed her whole. Regardless of this, she relented to the magnetic call of sleep.

In her dream, Pamela heard a voice. It was loud and commanding, like the voice of some authoritarian dictator or an overly enthusiastic congressman.

She jolted awake, her heart hammering against her chest and her palms clammy with sweat.

The loud conversation seemed to come from an ajar window in the kitchen—which was in such proximity that Pamela could see the artificial beam of the streetlight filtering through the half-closed drapes strewn across it.

Pamela's bones creaked like those of an old woman as she stood. She crept to the window, praying that the roaring noise was her imagination or people sharing a friendly conversation on the street below. She wasn't sure what she would do if the commotion had emanated from a burglar.

As she neared the sound and peered through the unwashed drapes, her heart caught in her throat.

There, beneath the illuminating gleam of the streetlights, stood Mr. Friedenberg. Five other men wearing dark overcoats and equally sinister expressions surrounded him.

The only man who wasn't dressed in an overcoat—but a sports jacket and flashy evening attire—was pacing back and forth as he combed his hand through his shadow-veiled hair. Pamela couldn't quite see his face as the streetlight missed his eyes, but she observed his lips curve upwards to reveal a demeaning smile and a set of perfectly pearly white teeth, like those straight out of a Crest toothpaste commercial.

"We don't want trouble," the man ceased his walk to size up Mr. Friedenberg, his voice gliding up to reach the kitchen window, "we do our business, and you do yours. That's all there is to it."

He spoke with the same thick brogue as Caterina, suggesting he was from the Italian part of Brooklyn.

"What can I tell you, fellas, to get you off my case?" The volume of Mr. Friedenberg's voice increased in his panic. "I need the trucks. I can't do business without them. I have an understanding with Roberto..."

"We know about the agreement." The man cut him off with a dismissive wave of his hand. "We need the trucks. We'll get 'em back to you when we've finished. That is our understanding."

Mr. Friedenberg opened his mouth to speak, but then closed it again, his upper lip trembling.

"Look, I understand you and the boss are friends. He respects your business. He says you're an honest fella." The man sighed, swiping a hand across his chin. "It would be an awful shame if anything happened to the store or your family..."

Pamela felt her heart beat faster. She had never witnessed something so terrifying, other than in print or at the movies. Who was *the boss*? Was he somehow even higher than Mr. Friedenberg? She hadn't known that Albright Trimmings was a franchise.

Mr. Friedenberg seemed to shrivel like a plant without water beneath the stony gaze of the dark man. There was no sign that he agreed, and if he did, he said nothing.

"Get 'outta here." One man spat at Mr. Friedenberg as he cowered.

"C'mon Mike, we treat our people with respect. Business is always to be done with the utmost respect, is that clear?" The man in the sports jacket barricaded himself between Mr. Friedenberg and the man who had spat at him.

Respect? Pamela wondered if he was being serious. Hadn't she just seen the fellow in the sports jacket attempt to threaten Mr. Friedenberg and his family?

One by one, the group dissipated into the darkness of the alleyway, until only the troublemaker in the sports jacket remained.

He stretched his back against the brick wall of the alleyway, raising his chin so it pointed up into the black sky like a dagger. He lit his cigarette and blew a plume of smoke out of his mouth slowly, warming his large hands in his pockets. He looked like a man without a care in the world, although he had just threatened an innocent business owner.

Pamela looked around frantically, hoping to find a telephone or something she could use to contact the authorities. She did not stray from her place at the window, however, and when she glanced back up, terror thrummed through her stomach.

Someone was looking at her.

She squinted through the window until she could see the man's blackened eyes searing into hers, and she almost lost her dinner.

The last thing that she saw as she crashed backwards onto the linoleum floor was the metallic stock of a gun peeking through his jacket.

CHAPTER 4

Johnny Siciliano had seen the girl. There was no doubt about it.

He thought about this as he sped across the Brooklyn Bridge the day after the shipment had come in and Old Friedenberg had complied with his orders.

He didn't know if she had been there all along, but he could still picture her face as he cruised over the East River from Manhattan to Brooklyn, Billie Holiday's raspy contralto voice humming through the lungs of his Becker Mexico car radio. The mounting waves below him glinted white in the waning autumn sun.

When Johnny noticed someone watching him, it profoundly surprised him that the busybody he detected in his trajectory was not an intimidating thug or a sharpshooter, but a young woman.

Johnny possessed eagle eyes—the kind that allowed him to shoot from far distances. His stellar vision had also helped him view the girl in great detail. From where he was standing, the streetlight had made the woman look almost ethereal, like an incarnate image of Selene: the goddess of the moon.

Johnny snorted.

He wasn't even sure why he remembered that; he had paid little attention in school and later dropped out in freshman year. Besides, his teachers had perpetually called him a worthless wop.

He rolled his eyes and looked out upon the city unraveling behind him, thousands upon thousands of bright city lights glittering across the canvas of the purple sky.

There was nothing Johnny loved better than the New York City skyline at night. It gave him an odd sense of comfort—knowing that though the night cloaked the city with darkness at sundown, the lights on the bridge and in the skyscrapers still shone. But that night, his memory of the mystery woman distracted him from admiring the breathtaking view.

Whoever she was, she had seemed terrified when he noticed her staring. Her soft features had hardened, her mouth going taut and her eyes widening with fear. Her forehead had creased, creating a worried line between her eyebrows and spoiling the serene face that had been there a fraction of a second earlier.

Meaning she had seen.

And heard.

She had shot at his instincts.

Nobody could watch that kind of business happen and rarely was Johnny watched. He was too good of a mafioso for such careless mistakes. He took great lengths to be discreet, unlike some of his brasher counterparts. He wasn't supposed to feel ashamed; it was just business, and yet, he had a sinking feeling dragging his soul down to the bottom of his feet.

The girl was afraid of him, and yet they had never had the chance to meet. If he had met her in passing at a dance or dinner club, he would've likely charmed her with his smooth talk and charm. But he had no such opportunity to do so now.

He banished these thoughts as he parked his car outside of a colorful stretch of taverns, produce markets and bungalows on Pioneer

Street, across from which lived his boss—the venerable Don Roberto Mancini.

People called Don Roberto "The Enforcer," to his face and "Blue Eyes," behind his back. Not that he disliked being called "Blue Eyes," it was more that he preferred being constantly reminded of his authority and the fact that the world could stop turning at the snap of his fingers. More often, the men referred to him as Don Roberto, or simply boss, for the sake of convenience.

The Mancini home was in a quaint block of tenements and red-brick buildings, with a flourishing olive tree out front and a patch of flowers that Roberto's wife, Isabella, cared for. Roberto had built a trellis out of planks of wood and metal to serve as a sanctuary for the grapes and other climbing plants he grew. The Mancini couple would garden together in the summers, producing olive oil from the olives they harvested. The hobby provided a sense of normalcy for their otherwise unconventional lives.

However unconventional, it was the life Johnny wanted. He yearned to establish himself as the respected don of a family, getting other people to do his business for him, and enjoying the comfort of a peaceful home on the weekends. He hoped he would bring in enough cash to buy a nice place for his *madre*, and set her up with a white picket fence rancher in a quaint suburb, away from the noise of the city. Perhaps he would even marry Carlotta, Roberto's eldest daughter, and carry on the Mancini line.

"Hey Johnny, what gives?"

Johnny spun around to face Tony Bellucci, the soldier assigned to protect the Mancini family, as well as his best friend.

Tony had not resented Johnny being assigned his own crew of soldiers, even when he became one of the very men Johnny commanded. Neither did he seem to mind that Johnny was twenty-four

—almost a year younger than himself, making the latter the youngest capo in the Brooklyn area.

The two men were close. Apart from titles, they were equals.

"Nothin.' What's up with you?" Johnny twirled his foot in a pile of gravel, his mind meandering back to the mystery woman.

"Nothin' to write home about. C'mon, I know something's on your case. Spit it out." Tony pushed Johnny's forearm lightly, something he used to do when they fought as kids.

Johnny didn't feel like telling Tony about the girl. If he did, he would tell Sal, and Sal would tell Roberto. If Roberto knew some doe-eyed girl had witnessed his capo coercing old Friedenberg, he wouldn't be pleased.

"Been thinking about the shipment, and hoping everything's in order," Johnny explained, hoping to derail his anxiety.

"Friedenberg take the bait?"

"Why wouldn't he?"

Johnny and Tony swaggered inside, crossing themselves as they passed a holy icon of Mother Mary, surrounded by images of various saints and cheap angel figurines. He thought Isabella kept them there to protect the house and her family from *maliocch'*, or the evil eye.

The Virgin's pious eyes seemed to follow him, her slender white hands clasped over her heart in ardent prayer.

He didn't believe in the stuff his mamma did—the angels, the saints, the all-loving, all-powerful God. It had never made much sense to him—he was too reasonable for all that ridiculous religious nonsense. He kept this to himself, though.

His mother would die if she found out.

She used to remind him she prayed for him every night, and when he came home in the morning, she thanked God he was still alive.

Johnny didn't go home much anymore.

He wanted to tell his mamma that his wits and his sense of self-preservation had kept him alive. He didn't need an invisible man donning a straggly white beard to protect him when he did it just fine on his own accord.

Johnny averted his gaze, away from the religious decor and towards the vicinity of the house. The interior of the abode was brick, indistinguishable from the exterior aside from the fact that the floors were carpeted and lace covered all the furniture.

Isabella Mancini appeared, her hands varnished in flour, and her cheeks a bright crimson glow touched pink by the heat in the insulated kitchen.

"Boys! Come on in! I've got *ganol'* in the oven, and some biscotti on the table. Help yourselves." Isabella Mancini rubbed her hands on her gaudy peach floral apron, briefly pecking Johnny on the cheek.

"*Grazie*, Mrs. M." Johnny returned her kiss and sauntered over to the table, grabbing a piece of soft crumbly pastry and swallowing it whole.

"How's your *madre*?" Isabella gushed, simultaneously marching over to reprimand her youngest son for teasing his brother by slapping him on the back of the arm.

"She's good," Johnny felt a twang of guilt with the blatant lie, "worried as usual."

"Tell her to come on over one of these nights. Why don'cha?" Isabella didn't seem bothered by Johnny's reluctance to talk about his mother. "I never see her."

Isabella was his mother's cousin. Contrasting with Isabella and the other Sicilian women, Johnny knew Silvia Siciliano wasn't interested in preserving the old ways. She had found herself a job as a maid in the city after Johnny was born, wanting to live an honest life. Even after

Johnny's father had left them, she had shunned the attempts of various relatives who wanted to give her mob money.

Johnny joining the mafia had been the biggest disappointment of his mother's life.

"Boys! There's more *ganol'*!" Isabella interrupted Johnny's rumination. "It isn't gonna disappear by itself!"

Johnny retrieved more cannoli from the table, out of respect for the cook.

"I hope you'll bring some home to your madre. Tell her we miss her. She shouldn't be working herself to death like that, poor woman." Isabella folded a handful of cannolis into a wax paper sheet, shoving them into Johnny's hands.

"Grazie, Mrs. M." Johnny knew his mother would never consider quitting her job. She was a proud woman and refused financial help from Johnny or Don Roberto.

"He upstairs?" Tony practically yelled over the roar of Italian opera music and the chattering of the younger Mancini children in the dining room as they did their homework.

"Where else would he be?" Isabella joked cheerfully, smoothing her hands over her dark perm. "Bring him some cannoli. I'm worried about that poor man. He has eaten nothing all day."

"He works too hard," Johnny commented off-handedly.

Don Roberto Mancini was a big man.

He was not large in stature or size, but his presence seemed to occupy every square inch of the office he spent most of his time in.

He was heavier than most men of his height and age, but that was because of his wife's lavish cooking. It was also because he had surpassed the age where he ran around New York City, settling disputes between the families as an underboss.

He was secure.

When his uncle, Carlo Mancini, died in his sleep of causes the doctors attributed to old age, Roberto was given the coveted position of boss.

Don Roberto had a paper cigarette hanging from the corner of his mouth at all times, followed by a wandering trail of smoke that oozed limply from his thin, gray mouth. He was well dressed, usually in a stiff, navy blue flannel suit along with his signature Rolex Tudor Royal steel automatic wristwatch.

However, Roberto wasn't one to waste money on frivolous things such as Cadillacs or dozens of expensive suits. His loyalty was to the Family, and that also meant the money he made went directly back into sustaining it. The watch was the one unnecessarily lavish thing he awarded himself. For this, he had gained Johnny's devoted respect.

Roberto's eyes were such a pale shade of blue that they appeared clear. It was especially unusual that he had that color of eyes, being a pure-bred Sicilian from the most southern region in Italy. What was more unnerving, even to Johnny, was that Roberto's eyes were almost always devoid of any discernible expression.

It wasn't that Don Roberto was heartless—Johnny had seen him warm up plenty of times when he was spending time with his kids or tending flowers in the garden with his wife—it was that he never flinched when he was doing business, even the trickiest kind of business.

The first time Johnny had seen a murder was when Don Roberto took him to a pool hall. There was another guy there, running his mouth to other families about what shipments the Mancini Family was hijacking. Roberto had noticed the guy and killed him with a cue stick.

The whole time, Roberto's face had been as glacial as Pond's cold cream.

Johnny was only a kid. Nausea had seized him like he had eaten some rotten meat. But he swallowed his disgust. Over time, the physiological objection had turned hard, like Don Roberto's eyes.

Then there was Lorenzo Palermo, Don Roberto's closest friend, and his consigliere. The two had immigrated from Sicily together, and as Johnny understood it, Lorenzo was the only one who could argue with Roberto, challenge him even.

Sal Palermo was Lorenzo's younger brother, and thus the underboss of the family.

They called Lorenzo "Doc," and Sal "Flash," because Lorenzo was the smartest brother and the only one out of all of them who had graduated from high school, and Sal was agile for his forty years, as well as that he liked to show off with flashy suits, gorgeous dames and sports cars.

Antonio Pugliesi, Luca Cattaneo, John Mancini and Marco Mancini were just a handful of the other capos who had been summoned to the meeting, being the most trusted by Roberto.

Perhaps it was because John and Marco shared the Mancini bloodline that Roberto had entrusted them with their soldiers. Some of the other men resented John and Marco. They were businessmen, not criminal masterminds. They hadn't fought in the trenches of the streets like the rest of them had; they hadn't had to gain respect for blood and loyalty.

"Boys," Roberto finally surrendered his cigarette to the ashtray beside him and readjusted his legs in his wide chair, "I've called you here about Friedenberg."

Johnny felt his pulse speed up while Tony remained poised and perfectly still beside him.

"You know that he and I go way back, and if there is one thing I would never do—that is to betray a good friend. But, sometimes that friend betrays you first, and you gotta get even. Show him he's gotten too proud for his own good. Too proud to accept the help of an honest man."

The room fell silent until Joey Romano, the sixth and most reserved capo, slipped into the cramped office, throwing his overcoat off and slumping into the chair at the back.

Roberto ignored him and went on. "Well, I'm an honest man. I take care of my friends, even when they don't wanna have me takin' care of it for them. I'm makin' Friedenberg an offer, and a very generous offer at that. We're gonna give him full protection, and he's gonna give us twenty percent of his business's earnings."

Johnny glanced at Tony through his peripheral vision. They both knew that Roberto had been meaning to get a hand in the textile industry and in the meantime, they had been using the trucks from Albright Trimmings & Co. for deliveries. Don Roberto had said that using Friedenberg's trucks would help them get a foot in the door.

"We keep using the trucks, and Friedenberg gives us twenty percent of each garment or product he sells. And of course, full protection for Friedenberg comes with that." Lorenzo added offhandedly.

"It's a shame, but the streets are a rough and bloody place," Don Roberto's pale eyes circled the room like a bald eagle looking for its next meal. "The least we can do is offer our services."

"You want us to send him a message?" Tony guessed.

"No, no. Old Friedenberg is a reasonable man. All we need is to talk some sense into him. Johnny, you visit him this afternoon. Make sure he knows you're loaded."

"No disrespect, boss, but don't you think I should bring some men along?" Johnny wondered.

"You'll be just fine on your own." Don Roberto dismissed him, then called back: "Don't disappoint me, Johnny."

The men paraded out of the office silently, leaving Lorenzo, Sal, and Roberto behind to deliberate.

Johnny began his descent down the stairs, swiping his hand through his hair and struggling with the cowlick in the front that just wouldn't stay in place. When he got home, he would add more grease. He didn't need to be looking like an unkempt adolescent when he was supposed to be intimidating a man twice his age.

"What was Papà saying to you guys?"

Johnny was startled senseless to bump into Carlotta Mancini, Don Roberto's eldest daughter. Her back was pressed up against the wall beside her father's office and her cornflower blue eyes searched his gaze for answers.

For a moment, he thought he was looking into the eyes of her father.

"Huh?"

Carlotta wasn't supposed to listen in when her father did business. Family and business were kept separate, with no questions asked.

"Don't play stupid with me, Johnny Siciliano. Tell me what he was talkin' about." Carlotta glared at Johnny, her hands planted squarely on her hips. "What is he planning?"

"A hello woulda been nice," Johnny said, hoping some banter might steer their conversation into safer territory.

She rolled her eyes. "Put a cork in it. Just tell me what he was sayin'."

"Carlotta, you know I can't... talk about this with you," Johnny whispered stubbornly from between clenched teeth, "our business is private."

Don Roberto would dismiss him if he disclosed secrets—or far worse if he violated the invisible, permeating line that divided family and business.

"Tell me, Johnny!" Carlotta repeated, clasping her hands together as if in prayer.

When he didn't answer, she stared at him for what seemed like an eternity.

Long, black waves of hair encircled a heart-shaped face, eyes piercing him with the might of a thousand brave soldiers. A beige pencil skirt and baby blue blouse adorned her appealing feminine curves, her body swaying ever so slightly as she stood in front of him.

She was too pretty for her own good. Even the men enjoyed letting their glances linger after her—avoiding the notice of Don Roberto, of course. Mob wives, sisters, and daughters were not to be touched. They were better off coveted in secret, and even then—men like Roberto were vigilant in protecting their women. A misplaced look or candid remark could land a guy at the bottom of the river.

Johnny himself couldn't help but admit that Carlotta was easy on the eyes, although she had an explosive temper and was always trying to insert herself into places she didn't belong. Naturally, he had always assumed that she was his future wife. They had known one another since they were kids, and it was the arrangement Roberto wanted.

Hopefully one day, Johnny would inherit the boss' throne with Carlotta on his arm.

"What are you smiling about?" Carlotta fumed, stomping her foot like a child. "*Maddiul*'!"

Johnny flinched at the insult. He could take the humiliation of getting into squabbles on the street, but it stung to lie to a woman he cared deeply about.

"Carlotta?"

Isabella appeared at the foot of the staircase, her ruddy face smattered with flour and the perfume of espresso escorting her. "*Lascialui*!" She chided, "Leave poor Johnny alone! You already know he can't speak to you about the business."

"Bye Carlotta." After leaving, Johnny climbed into his dark green Chrysler Imperial automobile and hastened across the city to pay Old Clyde Friedenberg a visit.

CHAPTER 5

The next morning, fear clawed at Pamela's heart.

She considered calling Sean on the telephone. Perhaps she could stay with him for a few days before finding a new, less complicated job, as a grocery store clerk or as one of the chipper girls selling lipstick in the Bloomingdale's department stores.

It wasn't characteristic of Pamela Anne Kelly to remain in such a compromising situation. Pamela was the type of girl who was often unpopular because of her beliefs and her adamant integrity, refusing to do anything that contradicted the rules. She had never cheated on a test or copied homework, never gossiped about a classmate, never lied to her dad, and had certainly stolen nothing from the school cafeteria. She hadn't even sat in a parked car with a boy before.

She wrenched herself out of bed, replacing her lacy nightgown with a conservative, plain white blouse and plaid circle skirt that ended at her calves. She comb her hair until it shone and used a ribbon to tie it back.

Perhaps the whole thing had been a misunderstanding. Perhaps the men who had threatened Mr. Friedenberg were, in fact, responsible for managing the business at a higher level and were angry with her employer for some horrendous wrongdoing. Maybe Mr. Friedenberg was a menacing criminal, and the men were honorable police officers who gave him a firm chastising.

But no matter how fervently she tried to convince herself of the opposite, Pamela knew something was wrong.

She frowned at her reflection in the glass-encased hand mirror, her hand shaking slightly as she held it.

The curtains were sealed shut, and even the paltry amount of light that crept into the place below the windowsill was swallowed up by the deep red paint that plastered the walls. As a result, her eyes were the darkest shade of green she had ever seen—resembling moss rather than their usual gray emerald. Her lips were chapped and pale, and her long honey-coloured hair fell around her head in unfashionable pieces.

She was just twenty-one, and yet a minuscule crease marred her forehead, a premature wrinkle her mother had said resulted from her incessant studying.

She should've cut her hair when her mother had told her to. Ironically, the Italian style was all the rage; short hair fashioned in feminine ringlets with bangs framing the face.

While Pamela was just settling onto her bed to do some leisure reading before her first work shift, Caterina burst into the room without knocking. Her raven black hair was pinned up in tight curls and makeup painted her face so thickly it looked like she was an actress and not a salesgirl.

"What are you dressed for? Church or somethin'?" Caterina scoffed disapprovingly. "You know, you could be really quite pretty if you wore something other than these..."

She scooped up a handful of clothes from the floor and inspected them with raised plucked brows. "Grandmother's clothes."

Pamela dipped her head in embarrassment. "They're all I brought."

"Isn't that a big tickle?" Caterina giggled. "Imagine that, a rich working girl from the Upper East Side who owns nothing but dowdy grandmother clothes. Where'd you get these hideous rags from anyhow?"

Pamela had never thought that her clothes were terribly ugly before. Humiliation flushed her cheeks, turning them a bright crimson.

Caterina apprehended her embarrassment and added quickly, "I didn't mean it like that. I just... think you could look like an absolute doll if you tried hard enough. You have quite the *classy chassis* if you ask me! But these clothes... they make you look like a thick-ankled headmistress."

The insult had already been fired, though Pamela knew her coworker was just trying to be nice. Caterina wasn't the type of person to think before speaking her mind.

"Try this little number." Caterina tossed one of Pamela's less frequently worn outfits over to her—a black swing dress and a string of pearls.

"I've only worn it once to a formal event at my father's country club," Pamela heard her voice quaver with uncertainty. "It's an evening dress... are you sure it'll be appropriate for work?"

Pamela disliked the dress for more than one reason. It was the gown she had worn on her first date with Timothy Atwell, a night that had started as an accompaniment to a formal dance and ended with Timothy drinking more than his fair share of liquor and relying on her to taxi him home. Halfway through the car ride, he had thrown up all over the skirt of her dress. It had taken ages for the fabric to regain its crisp black color.

Caterina disregarded Pamela's skepticism and tilted her head, inspecting Pamela's visage through narrowed eyes. "Really, you *are* pretty, Pamela. But those eyebrows need some work. Have you ever had 'em shaped?"

"I don't think I want to shape them..." Pamela grasped at the fabric of her frock as Caterina reached for a silver pair of tweezers. Her sister had tried the same thing on the first day of her senior year of high school. "Won't I be in an awful lot of pain before work?"

"Don't be silly," Caterina snickered. "How do ya think you're gonna impress the clients with those thick brows?"

Before she could protest further, Caterina was pulling at the thin hairs between and above her eyebrows with surprising strength, making Pamela wince with pain.

When Caterina had finished, Pamela held a mirror to her face, noticing that her eyebrows were now arched like in the movies. She had never looked so glamorous. Like Marilyn Monroe or Grace Kelly.

"That's much better. Now you're a sophisticated working girl as you oughta be." Caterina boasted.

Pamela ventured downstairs before Caterina, being told that she ought to practice opening up the store for the first time on her own.

Mr. Friedenberg had left a mysterious message with Caterina explaining that he would be away visiting family in New Jersey for some time. Though the time of his return was undisclosed, Pamela more than suspected that his disappearance had something to do with the infamous alleyway incident.

When Pamela had begged Caterina to help her, her new coworker and roommate had insisted that since it was a Monday, business would be slow, and she could call her down if she needed her help.

Luckily, the store was empty.

Pamela dug her heels into the carpeted floor, positioning her hands upon her hips as she took a mental survey of the room.

Her contemplation was muddled once a polished green automobile thundered and then rolled to a stop, parking in front of the store like a colossal beast.

Pamela watched motionless as she peered at the back of a man with a jelly roll of brown-black hair emerging from the impressive car. He was tall and possessed broad shoulders, which he wore well with an easy, relaxed gait, swaggering with the ease only movie stars could muster.

She wondered what kind of man shopped at a textile store on a Monday afternoon and guessed that he was running an errand for his wife he had forgotten before she woke up.

She smiled to herself, bemused by the prospect of such a thing. Her smile faded to an expression of vague horror, however, once the man turned to face her.

He was the man who had been intimidating Mr. Friedenberg in the alleyway, the man she had locked eyes with not long after.

His eyes were wide and dark, his complexion was a shade of olive, perhaps a shade or two lighter than Caterina's, his nose long and aquiline, and his face an oval shape. She would have categorized his features as remarkable if he wasn't so sinister.

Did he know she had seen him? Had he seen her? And if he had, did he recognize her now?

If he recalled seeing her, he made no sign of it as he flashed a charming smile.

Pamela unlocked the door and swung it open for him, keeping her eyes placed ahead and her chin upright. She would not allow him to perceive the fear pulsing through her with the might of a heavy freight train.

"Give yourself a break. I'll get the door," the man commanded as he neared the storefront, taking the door from Pamela with a steady grip as she scurried off ahead of him.

"Good afternoon sir," she replied, "what can I help you with?"

He leaned one arm along the aqua-blue counter, his soulful eyes appraising her. "Hey baby, is Mr. Friedenberg around?"

Pamela stiffened when the man nearly knocked over the tip jar. "He's in New Jersey, visiting his family. If the matter is urgent, I can take a message."

"When will he be back?"

"I'm not sure, sir, but I can take a message."

"Not sure, or won't say?" The man chuckled, the lights casting fragmented shadows upon his face.

"I don't know what you could mean." Pamela straightened her shoulders, willing herself to look up at him.

"Is that so? Guess I'll look around then." The man wandered through the aisles, scanning the rolls of fabric and flippantly caressing the textiles as he passed. With his every landed step, the floor reverberated against the soles of Pamela's shoes.

"He won't be back for a while, I'm afraid." Pamela reminded him as he paced to the other side of the store.

He ignored her, and so she tried her best to do the same to him, vacuuming the carpets, readjusting furniture, and cutting rolls of fabric. This went on for almost half an hour until the intruder seemed to grow agitated. He sat slumped with his back against the wall, drumming his fingers across his thigh and trying his best to abide by the No Smoking Indoors sign.

"I must remind you, sir, Mr. Friedenberg won't return until much later. I wouldn't want you to waste your time." Pamela cleared her throat, projecting her voice across the room.

He combed a hand through his hair and raised his eyebrows as he glanced up at Pamela. Then he came to reach his full height, more than a few generous inches taller than her.

His mood seemed to darken, and he twisted his mouth in anger. "Look, lady. As much as I would love to stay here with a nice broad like you all day, I don't have a lot of time to kill. I need you to tell me exactly where Friedenberg is before things get ugly."

The word *kill* made Pamela's breath catch and tangle in the back of her throat, like someone was strangling her voice with a rope. "Is that a threat, sir?"

"Is it a threat if it's the truth?" The man combed a hand through his dark hair, grinning menacingly.

Pamela could hardly contain her fury, but she wouldn't let him win in their battle of wits. She knew exactly what he was. She had read about types of men like him in the paper, and her dad had talked about their kind at the dinner table.

He was a mobster, a *mafioso*, a low-life criminal.

"Mr. Friedenberg is vacationing with his family, and is not to be disturbed."

"Yeah, I'll bet he is." The man laughed.

"You can wait for as long as you want, sir, but he won't be coming back anytime soon." Pamela articulated her words firmly and then swung around to walk in the opposite direction.

She heard padded footsteps behind her and wheeled around when she sensed that the unwanted visitor was approaching.

"I think we may have had a big misunderstanding," the man began, "I'm here to manage the company while Mr. Friedenberg is away."

Pamela wasn't stupid. She knew he was lying.

"I'm awful sorry for any distress I may have caused. Clyde is my business partner, and we have an understanding. It so happens that he hasn't met his end of the bargain, so I'm here to make sure he follows through with his word." The man continued as if his explanation was legitimate.

"I think I've seen you before," Pamela began, her words laced with indignation, "I believe we've met."

For the slightest of moments, a shudder seemed to seize the man, his brows sloping upwards and his eyes widening.

Then the moment vanished. A grin split his stunned expression, and his eyes became crinkled with feigned recognition. "Why didn't you say so before? I must've run into you at Copacabana."

Unintentionally, Pamela erupted into uncomfortable laughter. Certainly, she had heard of the Latin-themed nightclub on East 60th Street. Copacabana was one of the most famed places in the city, with Hollywood stars such as Lucille Ball and Sammy Davis Jr frequenting it. It was preposterous to suggest that a girl as introverted and bookish as Pamela Anne Kelly would spend her time there.

"Somethin' funny?" The man frowned, trying to understand in her personal amusement.

Pamela shook her head. "No, not exactly. It's just that... well, you must be mistaken."

"Mistaken? Why, of course, I'm not mistaken. I remember you."

Pamela yearned to tell the man that she had seen him in the alleyway that ominous night. She wanted to confront him, to ask him what he was doing there, but she knew that to do so would be utterly and completely foolish. Somehow, she suspected he had seen her that fateful night, too.

Then she noticed how silent it had become in the store. She and the sinister man were alone, and if he were to try something...

Pamela forced herself not to consider such thoughts. "I should return to my work."

The man seemed to sense her discomfort and balked away. "And I should be leaving. But before I do, I will tell my old pal Clyde that his new salesgirl is doing an excellent job. If I can get her name?"

Pamela noticed he had mimicked her Upper East Side accent, his lingering, gliding Brooklyn dialect and replaced it with hers, either unintentionally or intentionally and hoping to get on her nerves.

"My name is Pamela Kelly. And what shall I tell Mr. Friedenberg?"

"Tell him Johnny Siciliano wants... would like to have a word with him." The man, Johnny, reached for her hand and took it in his. He smacked his lips against her cold knuckles.

Pamela was so shocked by his unexpected gesture that she tore her hand from Johnny's grasp and slapped his wrist away.

"Oh! I'm sorry!" She exclaimed when she realized what she had just done.

Johnny reddened, taken aback by Pamela's sudden assault. "Uh, excuse me, Miss Kelly."

He sprinted out of the store; the door crashing closed behind him. Pamela watched in sheer horror as he hopped into his car and hastened past an angry horde of traffic.

Pamela was terrified.

The jarring reality caved in on her: she had not only insulted but assaulted a mobster, and perhaps one of the most powerful mobsters in New York City. She had hit him, and he had run off to do... what? To report her misdemeanor to his powerful friends and exact his revenge? And why had he turned red? Was it from seething rage, or was he shocked he had been challenged by a meek salesgirl?

When she heard Caterina return from the grocer, Pamela thought about telling her what had happened. But then she remembered Caterina was Italian and from the same part of Brooklyn as the mobsters spoke about in the paper often hailed from. What if she told Caterina, and then Caterina reported her to someone in the mob?

Instead, she decided to bring up Johnny Siciliano's name over a plated dinner of fried chicken and thawed green peas.

Caterina brightened at the name. "Johnny? Yeah, I know him. He and Mr. Friedenberg do... uh... business together here and there. One time, I almost successfully sold him a yard of Chambray for his girlfriend."

"He has a girlfriend?" The question sprang forth from Pamela's mouth faster than she could register that she had even said it.

Caterina cast her a strange look. "Not anymore, I don't think, at least. They broke up ages ago. But, Johnny is like that. Always dating one girl or another. You know how some men are." Caterina crammed a spoonful of peas into her mouth. "Anyway, Johnny and I grew up together. We're from the same part of Brooklyn. He was always playin' with my cousins, and I think I used to follow them around like a pest. Johnny was real good at using slingshots. He would put a row of cans on the top of the fence, and then knock them down, all in one go. We thought he'd enlist someday."

Caterina frowned, setting her spoon and fork down on the bright pink table mat. "Now that I think about it, Johnny stopped playin' with us when he left high school freshman year. He wanted to go do construction work, earn a little extra dough for his mamma."

"What about his father?" Pamela probed.

"His father wasn't around much, I guess. I think he left to find work when the stock market crashed and Johnny was still little." Caterina shrugged, tugging at her curls.

Pamela nodded, trying her best to absorb all the information that Caterina had fed her, along with the unappetizing thawed peas and greasy fried chicken.

That night, Pamela fell into bed, her feet dangling off the footboard. She was burdened by the plight of insomnia, and like many other nights she had spent wasting away in her bedroom on Seventh Avenue, she couldn't sleep. But this time, she wasn't worried about an arithmetic test or an impending English presentation. She kept seeing Johnny's imposing brown eyes gleaming in the forefront of her mind.

She tore herself out of an envelope of blankets and switched on the lamp on her nightstand, her frilly nightgown pooling out around her slender ankles. In her notebook, she jotted a phrase in small print:

TO DO:

Visit the New York Police Department. Tell them about Johnny Siciliano and what was noticed in the alleyway behind Albright Trimmings & Co. Inform them of Mr. Clyde Friedenberg's sudden absence. As promptly as possible.

She ripped the paper out of her notebook and folded it until it became as small as her thumb.

She stuffed the note into her purse and planned to tackle the matter in the morning.

CHAPTER 6

New York City, Brooklyn, October 1954

Carlotta Isabella Mancini stared at her bedroom wall.

A photograph of her mamma and papà, when they had married, was situated atop the mahogany dresser, guarded by a cracked china vase of wilting flowers.

Her then twenty-three-year-old mamma was the incarnate image of an angel with her pinned-up curls, her grandparents on either side of her youthful-looking padre, as if to intimidate him. It was captured in Milazzo, five years before Mussolini and his fascist regime had risen to power. Her parents had made a pilgrimage of sorts, traveling back to Italy to celebrate their union with a traditional Italian wedding. Her mamma had recalled that day fondly, gushing about the towering wedding cake and how the town folk had encircled them as they played traditional flutes and jaw harps until the scorching Sicilian sun slipped beneath the horizon, winking stars dancing in the sky.

Had her grandparents intimidated papà that night?

Carlotta giggled aloud at the absurdity of the thought. Nobody could intimidate Don Roberto Mancini, the man who single-handedly operated rackets all over New York City and silenced his enemies with just a look.

Did her papà frighten her?

She had never believed that her father was capable of any form of evil when she was a child. In fact, he had been the epitome of goodness. He had coddled her and indulged in her every ridiculous girlhood whim. He had made her believe he could give her a shooting star if she asked.

She remembered one distinct occasion when he had taken her on the ferry over to Staten Island. He had bought her cotton candy from one vendor on South Beach and insisted that his entourage walk slightly behind them so that their presence didn't encroach on his family time.

Back then, she hadn't been puzzled by the crush of cologne-drenched men that had continuously chaperoned their families wherever they went. They were Papa's friends. They cared about him, mamma, and the others, so they were her friends too. She loved making them laugh with the faces she made, pestering them until small dimples formed on their cheeks.

That day on the beach, Carlotta joined another group of children in a sand castle-building contest. At eight years of age and with a severe lack of experience, she had been thoroughly impressed with the citadel she constructed out of the sand.

However, another little girl and her brother were rewarded with the prize of the shiny new portable electric phonograph. Carlotta had bawled her eyes out until her papà had stormed over to the judges, convincing them that his daughter had been unfairly critiqued and demanded a recall.

Or, at least, that was what he told her.

Her father and his men had coolly accompanied the judge to the back of the Beachland Amusement Arcade. When they had returned, the judge was red and flustered, his palms open in defeat. An unexplainable bloom of crimson had painted the right side of his face

—a detail Carlotta had not understood in her childhood and yet remembered for years after.

Mysteriously, the disheveled judge had changed his mind, and Carlotta returned to her mamma with the pretty new phonograph, being convinced it was her sheer talent that had outshone the devastated little girl.

Carlotta rocked her head at the memory, her eyes flitting across the room to land on another portrait of her father.

She had always been proud of her father, as any proper Italian daughter ought to be. He was wise, and brave, and he provided for their family in how only a good padre could. He tickled her and bought her presents. She read him the newspaper in the mornings and brought him his espresso at night. They waltzed together in the living room to Frank Sinatra, whirling, until the two were paralyzed by their howls of laughter.

When Carlotta had found a gun in the bottom shelf of her mamma's bedroom drawer, she hadn't been particularly startled. She had made a casual inquiry to her parents, but they had informed her that the gun was only there for safety reasons. After all, Brooklyn was crawling with petty criminals, hooligans, and thieves. Her papà simply wanted to protect them if some troublemaker wandered into their home somehow.

In fact, she had been oblivious to the business until her eleventh birthday, when she was on the cusp of adolescence. Her father had called her into his office, territory she had never been allowed to explore before, and asked her what she thought he did for a living.

She had felt so small in that room, her head barely reaching the top of her armchair, and her papà gazing down at her from the comfortable view his six foot-four frame provided.

Carlotta had hesitated, petrified by the prospect of disappointing him with a wrong answer.

"No need to be timid, little Carlotta." Don Roberto released an intermingling of smoke and peppermint with his somehow unsettling words.

"I haven't really thought about it." She had swallowed, her fear hardening in her throat. "The business, I mean."

"Have the other kids talked to you about me? Any of the neighbors? Your teachers?"

Carlotta shook her head, clamping her hands together on her lap. Maybe one or two of her classmates had made silly allegations about her father—that he was in trouble with the police or that he was an illegal immigrant, but Carlotta always dismissed them as sheer nonsense.

"Carlotta, I have sacrificed my life for you and my family. I was only a young man when I left Milazzo." He stroked his chin thoughtfully, lighting another cigarette from the half-empty paper box on his desk as he did so. "You will hear questions. About me, about the Family, about my business. But, you must know, *figlia mia*, that my business is meant to protect you. Back in Sicily, we practiced the old ways. We fought for each other, we protected each other. Here, in America, we must continue to do the same."

Carlotta had been pleased to know that she was being watched out for, like how her mamma had told her that the Lord Jesus looked after them even when she didn't realize it.

However, she had taken her father's words with a grain of salt when she began junior high school.

Her classmates had fathers with jobs that they could talk about, while all she could say was that hers worked in construction, with his hand in the olive oil industry in Italy. He even possessed a fake business card to authenticate his fake address of employment. He brandished the forged rectangular paper to all of her teachers and the parents of her friends, almost as though he had been proud to lie about his profession.

Carlotta sighed, attempting to release the heavyweight within her.

Her room was like any other young woman's bedroom, with a floral quilt and a tall, white vanity pushed against the wall. It had changed little since her teenage years. Framed photographs of herself and her school friends lined the shelves. Posters of her favorite Hollywood actors hung above her bed like a shrine. A stack of unreturned library books was forgotten in a heap on the floor, and the phonograph from the beach supported a menagerie of records in the middle of her desk. Pretty colorful frocks dangled in her wardrobe.

Her papà had spoiled her. There was no doubt about it.

Around her, he was kind and generous, showering her with presents and attention whenever she wanted them. Yet something felt shallow about his type of love. It had outgrown her as one outgrows an old blouse or frayed dress.

"Johnny is a real nice young man." Her papà commented, wiping his mouth with a napkin over a dinner of *spaghett'* and meatballs.

"He's okay." Carlotta wiggled her toes in her black leather shoes, feeling the scrutiny of her family weigh down upon her.

Don Roberto seemed oblivious to Carlotta's discomfort and continued with an unapologetic testament of Johnny's person. "He's done well for himself, *figlia mia*. He's a true Sicilian, with a desire to honor his heritage and work hard in this country. I don't see what more a young Italian girl could want in a man."

"He's family, too." Carlotta's mamma added coyly, raising her fork in the air. "He knows us well, and would be an impressive addition to our *famiglia.* Trust me, dearest Carlotta. Marriage brings more joy than anything in the world. You could find it with Johnny."

"Kids at *my* school say that marrying a cousin is like marrying a sister." Teenaged Louis Mancini commented offhandedly. "They say it's *raunchy* and weird."

An expression of indignation roused some color into Isabella Mancini—Carlotta's mother's cheeks. "What kids? Your American friends? They know nothin' about our people. Besides, Johnny's ma is *my* cousin, and he's her son. That makes him your distant cousin."

Adrenaline rushed through Carlotta. She needed to change the subject. "Hey Ma, you know where my old rollerblades are? I was gonna give them to Louis."

"You used to rollerblade out on the street with Johnny, didn't you?" Roberto Mancini simpered, spearing his meat with his fork. "He taught you. I remember it. The both of you had so much fun back then."

Carlotta knew that her papà—like everyone in her family—had his heart set on her marrying the famed Johnny Siciliano.

Johnny was the youngest capo in the Family, in Brooklyn, for that matter, and one of the few men Don Roberto trusted, him being a second cousin of her mamma.

There was no doubt in Carlotta's mind that Johnny Siciliano was handsome. Every girl with a working pair of eyes could see that plain as day. And yes, he would likely become a boss one day if he wanted to and was ambitious enough to do it, but she couldn't fathom the idea of marrying a man she considered a brother.

These types of matches were made often, between the daughter of a powerful Boss, and one of the men aspiring to rise in rank. So despite American sensibilities, it wasn't uncommon for distant cousins or old family friends to marry for the sake of forging alliances. Maybe Carlotta had filled her head with the nonsense of American television and romance novels as her parents professed, but she *wouldn't* marry a man she didn't love.

"Carlotta likes someone else." Louis teased.

Carlotta muttered a string of curses in Italian and socked her brother in the arm, sensing her face grow warm with the truth of his words.

After dinner, Carlotta helped her mamma clear the table and wash the dishes.

She loved the sensation of warm water and a concoction of liquid detergent and soap mixed together, running over her hands like silk. It was the kind of soap that smelled of sunshine and lemons.

This was what Carlotta loved. Standing with her mamma, heads bent over the sink, chattering about both nonsense and wisdom and the in-between, loud enough for their confessions to be concealed beneath the crooning Italian music from the radio. The kitchen was her mamma's domain and so no men were allowed, including her father. If she could remain in the kitchen forever, she wouldn't be opposed.

"Gonna start preparing for the Christmas dinner?" Carlotta nodded towards a peeled-open recipe book lying on the kitchen counter.

"Of course. What d'you think I should make? A turkey? Pot roast? What did your papà like last year?"

"He liked the turkey. And maybe you could make some *frutta martorana* for dessert." Carlotta adored Christmas dinners with her mamma. She was the best cook in Brooklyn and began preparing meals ages in advance. For weeks before the Christmas feast last year, a powdery mixture of flour and sugar had blanketed the kitchen air.

"Turkey it is then." Isabella kissed Carlotta on the cheek, then held her shoulders to examine her at length, pinching her arms and sizing up the girth of her waist. "You're getting too thin, *bambina.* Do you want me to make more of that pudding you like this year? Fatten you up? You barely touched your plate of *spaghett'*! *Sesenta fame*?"

Carlotta shook her head in exasperation, drying a plate with the dishcloth attached to her checkered apron. "I'm *fine,* Ma."

It appeared even if she weighed a tonne, her mother would continually bug her about being too skinny.

"You don't look *fine* to me, Carlotta." Her mamma frowned, the creases on her forehead hardening. "Boys don't like skinny girls. You need to put some more meat on those bones."

Without further mention of the topic discussed at the dinner table, Carlotta hunkered down in the parlor while her father finished his meeting with the men upstairs.

She tried not to think about what they might be doing up in the tidy four-corner office. Likely, her father was assigning duties for each of the men to complete—pay off one of the many union labor leaders in the construction business if there was a new project, collect money from one business they had intimidated, meet with other family leaders, or hijack a shipment of goods and unload it in some abandoned warehouse.

Thinking about the type of activities her father was controlling from his little office and his thick leather chair made Carlotta's head spin. She had always possessed a sensitive feminine conscience, her mamma had told her, which is why she, and the other women, were prohibited from dealing in the business.

Or maybe they were just untainted enough to see how wrong it all was.

Carlotta tamed her nerves by mindlessly flipping through her younger brothers' comic books and her own romance novels, filling the quiet room with American music from the radio.

She stayed up later than she was used to, exhaustion nagging at her eyelids and her vision becoming blurred. Eventually, she was glad to hear the treading of footsteps through the door and into the hallway as her mamma whisked them away into the night with a pitcher of fresh espresso.

Finally, when the euphonious voice of her mamma had traveled the length of the hallway to the kitchen, Carlotta smoothed her hair and aired out her skirt, gliding into the main entrance way of the house.

She checked herself in the mirror before rounding the corner, admiring the way her black curls framed her face and the hourglass shape of her new dress. *Was it vanity?* All she knew was that she wanted to look her best. Being gifted with good looks wasn't a crime. In her world, her appearance had become one of the only things she could control.

Tony Bellucci was standing beside the door frame, his brown hair shining navy against the pleasant glow of the pinkish lamplight. His brown eyes were ringed with splashes of a yellow-golden hue, reminding Carlotta of a fading sunset.

Desire surged through her at the sight of him. How she longed to be in his strong arms and held close like the heroines in the pictures.

The pair shared a collective smile. Carlotta gave into her yearning and flailed herself into his arms, kissing his stubbled cheeks with a passion she hadn't known herself capable of. Then she pulled his mouth to hers—letting her soft lips crash against his rough ones. His determined hands ran along her waist until they pushed her away to take an unsteady breath.

"Carlotta, *aduzipazz*!" He whispered, "You are crazy!"

"Why?" Carlotta kissed him harder, the desire for him burning as a beacon within her chest. "Am I crazy to shower the man I love with affection?"

"Yeah, you *are* crazy," Tony joked lovingly, though quietly, finally circling her body with his muscular arms, "we are in your padre's home."

Carlotta pulled away, her lips tingling with his cool taste of peppermint and shaving cream. "Then, ask me out on a date. Bring me somewhere. I'm bored to death staying here all the time, waiting till everyone's gone to spend a few moments with you. I'm not a kid anymore. I'm a grown woman. I'm nearly twenty-three, for crying out loud."

How she had envied her high school friends and their boyfriends, making their love public and posing for photographs together on the dance floor at graduation. She had been forced to stand at the side of the gymnasium as a defeated wallflower, shooing away the boys who asked her to dance with them. But by that time, few sane boys were brave enough to flirt with the daughter of Don Roberto Mancini. Only Tony possessed the courage.

Tony and Carlotta had been going steady for a year now, but she had known him for most of her life. He was the finest-looking boy she had ever seen, next to Carey Grant, of course. She had sillily admired

Tony as a kid, and when they got older, she had been thrilled to know he felt the same.

"I can't now." Tony stroked his thumb along her cheek, sending shivers down her arms—through the tendons of her spine. "Your padre is waiting for me upstairs. Give me some time, and I'll take you on a drive, or out to the movies or something. I promise. But really, Carlotta, this kinda thing could get us in trouble. We gotta be careful."

"You promise then?" Carlotta raised a dark eyebrow, holding his firm hands captive until he nodded his head in the affirmative. "Promise you'll take me out somewhere?"

"I promise, *amore mio*. You think I don't want to be with you, alone? Of course, I do. Who could say no to the prettiest broad in Brooklyn?" Tony kissed the side of her neck, pulling her close.

Carlotta almost disappeared in his muscular arms. But the sound of footsteps and booming voices coming down the stairs disarmed their tender embrace.

"I love you, Tony," Carlotta whispered.

But she was speaking more to herself than to Tony, as he rushed over to the men, leaving her alone.

CHAPTER 7

Pamela tuned out the Blue Tango song, serenading her from the taxi radio and focused on the picturesque view unfolding outside of the automobile window.

She had endured an exhausting first week as a salesgirl at Albright Trimmings & Co, and Caterina had told her to use her first day off to have a ball.

She knew she should be out doing something more leisurely, or at least home curled up on the sofa listening to the radio or reading a novel. Sean had even sent her an invitation to join him for lunch at the greasy spoon he was working at in Greenwich Village. He received free portions of fries after every dishwashing shift.

Instead of doing any of those things, she was visiting the New York Police Department. She had an appointment with someone named Joseph Marino, or Sergeant Marino, to report what she had seen and heard in the alleyway, as well as her run-in with Johnny.

"This it Ma'am?" The portly cab driver dialed down the radio, drumming his stubby pink fingers on the dashboard.

Pamela peered up at a stone fortress, constructed in the style of a huge Romanesque palace. "Yes, this is my stop. Thanks for the ride."

"Hope you're not in any trouble." The cab driver cast Pamela a knowing look and tipped his hat to her. "Are you around bad types of people much?"

"Thank you," Pamela repeated redundantly, ignoring his nosy speculation.

"A pretty little thing like you shouldn't be hanging around a place like this, with crooks and criminals of the worst kind." The cab driver warned, examining her without concern for coming across as intrusive.

After redundantly thanking him for the third time, Pamela handed her driver a crumpled bill she had stuffed in her jacket pocket and stepped out of the cab, her short heels ramming into the hard concrete.

Pamela had dressed in a little black gown to compliment her willowy frame, accompanied by a string of white pearls and the reddest of lipsticks she could find. She tied her cornflower yellow hair above her head in a fashionable knot, and thick, dark lashes offset her green eyes. She was the prettiest she could ever be, she decided, and a well-kept appearance might benefit her today.

The damsel in distress was always the one to be rescued in the end, after all.

Pamela sucked in a breath.

She had never been to the police station before.

When she was in grade school, her mother had accused a young housemaid of stealing an antique Italian vase from the living room, but it was later recovered behind the sofa, where Pamela and her elder sister Cecelia had been playing tea party. Caroline had dismissed the maid, anyway.

When she thought about it long and hard, she realized her mother had possessed some kind of affinity for accusing people of things they hadn't done. Silverware and diamond-studded jewelry were all steadily misplaced and then recovered, with Caroline complaining that the servants weren't to be trusted. Whenever they went on vacation, she would insist the hotel's front desk guard her jewels—though always said something was missing at the end of their stay. In turn, she gained notoriety as the wealthy socialite who cried wolf.

Could Caroline's habit make Pamela seem less trustworthy? Would the cops even believe her?

Pamela shrugged the thought off as she entered the waiting room of the police station. After telling the secretary that she had an appointment, she sat down in a burgundy armchair, gazing up at the plaster ceiling.

Not long after she had flipped through a glossy fashion magazine, the secretary called for her to join Sergeant Marino in his office.

Following the secretary through a maze of winding hallways and corridors, they came to a small corner office with the name **MARINO** written in bold uppercase letters across a brass sign. The secretary rapped her knuckles on the wooden door, and a deep male voice yelled: "Come in!"

The secretary gestured for Pamela to comply, and she quieted her nerves before opening the door, her heart quaking.

She prayed for courage.

"Pamela Kelly?" Sergeant Marino wasn't the man she had in mind when she thought of a police sergeant.

For one, he was young, in his late twenties at most. Second, he was handsome and trim, if she dared admit it. He was the type of man juvenile girls like Pamela had pictured as the lead of romantic Western novels and daring detective stories, with his blinding white smile and magnetic gaze.

His athletic figure was cut in a beige overcoat and suit, much like the one Johnny had worn the first time Pamela had seen him. She suspected he was an undercover officer, or maybe he could wear civilian clothes because of his high rank.

He stood to greet her, extending a hand. "My name is Joe Marino. I've been meaning to bust Mr. Siciliano and his gang for quite some time now, and when I got your call, you can imagine how pleased I was."

Though it wasn't pronounced, there was a kind of quickness and drawing out of vowels that lay beneath the surface of Sergeant Joe Marino's polished Manhattan speech—the repressed remnants of a Staten Island or Brooklyn cadence.

"Nice to meet you. And yes, I've been eager to speak with you as well." Pamela agreed formally.

"You want something to drink?" Sergeant Marino offered, looking slyly at a bottle of champagne atop his desk. "I have nothing to celebrate. One guy brought it over as a going away gift."

Pamela wasn't sure whether it was professional for him to be drinking on the job, but she assumed the latter. "No, thank you."

Sergeant Marino leaned back in his chair, his palms on his legs. "So, tell me exactly what you saw that night, and what happened afterwards."

Pamela recounted the evening in the alleyway, how Mr. Friedenberg had reacted, and how he still hadn't returned from his supposed family vacation.

When she was done relaying the tale, Joseph Marino shook his head in disbelief, his forehead creased in worry.

As he stewed in contemplation, Pamela observed her surroundings.

His office was small and clean, with no family photographs or potted plants to testify that anyone had ever worked there. Pamela noted a stack of newspapers in the room's corner, each with a cover having to do with the mafia or murders committed in the city, which had increased in recent years.

"Thanks for filling me in," he murmured as if lost in his thoughts. "I wouldn't want to keep you waiting for any longer but if you have questions..."

"Am I in any danger, Sergeant Marino?" Pamela tried to swallow the insoluble lump that had been growing at the back of her throat. She tasted charred toast and orange juice from her breakfast that morning.

Joe Marino chuckled, crossing one leg over the other. "Please, it's Joe to you. Don't call me Sergeant Marino. That's what everyone called my dad, and I don't want a dame like you thinking of me as some old miser."

Pamela detected a thread of flirtation weaving through his words, but she tried her best to shrug it off. Ever since Timothy, she had been wary about men paying her any kind of romantic attention. She possessed a yearning for romantic love, but she was so used to being in the shadow of the other Kelly women she had convinced herself she was invisible in that arena.

He paused before standing and pouring himself a glass of lemon water, offering the pitcher to Pamela for her to do the same.

She mumbled a polite denial.

He continued. "I would be lying if I said you're not in hot water. But I wouldn't want a kitten like you to worry. But now that you've told me everything, I guess you should know who this Johnny Siciliano is."

Pausing, Joseph Marino pulled a drawer open under his desk and retrieved a thick stack of papers and photographs. "These are all the things I've collected on the Mancini family, the crime syndicate Johnny works for. It began when Roberto Mancini immigrated from Sicily. Roberto had family connections here in America, and instead of making an honest living as any decent American citizen would, Roberto used these connections to involve himself in illegal sales of alcohol, racketeering, loan sharking, hijacking, bribes... the works. He has ordered the killings of up to a thousand of his enemies and rivals. He murdered a witness to a bank robbery in 1945 because he doesn't like squealers. Now, he has a handful of dangerous men working for him, and Johnny Siciliano is just one of them."

The photograph was a family heirloom, taken of a young couple on their wedding day. It showed a beautiful young woman with black curls and her serious groom being crowded by giddy family members on the cobble-stoned streets of Italy. Below it, in red ink, were the names of the people pictured: Roberto Mancini and Isabella Fiastri.

"Where did you find the picture?" Pamela inquired, "I would imagine such artifacts are difficult to get your hands on."

Joseph Marino replied without pause. "Immigration. Ellis Island."

If she didn't know any better, Pamela would say that they looked happier than her parents ever had.

"But, if you know all this, why can't you arrest him?" Pamela wondered aloud, searching Joe Marino's faraway gaze. "If you know that he's had people murdered, isn't that a crime enough to send him to jail for life?"

"If only it were that simple," Joseph Marino laughed cynically, "not only is Roberto a criminal mastermind, but he is also a practiced businessman. He and his cronies cover their tracks well, and if we were to arrest them, we would need some solid evidence to hold up in court. Tax evasion charges, arson charges, damage to property and goods, eyewitnesses. Anything to prove that Roberto Mancini and his friends are breaking the law. If it were up to me, I would deport the lot back to Sicily where they came from. But, we've got nothing. Nada." he raised his palms to her in defeat.

Pamela tried to figure out why Joseph Marino had summoned her here if he hadn't any means of developing a solution.

He silenced her unspoken fears with a statement. "Everything changes now that we have you."

"Me?"

"Yes, you, Miss Kelly." Joseph Marino circled his desk, his gaze pressing into her. There was something more than flirtation in his stare: something menacing. He wanted something from her.

"I don't understand..."

"I'm sorry, Miss Kelly. I should explain myself. What I mean is that now that we have you, a young, attractive woman in contact with one of the mafioso, we have a promising lead. We can use your closeness to Johnny and his crew to infiltrate the mob, and bring down the Mancini clan once and for all." Sergeant Joseph Marino folded his arms across his desk and leaned forward. His incessant shifting made Pamela nervous.

"If you're implying that Johnny Siciliano and I are in some sort of relationship... you are most definitely mistaken." Pamela could not imagine herself ever considering having a romantic tryst with Johnny Siciliano.

The man frightened her half to death! Besides, he was a mafioso. What would they talk about over dinner? Not the economy as she had with Timothy, though the topic had bored her half to death. She doubted that Johnny Siciliano would ever see her in that way, either. Few men did.

"I don't imply. I know that with Johnny's track record, he's bound to take the bait if we have a pretty girl like you working on the scene."

"Working on the scene? I'm not sure I understand you. And, I don't believe you understand me, either. I work as a sales assistant. I'm not a detective." Pamela's tone grew more urgent and far more intentional. She was not happy with Sergeant Marino talking about her as if she were a pawn in a trivial game of chess.

"Yes, but you are a good citizen. And good citizens work under the rule of law." Joseph Marino tilted his head sideways as if to take a better look at her. "I'm not saying you have to help me. I can't force you to do anything. But, now that you've reported all that you've seen, you can help us stop this guy once and for all. You'd be willing to do that, now wouldn't you?"

Pamela tried to comb through the thoughts that were wildly gallivanting through her mind. She had hoped that coming here to talk to Joseph Marino would vanquish her anxiety, while instead; it had turned her into a nervous wreck.

"I hope you're not under the impression that Johnny Siciliano and I are... romantically involved," she repeated frantically, massaging her temples as if to comfort herself, "he hardly knows me. I mean—we only met only a few days ago, and there is no guarantee that he will even come back to the shop."

A sinister look blighted Joseph Marino's otherwise handsome countenance. "He'll come back. You can be sure of that."

After being escorted out of Joseph Marino's office and into the dusk-ridden streets of New York, Pamela contemplated his last words to her while she tried to hail a taxi.

"I'm not asking you to do much, Miss Kelly. You don't even have to go out with the man. Just to record everything Johnny Siciliano tells you. Everything you overhear, remember it. I'll take care of the rest and see you when I get the rest of my business sorted out." He had said before closing the door of his office.

Pamela wanted to believe Joseph Marino. But she was scared out of her mind. The illegal activities she had witnessed were far worse than she had suspected. When she had taken the job at Albright Trimmings & Co., she had never expected to end up amid an intricate crime network. She had wanted to become someone other than the socialite wife her mother wanted her to be.

Admittedly, she had yearned for adventure. But this kind of adventure was far more dangerous than she could ever have imagined.

CHAPTER 8

New York City, East 60th Street, November 1954

I should never have come. The thought was all Pamela could consider as she zigzagged through crowds upon crowds of beautiful female salsa dancers and dapper Latin orchestra band members, sporting their trumpets and miniature drums like colorful accessories.

Why did I ever agree to this? She asked herself. *Why couldn't I have just stayed home to read? Washed my hair? Listened to the radio? Or done anything else?*

It was a Thursday night, and she had work the next morning. The Copacabana was the spot Johnny and his crew hung around, and Pamela had no interest in running into the man after the humiliating spectacle back at the store. However, Caterina had convinced her that Thursdays at the Copacabana were always fun and that it would do her some good to come dancing.

The Copacabana was oozing with activity. It wasn't like the old money nightclubs that Timothy had taken Pamela to on some of their dates, where the staff wouldn't serve you unless you were from one of the wealthy white families in the Upper East Side.

The people running the Copacabana called themselves *progressives* and *the voices of the young.* They claimed to cater to all the richest and most influential people in New York City of every creed and color.

They also played Latin music, adorned the walls in safari animal patterned decor, and served steaming hot plates of Chinese food.

Young columnists made a sport of writing about the happenings of the Copacabana in the newspaper, providing old ladies and young homemakers with silly gossip over what awful thing Frank Sinatra had said to his latest girlfriend on Monday, or what gorgeous hairstyle the Copacabana girls were trying out on the weekend.

Several men in red uniforms were scattered around the room, barely visible beneath the constant swarm of people and pounding music. Caterina had said that they were there to guard the celebrities who frequented the Copacabana, as well as to break up fights if they ever arose.

Despite its self-proclaimed status as a progressive New York hotspot, the Copacabana was still an exclusive nightclub, and nearly impossible to get into unless you were a celebrity or had affiliations with the mob. Luckily, Caterina's father knew one bouncer, so to some of the other patrons' irritation, the girls could skip the long line forming down and around the block.

"Come on!" Caterina shrilled, ushering Pamela over to a small, circular table shoved against the backdrop of black and white zebra-stripe decorated wallpaper.

Pamela gathered the crinoline skirt of her red circle dress, smoothing it so that she could park on the chair without creasing the fabric.

"You look like an absolute doll!" Caterina let out a low whistle, eyeing Pamela's curled blonde hair and the pearls she had slipped through her earlobes. "Not half bad for a cube from the Upper East Side!"

Several men standing nearby swung around to signal their approval.

Pamela ducked her head, her ears burning. "I still don't look half as glamorous as you, Cat."

"Beauty is an art, Pam. It takes practice." Caterina winked at one man as he pretended not to eavesdrop.

The two had become an unlikely pair of friends. Pamela cherished Caterina's company more than anything.

Pamela had grown lonely after moving to the Ave. Without the friendship of Lorna or her old high school friends, if nothing else, she appreciated the bubbly and talkative personality of Caterina De Lorenzo. It meant that she didn't have to talk that much herself. Rather, she could fill the silences of her own life with Caterina's ceaseless chatter. The stories about the boys Caterina went out with, her beauty tips and fashion icons, and her growing annoyance with Mr. Friedenberg's prolonged absence all entertained and distracted her.

Caterina smiled, twirling her dark hair around her finger and scanning the room with her eyes, fleshing out the attractive young bachelors of the night. Before leaving, she had promised Pamela that she would find a dreamboat for both of them to dance the night away with.

"Look over there!" Caterina lowered her voice and nodded toward a group of stunning women, all dressed to the nines in diamonds and pearls.

Amid them towered a handsome man with a combed-back hairdo and a comfortable smile. His teeth were a blinding white, the kind one saw in Crest toothpaste commercials. "Cast an eyeball over there. That's Leonard McCoy! Isn't he an absolute *dream*? He's directin' a film with James Dean as the lead. All those gals are actresses hoping to be cast in the movie as if they have a chance. Huh!"

Caterina stirred her water and shook her head vigorously, her eyes still trained on the promising young director and his posse of female admirers. He appeared bored by the girls corralling him like a penned-in farm animal. Suddenly, Caterina seemed to catch his eye, and he raised a brow in interest. She smirked coyly, daring him to approach.

Pamela was shocked by her friend's audacity because she seemed to have undying confidence that never wore off. Pamela would never be able to flirt so openly with anyone, let alone a famous stranger. She didn't think she'd want to, either.

A young server with charcoal eyes and walnut brown skin obstructed the young Leonard McCoy from view. In his gloved hand lay a tiny notebook and pen. Irritated, Caterina groaned, but the waiter couldn't hear her over the pulsing cacophony of noise.

"Welcome to Copacabana! What can I do for you, ladies?"

"A glass of gin, please," Caterina drawled in her Brooklyn accent, her dark lashes fluttering flirtatiously, her aim shifting.

"Oh! And add a plate of dumplings. Elizabeth Taylor said they were one of the *best* things she's ever had." Caterina giggled as though she and Elizabeth Taylor were personal best friends. The waiter hardly seemed phased, jotting down her order.

The waiter smiled pleasantly toward Pamela. "And for you, Miss?"

"Water, please." Pamela was humiliated. She didn't have enough money to spend on soft drinks like the Coca-Cola she might usually order. She hadn't gotten her first paycheck yet, and she couldn't possibly think of going back to her parents and asking them for money after her unexpected disappearance.

"Get the young ladies anything they want."

Astonished, Pamela froze and watched a dark figure looming in her periphery. From the voice, he was male, and from the expensive charcoal suit, he was wealthy. Before she could turn around, she heard Caterina's energetic greeting.

"Johnny! Fancy seeing you boys here!"

Pamela peered up at Johnny Siciliano. His brown eyes, framed by lashes a woman would envy, flashed violet beneath the flicker of lights. His grin settled upon his olive face. He swept a hand through his dark, slicked-back hair, like a bonafide greaser.

Something electric shot through her.

He appeared far merrier to her than he had when she formally met him in the store. She wondered if he had forgotten their strange interaction and her brash reaction, or if he was just shrugging it off.

Behind him, a group of men in black suits waited, the group that had been in the alleyway on that long-ago evening. Idling behind the men was a group of women, many of the same young actresses who had been talking with the famed Leonard McCoy. One of these women gripped Johnny's arm, her neckline plunging and her head resting on his sturdy shoulder.

"There is no need," Pamela insisted as Johnny shooed the woman away, handing the waiter a stack of paper bills.

The girl pouted and moped, but Johnny paid her no mind.

"Of course there is. We're at Copacabana, New York's finest who's who!" The men raised their glasses and cheered.

"No, really, Mr. Siciliano..." Pamela met the eyes of the kind waiter and finally agreed to place an order. "Then, I suppose I'll have a Shirley Temple."

"No, no, we need some alcohol here. The lady will have your finest Pink Squirrel, and for me, a gin and tonic with ice." Johnny demanded, winking in Pamela's direction.

It annoyed her that he had changed her order without asking, but before she could protest, the server grinned and waltzed away, stuffing the cash into his pocket. A malignant question came to Pamela.

Where had Johnny gotten the money? From some other poor, tired New York business owner?

Without asking, Johnny and three men plopped themselves down beside Caterina and Pamela. One man had his arm around the slender waist of a ditzy-looking blonde, and Johnny claimed the chair across from Pamela. The moping woman had vanished.

"Introduce Pamela to your friends, Johnny." Caterina cooed, fiddling with her plastic straw.

"This is Lorenzo." Johnny gestured to the middle-aged man holding the blonde like a trophy in his possession.

"And this is Tony and Mike." Johnny pointed to two younger men with prominent Italian features and brown eyes.

Caterina pointed her gaze toward the young man named Tony. "I'll never forget your name, dear Tony. I was always sweet on you, even when all the girls liked Johnny!"

It seemed as though Tony squirmed under Caterina's prying eyes, trying to keep her from noticing him.

"Don't bother with Tony, baby." Lorenzo addressed Caterina directly. "He already has a girlfriend, and he's stiff. Refuses to leave the old ball and chain."

Caterina sighed exaggeratedly, tilting her large brown eyes up to Lorenzo.

"Me..." Lorenzo's lips quirked into a menacing smile. "I'm completely available."

Johnny cast his earnest gaze towards Tony. "Hey! My best pal has a girl? Where is she tonight? Why didn't ya invite her here to be with us?"

From where she was sitting, Pamela could see Tony kick Lorenzo in the shin.

"I dunno, never met the dame," Lorenzo admitted, raising his shoulders in a shrug.

"She lives in the Bronx." Tony flushed, looking away. "Has to stay home to take care of her ma. She's real busy."

"And who is this little darling?" The man named Mike kept Pamela in his trajectory, inching so close to her that she could feel his hot, foul-smelling breath on her face.

Pamela edged away from Mike, uncomfortable with his hand moving treacherously down her waist.

"Mike, take it easy, okay? They work at Friedenberg's place, real nice girls." Johnny reprimanded Mike, who then shrugged and wrangled his hand away.

Eventually, Mike and Tony rejoined a gang of men and women on the dance floor, while Johnny stayed back and folded his long legs under the table.

Once Caterina exited to the lady's room to freshen up, Johnny and Pamela were left, sitting across from each other in tense silence.

Johnny got up and hunkered down beside Pamela so that he could get a better view of the musicians and their orchestra, bringing his gin and tonic with him. He tapped his foot to the music, humming along pleasingly.

"What a song, huh?" He brought his hands together and clapped when the band had finished. The musicians relished in his wild applause, beaming at him with pride. It seemed everyone in the room knew exactly who Johnny Siciliano was and understood the power he wielded.

She noticed Johnny was sitting too close, his leg snagging the long skirt of her dress. She inched away, pretending to reach for the alcoholic beverage she hadn't yet touched.

"I'm sorry if he made you uncomfortable," Johnny apologized after a long silence. "Mike, I mean. He's a real Casanova. Or at least he thinks he is."

"I'm sorry about how I... hit you at the textiles shop," Pamela blushed.

Johnny burst into genuine laughter, crinkles forming at the corners of his eyes. "If we're still saying things we're sorry for, I'm sorry for leaving so quickly. It startled me, that's all."

A slow love ballad hummed through the air. The din of the room melted into more of a mellow susurration as people ceased their conversations to listen, transfixed by the sultry voice of the singer atop the stage.

"I wanted to ask..." Pamela began but lost her courage and buttoned her mouth shut once again.

"What?" Johnny dropped his fork to his plate, correcting himself. "I mean, what did you want to ask?"

"You said you're in business with Mr. Friedenberg. Do you know when he's coming back?"

Johnny didn't answer, his face becoming dismal and removed. A secret flashed within them. He knew something.

Of course.

He feels guilty, Pamela reminded herself. *Or do mobsters feel remorse at all?*

"I know I shouldn't ask. I'm just wondering because, well, I haven't been paid yet, and I've been wanting to get a train ticket to see my sister and her husband in the suburbs." Pamela explained. The last part wasn't completely true. Her sister had invited her to come to visit the kids, but she had no intention of going. Not now that she had been virtually disowned by Mother and Father.

"I'm awful sorry, Pamela. All I know is what I've been told, which is that Old Friedenberg, I mean Clyde, left to visit his family and never came back." His eyes got darker, and he turned to examine the dance floor.

"Have you worked with Mr. Friedenberg for long?" Pamela dared to ask, adrenaline pumping through her.

"No." Johnny hesitated. "Well, sorta. My boss knows him. They've been friends for a long time."

"Maybe your boss would know where he was?"

"I haven't asked. But talking about these types of things only stirs up more trouble. Mr. Friedenberg is safe and sound, enjoying an extended weekend away from work. Who'd wanna bother a man enjoying some well-deserved vacation time with his kids?"

"I hope that's the case." Pamela wasn't convinced.

A new song throbbed through the Copacabana, the music of steel drums, saxophones, and electric guitars melding in an entrancing symphony of noise. Couples charged to the dance floor in a plethora of pink crinoline and black leather, men swinging their partners up to the heavens.

Johnny rose from his chair and grabbed Pamela's hand. "This is a real groovy beat! Forget the business talk and dance with me."

Pamela gulped down her Pink Squirrel along with her suspicions and took his hand, following him out to the dance floor.

Johnny set his hands on her waist, and gingerly Pamela held onto his muscular shoulders as he swept her around the dance floor.

The music sped up.

His face was transformed by an exhilarated smile, the joyful light in his eyes pulling at the edges of her lips.

He looked like a different man, and Pamela decided he was handsome. Dark, tousled hair was gelled across his head, his eyes the color of warm, melted chocolate. He threw his tailored sports jacket to the side and lifted her, spinning her around until she lost her breath in a fit of dizziness.

She felt mystified. She couldn't look at him for fear of breaking into a blush.

A small crowd of people had gathered to watch them, impressed by Johnny's polished dance moves and her good sportsmanship. The gossip columnist Caterina had pointed out earlier was watching intently, his hand moving rapidly as his pen ran across a small notepad. Pamela hoped he would not reveal her identity in the paper. The last thing she needed was for her mother to hear about her dancing with a gangster at the Copacabana.

In the corner of her eye, Pamela saw someone familiar.

Sergeant Marino.

He was watching them with a knowing expression, and when he noticed her looking, he turned away to talk to a waiter.

"I need... a breath of fresh air."

"I'm sorry that I tired you out." Johnny apologized, a grin still plastered to his now amiable face.

"It's okay. I just haven't danced like this in a while." Internally, Pamela corrected those last two words to ever. She had never danced like that before.

Was it wrong that she had enjoyed it?

In the crisp New York night air, Pamela tried to collect her strength. It was no use. She was utterly exhausted, both physically and mentally.

What had she been doing, dancing with one of the most dangerous made men in the city? And had she enjoyed being in his arms, his eyes locking her into a state of near-paralysis, helplessness, and magnetism?

She had felt something dancing with him she had *never* felt before; not with Timothy, not with *anybody*.

"Pamela." Sergeant Marino caught up with her, nodding in acknowledgement and taking off his hat.

"Hello, Sergeant Marino."

"Chilly night." Sergeant Marino offered.

Pamela nodded in mute agreement.

"We've found Mr. Friedenberg, your employer."

Pamela's breath sped up, and she waited for him to elaborate.

"But... it isn't good." Sergeant Marino inclined his head, wiping his handkerchief across his forehead.

"What happened? Is he ill?"

Sergeant Marino looped an arm through her waist, noticing her nervousness, or perhaps preparing to catch her if she were to faint from some dire news.

"Not quite. It pains me to tell you this... well, I wish I didn't have to tell you at all. We found his body off the banks of the Hudson River. He's dead."

Pamela stared at him, her head spinning with the news he had just relayed. He was staring back down at her, gripping the back of her arm as if to steady her beating heart.

It wasn't any use.

She was left paralyzed by his words, and not for any of the proper reasons. She knew she should feel sorry for Mr. Friedenberg and the terrible fate that had gotten the better of him, but she was more concerned with her safety, and more afraid that she might be the next one to suffer the consequences of her emerging affiliations with the mob.

And she was angry. She should never have danced with Johnny Siciliano. She had always known that he was a mobster, a mafioso.

He can't be that bad, can he? She had asked herself, hoping to sympathize with an evil man. She felt sick to her stomach knowing that the man who had held her close on the dance floor was the same man behind the murder of her now-deceased employer.

"Was it Johnny?" Pamela beseeched, but she already knew the answer.

Officer Marino examined her with sympathetic eyes. "We don't know. I suspect that the Mancini family was involved, but considering their history with avoiding charges, I'm sure that they will get out of this fix too."

Pamela realized that Officer Marino's hand was still resting on the small of her back. She took a firm step away from him.

He seemed to notice her sudden movement, but rather than being irked by it, he laughed. "Well, go back in there and dance with your boyfriend. Any information he gives you is evidence we can use to press charges in court."

Pamela focussed her eyes on the dim scenery behind him.

Streets snaked up and down hills and around the curves and edges of buildings, squeezing like a boa constrictor or tropical snake that could suffocate the entire city, snapping its neck with one wrong move.

"He isn't my boyfriend, Sergeant Marino." Pamela knew he had told her not to call him that, but she didn't care. "And I'm certainly not his girlfriend. One dance was all it was."

Joseph Marino shrugged. "Look. I want to reiterate that my intention was never to put you in any danger, Miss Kelly, but if you can elicit any information from him about Mr. Friedenberg's sudden death... then I would be grateful."

"I won't go back in." Pamela objected, folding her arms across her chest like a child. There was nothing he could do to make her. Sure, he was an officer of the law, but what could he do? Tie her up and drag her back inside?

"Don't be unreasonable, Miss Kelly." He continually addressed her with the voice of one who considers themselves to be a grown-up, acting as though she were decades younger and less experienced than him. It irritated her that he was putting her in so much danger, and yet speaking to her in such a patronizing, didactic, condescending tone.

Sergeant Marino fixated on her with a particular message projecting from his eyes: *don't be difficult.* "I'm right here, okay doll? You don't need to worry about a thing. I'll follow you shortly to make sure you are safe. But not to worry, I'll stay just close enough so that they don't notice me. I'll be invisible, okay?"

As if she was a puppet being controlled by someone other than herself, Pamela walked back inside Copacabana.

The music had increased in pitch and volume if that was possible, and men were swinging their female dance partners up and around, throwing them and catching them mid-air like rag dolls.

Pamela's gaze darted across the room, yearning to catch a glimpse of Caterina so that they could go back home. Well, the apartment wasn't quite her home yet, but it was more of a home than anywhere else.

To her surprise, Johnny was not at the table anymore, and neither were his cronies. Each of them was on the dance floor, their arms looped around women with gowns swelling with gaudy tulle and sequins.

Johnny himself had his hands set on the waist of a petite raven-haired woman. Johnny was beaming at the woman in the same way that he had looked at her earlier that night, or perhaps he exuded even more exhilaration.

As he swept her around, Pamela noted she was stunning. She looked like Elizabeth Taylor. *Maybe she was Elizabeth Taylor!* No, she was too short. Her waist was minuscule. Pamela guessed Johnny could encircle it with a single hand.

An awful feeling overcame her, something she had experienced little of before, like needles puncturing the insides of her stomach and a mixture of anger, dread and anguish climbing up her throat. She had felt nothing like it since the times she was compared to her elder sister, or when her friend Nance had gone out with a boy she fancied from afar. She knew what it was, but she wouldn't allow herself to conceive the thought. But in her subconscious, the word arose.

Jealousy.

She was envious of that girl, dancing with Johnny and peering up at him through those layered eyelashes. And yet, she didn't like Johnny in the least. He was a murderer. He had killed her boss, and he could do the same to her. Perhaps she was nervous about the girl's well-being.

"What's a pretty girl like you standing off here in the corner like a wallflower without a fella?"

Pamela urged herself out of her jealous trance, acquainting herself with the tawny brown eyes of a short man distinguishable by a mop of wheat blonde hair and a lopsided grin.

"Uh... I'm just about to leave. I'm exhausted."

"Nonsense! While you're all chrome-plated, how about giving me a dance? And then I'll leave you to it." He rasped, jutting his hand out as a forceful offer.

Without the stamina to decline, Pamela let him escort her to the heart of the dance floor, where he placed her hands on his sweaty shoulders and began swaying with her, back and forth, to a slow ballad. He was so short that whenever she sought to reach his gaze, her eyes landed on the top of his head where a shiny bald patch had materialized.

He raised his stare to look at her face, attempting to make light conversation. "You a real New York girl, huh?"

"I suppose so."

"The name is William. William Evans Junior. Named after my old man. I'm from Chicago, the Windy City if you like. Pleased to be at your service." William Evans blabbered emphatically as he gazed up to gauge Pamela's reaction.

She concocted a polite giggle, though it came out as more of a disappointing squeak than anything. Johnny had disengaged from Elizabeth Taylor's stunt double and was watching them from across the room.

"Hey! Who is that guy? Is he your boyfriend, or something?" William Evans wasn't as dense as he let on, and he had noticed Johnny staring at them, too.

"I don't know him in the slightest."

It was half true.

Pamela aggressively grabbed William Evans by the shoulders and pranced him to the other side of the dance floor. She kept time with the music, her clunky high heels battering against the linoleum floor.

"Wow! You're really something!" William Evans proclaimed, impressed by her performance. "Who woulda thought a wallflower like you was a real dancer?"

Unfortunately, Johnny kept up with them and without missing a beat, tapped William Evans on the shoulder.

"Mind if I steal her from you?" It was more of a demand than a question. Johnny towered over William Evans and knew it, straightening his shoulders to fill his lanky stature.

"Give me a break," William Evans groaned under his breath, refusing to let go of Pamela. "She's mine. *I* saw her first. And she said she doesn't know you. So scram!"

At that moment, Pamela wanted to applaud the courageous, outspoken William Evans, the only man in New York to ever work up the nerve to stand up to Johnny Siciliano, even if he was from Chicago.

"Do you know this guy? Want me to get him outta your hair?" Johnny directed the question to Pamela.

Before she could answer, the expression on William Evans' face transformed to one of pure terror. The blood rushed out of his skin like a lemon being squeezed. Johnny's group had descended upon them, surrounded them like a pack of wolves ready for the slaughter.

"Aw... gee, I didn't realize..." William Evans blew out a low whistle and dropped Pamela's hand. "With all due respect, I've gotta get going, Miss. But it was real nice dancing with you."

Before she could object, William Evans had scurried out of sight, vanishing into the vast swell of people.

With Johnny's silent instruction, his men also melted away, returning to their cocktails and giggly dance partners.

"What was that all about?" Pamela growled, tightening her arms around her waist.

Johnny cocked his head to one side, feigning innocence. "I don't know what that guy's deal was."

"No, I mean, why did you follow me onto the dance floor?" Pamela realized it was a convoluted question as she presented it to him.

"I was just being courteous. I wanted to meet your new friend."

"No, you were rude. You and your friends scared him out of his mind!"

Johnny stepped towards her until his rough face was mere inches from her smooth one. He didn't like being challenged. It was a new sensation, but not one he'd want to get used to. "What? I was respectful. I just asked a simple question."

Pamela took a step back, biting the bottom of her lip. "Anyway, I don't care. I'm tired. It's been a long night. I want to go home."

"Let me drive you." Johnny commanded rather than suggested.

"You've been drinking. It isn't safe to drive intoxicated."

"The alcohol has worn off. It's the least I can do for scaring off your new friend." Johnny looped his arm through hers and maneuvered her towards the door.

Pamela scanned the room for Joseph Marino, but he was nowhere to be found. Her heart pounded against her chest as if it wanted to break free.

"No, I'm going to wait for Caterina. She might need me." Pamela searched for her friend, but her quest failed. Somehow, she suspected Caterina was already at home.

"She left ages ago with some guy. Are you sure I can't give you a ride?" Johnny confirmed her prediction.

Pamela didn't say a word, and Johnny took that as acceptance. He retrieved their coats from the coat check and tipped the server one last time. "I'll go pull the car around to the front. Don't move a muscle."

Pamela watched as Johnny disappeared around the corner. Her intuition was warning her to make a run for it, but her legs felt heavy: two pillars of lead welded to the ground.

Johnny followed through with his word and soon she was tucked under a fur blanket in the passenger seat of his flashy automobile, her pale legs sticking to the leather seat from the sweat clinging to the backs of her knees.

"Beautiful," Johnny hummed as he cruised through Midtown. Pamela assumed he was referring to the Christmas lights strung across telephone poles and on the tops of buildings, evidence that the holiday had trickled into the city again.

"Christmas has never been my favorite holiday," Johnny said, in complete contrast to what he had just stated moments earlier.

Pamela waited for him to digress.

Johnny glanced at her through his periphery.

"Christmas at the Siciliano house was a dire affair. I guess it was cause we were poor. Or maybe it was because I was a kid during the '30s, and you know, money wasn't in unlimited supply. Anyway, it was always bitter cold, and on the coldest nights, the furnace was never any good. Nicest thing I got for Christmas was a pair of ice skates. Problem was, I didn't know how to use them." He laughed cynically.

Pamela didn't know what to say.

She had never known what it was to be poor. She had grown up with Lorna, and an abundance of maids and nannies at her disposal. She had never been cold, despite being born shortly after the stock market had plummeted. Her father had always provided the family with an excess of luxury. It appeared no matter how bad the economy got, houses still needed to be made, and that's where Stuart Kelly & Sons came in. Her father had been poor before he made his money, but they never spoke much of it.

"It must have been very difficult, growing up that way." Pamela sympathized, moved by the vulnerability in his voice.

"You know, growing up poor taught me more about how to fend for myself. How to do business the right way without getting pushed around by the big guys." Johnny slammed his foot on the brake as they neared a red.

Pamela had almost felt sorry for him. Almost. And then he reminded her what he was.

"I'm sure Mr. Friedenberg felt that way too," Pamela prickled. "He was a good man. Doing his best for his business. And yet, his life ended so tragically."

The substance of what she had just said expanded in the frosty November air.

Pamela hoped Johnny couldn't hear her heart thudding against her coat.

"How do you think his wife feels, mourning the loss of her husband?" She asked, metaphorically lifting a shovel of dirt in the air as she dug her own grave.

Johnny's fingers trembled against the steering wheel. They had pulled in front of the shop, the *Sorry We're Closed* sign still hanging, defeated above the door.

"You can't tell anyone you know about this," Johnny whispered, pulling her ear against his lips, "*they'll kill you.*"

CHAPTER 9

The three words echoed in Pamela Kelly's mind as she stared into Johnny Siciliano's eyes. She knew she should look away, but something in his gaze was magnetic, drawing her into him like a bee to honey.

"Do you mean to tell me I'm going to die?" Pamela choked out, turning to face Fifth Avenue.

The street was still, aside from a few stragglers who had returned from parties and dancing. The outline of a tall, concrete building with many rectangular windows overhung above them, with all the windows being dull and empty. The outline of the American flag blew in the wind, and Pamela wiggled around in her massive fur jacket to conserve her warmth against the powerful gust.

If Johnny were to reveal a gun and pull the trigger, Pamela realized that nobody would notice. He was probably already reaching for one. It was only a matter of time before he used it to dispose of her, as he had with Mr. Friedenberg.

"Look, Pamela. I think you're a nice girl. Perhaps not the wisest of girls, but I know you only have good intentions, and you were caught up in the middle of this to no fault of your own." Johnny sucked in a breath sharply, moving his hands slowly through his gelled black hair.

She watched as his gold crucifix caught in the streetlight. How could he wear such a thing when he actively murdered and hurt innocent people without remorse? Did he even know what it meant—that little golden cross?

"I don't understand..." Pamela trembled. "Aren't you going to kill me yourself?"

"I'm not gonna kill you," Johnny said as though he hadn't done so to other people many times before.

"Then what?" Pamela choked, "Should I run away?"

She had already imagined herself buying a ranch somewhere in Southeast Texas, or perhaps moving overseas... to somewhere like Australia or New Zealand. When she was a little girl, she had seen a brightly painted postcard with an image of a sandy yellow beach on the front, and people swimming and surfing past the sparkling blue shore. She had fantasized about the postcard and wondered if she would one day be an elegant lady, basking in the sun with a wide-brimmed sun hat and nylon striped swimsuit.

Johnny shattered her simple dream with a single sentence.

"Runaway? If you run away, they'll find you." He shook his head vigorously, lighting a cigarette and tapping his fingers on his knee. "If you show any sign of fear, they'll know that you've done something wrong, or that you know more than you should."

"So what would you suggest I do?"

Johnny's mouth was half-open in a forced smile, the type of smile you give someone when you're trying to be polite or conversing with strangers. Even with such a small contortion of his face, the streetlight revealed a dimple in the side of his mouth. She noticed the prominent mole on his left cheek.

"Stay put. Continue with your job as a salesgirl, pretend like nothing is awry. I won't say anything to anyone, and you should mind you do the same. You don't know who you can trust in this city, especially the cops." Johnny finally spoke, exhaling, as he quickly blew a gust of smoke from his mouth.

Whose side was he on, anyway? He hadn't mentioned why he was helping her, or why he even cared what happened to her.

"Why are you helping me?" Pamela asked as she moved closer to Johnny, wanting to gauge his true feelings about the situation. "What I mean to say is... I'm practically a stranger. You don't know me, and for all you know, I could bring this to the police. So why haven't you turned me into your superiors? Why are you being so nice to me?"

"Are you some kind of cop, Pamela Kelly?" Johnny accused, slamming his hand on the steering wheel. His expression was half-joking, half sincere, but Pamela instantly felt the need to banish his suspicions.

"No!" Pamela objected, "I'm sorry. I don't know why I'm asking so many questions. I'm just... unused to being helped like this."

Especially since Johnny Siciliano was a mobster. She knew he had probably killed people before, so she found it strange that he would not do the same to her.

"I dunno... I guess you're a nice girl, like I said. And, I'm sure you've got family who are worried about you. If you were to mysteriously vanish... I'm sure that they would send the fuzz to overturn all of New York in a jiffy. Despite what you may think, I'm not heartless. And I'm certainly not stupid."

The two were silent for a moment.

She wouldn't tell him that her parents probably couldn't care less where she'd disappeared. By now, they probably suspected her to be dead. There was Sean, but he was hardly in the position to send a search party after her.

Pamela sensed a drop of silver fall delicately on the tip of her nose as she raised her head to the sky, and soon it was pouring, rain thrumming down, creating a ballad brimming with percussion and shrieking city girls, giddy with the sudden change in weather and eager to run for cover.

Johnny struggled for a moment to pull the top of his prized convertible up, and when he ceased his efforts, they slipped over to Albright Trimmings & Co. Johnny unlocked the door with a small brass key Pamela hadn't realized was in his possession.

"Come in. I'm desperate for a hot cup of Joe." Johnny said, holding the door for her like a gentleman.

Pamela followed his instruction and closed the door behind them, glad to find a sheltered place to wring out her soaked hair.

Soon Pamela and Johnny were sitting next to the television in the crummy apartment up the stairs from Albright Trimmings & Co.

Pamela turned on the coffeemaker and put on the coffee, praying that the sleek-looking machine wouldn't break down like it usually did. It was a dire moment, and the last thing she needed was a broken coffee maker and an unhappy mobster in her living room.

She settled in the living room beside Johnny, crossing her legs, and waited for him to continue the conversation. Instead of turning to the matter at hand, he attempted to deflect her attention to other trivial things.

"Nice little place you have here," Johnny commented offhandedly, struggling to dial up the television.

"It hasn't been working all week."

"Really?" Johnny frowned, smoothing the crease in between his eyebrows with his hand. "No television? What do you do to pass the time?"

"I read, I suppose."

"Read? Well, you sure are from the good ol' days then." Johnny teased. "I haven't read since grade school. What do you read, anyway?"

It was such a sudden and unexpected question that Pamela found it hard to answer immediately. She hadn't had the time to read since she left home.

"I enjoy the work of Hemmingway, Steinbeck, and Tolstoy." Pamela didn't dare mention the many romantic novels she adored, like *Jane Eyre* and *Pride and Prejudice.* She wouldn't mention the obscure books either, ones she had found in the library as a child, about archaeology and forgotten moments of history.

Johnny nodded, grappling for words. When he finally recovered, he leaned back and smiled at her. "The only book I ever read was a textbook. I was never the best at reading."

Pamela was surprised by his sudden vulnerability, but it also consoled her. If he was willing to be open with her about his weaknesses, perhaps he would be honest about other things, too.

"Reading isn't entirely difficult," Pamela said, hoping her voice sounded comforting. "You only need to find something you are interested in and find a book about it."

Johnny considered this, his dark eyes pensive. "I guess so."

When Pamela smelled the consoling aroma of hot coffee wafting through the apartment, she traversed to the kitchen and each of them a cup. She turned her coffee caramel-brown with some cream and sugar but kept Johnny's black as he'd requested.

"Smells great." Johnny grinned once she returned to the living room and handed him a cup. "Thanks for keeping mine black."

"You're welcome."

Silence encompassed them for a few minutes more. The rain had softened on the roof, the gentle pitter-patter lapsing into an occasional drip-drop. Johnny uncrossed his legs and then crossed them again.

"Look, Pamela. I know you must be afraid." Johnny said, after taking a sip of his hot beverage. "But there's no need to be scared.

Here and now, I'm giving you my word. An Italian's word is a very sacred thing, you know."

"I know you're sacrificing a lot to help me, not to turn me in," Pamela admitted, stirring a packet of sugar and a drop of milk into her coffee. The caffeine would keep her up, but she wouldn't be able to sleep, anyway. "I guess I'm just scared. I don't understand why you're helping me if you're not getting anything out of it."

"Maybe if you knew I wasn't just doing this out of the kindness of my heart, you'd feel more reassured," Johnny suggested cautiously, gulping down his black coffee. He preferred to drink it that way, he had told her.

"I suppose..." Pamela's voice meandered into the blackened night.

She wasn't sure what he was implying. She had heard of gun molls, the shameless girlfriends who knowingly assisted their incredulous mob boyfriends in accomplishing the most despicable of crimes, insisting on their innocence in court with mascara smudged eyes. What if Johnny was suggesting a similar type of arrangement?

Pamela straightened, hoping to appear as cold as possible. She didn't want Johnny getting any ideas.

"Ever since Mr. Friedenberg's disappearance, we haven't had a way to collect the earnings he owes us. Perhaps you could deliver twenty percent of the earnings to us every week. And since you still work here, you could authorize our use of the trucks." Johnny seemed to have already thought about the proposition well ahead of time.

Pamela wanted to sigh out in relief, glad that he wasn't propositioning her for anything more brazen. But the offer was still illegal, and morally dubious.

Suddenly, Johnny drew a metallic pocket knife from his coat. He proceeded to use the edge of the blade to draw blood from his hand.

"You mind?" He questioned as he took her hand, cradling it.

Before she could deny or accept the advance, he had cut a neat slice of crimson red blood from her lily-white wrist. It stung terribly at first, but the longer she stared at the injury, she became numb to it like it had never even happened at all.

Pamela flinched as Johnny pressed a large thumb upon the place he had cut to prevent it from bleeding out.

Johnny's gaze didn't change. He appeared completely oblivious to the fact that the act seemed like an absurdity to Pamela. His usually expressive face was masked with indifference, his brows creased in determination.

He grasped her fingers and gave a firm handshake, shooting shivers through Pamela's spine.

"Not too painful, was it?" Johnny coaxed, as if he was a school nurse who had just administered a simple tetanus vaccination.

"I just wish you had warned me first... before you pricked me."

"It's called a blood oath. So you know I mean business." Johnny stated grimly.

After agreeing to the plan that Pamela was to meet with Johnny every Wednesday in the alleyway at six in the morning with an envelope of twenty percent of the earnings from Albright & Trimmings Co., Pamela showed Johnny out and then changed into her nightgown.

Her hand was still dripping with remnants of Johnny's blood, and she stood in front of the vanity mirror, the bathroom light artificial and bright, exposing the fear from deep within.

She felt incredibly overwhelmed, and though she had done nothing wrong, a strange sense of guilt gnawed at her and refused to let her sleep. She knew she was in scalding water, and agreeing to Johnny's plan was the only reasonable thing she could have done. Still, she couldn't help but acknowledge that she was breaking the law and fuelling a tremendous evil in the city.

She used a washcloth and scrubbed the blood from her hands until they glistened clean once more.

CHAPTER 10

A couple of days after Copacabana, Johnny was invited to a family gathering at Don Roberto's house with the rest of the crew.

Johnny was both relieved and regretful to have told Pamela about the business, or at least in vague terms. She didn't know half of it, a quarter of it even, and she never would. However, it wouldn't hurt to have a middleman down on Fifth Avenue handling operations within the store now that Friedenberg was gone. Johnny also knew that Pamela was too scared to leave, and if she ever dared to, he could blackmail her with her newfound knowledge of the mob, though he hoped it wouldn't come to that.

Johnny had told Roberto about the arrangement, but had left out the part about Pamela knowing too much. Besides, she was a nice girl, the kind who seemed to care about other people more than herself. If Johnny was able to forge some kind of friendship with her, he was certain she would remain compliant.

Lorenzo and Sal, Tony, Antonio, Luca, and Marco: the respective underbosses and capos of the Mancini clan had accepted Don Roberto's invitation for some good Italian food and wine, except for John, who claimed a sore throat. They all hunkered down around the table, ready to enjoy the food.

"So, how's John?" Isabella asked as she sat down to eat.

Once again, Isabella Mancini had outdone herself.

Steaming spaghetti, meatballs, tomato sauce, tortellini, risotto, gnocchi, arancini, cassata, and cannolis amassed the sprawling oak table, carved by Roberto's expert hands. Defrosted green grapes from Roberto's vineyard were placed at the center of the table, proving that he contributed at least a little to the massive feast his wife had prepared all day.

Though he had never actually been to Italy, Johnny decided that the celebratory meal smelled just about as Italian as any kind of nourishment could get.

The Mancini abode was ready for Christmas, complete with a Christmas tree from Jersey, ornaments, lights, tinsel, and an oversized plastic Santa perched out on the pillowy, recently snow-covered lawn.

A pitcher of alcoholic eggnog was left on the kitchen counter, but every time the Mancini kids attempted to steal a little, their mamma reprimanded them with a harsh warning and a sharp slap to the head.

Tony and Johnny exchanged a glance at the mention of the enigmatic John. They had both complained about John's lecherous presence within the family. He rarely attended family meetings, and when he did, he was completely obtuse and ignorant.

Behind Don Roberto's back, the rest of the crew had fondly nicknamed John Mancini *facciabrutt'*, paying homage to his uncomely features and terrible body odor. To make matters worse, John was a self-proclaimed *medigan'*, an Italian-American who had lost his roots. To his family's disgrace, he didn't speak a word of Italian and often declared that he was a red and blue-blooded American.

"He's been sick, the poor kid," Roberto said sympathetically, though a sharp frown revealed his distaste for the subject. However unhappy Roberto was with having John as an underboss within the Family, nothing could remove the reality that John was Roberto's nephew.

Johnny still didn't understand why Roberto wouldn't just demote John into a capo, but he wasn't about to make the Boss' decisions for him.

Marco Mancini stiffened at the expression on Don Roberto's face, clearly uncomfortable at the mention of his brother.

Blood is thicker than water, Johnny heard Roberto say in the back of his mind.

"Poor thing," Isabella sighed, dropping a helping of dull yellow gnocchi onto Johnny's plate, although he hadn't asked for more.

"Yeah, yeah, he'll be fine. He always is." Marco reassured. "I'm sure he's in bed watching *I Love Lucy* and drinkin' hot soup as we speak."

The group laughed, and Tony passed a tiny alcohol flask to Johnny under the table.

Tony winked, but Johnny shook his head, declining the offer. He didn't like to drink at Roberto's home for fear of making a fool of himself in front of Isabella and the kids. He did stupid things when he drank.

"That show is hilarious. Carlotta is always watching it, I can't get her to turn off the darned television!" Isabella chuckled. She wiped the corner of her lips with her napkin. "Carlotta—tell Johnny about that Cuban fella you're sweet on... what was his name? Ricky something? He looks kinda like Johnny, wouldn't you say?"

Carlotta, who hadn't taken part in the conversation for the entirety of dinner, glared at her mother with a luminous blue-eyed look that could stop an army. Her cheeks flushed. But Johnny knew it wasn't because of adoration or girlish embarrassment.

"Ma! I don't know what you're talking about!" Carlotta exclaimed, crossing her arms.

"Don't talk back to your mamma," Roberto warned sternly, though his perpetually roughened expression turned soft as he gazed upon his daughter. He loved her. Though she was a girl, she was his firstborn, and because she was a girl, her father regarded her as some sort of heaven-sent, angelic being.

"Carlotta! I was just making conversation!" The impossibly outgoing, chatty Isabella laughed, oblivious to her daughter's seething rage. "We all know how sweet on Johnny you've gotten over the years. You know, I was just like you when your father came calling, as they say. I refused to marry dear Roberto at first because he said my spaghett' was dry. Can you believe that man? Anyway, I know my sweet Johnny is a good boy, and one day you'll come to love him as more than a brother."

"Listen to your mamma child." Roberto pinned Carlotta with a look.

It was obvious to the rest of the table that Carlotta was humiliated, and not in the least bit impressed with her mother's attempts to set her up with Johnny. It mortified Johnny.

He had never made it a secret that he intended to marry Carlotta one day, but he had never gauged her as being this opposed to the idea. Wasn't it her who had offered him his very first kiss, after a long day of riding the neighbor's bicycle in the blistering sun? Wasn't it her who had insisted he pretend to be her husband when they played family in the backyard?

He had known Carlotta since their days as a youth, playing on the streets of Brooklyn, sneaking into the back of fancy movie theaters, and stealing pockets full of ice from the iceman on early Saturday mornings. He knew her well enough to conceive that she did not yet like him the way a girlfriend ought to like a boyfriend, or a wife ought to like a husband.

It hurt worse than a gun wound, but Johnny was too proud to admit it.

Carlotta stood up, slamming her chair back, her lustrous black hair bobbing with her sudden, jarring movement. "Excuse me. I'm tired. I gotta go upstairs."

Soon after dinner had ended, Don Roberto called another meeting in his office, but this time, it was private: with only Johnny's presence requested.

While he paced the hallway, waiting to be called in, Johnny could hardly pretend that he wasn't nervous. He had known Roberto for the greater part of his life, but he still couldn't help but squirm when he was with him, alone, in a room one-on-one. Johnny was never nervous around anyone, but as soon as Don Roberto was reviewing his earnings or talking to him about business, the dynamic shifted. Soon Roberto muttered his name, and Johnny entered.

"Sit down, sit down." Roberto insisted, his heavy form sprawled against the back of his chair.

"First, I want to apologize for my daughter and her behavior at the dinner table." Roberto blew out a smoke-laden breath slowly, his piercing blue eyes scanning the room as if he were looking for something, or someone in particular. "Isabella tells me she's been acting crazy, slamming doors, keeping secrets, staying out late. We think it has something to do with a certain boy she's seeing. And believe me, I'm not happy about it. Whoever this worthless *giamocc'* is, I can guarantee you, when I find him, he is already finished. Gone."

"Does Carlotta know?" Johnny questioned, propping an elbow on the table. "What I mean to say is, won't she be devastated when she finds out that her alleged boyfriend is... gone?"

Roberto erupted into deep, rumbling laughter, his face splitting open with a smile, his chest heaving with delight.

"Dead? Do you think I mean dead? What do you think I am, Johnny? A monster? No, no! I'm a civilized man. What kinda father goes around whacking his kid's boyfriends, anyway?" Roberto wiped runnels of tears from his cherry-red cheeks, uttering another hearty chuckle under his breath. "No, no, I'll get Tony and some guys to follow her around for a while, see who she's been hanging around with."

"Tony is just the man for the job." Johnny agreed. His best friend was honest and a trustworthy fellow. He could be quiet sometimes, but Johnny supposed it was because he had a reserved personality by nature.

Conversation switched to the construction business: namely the construction companies in Manhattan and Brooklyn the Mancini syndicate was given authority to operate. As Johnny saw it: this included providing security and trucks to move supplies, but everything came at a price and each company under Roberto's control would pay the Family twenty percent of the earnings in fees. It was the same with Albright Trimmings & Co., and the other textile companies on Fifth Avenue they provided trucks for.

"I've had some trouble..." Roberto explained candidly, loosening his shirt tie, "mostly with an Irish fella named Stuart Kelly. He hasn't taken too kindly to our offers of business. He hasn't cooperated with any of the other families either and refuses to discuss business terms. Even when his gypsy truck drivers disappeared, he hardly batted an eyelash."

"The name rings a bell," Johnny admitted thoughtfully.

"That's because his daughter, Pamela Kelly, works at Friedenberg's old place. The one you put in charge of collecting fees. Anyway, I've heard from the crew that the girl has taken quite a shine to you. If you manage to, you know, date her... at least until she introduces you to her old man, then you'll be able to offer him our services." Roberto winked, placing his hands against the back of his head.

Johnny reeled back with shock.

Sure, Pamela was a sweet girl, and he couldn't deny she possessed the kind of eyes that could make a grown man weep, but he had never suspected that she thought of him in that way. They had danced all night at the Copacabana, and at one point or another, he had felt his heart do cartwheels as she gazed up into his eyes. He had felt a powerful desire for her at that moment.

But he wanted Carlotta.

That was that.

"Doesn't this seem a little... contradictory, Boss?" Johnny swallowed the lump building in his throat. "I mean... wouldn't dating Pamela to get to her father be mixing pleasure with business?"

Roberto's reply came out instantly. His tone was laced with a removed brutality that Johnny found hard to stomach. "This is business."

Johnny turned to leave, but Roberto stopped him. "I need you to visit Mr. Murphy in Levittown, Johnny. He hasn't been paying up. Put his contract out, enough is enough with that guy. I won't tolerate his disrespect any longer."

Roberto handed Johnny a folded piece of paper, and Johnny shoved it into his pocket dutifully.

Suburbia encompassed Johnny Siciliano as he cruised through Levittown, Long Island. The tires on his automobile swiveled as he curved around a bend in the cement road, elapsing baby blue bungalows and buoyant ranchers.

Every block was the same.

Each home was fronted with a fence-like hedge—pristinely trimmed despite leaves being encrusted with ice because of a recent series of storms that had ravaged the East Coast. It was quiet, with children off at school, housewives inside with their brand new vacuums and furniture polish, and husbands working nine-to-five jobs in the city.

The only noise that reverberated through the utopian neighborhood was the barking of a family dog.

The bizarre sameness and unruffled wealth unnerved Johnny. Did these people know that only a short drive away, real people were suffering—living paycheck to paycheck in cramped tenements? Did they know some people didn't have the luxury of backyard swimming pools and automatic washing machines?

And yet, they were the ones to call men like Johnny Siciliano morally depraved.

He snorted.

Johnny parked outside one of the inconspicuous ranchers, unfurling a crumpled scrap of paper from his pocket to ensure he had singled out the correct address.

Pulse leaping up in his neck, Johnny let himself out of the car and pursued the narrow concrete pathway up to the front door as discreetly as he could. He wasn't certain why he was so nervous. He had done this many times before.

Johnny tried the doorknob with bunched fingers, and it worked. Apparently, residents of Levittown didn't fear break-ins or burglaries.

The open door displayed a home as polished as its exterior, with golden yellow wallpaper, stucco ceilings, and patterned beige Beauvais carpeting.

Muffled voices coming from the living room attenuated Johnny. He slid his hand around his pocket gun, boldly taking a step forward. It didn't matter who was in there. With a gun and the element of surprise, he had the upper hand.

"Discover the clean difference—the clean difference with today's smoking Belair cigarettes!"

"Breathe easy! Smoke clean with Belair! Air-fresh menthol blend: the clean difference in taste!"

"Gee Joe, don't you just feel wonderful?"

"Yes, I do, Mary, now that I can *smoke clean* with Belair!"

Johnny's pulse returned to normal. It was a stupid television commercial.

He entered the living room, children's playthings strewn across the carpeted floor. A woman's magazine lay open on the baby blue sofa—advertising winter frocks and aprons. On the opposite side of the chamber was the back of a man. He was the one watching the television, a newspaper spread wide across his lap.

Johnny readied himself. "Hello, Mr. Murphy. Turn off that television, why don't you?"

The television screen became black.

Mr. Murphy rose, dropping his paper on the table as he whirled around to confront Johnny. Angry creases gilded his tanned forehead. "What in the world are *you* doing here? In my *house*?"

"You know why I'm here. Roberto won't tolerate your disrespect any longer, and neither will I." Johnny held the gun out, aiming for Mr. Murphy's suited chest.

Mr. Murphy raised his thin arms so that his hands were above his head, his cheeks pale. "I told Roberto, I'd have the money to you by Christmas. Business hasn't been good, you know. I've had to lay off some of my workers just to make ends meet."

"You can afford new carpet but you can't afford to pay up?" Johnny gestured to the living room—the modish wallpaper and ceiling, the toys, the television. He wasn't sure why he was making conversation. Usually, he would just get the job done without complicating things with small talk. There was no point in conversing with a man who would be dead moments later.

"Look, please. My kid is home sick today. Come back tomorrow, or the next day." Mr. Murphy lowered his voice, a look of pleading softening his features. "I told my wife I'd look after him while she's out at the store."

Roberto didn't say there was gonna be a kid involved. Johnny's heart thumped against the barrier of his chest.

A child, dressed in pajamas and clutching a teddy bear, drifted into the living room. He couldn't be more than six-years-old, with a cluster of freckles fanning out around his large dark eyes.

A memory flashed across Johnny's consciousness—a photograph his mamma had taken when he was about the same age. It was the only photograph his madre could've afforded—the only one she really cared about having taken. In it, he had been standing in the sparse backyard of their tenement, a shock of wild dark hair peeking out from underneath his cap. A baseball glove and ball snug in his tiny brown fingers.

The Murphy boy's caramel brown eyes swept sleepily around the room and widened when they landed on Johnny. "Pops? Why is he holding a gun?"

"Go to your room, son." Mr. Murphy snapped, his right arm descending to shield the boy.

The pistol in Johnny's fist became weighty, despite it only being a simple handgun. Perspiration dampened his fingers. He lost his grip. *What* was happening to him? All he had to do was shoot a guy, and he was usually unruffled, with far worse.

"Just pay up, alright Mr. Murphy? I don't wanna have to come back here." Johnny retreated, walking backwards, until he got to the door.

He sprinted back to his automobile, his breath ragged.

Risking a sharp reprimand, and possibly worse from his boss for failing to follow orders, he pressed his clammy hands to the steering wheel and slammed his foot down on the accelerator.

CHAPTER 11

Pamela's work week lagged. Her mind was riddled with thoughts of Johnny and the deal she had accepted while she sorted countless buttons, mended drapes and cloths, and ironed textile sheets to creaseless perfection. She dreaded the day she would have to deliver twenty percent of the store's earnings to him, along with handing him the silver and brass keys that provided access to the delivery trucks.

She considered finding a new position as she had fantasized about before, but every time she scanned job advertisements in the newspapers, her search came out flat. No place in New York was hiring young unmarried women with minimal experience.

So, she resolved herself to silence, talking only when she was required to do so, and retiring to bed early for fear of exposing the truth to Caterina.

Pamela attempted to subdue her anxieties by keeping herself busy when she wasn't required to do so by folding, cleaning the countertops, and prepping the polished display cases. It seemed to work, as she forgot everything except what her hands did while they accomplished menial tasks.

Her fingers had become sore and calloused from needlework and stitching, long hours of labour imprinting themselves upon her flesh as if to serve as an eternal memory.

When she closed her eyes tight enough, she was transported to a simpler time: where she worked with Lorna in the kitchen, crafting scrumptious chocolate peanut butter squares and peach cobbler for her parent's dinner parties. Sometimes, she would lick the batter from the spoon and Lorna wouldn't scold her, though, of course, her mother would have a fit if she knew.

One day she was so embroiled in the role of mending a torn bolt of periwinkle-striped linen that she didn't hear Caterina calling her for supper.

Caterina shook her out of her stupor, drawing her to consciousness once again. "Pamela Anne Kelly! What has gotten into you lately?"

Pamela braved a timid smile and shrugged her shoulders halfheartedly. "I'm peachy, Caterina. Just a little tired. I haven't been able to sleep much lately."

"If you didn't work so much, maybe you would find the time to sleep." Caterina chastised. "The bags under your eyes are getting darker."

"I'm fine! Really!" Neuroticism took hold of Pamela, combined with a lack of sleep. "Sorry, Cat. I don't mean to sound crazy or anything. But, believe me, I am perfectly fine."

Caterina glared, making her incredulity known. "All I'm saying is there's no need to work when we aren't even getting paid. Some of the other girls are considering quitting, and finding jobs with steady pay. Johnny said we'd get our share at the end of the month, but some of us can't wait that long."

The news surprised Pamela. Surely she hadn't been so oblivious to the surrounding happenings.

When the two girls were upstairs, Caterina guided Pamela to the sofa, hooking an arm around her slender shoulders.

"What's bothering you? Is it poor Mr. Friedenberg?" Caterina inquired softly as she crossed herself.

All the girls had heard about Mr. Friedenberg and his untimely demise. They had received a formal letter from his family which included news of their employer:

Dear Albright Trimmings & Co. staff,

With great sadness in my heart, I am writing to inform you that my husband, Clyde Friedenberg, has passed away. We aren't willing to share the details of his death but remain assured that with great confidence, we will pass the position of store management onto a new hire. Please do not reply to this address, as we will be unreachable and are grieving.

Sincerely,

Ellen Friedenberg

"Not Mr. Friedenberg, though I am sad about his death..." Pamela said cautiously, "I suppose I'm just unused to the men, Mr. Friedenberg's former associates, who stand idly by and tease us as we work."

No news report had been penned regarding Mr. Friedenberg's death, and no suspects had been charged with the crime of his slaughter, but it wasn't a secret that his death wasn't by accident. Mancini's trench coat-clad soldiers had been congregating outside the shop for the past two weeks, flirting with the salesgirls and egging on pedestrians who didn't want to cause any trouble.

Caterina laughed at her friend's innocent remark. "They mean well."

As far as Caterina was concerned, the men didn't bother her as long as her bank account wasn't empty and some kind of remotely static system at the business had been implemented.

Despite her knowledge that the Mancini Family was not legitimately recognized in the eyes of the law, she was thankful for the cash slipped under the table to keep her mouth shut and the promise of protection from petty crooks, thieves, and gangs around Brooklyn. Whenever she visited her mamma's house on Cobble Hill, no one would so much lift an eye to her once she mentioned Mancini's name.

Besides, she enjoyed some good banter and even a little flirting. Compliments about her dress or her red lipstick made her feel appreciated as if she mattered somehow. No matter how hard the men tried to deny it, she seemed to cast some kind of spell on them, and she enjoyed it. It gave her control, and for a working girl, control was scarce.

Regardless of Caterina's ease with the subject, Pamela's expression was still contorted in fear. Caterina placed a palm on her arm to console her. She knew how delicate and introverted Pamela was, as opposed to her bold and extroverted personality. "Trust me, Pamela. They're absolutely harmless. More bark than bite, as they say."

After turning up the volume dial on the radio, Caterina reigned in Pamela's attention with another statement. "And, I hear that Mr. Johnny Siciliano has his eye on you. Be careful, that man is crazy with girls!"

On Wednesday at six in the morning, prior to the sun painting the sky a pleasant golden hue, after a fresh snowfall the night before that made the streets pure and shoved spring dormant beneath the ice-glazed Central Park Lake, Pamela roused herself awake.

She smoothed her wheat blonde hair back into a long ponytail. She slipped into a gingham dress and forwent lipstick and mascara, leaving her skin bare and touched red by the nipping cold.

Did she care what she looked like? She didn't have an answer, but she didn't want Johnny to get any ideas, especially considering that he supposedly 'had an eye on her'. What did he see in her, if he saw anything at all? After all, Caterina was prone to lying, and exaggerating she called it, and she could just be making the gossip up.

Pamela leaned close to the vanity, her body angled over the chipped bathroom sink so far that her nose grazed her own reflection.

Timothy had once teased her it was a wonder she was born into a family of beauty queens. The comment had wounded her, unearthing years of schoolgirl taunts and parental chastisement. She had spent hours trying to appear as effortlessly elegant and beautiful as Cecelia and Caroline Kelly but had never succeeded. Some women possessed the talent of perpetual confidence and poise, and others, like Pamela, did not.

What did Johnny Siciliano see in her, if anything at all? Was she just another challenge that he wanted to add to a diabolical mental list? She winced at the thought.

Pamela took a deep breath and tottered to the kitchen after slipping on a pair of high heels, careful not to wake Caterina.

She followed Johnny's instructions and waited for him outside, folding her back against the alleyway wall, her gloved hands clutching the crisp white envelope neatly folded between her bent fingers and concealing the nerves quaking through her bones.

She peered across the street, where street vendors and fashion stores had not yet opened their doors to their patrons. Impervious bulwarks of steel bars and grilles encased the storefronts. A lone worker slinked across the street, his steps long and unhurried.

For once, the city was silent.

No one was there to witness the transaction between Pamela and an unpredictable gangster, and it made her extremely nervous.

Minutes later, a lone figure emerged from the darkness, masked by black shadows that bounced against the ice-enameled walls.

Pamela's heart sped up, and she prayed for courage. She would not appear afraid or unsure in front of him. Ever.

"You're late. I've been waiting for half an hour."

Pamela looked up to match the searing brown eyes of Johnny. The scowl on his face insinuated he was in a bitter mood, perhaps provoked by the blistering cold streets of Manhattan.

"I set the alarm for six sharp. I was on time." Pamela declared, presenting the envelope to him grandly, extending her arms in one graceful flourish of a movement. She knew she had to seem self-assured and confident: she couldn't show him she was afraid.

"Alarm? You know, that could've woken Cat. We don't need another employee getting suspicious." Johnny scolded.

"She sleeps like a dead man," Pamela assured him, suddenly realizing the double meaning of her words.

"Well, maybe I'm wrong. Is everything in here? The full amount?"

"Yes, I counted it all last night."

They stood facing one another for a few moments longer, clouds of breath intertwining to become one large puff of dappled chimney smoke.

Johnny's nose was long and pointed, and his eyes were full and down-turned, the size of two large almonds. His clean-shaven face was straggly with the beginnings of a beard, and Pamela guessed he hadn't shaved for some time.

Pamela noticed how she had been staring at Johnny. An embarrassed blush rose to her cheeks, and she hung her head, focussing her vision on the toes of her black winter boots.

This action seemed to perk Johnny up, and he cleared his throat. "Sorry, Pam - Pamela. I can call you that, right?"

Pamela nodded. She hated the name, but she wasn't about to tell him he couldn't use it.

"I was wondering if you'd maybe... wanna grab some breakfast with me."

Pamela felt her heart speed up to full alarm. She remembered what both Caterina and Sergeant Marino had said about Johnny, that he was both an infamous flirt and relentless with girls. How would he react if she declined?

She was about to find out.

"I shouldn't." She steeled herself for his response, trying to see past his towering frame into the distance and hoping that someone was there to witness if he were to get violent. "It isn't decent to fraternize with an employer."

Johnny's forehead creased in confusion. "I gotta be honest with you, but I don't know what that means. Even if I did, I still insist."

"Please, Johnny." Pamela whirled around, turning to leave. She wasn't sure how she had mustered the courage. Perhaps her prayer had worked.

She felt his hand on her shoulder, gentle but insistent.

"C'mon, cut me a break, would you?" Johnny pleaded, his eyes softening and warming in the cold. "I'm starved, and I don't wanna eat alone."

"But I have to..." she began, hoping to scramble through the lengthy list of excuses in her mind she had used with Timothy.

She couldn't find any, so she agreed.

Donna's Diner was a quaint restaurant somewhere in the middle of Brooklyn, one borough Pamela had never visited before.

She had driven through Brooklyn a few times, but she had never walked around, never passed the tall, brick-red buildings with greenery out front and children playing and screaming outside. There seemed to be more Italians, Portuguese and Irishmen in Brooklyn than in the Upper East Side. The only neighborhood she could compare it to was Lorna's vibrant residence in the Bronx.

The diner itself was alive with men guzzling cups of coffee before dashing off to work and women catching up on the latest neighborhood gossip. The floors were black-and-white checkered, the panels stainless steel, and the booths a pleasant light blue in color.

The scent of pancake batter and sizzling bacon threaded through her lungs, and her stomach growled in anticipation.

Johnny sprawled himself in the booth across from her, his feet planted wide apart. He looked so comfortable as if he went there for coffee every morning before catching the bus in the city.

He signaled over to the waitress with a limp wave of his hand and asked her to bring a couple of waters.

Pamela found it funny how she came running and greeted him with a shadowed grin. Everyone in Brooklyn was friendly with Johnny or was too afraid of him to feign oblivion. In droves, others passed by, staring at them doe-eyed.

A group of kids came over to ask Johnny to sign their baseball mitts as if he was some up-and-coming Joe DiMaggio or Jackie Robinson. Johnny turned them away, but not before giving them some pointers on how to pitch a baseball.

"So, you must be famous around here," Pamela said, her eyes glued to her menu as the boys scampered away.

Johnny chuckled, no doubt pleased with her recognizing his celebrity. "Not famous. Just well-known, I guess. Kids like to see an Italian fella from Brooklyn make it big. Gives 'em somethin' to look up to."

Pamela pulled her cardigan around her shoulders, saddened by the idea that the kids believed the only way for them to make it big was to become a mobster. Weren't there other ways to make money? Honest ways?

"Do you like music?" Johnny inquired spontaneously, swirling the glacial cube of ice around in his lemon water before taking a sip.

"Doesn't everyone?"

Johnny chuckled. "I just mean—what's your favorite type of music? What do you listen to on the radio?"

"I don't have a favorite type. I listen to anything that's playing." Pamela answered, hoping to keep her responses short and invulnerable. She felt like she was being interrogated, and she didn't enjoy the uncomfortable sensation it produced.

The server returned with a little notebook cupped in the palm of her hand, a pen lingering above the paper in anticipation.

Johnny ordered a shot of espresso and steak and eggs with a side of bacon, and Pamela requested a stack of buttermilk pancakes topped with blueberry compote.

"You sure are hungry," Johnny commented on her breakfast choice when the waitress had left the table.

"Not hungry enough to order steak and eggs," Pamela said, realizing that her honest quip had sounded more like a playful jab.

To her relief, Johnny chuckled and took a swig of his ice water.

"All I meant was, you eat more than the other girls I've taken on dates. They want nothing but water and carrot slices, maybe 'cause they're afraid of getting their lipstick messed up or something." Johnny shrugged.

"So... this is a date?" Pamela asked, concealing her alarm with flirtation.

"Uh... no... it's a business meeting." Johnny's voice quavered, perhaps not realizing he had referred to it as a date.

Pamela shook her head, sipping from her own water. "I guess I just miss Lorna."

She surprised herself. She didn't realize that she had said it aloud.

"Lorna?" Johnny asked.

"She was... my housekeeper." Pamela sensed her cheeks brighten in a flush. She knew that if she was to explain her family's backstory, she might get in trouble. She recovered quickly. "I mean, she was one of my mother's friends. She would always make the most delicious buttermilk pancakes, and she always added a dollop of blueberry compote on the top. I miss home cooking or any sort of cooking at all. Cat and I eat Swanson television dinners and canned beans."

The waitress paused their conversation as she placed their meals in front of them.

"Sounds like a nice woman." Johnny continued where they left off, cutting his steak into smaller pieces. "Was your ma nice too?"

Pamela hesitated as the moment stretched between them, unsure of how to describe her relationship with her mother. "She cares about me, I suppose. But she's never been the warmest woman. Sometimes it's difficult to know how she feels."

"Still, you must miss 'em. Your family, that is." Johnny prodded, leaning closer. His eyes were the darkest shade of brown, a fountain of ink pooling in them.

Pressure bloomed in her stomach, and she swirled a piece of pancake around in an indigo pond of compote. She nodded, looking at him and then breaking their shared gaze for a moment to slice the buttermilk pancake in half.

"So, why not go visit?" Johnny challenged as if it were that easy. The scent of hot bacon whirled around him.

Pamela grimaced, not sure how to hide her life from him any longer. "Perhaps I could."

"I could bring you." Johnny insisted, clasping his hands over hers, cupping her warmth in his grasp. "Now that we're goin' steady, it's about time I met your folks."

"Going steady?" Pamela laughed. Are you out of your mind? Was what she wanted to demand.

The cool touch of flesh upon flesh reminded her he was still holding her hands. She eased her fingers away from his and laced them together in her lap.

"I'm kidding." Johnny rolled his eyes, then directed them back at her. "But really, I can bring you to visit your folks. We are business partners now, after all."

She wasn't sure what came over her, but Pamela accepted his request. If she wasn't dead already, she knew she would be soon if she didn't go along with what he wanted.

Johnny was full of merriment when she agreed to his proposal. Along the car ride home, he dialed up his car radio and chanted along to all the songs, urging her to sing along with him. Pamela did, but her voice was shaky with uncertainty. For one, she didn't understand why Johnny was so giddy about meeting her parents. Second, she knew she had to devise a plan. She could never introduce her family to a mobster, even if she was still in contact with them.

When Pamela reached the door of her apartment, she slid off her heels and bounded into the closet, pulling the phone with her. She dialed up Sean so urgently that her fingers hurt.

He picked it up, answering with a deep, sleepy voice. "Hello?"

"Sean!" Pamela whispered, "I need your help."

"What? You realize you woke me up from the best dream I've ever had? You can't just call without giving me notice. I live by the clock of my imagination, Pamela."

Pamela snaked the cord of the telephone around her elbow, trying her best to disregard the absurdity of her older brother's statement. "Tomorrow afternoon, 2 o'clock, I'll come over and get everything ready. I'll explain then."

CHAPTER 12

"I can't believe he got you to look after me like I'm some silly school kid." Carlotta snorted, standing with her back to Tony.

Her father had humiliated her, and she hated him for it.

She had made plans with a friend to meet at Fulton Park, across from the Boys and Girls High School, then take the bus to Manhattan and shop for clothes in the afternoon. Instead of seeing her good friend Francesca, she had been startled to see her boyfriend sheepishly hunched behind the wheel of his automobile in a leather jacket.

"Sweetheart, you know your papà told me to look after you. He's getting suspicious, and if I said no, he'd find out 'bout us." Tony stroked his thumb across her exposed arm, sending shivers down her spine. She turned away, sinking into her winter coat.

"He thinks you're goin' steady with some *disgraziat'*." Tony elaborated, his lips curling up into a grin.

He's not wrong, Carlotta thought to herself.

"You were spying on me." She repeated, resisting his grasp on her arms.

"I was only protecting us." Tony contended. "What do you think, *amore mio*? Do you expect me to tell him no when he asks me to do somethin'?"

Despite her momentary fury at his secrecy, Carlotta couldn't deny that she wouldn't stay mad for long. Tony was the man she loved, and she knew what he said was true.

She just didn't understand why her papà had sent his men after her. Sure, it had happened before, but she was a girl back then. Now that she was a grown woman, she needed her privacy, her own life. Or, perhaps, no matter how old she got, her father would never understand that.

"I love you, Tony. I'm sorry we fought." Carlotta relaxed her shoulders, welcoming Tony's hands to rest upon them.

The park was silent. All the kids from the school had gone in after lunch, but from experience, she knew anyone could listen to them, night or day.

"Believe me, sweetheart. If the boss found out about the two of us, that you are my *gumad*, he would never speak to me again." Tony locked her into an embrace, combing his hands through her curled hair and kissing the side of her neck.

Carlotta bristled and jumped back.

She hated the word *gumad*. It was the same word she had heard some men call their mistresses and flings: classless American women who dated wise guys for money and lacked respect for themselves or their men. Carlotta was *not* a fling or a *gumad*. She was an honest woman like her mamma.

"Hey, what gives?" Tony angled his head sideways to secure a better view of her countenance.

"Nothing!" Carlotta lied. "I just wish you woulda told my papà about us by now, that's it. If we had gotten his blessing a long time ago, none of this woulda happened."

She knew it wasn't true.

Her papà had a way of blowing things out of proportion, especially with the boys she dated. Though Tony was as close as a son to him, he wasn't Johnny Siciliano, and it would humiliate him that one of his men was courting his daughter without his permission.

Tony blew a breath out of his mouth and sighed. "C'mon, I can't just do that."

Carlotta inched away from him, almost tipping over in her stiletto heels. "What do you care more about, Tony? Me? Or your stupid, dead-end job?"

Tears flooded her eyes. She didn't know if she could hold them back for much longer.

Tony groaned in exasperation, infuriating Carlotta even more.

"I work with the famous Don Mancini," Tony snapped, "somethin' I wouldn't get anyplace else."

"Don't say that. Come away with me and we'll find out together." Carlotta said, twisting her mouth into a knot.

"Not that simple," he said slowly, pronouncing the words tentatively and clearly as if she didn't speak fluent English and needed her to understand.

You do my papà's dirty work and get paid for it, Carlotta wanted to remind him.

"We can get out of here. Right now. Let's get in your car and drive to Boston. I'll work at one of those little motels or diners, and you can become a mechanic. We'll get married without my papà's permission. We don't need him." Carlotta ran her soft gloved hands over Tony's chest, her voice growing more and more animated. "I have money left over from relatives, you have money from... work. We can make it there in under a few hours."

"What about Johnny?" Tony begged, clasping her slender shoulders with his broad hands.

"What about him?" Carlotta fought the overwhelming urge to roll her eyes. Johnny had a way of interfering with her personal life, even if he wasn't doing it on purpose.

"He's my best friend. I haven't told him about us. He'll be... upset if he finds out some other way. Besides, he's always been sweet on you."

"I don't care what Johnny thinks, and you shouldn't either. If he was your best friend, he'd be happy for us." Carlotta demanded.

Tony didn't speak for a long moment, hanging his head and staring at the concrete sidewalk. Then he sucked in a breath, rubbing his temples with his fingers.

She hoped he was considering her offer, but when he turned back to face her again, his eyes were misty with remorse.

"Please," Carlotta rasped. Any other words she possessed the capacity to say had become locked away in the prison of her heaving lungs.

Lord, please, she prayed ardently as she squeezed her eyes shut for a moment; *you know how much I love Tony. If you give me this chance, I will never ask you for anything else.*

Tony turned to leave, but before he did, he whispered into her hair. "Meet me at our old secret place, one hour from now. Don't tell nobody."

Carlotta had never felt so ecstatic in her life. She was doing something wonderful, for herself and for the man she loved. She would never look back, never regret taking her livelihood into her own hands.

From the moment she was born, she had been under the guard of her papà. She could not visit the park on her own, play games with the daughter of a family with whom her papà had trouble, or even talk about the family business. She had been followed, stalked, by the men working for her father, and sometimes it appeared she wasn't even allowed to breathe without someone watching her.

Tony had been a lifeline.

She had caught him staring when he wasn't supposed to, and she had gazed at him longingly, a silent act of defiance, whenever her mother had invited the men over for dinner. It had begun as an innocent mutual pondering, the beginnings of the disseverance of a possibility. She would watch him with the knowledge of how forbidden their love would be, but she knew that all the best love stories spoke of star-crossed lovers.

Somehow, in the garden on a humid summer night when everyone else had gone to Coney Island for ice cream, he had kissed her. She had been sweating like a teenage boy with her hair knotted crudely at her waist, but it had still been magical.

She stared at herself in the mirror, smiling a real, toothy, genuine smile, and buttoned up the back of her white Sunday dress. To avoid suspicion, she embellished the outfit with a pair of gold-encrusted ruby red earrings and a peach pink cardigan.

She swung a purse stuffed with clothes and cash over her shoulder, mentally saying goodbye to the little childhood room that had carried out her prison sentence for so many years.

Just when she was at the threshold of her bedroom, the gruff voice of her father bellowed out to her. "Where are you off to?"

He had crept out of his office, cigarette in hand and a stack of papers shoved underneath his arm. He looked older than he had before, with deep lines carved into his forehead and the olive crevices of his face. His pale blue eyes glared at her as if he could see right through her little scheme.

She braced herself and straightened to face him. "I'm going to the movies with Francesca."

"Francesca? Lorenzo's girl?" Her father demanded, a worried look crossing over his distinctive features.

Carlotta nodded. "We're going to the cinema downtown."

"The cinema?" Her father continued as if the words had two different meanings. "Don't speak to anyone other than Francesca, understood?"

"Yes." She cleared her throat, pretending to busy herself arranging her hair. "We're only gonna see White Christmas."

"Take off that lipstick. It's too dark for you." He adjusted his tie and thrust a handkerchief at her from his suit pocket. "We don't want anyone getting the wrong idea about my daughter."

She wanted to yell and raise her fists in protest, but she knew it was the last time she would ever have to follow his orders. "Okay."

She pressed the tobacco-scented fabric to her lips, instinctively memorizing his smell. Not as a nostalgic sentiment, but because she wanted a memento from the day she finally broke free.

"Carlotta, you remember people see me when they see you." Roberto reminded her, taking the fabric from her to wipe the powdered blush from her cheeks. "You are my daughter, and you must not forget that."

"Yes, Papà," Carlotta said, looking down at her feet.

"Don't stay out too late. There are too many creeps downtown these days." Roberto ordered.

Carlotta sensed a thread of sadness in his voice.

Surely, he too had noticed how they'd grown apart. Ever since he'd told her the truth, she had been wary of him. It was as if she'd become an adult overnight, and no longer had the desire to read him the newspaper in the morning or seek his advice.

Against her will, Carlotta felt a pang of sadness in her chest, but the two parted ways, and her father's words rattled in her brain: *I need you back here with me.*

She shook off the nostalgia and walked downstairs, kissing her mamma goodbye, then her little brothers. She embraced her teenage brother, Louis, the sibling whom she'd known the longest.

"I'll miss you all. Be good to Mamma, will you?" she called out to them, meaning it.

In her heart, she knew her parents would metaphorically kill her when they found out she had run away, but with time, she hoped they would come to understand. Her mamma had talked about being young and in love against her parents' wishes. She would sympathize with Carlotta, and then accept Tony into the household as a son-in-law.

Her father's reaction would be a different story.

He would be angry, livid perhaps when he found out, but afterwards, he would realize that his love for his daughter surmounted any unwritten rules of respect and oaths. Soon after, they would all cry laughing about the time that Carlotta had eloped, and be glad that the events unfolded how they did.

Tony and Carlotta married that night in a quaint chapel right outside of Boston. They parked their car on the side of the highway beneath a magnificent weeping willow, leaving Carlotta's overstuffed purse and Tony's black leather suitcase in the trunk. The priest had been asleep at his tiny chapel desk when they arrived, and they had wakened him, insisting that their vows couldn't wait till morning.

He had frowned at them in irritation, then placed his spectacles on his nose and rummaged around in his cabinet for the documents.

The parish secretary acted as their one and only witness, dabbing joyous tears from the wrinkles at the corners of her eyes and remarking repeatedly about the ecclesiastical beauty of the new young couple.

They had been pronounced husband and wife, in the eyes of God. *Forever.*

Carlotta had never felt happier in her life. The radiant beam plastered to her exuberant face announced her as the prettiest girl on the East Coast that night.

By the time they walked back to their car as a married couple, arms intertwined, it had snowed, coating the already fluffy streets with another layer of minuscule crystal snowflakes. Lyrical curls of smoke from the chapel chimney weaved themselves through winking stars in the twilight sky, and their boots crunched on mantling ice. Tony draped his jacket around Carlotta's shivering arms, though she wasn't thinking much about the cold.

"This is perfect." Carlotta's tone was soft and warm, like fresh cookies out of the oven. "Our wedding, a day we'll never forget."

"The day I became the luckiest guy in Brooklyn." Tony grinned, his eyes reflecting the stars.

"We're not in Brooklyn anymore." Carlotta reminded him solemnly.

"Right. Then I'm the luckiest guy on the East Coast." Tony threaded his hands through her dark hair, admiring the celestial sheen and the supple curls that coiled right around his fingers.

"You're the luckiest guy in *America.* And I'm the luckiest girl."

When Carlotta glanced up at him, her almond-shaped sapphire eyes radiating light, he seemed to remember her father and the terrible thing he had just done by breaking his oaths. "You sure you don't want me to take you back to your papà's house to get his blessing? He'll be awful mad when he finds out we're gone."

Sometimes he's as dumb as a brick. Carlotta swallowed her annoyance and sweetened her tone, shushing him with a quick peck on the lips. "Why would I want to go back there? He'll never give in."

"You're right. We don't have to go back there. Let's stay out here in the stars forever." Tony cradled her to his chest, his heart thumping against her chest.

They began to dance.

CHAPTER 13

Pamela paced across the sagging pine planks of Sean's Greenwich apartment floor. Her eyes were trained steadily ahead at the door. She had arrived early to clean the place, organizing plates and cups into the cupboard and removing cluttered stacks of unreturned library books and literary journals from the shelves. She had informed Johnny that she wouldn't need a ride, simply because she was meeting Sean for an early breakfast.

That was a lie.

Sean rarely ever had breakfast, since he slept late and woke later. When Pamela had let herself in through the unlocked door, he had been asleep on the couch, snoring with his mouth hanging wide open, his chin tucked into his neck, a trail of saliva landing on his pajama shirt.

There had been no sign of his girlfriend, so Pamela presumed they had parted ways.

Pamela hadn't told her brother more than he needed to know; that she had a gentleman friend who wanted to meet her family. Since her parents had practically disowned her, Sean had been the only plausible option. On the telephone he said he wasn't surprised, reasoning that their family history was too burdensome to explain to a new acquaintance. She had made him swear he would keep the visit brief, and tell Johnny only that their parents were out for the day.

Now all there was to do was wait.

Waiting was excruciating. Pamela kept on checking her wristband watch, then switched her gaze to the knockoff mahogany wall clock Sean had purchased at a flea market in the Bronx. Three o'clock came and went; which was the time Johnny had promised to arrive.

Finally, at half-past three, the doorbell rang.

Pamela adjusted her nylons and then aired out her pastel blue swing dress in the mirror, a tremor of fear pulsing through her entire frame. In a fluster, she called out for Sean in a mock whisper and took a deep breath.

Johnny was standing outside the door, his hair slicked into a side part with plenty of castor oil. The cowlick dangling in front of his forehead had itched itself loose, and somehow it made him less intimidating. His endearing brown eyes were clouded with indifference, concealing any trace of emotion.

"Hi Pamela," he said gruffly in his thick Italian Brooklyn accent as she opened the door, stepping gracefully to the side for him to enter.

"Hello, Johnny." She blew out a breath, making a mental observation of his dark sports jacket and dress pants clothing his athletic frame.

He had taken the occasion as a formal affair rather than a casual lunch, as she had understood it to be.

Then again, she supposed that meetings with mobsters were always glamorous, like the romanticization portrayed in radio broadcasts and newspapers.

She followed Johnny's quizzical gaze as he surveyed the small, outdated kitchen and modest living room. Confusion stamped his countenance.

"Is everything alright?" She asked.

"Yeah," Johnny started, pinching the bridge of his nose, "this your parents' place?"

He did not hide his surprise at the crude apartment.

Surely he hadn't suspected her to be from a rich, upper-class family, simply from her speech and dress. She had tried her best to disguise her accent, quickening her speech and pronouncing vowels like Caterina did. But she was not a good pretender.

"Yes," Pamela frowned, surprised at the provocation in her tone, "is there something wrong with it?"

She couldn't see Johnny's face as he turned towards the window.

"No, no, it's nice." He answered, though his eyebrow quirked in suspicion.

"I'll go fetch the tea. Please, make yourself comfortable." Pamela chirped, pretending to ignore the delicate tension building up between them.

When she reached the kitchen, she swung around and Sean lumbered towards her.

He was dressed even more casually than she was. A pair of denim overalls was fitted over his long-sleeved black turtleneck. He clutched an anonymous book of free verse poems beneath a hooked arm and stroked his stubbled chin with his right hand.

When he saw Pamela's wary expression, he laughed. "What? You said this kid was from Brooklyn. I dressed the way I usually do."

"I said nothing," Pamela sighed, pouring boiling water from the kettle into two chipped teacups, keeping the one for herself empty so that she could use it for tap water.

She raised her eyes to watch Sean saunter into the living room, extending a hand to Johnny, who had been lounging on the red velvet sofa. Before his arrival, she had moved the pillows around on it to cover the stains left from coffee spills and cheap wine.

"So, what business do you have with my kid sister?" Sean shook Johnny's hand with a tense grip.

Johnny had risen to his six-foot height, Sean only taller by a couple of inches.

Sean balked a little, perhaps surprised that another man was challenging his invisible act of dominance.

"We work together." Johnny returned Sean's firm handshake with one of his own.

"Is that so?" Sean released Johnny, his hands dropping to his sides, giving up. "Well, my good fellow, whatever your intentions are with her, I hope you've made them clear. We don't want any trouble befalling you, now do we? I wouldn't want a nice chap like you ending up in a dumpster somewhere along the lower East Side."

Pamela winced as the sentence dangled between the three of them.

A smirk curled up the corners of Sean's lips. But Pamela wasn't sure whether Johnny knew he was joking. His sense of humor required an acquired taste, one she wasn't sure Johnny possessed. She felt like rolling her eyes. Whatever her brother was trying to do, he thought that the whole thing was some kind of practical joke. He was treating the exchange like an exercise through which to portray a character from his books.

"I give you my word," Johnny promised. It relieved Pamela when she saw a smile illuminate his face. "No harm will come to her if I have anything to say about it."

"Very well, sir." Sean chuckled, imitating the Queen's British accent.

After distributing the tea, Pamela found a seat on the rocking chair across from the two men. She waited for the silence to subside, hoping they would persist with the conversation. She wanted the whole thing to be over with.

Johnny was the first to talk. "Are your folks home?" He asked tersely, lifting his eyes to Pamela but addressing the question to Sean.

"Nah, they don't come home much. It's been like that since we could walk, though." Sean shrugged, his tone becoming theatrical like it had when he performed a monologue in the school play. "Pops is a real gin mill cowboy. He doesn't come home till early in the morning, and then he goes off to work as a tie salesman, breaking his back for corporate America to put bread on the table. Ma hasn't been around since the war. She was a Red Cross nurse overseas, and you know, it hit her real hard."

Did Sean think up this entire fabricated story before I came over? Pamela asked herself. Regardless, he would get a stern talking to when Johnny finally left, and at the rate they were going, that wouldn't be until midnight.

Johnny looked slightly amused. Pamela could tell that he wasn't buying the fancy charade and watched as Johnny raised an eyebrow in mock sympathy. "What a shame."

Sean nodded his head, wiping pretend tears from his eyes. "It's been a real zonk in the head."

"Where does your pops work?" Johnny interrogated, though Pamela wished he would just drop the subject.

What was he so interested in her family history for? And why on earth had he planned this intrusive meeting in the first place? When she had told him she could take the bus to visit her family, he had resisted still, insisting on meeting her after. But what for? They weren't going steady as far as she was aware.

"Down by Union Square."

"Really? I get my ties from a little shop around there. Never come across a fella named Kelly, though."

Pamela was desperately trying to lock eyes with her brother in warning.

The one thing he had promised to do was keep his mouth shut, and yet, he had insisted on playing his own game of make-believe. She knew he didn't realize that he was compromising much more than her pride, but she was equally agitated.

In desperation, she faked a series of hoarse coughs, and Johnny offered her his napkin.

"I'd best be leaving," she announced, once her faked coughing fit had expired. "I have a lot of things to do at work that can't wait."

Sean wasn't half bothered by the announcement, leafing through his miniature book of prose.

"There really isn't any need to work today, Pamela," Johnny interjected, leaping to his feet immediately. His eyes were cold and hard like granite, sending a silent command.

Pamela blinked at him, biting the corner of her lip in consideration of what to say next.

"You know, ever since Mr. Friedenberg's accident, I am your boss, and I say you take the day off," Johnny added lightly, though the magnitude of his words rang in her ears.

He was not her boss. He would never be her boss.

Mr. Friedenberg had been her boss until Johnny had sent his men to kill him.

"Accident?" Sean frowned, an expression of confusion infiltrating his one-man play.

Pamela glanced at her brother, then back at Johnny again. If she didn't leave soon, she was certain that Sean would say too much and disclose more to Johnny than she ever wanted him to know. Besides, she was uneasy with Johnny's determination to investigate her family life.

Is he planning to kill me, after all? Or perhaps attempting to track my whereabouts if I am ever to try to escape? She shuddered.

"Thank you for the breakfast, Sean. It was lovely," she smiled, avoiding eye contact with Johnny and instead fixing her gaze upon her brother. "Johnny, would you mind giving me a drive home?"

The car ride home was quiet.

Johnny turned up the radio and drank out of a glass Coca Cola bottle, though Pamela wished he would keep both hands on the steering wheel.

New York City rushed past them as Johnny's automobile sped through the streets. The wintry sun bounced off glass and steel towers. Men in charcoal gray suits walked in and out of the doors below, either coming from or going to work. Women gathered like hens around the windows of stores, and children clung to their mothers' skirts in fear of their hectic new surroundings.

Johnny took a detour, and they entered a residential part of Manhattan.

School kids were returning from class, carrying lunch pails and satchels strung across their backs and clutching thick geometry and biology textbooks to their chests with mitten-covered hands. Boys tossed a football back and forth, causing a nearby car to honk in frustration when it contacted a windshield. Girls giggled and swung their arms gleefully in the air. Their eyes sparkled with elation.

Pamela felt a pang of nostalgia at the sight of them.

She dearly missed being a student, when all she had to worry about were strict teachers, school papers and final exams. She had been good at school, and unlike many of her peers, had found comfort in her studies and learning. She had hardly known what a mobster was back then, other than from romantic descriptions in fictional works read in the comfort of her sealed bedroom.

She had been innocent and sheltered as the schoolgirls passed across the street in front of her, with rosy cheeks and pigtails. Life had been unknown, and unthought of, as each day was marked in her school calendar and she knew what to expect.

"Hey, you know that guy? Is he related to you?"

Pamela's thoughts were impeded as she followed Johnny's pointed look toward a construction site on the other side of the road.

A large yellow sign obstructed traffic in the lane adjacent, reading STUART KELLY & SONS CONSTRUCTION COMPANY.

"Why would I?" Pamela veiled her panic, turning her head in the opposite direction.

"He shares your name. Your name is Kelly, right? What is that, Irish?" Johnny tapped his hand on his knee in rhythm to Mister Sandman.

"Well, yes, I suppose I am Irish. But not by birth. And... only on my father's side." Pamela thought her response was innocent enough. Besides, there were hundreds of Kellys throughout New York City, and more Irish. How would such an insignificant fact be useful to him?

"No need to defend yourself, Miss Kelly. I'm not mocking your heritage." Johnny teased. The light turned green, and Johnny slammed his foot onto the accelerator, the force of inertia knocking her back against her seat.

"Hey!" Was Pamela's automatic reaction. "Are you crazy?"

He passed Albright Trimmings & Co. He barrelled through what seemed like all of Manhattan and sped ahead onto Brooklyn Bridge.

"Where are you taking me?" Pamela cried, becoming more and more anxious. She felt her lungs expand and fall, and she squeezed her eyes shut. If he was going to shoot her, she wished he would just get it over with.

"I'm not gonna kill you," Johnny said, reading her thoughts. "Why are you lying to me, Pamela Kelly?"

"I am not lying to you." Pamela resisted.

After crossing the bridge, he pulled over onto the side of the street at the base, directly beneath the side span of the steel-wire giant.

She surveyed her options.

She could unlock the door and make a run for it. Unfortunately, there weren't many people around, and Johnny had parked in the most secluded spot he could find.

Johnny sighed and lit a cigarette, gazing out at the view of New York City in all its glorious entirety. He knew as well as she did it was too much of a risk to escape. "I know who your dad is. As funny as your brother's gaffe was, I know that your family owns the biggest construction company in the City. Patrick Kelly & Sons are well known around here."

"I..."

"Don't make up some fake excuse. I'm your boss, aren't I?"

Pamela wanted to slap him.

Instead, she let her head fall onto the back of the seat, listening to the rattling of automobiles over top. "What do you want? Is it money? Because I can assure you I have nothing to give."

He dipped his cigarette into the automobile's ashtray.

His silence perplexed her.

"Then what? What is it you want?" Pamela begged. She wanted him to leave her alone, but she knew he wouldn't do that until she gave him whatever he required of her, whether that was money or another favor working at the textile store.

"Nothing." Johnny shrugged. "I don't want nothing."

Pamela gaped at him in shock. Surely he wasn't telling the truth. "I don't believe you."

"I expected as much." Johnny leaned back in his seat, his brown eyes lifting sideways to a slab of blank gray sky.

It was freezing cold, as any winter afternoon in New York was. It was then that Pamela remembered it was almost Christmas, and yet she didn't have anywhere to go. She felt like crying, but she would not show that side of herself to Johnny. He wanted her to trust him, but not out of the goodness of his heart. He wanted something else, though she didn't know what yet.

"Hasn't anyone ever done anything nice for you before? With no reason?" Johnny swung an arm around the back of her seat, facing her.

Pamela wasn't sure whether he was flirting with her or simply asking an honest question. Maybe Caterina had been telling the truth when she said that Johnny was interested in her.

What if he tried to kiss her?

"If you must know, yes. But he hadn't been a mobster, trying to win my good graces in order to secure a favor." Pamela retorted icily.

To her relief, Johnny laughed. "Listen, Pamela, would you like to... I dunno, come meet my mamma for an early Christmas dinner?"

Pamela startled, sitting upright in her seat. "Your mother? Why?"

Johnny chuckled again.

Pamela was glad at least one of them was enjoying themselves.

"She's awful lonely and wishes I would bring home a nice girl. I know you're not Italian, but she'd be delighted to know that her son keeps company with at least a few respectable people." He propositioned, meeting her eyes with a smile. "And she makes a darn good Sicilian cheesecake."

Pamela heard herself say yes, and Johnny drove her home.

CHAPTER 14

New York City, Brooklyn, December 1954

Pamela stood before Johnny's mother, with her skin nipped by the cold and her teeth chattering from trekking through the snow for so long. The wool socks inside her boots were soaked through with melted ice, and she desperately wanted to warm herself by a furnace or any source of heat.

But she wouldn't be able to do so without a confrontation.

Johnny's mother was a slight woman with graying black hair wound around her ears beside her temples, and a horizontal crease carved neatly across her forehead. She had eyes identical to those of Johnny, but a pair of wire spectacles and hard-set laughing marks framed her face. Her complexion was also lighter than Johnny's, her cheeks olive-pink instead of beige.

She wore a worn white blouse tucked into a long navy blue skirt: an outfit that had not been in fashion for years. Her silver-black hair was also long and uncut, swinging at her waist and making her appear like an American pioneer from one of Pamela's old childhood stories.

"You the Americana?" She twisted her lips, crossing her arms across her chest and puncturing Pamela with a glare.

"Yes..." Pamela found her voice, sticking out her hand to greet her. "My name is Pamela Kelly. Johnny invited me. I-I'm sorry if I'm causing you any kind of trouble."

Without speaking, Johnny's mother looped a sturdy arm around her back and led her through the tenement room. Though she was at least a head shorter than Pamela, she walked with such compact strength and determination that she reminded Pamela of Napoleon the little general.

The tenement's walls hung low and lights gleaned dimly. The furniture was at least three decades old. Perhaps they had been purchased when Johnny was in diapers. The building itself was archaic —tenements like the one Johnny's mother lived in had been prohibited by New York State law back in the thirties for their poor living conditions.

Pamela had only ever read about the atrocious excuses for housing that had lacked bathrooms and were meant to contain poor immigrant families recently arrived in the country.

Regardless of its shabby appearance and cramped configuration, the particular unit was warm and clean.

There was one, rectangular-shaped radio in the corner, the type that Pamela's parents would have listened to during the Great Depression. The red-carpeted floor bore no stains or spots. The drapes were pristinely ironed, and a small potted plant dwelled atop the mantle, where heirlooms and family photographs encompassed it. The kitchen was to the left of the living room and contained a miniature fridge and a single table and chair in the center.

Pamela wondered why Johnny hadn't paid for more suitable accommodations for his mother. He could certainly afford to. His suits were always expensive and his automobile was one of the newest models. Why had he covered the costs of personal frivolities and neglected to fund the basic needs of his mother?

Disgust rose in her throat, and she remembered how unsavory his character was. How could she flirt with the idea that he was anything but? He didn't deserve her admiration.

Johnny's mother drew her from her contemplation. "Do you cook?"

Pamela raised her eyes to Silvia, lifting her chin. "Not very well. I can boil an egg, put together a sandwich, or make a stew if I have to. But..." She was about to add that the help had always taken care of her culinary needs, but she thought better of it.

Silvia was critical, her deep frown revealing she believed that any young woman should be able to cook for her husband and family—not that Pamela had any to show for it.

"Us Italian women cook to make sure that our men always have full stomachs," Silvia explained. "you Americans buy your men frozen pasta from the grocery. No wonder."

The generalization seemed like a vague insult, but Pamela wasn't offended. She had no intention of ever cooking for Johnny, and so she didn't care what Silvia thought about her in that respect.

"How about cleaning?" Silvia appeared to brace herself, dropping into a rocking chair and pursing her lips.

"Yes, I can clean," Pamela stated.

She could clean, but she had never learned or needed to until recently. Before she had been forced to care for the apartment, she had thought cleaning and housekeeping were easy. How wrong she had been. She had wasted hours scouring Lady's Housekeeping magazines and articles to no avail.

"Good." Silvia softened ever so slightly. "At least you'll be able to take care of Johnny's cleaning. I want to know that my son is taken care of, you understand."

Pamela winced, disliking the implication of her statement. "We *aren't* married, Mrs. Siciliano."

When Silvia pierced her with a lethal look, Pamela discovered where Johnny must've inherited his commanding brown stare from. "He invited you here, didn't he? What kinda man brings his girl over to his mamma's unless he's gonna marry her?"

"I can assure you, I am not going to marry Johnny."

Despite Pamela's cold tone, Silvia still cocked a suspicious brow in her direction.

The sound of water boiling in the kitchen interrupted them, and Silvia gathered her skirts to go check on the preparations. She returned with a tray of biscuits and tepid water with lemon, inside of chipped and faded china.

"Be careful with it," she instructed sternly. "this china has been in my family for generations. It was my mamma's and belonged to her."

Pamela nodded, taking care to steady the teacup in her hands before lifting it to her lips.

"I know you work with Johnny." Silvia impelled, stirring her water with a spoon. "And I know how he makes his money. I know what he does, and that he isn't working as a construction worker or salesman as most other boys his age."

Her eyes were dull and passive, and her mouth was constrained. An expression of deep sorrow settled in the crevices of her face, and Pamela understood that she must disapprove of the way Johnny made his money.

Or perhaps, as any reasonable mother would be, she was frightened. Mobsters were killed all the time, and Johnny was not immune to the threat simply because he feigned invincibility.

Pamela dropped her eyes to her lap, her cheeks burning in a flush. What could she say? She had assumed that Johnny's mother was like Caterina; content to remain silent, unwilling to stir the pot.

"I work at Albright Trimmings as a salesgirl," Pamela said blankly, "Johnny is my... boss. I know nothing more of his work than you do."

"I am not slow, Pamela. I know what my son does, and I know what Roberto Mancini has been doing all these years." She spat. "I know how girls like you act. You date wise guys, enjoying their money for your pleasure. Then, when they are killed, you find the next one to use. I want you to know that I do not approve. I love my boy, and I resent any woman who wishes to take advantage of his generosity."

Malice and disdain seeped through Silvia's words, cleaving into Pamela's heart.

"I am not like that, Mrs. Siciliano." Pamela defended wearily. "Months ago, I was a normal girl. I wanted to go to college. I liked going to the movies, and I loved to read. I never wanted to find myself here, with this injustice and chaos. I... simply wanted a job. I didn't know that all *this* would happen."

Silvia was quiet, staring into the corner of the room with her hand on the side of her neck.

"I didn't want to end up in the middle of all this, but somehow I am." Pamela continued tentatively. "I'm a law-abiding citizen. I really don't agree with your son's business at all."

The honesty provided a catharsis. She had not confided in anyone since Sean, and even then, he had hardly been receptive to her words. Besides, he only knew a fraction of the truth. Silvia was intimately familiar with the workings of the mob for better or worse.

"I... I didn't know you weren't compliant." Silvia admitted quietly, guilt permeating her hard gaze. "I am sorry for the misunderstanding."

The door swung open and bounced against the wall, and Johnny's deep voice came rumbling through the one-bedroom abode. "Mamma!"

Pamela craned her neck to see Johnny around the corner, his back turned to her as he placed his coat on the coat hook.

Immediately, Silvia's countenance brightened, like a tired light being switched on. She jumped to her feet and ran over to embrace her son, burying her face in his chest. Her tiny frame disappeared in his wide embrace.

"*Cucciolo*!" Silvia exclaimed, mussing up his hair with her hands. "What took you so long? Is your car okay?"

Johnny laughed, kissing his mother in return. "Nothing's wrong with my car, Ma."

"You're thin. Tell me you've been eating enough!" Silvia gasped, pinching Johnny's side with her fingers. "Have you not been following the recipes I gave you?"

"I'm fine, Ma." Johnny chuckled. His face swiveled towards the living room, where his eyes locked with Pamela, and his expression changed.

He didn't know I was already here, Pamela realized.

Suddenly, she felt like an intruder, encroaching upon a very special family reunion.

"Hello, Pamela." He delivered dryly, like an actor tired of rehearsing his line.

"Hi, Johnny." Pamela forced herself to stand, and Johnny took a few paces towards her, shaking her hand.

It was cold.

He seemed to hold her gaze for a moment, and she felt her heart flutter, the same sensation she had felt around him.

Was it fear?

She had felt nothing like it before.

"You look swell." He muttered.

"So... do you." Pamela played with her clutch nervously. It was true. He was attired well, in a formal sports jacket and navy blue pants. His hair was not slicked back as per usual; it hung above his eyes, some strands reaching below his eyebrows. Somehow, the hairstyle made him seem more boyish, less threatening.

Silvia delivered them from the awkward exchange with an announcement.

"I've got food in the kitchen on the stove. Help me bring it out, Pamela."

Pamela followed Silvia through the narrow room as they gathered peas, carrots, pasta, meat sauce, soup, sausage, roast potatoes, and loaves of garlic slathered bread. The size and variety of the cuisine were impressive, and Pamela found it hard to believe that Silvia had prepared all of it for just the three of them. She could hardly afford to repaint her ceilings, after all.

"Before we eat, I would like to say grace." Silvia declared, though the determination in her voice revealed she didn't need anyone's permission.

The suggestion gladdened Pamela. Perhaps because of Lorna's influence, she had prayed every night on her knees by her bedside, finding much courage and comfort in her Christian faith. She had even attended one of the preacher Billy Graham's crusades with her school friends and had committed her life to Jesus Christ.

Johnny, on the other hand, appeared perplexed. He stiffened in his seat, his muscular shoulders prominent under the thin material of his shirt. Pamela didn't believe he was a religious man. He had never talked about God, and from the way he lived, she suspected he didn't want to.

After praying, Johnny and his mother talked as if they hadn't seen one another in years. They grew animated discussing past events, Johnny's childhood and growing up, Brooklyn, Italian relatives across the sea, and neighborhood gossip.

They made no mention of Johnny's father, nor the Mancini Crime Family, and their dealings across the city.

Pamela continually felt like an outside observer—as if she was watching a family television show from the sofa in her leaky Fifth Avenue apartment. If she were a completely unbiased and uninformed witness to the scene, she would have thought they were the perfect replica of a family.

She would have been jealous.

Her mother had never looked at her as Silvia studied Johnny—her eyes teeming with pure affection, as if she regarded her son as the most precious being on earth.

The one time her mother had been proud of her had been when she started going out with Timothy Atwell. She had regarded Pamela with a newfound sense of respect, even if that respect was subdued.

When their chatter diminished, the two peered at Pamela, as if annoyed by her presence.

"I'm sorry we've left you in the dark," Johnny clued in, scraping his plate clean as Silvia dumped another pile of potatoes onto it. "I haven't seen Mamma in a long time."

"If you visited more..." Silvia sobered, her brown eyes glimmering coppery with emotion.

"Work, Ma. It keeps me busy." Johnny chuckled.

Silvia stood abruptly, her skirts rustling. She grabbed some of the empty dishes from off the table and excused herself.

Pamela and Johnny were left swimming in silence, unsure of how to proceed.

"I shouldn't have brought you here," Johnny growled, raking his hand through his hair.

"Then why did you?" Pamela whispered shrilly.

"I... I like you, and I wanted you to meet my mother." Johnny maintained, tapping his hand on his knee. "If she met you... she wouldn't be so worried about me all the time."

"She knows as well as I do I do not influence your life." Pamela cleared her throat. "Besides, if you cared what she thought, why wouldn't you quit... that job?"

Referring to Johnny's business as a mere job was unsettling.

"I do what I do because I care." Johnny reviled.

"You care about your mother, and yet you won't pay for a nicer home?" Pamela challenged indignantly.

"She is a proud woman. She won't take my money. I'd do anything to help my ma, know that."

"Then why not quit?" Pamela set her chin. "She told me herself that she hates worrying after you."

"I love my ma, Pamela, and you're a stranger to her. Don't act like you know what she wants." Johnny jerked his arm from the table angrily, causing one of Silvia's china plates to collide with the floor.

The precious family china, carefully brought from Italy, was gone in just a moment.

Pamela stooped down to help Johnny and Silvia retrieve the pieces, but the damage was done. The shards of china were tossed into the waste-bin, never to be seen again.

Silvia appeared, her eyes rimmed with crimson and her lips parted in shock, gripping a handkerchief close to her chest like a shield.

"I'm real sorry Ma." Johnny trembled like a little boy, gathering the pieces with his hands.

"I don't care about the plate, *bambino*." Silvia sighed. "I am just glad you are here with me after all these months. You don't visit enough."

They resumed their conversation as if nothing had happened, and Silvia made a noticeable effort to include Pamela in the festivities. Pamela even found herself laughing at Silvia teasing Johnny about his antics as a young boy; how he had used crayons to draw pictures all over the walls when Silvia was out.

"Ma, I got you somethin'." Johnny effused after a delicious dessert of pudding and cakes had been served and consumed.

He revealed a wrapped red gift box with a velvet bow, one which had surely been bought at a store.

Silvia unraveled the paper and opened the box to find a sleek pair of silken black gloves. They looked like the most expensive item in the apartment.

"Oh, Johnny, how *beautiful*," she cooed, leaning over to kiss him on the top of the head. "Just as elegant as the gloves in the department store. I've been eyeing them for so long. How well you know me."

Silvia kissed her son, mussing up his hair with her withered hands.

"Now it's Pamela's turn." Johnny quipped, egged on by his mother's enthusiasm.

"Oh... I'm sorry, I didn't bring anything," Pamela blushed. Even if she had wanted to bring a housewarming gift, she wouldn't have been able to. She wasn't paid very much on her salesgirl salary, especially with such much of the business's profits going to the mob.

"No, I mean you can open my gift to you." He pulled a long black case from on his lap and handed it to her, their fingers brushing against each other for a moment.

"Johnny y-you didn't have to." Pamela sputtered. To what lengths would he go to carry out this charade? Was it all an act, or had he thought they were dating?

"Open it. I paid good money." Johnny reprimanded jokingly.

Pamela pried the case open to expose a gold and ruby bracelet. She ran her finger along it, tiny diamonds grazing her flesh. It was expensive, no doubt, something a husband gave to his wife on an anniversary.

"I... I really can't accept it." Pamela gulped, folding the strand and placing it back inside the case.

"Sure you can," Johnny pressed, his brown eyes somber. "I'm giving it to you as a token of our... friendship."

Silvia stifled a laugh, patting Johnny on the back. "That isn't a gift of friendship, *passerotto*. That is a gift of love."

Pamela dipped her head to conceal her flushed skin. "Regardless, I cannot accept it. I didn't bring you anything to exchange."

Johnny surprised her by swaddling her small hand with his large one and leveling her with a tender eye. "I want you to have it, Pamela. There's no one else I would rather give it to."

Pamela had never been looked at in such a way by anyone, and it felt like warm soapy water rushing down her back.

She gaped at Johnny and realized that yet again there was nothing she could do but comply with his wish.

"Thank you," she uttered. "Really, Johnny, I wasn't expecting a present."

"Let me help you put it on," Johnny said, chuckling.

He captured her hand in his once again, firmly embedding his thumb in her palm as he slipped the bracelet around her wrist. She shivered at his touch, convincing herself it was from the cold.

After fastening the clasp, she raised her hand, letting the light scour the crimson rubies and the dainty diamonds.

"It's beautiful." Silvia gushed approvingly, smiling at her son. "I think the next thing you'll be giving her is a wedding ring."

Johnny cleared his throat and peered down at his wristwatch. "Wow, it's late Ma. I have to get back to Manhattan. I'll bring Pamela home."

Pamela knew she couldn't refuse, and so they thanked Silvia for dinner and the good company.

After Johnny helped put on her winter coat, Silvia gathered Pamela into a parting embrace and whispered into her ear. "God goes with you, dear, and so do all my prayers. Take care of my son."

Pamela smiled and thanked her again, knowing she could never fulfill such a promise. She was playing along, but she would rather die than give her heart to a mobster like Johnny Siciliano.

As they walked back to Johnny's automobile, she reminded herself that she was still pretending and that soon, after Officer Marino and his men arrested Johnny, she would go back to living like normal.

However detached she wanted herself to remain, she felt guilt carving out her stomach. She imagined Johnny's mother on a bench in the courthouse, clutching a rosary with tears surging from her ruddy eyes.

Would Silvia blame her when Johnny was locked away for good?

The golden tinsel of a Christmas tree flashed in her periphery, and she let her head fall on her hand as she regarded the view outside of Johnny's automobile. Old tenements like the one Johnny's mother lived in sprinted past them, poking their brick heads above mounds of snow. The sweet voices of Christmas carollers rode in on a gust of wind, singing of Jesus' birth on a midnight clear just like that night.

Johnny was quiet, and he didn't turn on the radio to listen to music as he had done before.

When they reached Fifth Avenue, he leaped over the car door, almost slipping on the ice and making her laugh, and helped her disembark so that her heels didn't catch on the pavement.

"I had a nice time Pamela."

Johnny didn't release her hands and squeezed them. She felt another shiver crawl up her spine and recovered her hands.

"So did I." Pamela confided. It was the truth. Though the visit had been thoroughly uncomfortable at times, she had sincerely enjoyed the food and laughter, something she missed since she had last seen Lorna.

"May I?" Johnny stepped towards her, his eyes narrowing in on her face with surprising earnestness, so different from the way Timothy Atwell had always looked upon her.

Pamela wasn't sure what he was asking until he gathered her face in his hands. His breath was pregnant with the red wine his mother had given him as a present. The midnight sky cloaked his tall figure, leaving only his magnetic eyes and handsome face for her to see.

He kissed her.

His kiss was gentle and nervous, his lips brushing against hers for only a moment before Pamela broke away.

Pamela's heart drummed against her chest, and she waited for him to break his stare so that she would no longer have to look at him.

"I'm sorry," he said, his voice low with embarrassment. "I thought..."

"Please. Don't." Pamela silenced him, stepping backwards. “I—I don't think we should ever do that again.”

Johnny looked as though he had been shot. His brown eyes were circles, the pallor of his skin a stark contrast from his usual spirited appearance. He drew away from her, his face downcast and bereaved by her sharpness. His lip began to tremble.

Pamela had never been kissed before. She had stopped Timothy on the rare occasions he tried to kiss her, but that was because he was a terrible oaf. She had dreamed of this moment for years, but had never thought it would be shared with a mobster on the streets of Brooklyn: a place her mother had decried as dangerous and full of unruly immigratns.

Even though she wanted more than anything to bury her head into Johnny's shoulder and hold herself against him, she knew she couldn't. Sorrow and desire and shame washed through her all at once.

The next moments between the kiss and her rejection were blurred as Johnny walked her to the door of the shop to ensure she got inside and out of the cold.

"Merry Christmas." He murmured as she climbed up the stairs.

"Merry Christmas."

CHAPTER 15

New Hampshire, January 1955

Once they married, Tony and Carlotta drove down a series of winding mountainous roads, steering away from craggy cliffs and boulders, tires bumping against eroded cement. They were unsure of their intended location, but Carlotta proclaimed she would know where they would settle when she saw it.

She chose Merrimack Valley.

Merrimack Valley was a humble enclave, hemmed in between snow-capped mountains and a meandering river. It was unlike anything Carlotta had seen before, posing a great juxtaposition to the Brooklyn of her childhood, which is precisely why she had selected it as their new residence.

Oak, beech and maple trees fanned out above them in a canopy of snow heaped leaves; which had been eaten away because of a recent series of blizzards and rough winter winds. The harsh scent of peat saturated the air, making everything seem earthy and untouched by the pomp of the city behind them. Only a few gas stations and one or two churches passed them as they sped by. Other than a handful of farmers and bicyclers, they had spotted few people.

The couple drove further, through the woods and down Interstate 93, sinking deeper and deeper into a wilderness they had never known.

They reached the barren town of Hooksett. True to its name, Hooksett was hook-like watershed land buried into the belly of a peaking mountain and embraced by the Merrimack River and Heads Pond. The town was more of a village than anything, for many of the inhabitants were lumber mill workers who had left in mass exodus when their jobs began disappearing to southern states.

When the engine of Tony's automobile began sputtering and gasping for fuel, they pulled over to a Texaco gas station to appease it.

While Tony went inside to pay a lumberjack looking man with a flannel shirt and a tawny beard, Carlotta sauntered over to the other side of the road, peering down at Hooksett from above. She was eager to stretch her legs—they hadn't ceased driving in hours, and the freezing morning air felt good against her naked face.

The town below didn't house many buildings—only a few shack-like homes and a couple of convenient stores, grocers, and a single old-fashioned schoolhouse with a long, triangular roof. It was nothing like she had ever seen before.

Carlotta's heart fluttered as she pictured her new life. She imagined it, with their humble one-story bungalow and bundle of giddy children but reminded herself that she no longer needed to. Her dream of eloping with Tony Bellucci was becoming her reality. She wanted to squeal and giggle in a fit of euphoria.

Married life was more wonderful than she ever could've imagined. She adored being with Tony. Knowing the love of a husband was better than described by love poems and motion pictures and novels—it was too good to be put into words.

She whirled around again to face the gas station, watching Tony and the lumberjack man exchange a stiff handshake.

Tony ushered her over with a quick movement of his hand.

She gladly complied, joining him at his side. He looped an arm around her, his powerful frame against her soft one, reminding her once again that he was *her* husband.

Nonchalantly, he combed his hand through her dark curls, not caring about being in the presence of a stranger.

He had never been so bold when they were going steady for fear of being found out by her father or the other wise guys. Now that they were free, he could smother her with affection in public as much as he wanted.

Once again, Carlotta felt a tremor of happiness jolt through her.

"Carlotta, this is Ed." Tony introduced Carlotta to the lumberjack man. "He says he knows someone willing to let us rent for a couple days before we get back on our feet."

"How d'you do?" Ed grinned, shaking Carlotta's hand firmly as he had done to her husband. "Must be real different from the big city down here in Hookline Falls."

"I'll say." Carlotta laced her fingers through Tony's, enjoying the rough skin of his hands. "We haven't seen much yet. Is there anything to look for in town?"

"There's a real nice drive-in a few miles north," Ed replied. "And you can visit the old mill."

"We will," Carlotta smiled. "Thanks for the suggestion."

"What's the accent, anyhow?" Ed stroked a finger along his chin, tilting his head to inspect the couple. "You folks got a funny way of talking."

"We're from New York." Tony flicked a glance at his watch, pretending to check the time.

"You don't say," Ed's eyes widened with excitement, "I've got family up there. They don't sound like you two, though. Must be from a different part of the city."

"It's a real big place," Carlotta suggested. "Lots of different people up there."

"We're Italians." Tony asserted, his voice carrying a defensive note.

"Italian *American*." Carlotta corrected, hoping the man would continue their previously friendly charade.

A tendon in Ed's jaw tightened. His arms stiffened, clenching to his sides. "We don't have many *dagos* around here for a reason. You said you wanted to settle in Hooksett, that right?"

"*What* did you just call us?" Tony stuck out his chest, his nostrils flaring.

Carlotta felt her muscles tense up, knotting all along her back and shoulders.

"See, they stationed me in Italy during the '40s," Ed growled in a hostile manner, as if the fact justified his unease. "You crazy Italians got what was coming to you, damn *wops*."

The baldness of his words frightened Carlotta. Sensing her fear, Tony stepped in front of his wife.

"We had nothin' to do with Mussolini's fight." Carlotta inched forward, covering Tony's fisted hand with her fingers. "Our boys fought for Uncle Sam too."

Ed ignored her. His eyes were roving across the mountains with a wild light in them. She had never seen such a terrifying look on a man. Clouds were gathering, dappling the sky with black, an unnatural hue of violet crawling towards the river—matching the ferocity in his stare. "You know, this country used to be great before immigration turned soft. The papers say a bunch of greaseball Italians brought their criminal activities to the cities, stole away the lives of honest, hard-working people. We should send you back to where you came from. I didn't fight that damned war for nothing."

Carlotta could feel Tony stiffening beside her, the muscles along his back pulled taut like a wire rope. She stepped closer to her husband, hoping her mere presence might mollify him. "Please, sir. We're good people. Just let us pay for our gas and we'll get outta your hair."

"*Woman*, there is no way I'm selling *anything* to a pair of *black dagos*."

Shock glistened on Carlotta's skin. She had never heard the slur said with such unabashed malice before. She had grown up in an Italian neighborhood, where the word was said as a mean joke between male friends or read in the papers when columnists complained of Italian immigrants filling the tenements of Brooklyn. Even then, it had never terrified her as it did now.

"Don't you say another word to my wife!" Tony lunged forward. He grabbed Ed by the collar of his plaid flannel shirt and pummeled him to the ground. He punched Ed so hard that Carlotta saw a mark of red bloom on his creased forehead and a crimson ribbon trickle down from his nose.

"Tony!" Carlotta screamed.

She stood frozen as her husband reached for the gun in his back pocket, his hand shaking violently as the man squirmed from beneath his weight. He pressed the gun to Ed's neck, pushing it deeper and deeper into his red skin until Carlotta was sure that the man's flesh might be punctured.

"Say it again," Tony grunted, "I dare you to say it again, you damn old hillbilly."

Ed cursed, clawing at Tony's face like an animal. His eyes rolled back in his head, showing white. “Damn dagos.”

Tony retaliated, a firm punch wiping all the color from the man's face.

"Tony!" Carlotta yelled again, throwing herself forward to rip her husband away from the attack.

Oh dear God, don't let Tony kill him.

With a quaking heart, Carlotta wrenched the gun from her husband, using all her strength to throw it away, where it landed near a mass of shrubs and wildflowers on the other side of the gas station.

"For crying out loud!" Carlotta yelled when she pried Tony away from the fight. "You were gonna shoot him!"

"I was gonna teach him a lesson." Tony seethed, wiping the moisture from his palms upon his trousers. "*Ammonini!*"

Ed thrashed about on the pavement, his hands pinched into futile fists. "See what I mean? Yer all animals."

Tony whipped around, clenching his jaw as Carlotta grabbed his hand. "C'mon Tony!"

She had to force him back to the side of the road, as he trembled and shook with rage. By the time they were in the safety of the car, Carlotta was crying. Tears soaked her face. Her heart squeezed as she released a wail of grief loud enough for everyone in New Hampshire to hear.

"Please Carlotta." Tony groaned, slamming his foot onto the gas. "Leave the damn thing alone."

"You've never been like that around me before..." Carlotta's head dropped into her lap as she sobbed, "you were always the gentle and kind one. Always sweet and good."

She had never seen the angry side of Tony. She had never seen the violent side of the men her father worked with—it had been forbidden. Family and business were strictly separated from one another, so the violence had never been tangible to her. She knew it was there, of course, but it was always churning beneath the surface.

Now it had erupted.

"Have you ever killed a man, Tony?" Carlotta whispered hoarsely.

She raised her pale eyes to him. They were two sparkling pools of periwinkle tears.

He avoided her gaze, his eyes trained ahead. His lack of response dangled between them.

"Oh, Tony, you couldn't have." Carlotta rasped. "God forbids murder. You wouldn't."

"Don't play stupid, Carlotta. It was my job. I was a soldier. That's the way I made my money. The money we're using now for our new life. How else would you expect an Italian kid from Brooklyn to make a livin'?"

"Besides," Tony added, "your own padre..."

Carlotta knew her father had killed men, but Tony wasn't like her father. He was good and pure, different from all the others. He had never been corrupted by the business as the other men had. Sure, he had gone along with it all in public, but deep down inside he had been full of goodwill and kindness. Hadn't he?

"Don't talk to me about my father." She snapped her head around to glare at him. "Just 'cause my papà did something doesn't mean you had to do the same."

"I made an oath." Tony moved his eyes from her. "I promised I would never break my loyalty to the Family. I got my badge when I spilled my blood over a picture of one of the holy saints and swore that I would never lift an eye to another fellas girl."

Carlotta was not unfamiliar with the proceedings of the ritual, all mafia members were required to take part in. To her, the entire ritual was sacrilegious. The men would spill their blood over a picture of a saint, then burn the image, claiming that if the wise guy should ever break their vows, they would burn like the saint.

"I'm not my father's woman," Carlotta argued, feeling sick imagining her husband at such an obscene ritual. "I'm his daughter, and that means I can make my own decisions."

"It doesn't matter, Carlotta. It's the same thing."

"How can you think of me that way? It wasn't my choice to be his daughter. Just like it wasn't your choice to grow up a poor Italian kid."

Tony's lip trembled. He looked like he was about to cry.

Carlotta felt her heart drop, realizing she had hurt him. But there was no turning back.

"You made an oath to me, Tony." Carlotta persisted, softening her tone. "You promised you'd be loyal to me, your *wife*, and keep nothing from me."

Her husband—the same man who held her, kissed and embraced her tenderly, was a murderer. She knew what he had been, but she had never fully registered the meaning of his role before. Perhaps she had been naïve, hoping her unspoken fears remained unconfirmed.

"You saw how he thought of us, how they all think of us," Tony said, veering off onto the major highway as their car bumped against the unpaved road they left behind. "We're greaseballs to them. *Our* old ways repulse them. *Our* ways, Carlotta, the ways of our forefathers, repulse *them*. Quittin' is just what they want us to do."

"They aren't our ways." Carlotta shook her head. "They're my papà's ways. And he can't tell us how to live anymore. We're gonna start a new way, Tony, a new life. The Lord forgives if we repent. And we are gonna repent, aren't we? With His help, we can turn our lives around…"

She knew Tony had never really shared her faith. He went to church and prayed the same prayers she had, but his had been said out of duty rather than devotion. Still, he was a gentle and kind man with the desire to help his family and fellow man. She had always admired his character, but now she wondered if it had been a ruse.

"You gotta remember Carlotta." Tony took in a sharp breath as he veered back onto the highway. "We can't run away that easy, without your dad putting up a fight. They are family, whether you like it or not."

Merrimack Valley faded into the rear window along with New Hampshire.

Night came, shrouding the car in black, and despite her agony, Carlotta drowned in a river of sleep.

CHAPTER 16

New York City, Fifth Avenue, January 1955

The public library had been Pamela's second home since she had learned how to read.

Lorna had brought her there during the afternoons when it was too cold to go to the park or visit the zoo, dressing her up like a china doll in prim white blouses and frilly pink skirts, though Pamela squirmed and sulked in revolt.

Annoyance ceded to the warmth of familiarity when the marvelous coliseum-like building rose above their bus. Lorna would clutch Pamela's hand to signal their upcoming descent, moving with a wave of commuters to the front.

Though intimidating marble lions guarded the building and black paper lined many of the library windows during the war, Pamela, a timid child, had always enjoyed the excitement that came with a trip to the library.

While Lorna traded recipes, laughter and stories with the other nannies of the Upper East Side, the rambunctious children in their care would slide down banisters and play war, causing general affliction for library patrons and staff.

Pamela, ever-contented to be alone, would steal away to some unoccupied corner chair, and read whatever book leapt out at her from a shelf. Fairy Tales, poems and myths were at first her favorites, but then she enjoyed *Anne of Green Gables*, *the Hobbit*, and *Nancy Drew*. Fiction became her escape, though, with history and language, non-fiction could also satisfy her ever-expanding intellectual appetite.

In her formative years, Pamela came to cherish the librarians and regular patrons. There was Mrs. Boyce, a middle-aged mother of twin boys fighting overseas, who took on extra shifts to support her sickly daughter, Violet. There were Larry and Henry, the kind janitorial staff who would slip her hard candy wrapped in shiny colorful jackets if she asked nicely. There was Ms. Czerwinski, a Polish Jew who had, fortunately, fled her homeland in the early thirties, but still mourned the disappearance of a sweetheart and countless relatives she left behind.

While her mother had been preoccupied with planning dinner parties and her father at work, Pamela had grown up under the care of the library and her beloved Lorna.

The bliss was temporary.

One day, Pamela had returned from an afternoon at the library to find her mother and a meddlesome neighbor called Mrs. Sanders exchanging formalities in the living room.

Lorna had sensed the cold ambience in the room. She had grasped Pamela's hand and brought her to the kitchen, where the two of them mixed cookie batter. While Pamela licked dough straight from the spoon, Lorna dialed up the radio to listen for updates on the invasion of France by the nazis.

After a few moments of tension veiled by light conversation, Mrs. Sanders had cleared her throat, nodding towards the open kitchen door.

"For crying out loud, turn that wretched thing down, Lorna," Caroline commanded more sharply than usual. When she recovered her polite hostess voice, she added jokingly, "Lorna, you are as bad as my husband. Come here, Lorna, and Pamela too. I must speak with you."

The buzz of the British voices on the radio cut to silence and Lorna emerged from the kitchen, her head inclined and her dark lashes casting shadows upon her caramel skin. Pamela followed her guardian obediently, licking the last bits of batter from her fingers before her mother could see.

"Now, Lorna," Caroline Kelly had chimed rather pleasantly, "I want to ask you a question."

"Yes, Ma'am."

"Mrs. Sanders has informed me that my daughter has become a recluse. She spends hours at the library reading while the other children play. Is this true?"

Lorna bent her head, though Pamela could see her nostrils flare as she took a breath.

"Yes, Ma'am. But I'm never far, and Pamela—Miss Kelly loves books. She is smart, like Mister Kelly. Her teachers all say the same thing—she is as bright as a star."

The mention of Pamela's father made Caroline stiffen. "If you are to rear my child, you must socialize her. She is never to be brought there again."

"But Mother!" Pamela had spoken out against her mother for the first time, her voice caught in desperate tears. "What else will I do during the afternoons? The other children go to the library too."

Caroline Kelly had blanched, mortified by her daughter's overt insubordination. "That is quite enough, Pamela Anne Kelly. You may visit the park, or spend the afternoons at the other children's homes. I will not tolerate my daughter wasting her life by dreaming in a library."

Pamela had cried that night. Her eyes had stung and her chest had ached. Lorna had hummed gospel songs and prayed over her, words of the Almighty warming her back to life.

Pamela wasn't sure if she had ever forgiven her mother. She wasn't sure if her mother cared what she felt either way, now that she was gone without explanation.

A library worker pulled her back to the current with confusion in his voice. "You need help, Ma'am?"

Pamela giggled with embarrassment, realizing she was blocking his cart full of books. She stepped to the side to let him pass, embarrassed by her inconveniencing him. "No, I'm just looking."

He shrugged and continued his work, allowing Pamela to return to her thoughts.

When Johnny kissed her, she had been aghast.

There were many descriptions of kisses in the novels she read and the films she watched, but this had not been one of them.

It had been amateurish like Johnny was a nervous schoolboy who had never kissed a girl. It had felt like he feared her as if his fate rested in her hands.

Of course, none of that could be true.

Johnny Siciliano was a man of the worst kind, and he had surely kept company with many unsavory characters. He was also flirtatious and morally misguided, as Lorna would say.

So, why had he set his intentions upon her?

With so much uncertainty and change thwarting her life, she needed advice from a trusted source. She had spent some time trying to find Lorna's information in Caterina's phonebook, but to her utter shame, had realized that she didn't know what neighborhood she lived in, or even her last name.

Looking back, she realized she had known little of Lorna's life outside of her own. She knew she had lived in a building downtown with her children and ailing mother and that she attended a Baptist church on the Sundays she didn't work. She knew Lorna had faith as strong as any, and loved Jesus with all of her heart. It was from Lorna that Pamela had first learned about the resurrection story and the love that transcends all others.

Pamela sighed, sadness ebbing through her conscience for the person she had loved most in the world.

She had tried to contact Sergeant Marino again, but the secretary on the other line had informed her he was busy. She had begged for another way of contacting him but had been refused and told that the Sergeant would only speak to those on some kind of designated list.

Pamela knew it was too dangerous to turn to the authorities again. If Sergeant Marino was unwilling to fulfill his end of the bargain, what was stopping other officers from doing the same?

With nowhere else to turn, Pamela had to hope and pray that the New York Public Library staff she had loved so long ago remained.

She lingered at the base of one of the two grand staircases in Astor Hall for a moment and then gathered her courage to walk to the other side of the massive room where a small reception desk endured.

"May I assist you with something?" An unfamiliar woman with gray hair and wide-rimmed spectacles smiled up at her from her leather seat.

"Yes," Pamela said and then remembered her manners, "thank you. I have some old friends who were employed here, and I was hoping to speak with them."

"Of course." The woman nodded as she adjusted her spectacles. "Might I ask your name?"

"My name is Pamela Kelly." Pamela swallowed the lump in her throat and felt it disappear. "You can tell them that. I'm sure they'll remember me."

They would remember her name.

They always had.

The librarian looked up from her notes as she inspected Pamela. "Who are you looking for?"

"Mrs. Boyce. I remember she worked here during the war." Pamela waited expectantly, her heart stretching with hope.

"Mrs. Boyce? She left here years ago to live with her son in Minnesota after her daughter passed. I can try to locate her address if you would like."

"No, thank you. How about Larry and Henry? They were part of the cleaning staff when I was young."

"I don't know anyone who works here by those names. You must understand, we experienced massive turnover in staff after the war."

Pamela drew a breath, panic pricking her arms and chest. Blood rushed to her ears. "Then... Mrs. Czerwinski?"

From the librarian's expression, Pamela knew she recognized the name, but she shook her head. "I'm afraid Mrs. Czerwinski passed away last April. She was a dear woman, God rest her soul."

"Oh no..." Pamela fidgeted with her gloves, her upper lip trembling as it did when she was about to cry. She had never felt so discouraged or so frightened. She had no one left, not even an old teacher or friend who might help her.

She was trapped.

"I am very sorry dear, I'm sure they would have loved to see you." The librarian handed her a tissue, perhaps sensing her urge to cry.

"I'll be just fine. Thank you for your help." Pamela said, taking the tissue to dab her eyes.

Pamela left the New York Public Library without a book for the first time in her life.

She hailed a taxi, digging through her handbag for change, and drove back to Albright Trimmings & Co. without a choice.

Men were standing outside smoking, as usual, the collars of their black overcoats lifted above their ears for protection against the persistent winter cold that refused to give way to spring. Somehow, their ominous presence did not deter business, with female cousins, mothers, daughters, girlfriends and wives of the Mancini family flocking to the store in hordes. Other women, unaware of the dark hidden truth of the business, continued to shop without hindrance, pleased by the uninhibited supply of gauze, chiffon, silk, wool, and even exotic Canadian furs.

Johnny had not returned to the store after the night Pamela had rejected his kiss. Pamela didn't care to guess why, but only hoped that his business would keep him elsewhere for the rest of the time she spent in Fifth Avenue.

As Pamela tipped the cab and climbed into the street, smoothing her plain blue skirt and permed hair as she did so, she noticed the men staring at her with disconcerting intensity.

She knew they weren't looking at her because of her figure or her pretty face; there were more boldly dressed and beautiful belles to admire. There was something more sinister than lustful appreciation in their leers, something lethal.

Pamela met the eyes of one man, familiar to her because of his presence at the Copacabana. He was the man who had touched her waist to Johnny's rebuke; the man named Mike.

Pamela refused to look away, casting a dark look towards him with an angry intensity she was sure out-competed his.

Instead of relenting, Mike held her gaze. His eyes narrowed with a lecherous smirk that made her stomach drop.

Pamela looked away, pushing the door open and letting it crash behind her as she felt the examining eyes follow her.

"Where have you been?" Caterina gasped, bumping into Pamela as she entered. "I've been looking everywhere for you. Have you lost your marbles? You were supposed to start work half an hour ago."

Pamela sighed, tying an apron around her waist to stand behind the till. "Sorry Cat, I was visiting some family."

"Lucky for you, it's been too busy for Johnny to notice anything amiss." Caterina winked. "Although he will be awful worried when he realizes his girl has been running around without his knowledge."

The air in Pamela's lungs went stale as she absorbed Caterina's words. She placed a hand to her heart, feeling it thud against her chest. "Johnny? He's here?"

Caterina rolled her dark eyes, ducking behind the counter to pull her glossy ebony hair into a ponytail. "Of course Johnny's here. He's working in the back. He asked for you to come see him when you get a chance."

Pamela could hardly think as she tracked sales and counted change, fearing the nearness of Johnny just a door down.

When the patrons dissipated with the evening, going home to their safe lives and comfortable families, Pamela wished she could beg them to take her with them.

Instead, she released a terse breath, applied a fresh coat of lipstick and drifted to the back corner office like an apparition to meet her fate.

Johnny was hunched over a stack of papers, circling numbers with a faded yellow pencil and surrounded by a group of four men. One man sitting on a stool outside the glass-covered door, presumably a guard, stood when he saw Pamela and let her in.

She tried to ignore the naked gun in his hand, and harder still to dismiss the throbbing pain in her chest.

Johnny surged from his chair, his pencil clinking against the wood of the table and his eyebrows lifting in surprise as if he wasn't expecting her. The horde of men around him raised their brows and smiled. "Fellas, disappear for a few seconds, would ya?"

The menagerie of men obeyed his order and scuttled off, leaving Johnny and Pamela alone.

Johnny did not look like himself. His shirt was crumpled and stained, his hair disheveled, as if he had just woken up. Dark circles shadowed his brown eyes. The mole on his face looked pitch black against the pallor of his skin, and his lively brown eyes were sedate for once.

He was the antithesis of the man Pamela had seen at Christmas Dinner, the man who had laughed and reminisced with his Mother as he let the merriment of the night engulf him.

Still, Pamela felt a pang in her heart for him, an indescribable affection and sorrow that she would forever keep a secret.

There was no reason for her to feel this way about a man who plagued her thoughts. The only explanation that she could give herself was that there were moments that had revealed in him an endearing heart. Or at least parts of him that were still uncorrupted and pure.

It had been when she had spent Christmas Dinner with him she had seen the young boy he must've been; the boy who had loved his mamma, and when she had danced with him at the Copacabana.

Pamela banished the pesky feelings from her mind and focussed back on the present upon the man who all but had stolen her life from her.

Before Pamela could speak, Johnny stepped forward, his hands tied together. "I wanted to apologize."

Did he feel the same desire to apologize to the countless victims of the mob that terrorized the city? Did he feel the same desire to repent of his sins against God and mankind? The same desire to look after the late Mr. Friedenberg's poor widow and her children?

"I guess I was too forward in... kissing you that night. Maybe I was wrong in reading your happiness as... something else." Johnny winced, glancing away from her.

"I was only surprised," Pamela admitted. "I... I've never really been kissed before."

"You haven't?" A look of surprise flashed across his face.

Pamela shook her head, hating the vulnerability in her confession. "Why are you surprised?"

"I haven't met a girl as pretty as you who hasn't been kissed," Johnny claimed. His dark eyes pressed into her.

"You don't need to flatter me." Pamela groaned, wanting to plug her ears. She hated how he stared at her so as if he was trying to read her mind.

A swell of confidence seemed to overcome Johnny. He grabbed a wrapped golden bouquet of roses and pressed it into her hands.

They were the deepest shade of crimson red, and smelled beautiful, like he had plucked them from a summertime garden.

Pamela didn't ask why or how he had gotten them in the cold of mid-January.

"Thank you Johnny, but... I can't accept them." Pamela cleared her throat, stretching her arms out to decline the flowers. "You said that all that this was is business, and yet you are treating me like a girl you want to court."

Johnny grimaced at his hurt pride, his brown eyes flooding with disappointment.

"I don't understand why you're trying to win my affection," Pamela swallowed, staring up at him, "when I have nothing to offer you. Just let me leave here, and this will all stop."

"I'm not pretending to like you." Johnny said the words so quietly that she had to strain her ears to hear him.

He refused to look at her, turning around with his hand upon the desk. "I do like you, a lot. Under different circumstances..."

His voice fell into silence until he cleared his throat. "But if I let you leave now, the other guys will see you as a witness to be used in court, with enough valuable information to lock up the entire Mancini family for years. Including me."

"What... could they do?" Pamela hugged herself, her skin bristling.

"You know what they're capable of." Johnny sauntered around the office, completing a circle that ended with her. "They could do what they did to old Mr. Friedenberg."

Horror seized Pamela.

"I'm being honest with you." Johnny cut her off, his eyes dark and unreadable. "Trust me."

Pamela could scarcely hear anything else he said. He was moving his mouth: speaking rapidly, moving his hands to reassure her, but all she perceived was more silence.

"I can go back to the police," Pamela threatened, though she knew she could never follow through. "I can tell them what you've done. How you've slaughtered Mr. Friedenberg and left his wife a widow, his kids fatherless."

"The cops won't do anything." Johnny looked at her as if she was stupid. "Half of them are paid off. The other half are too scared to cross us."

Pamela didn't believe him. Sergeant Joseph Marino was already helping her, behind the scenes. He was a good cop.

Johnny shook his head. His forehead creased in exasperation. "All I need is for you to bring me to meet your father. I care about you, Pamela. You gotta understand. I wouldn't have to spare your life if I didn't want to, and I do."

His gaze pierced her, and she realized that there was nothing between them anymore. Her life was in his hands, and she couldn't do anything about it.

"What do I have to do?" Pamela begged, searching his eyes for answers.

"Follow my lead, and pretend that we're engaged to be married. That way, I'll gain your dad's respect and the guys will have no reason to kill you. I shouldn't be telling you this, but my boss needs me to secure a deal with Stuart Kelly, and by pretending to be engaged to you that can be accomplished. After that, you can go back to the life you loved so much." Johnny took her hands in his large ones and kissed her fingers, sending shivers up her spine.

His words were calculated and measured. He sounded like he was presenting her with a recital for a play, or a business deal. That was what his proposition was, wasn't it?

Before he let her go, Johnny dug through his pocket and displayed a stunning silver ring with a diamond large enough to make the Queen of England envious.

He slipped it onto her ring finger gently and circled his arm around her waist.

When he let the other men back inside, he bellowed and cheered with such exuberance that Pamela almost believed they were to be married. "Champagne! For the future Mrs. Siciliano!"

CHAPTER 17

The men parted for Pamela as she descended the stairs from her apartment to the ground floor of Albright Trimmings & Co.

Johnny imagined his jaw-dropping like in some stupid cartoon as she tottered down the stairs, appraising her glamorous appearance.

Her thick blonde hair was swept up into a bun, half of it cascading down her shoulders into loose tresses around her slender neck. Her makeup was simple but flattering. Lashes combed up with jet-black mascara framed her lovely eyes, a flicker of light in the room making them catch gold. Rouge coated her dark lips, darker than anything Johnny had seen her wear before. She wore a fitted swing dress the color of dawn in a wide tulle skirt, complementary to the soft, feminine curves of her figure.

Johnny sensed his heart gallop within his chest and his palms grow sweaty. He felt like a schoolboy again, fostering a crush, yet too entranced to speak of his affection. *She's beautiful.*

She didn't enjoy being the center of attention because when she saw the crowd of men and women gathered to wish her congratulations, her cheeks burned pink and she ducked her head.

Pamela's glamorous appearance wasn't missed by Johnny's peers. The men elbowed him and slapped his back, whispering crude innuendos and whistling.

Johnny shoved them away, sickened by their coarseness.

Caterina De Lorenzo followed behind her roommate, her face flushed with exertion. Johnny suspected she must have helped Pamela with her preparation for the evening.

Upon Johnny's announcement, the men had been pleasantly surprised and demanded a celebratory party. Of course, they had known about the financial arrangement and how Pamela had been in charge of setting aside twenty percent of sales for the Family, but Johnny doubted they knew about the construction tycoon, Stuart Kelly.

As he saw it, theirs was a relationship of mutualistic benefit. If Pamela bridged the gap between the Mancini Family and her father's construction business, Johnny would honor his end of the bargain and keep her from harm. If the men believed Pamela had fallen in love with him, there would be no further reason for them to suspect her capable of ratting on their operations and what she had been privy to.

"What are you waiting for? Kiss your bride!"

Johnny whirled around to perceive the wide, beaming face of Sal Palermo, his sweaty shirt plastered to his skin and his arm loosely around the shoulders of a young woman.

Lorenzo Palermo was there too, along with his long-suffering wife Victoria. So were Mike, Luca, Marco, John and Antonio. Even quiet Joey Romano had shown up with his wife Giovanna, despite his perpetual aversion to large social gatherings and parties.

Some soldiers Johnny didn't know well stood by the door, their hands dug into pockets, no doubt containing guns.

It was then that Johnny noticed Tony Bellucci's absence. Tony had been around a little lately and had disappeared after Christmas. Johnny had assumed it was because he was with family for the holidays but found it strange that he hadn't heard from his best friend in over a week. Even if this was a fake engagement party, Tony wouldn't have known that, and Johnny would expect his friend to attend out of loyalty.

Roberto wasn't present either but had been the one to recommend a proposal. He had called Johnny into his office with a distracted expression and advised him to coerce Pamela into an engagement. As a future son-in-law, he would have to be accepted by the untouchable Stuart Kelly.

"*Andosh*!" Lorenzo yelled, clapping his hands together. "Let's go! Give the girl a smooch!"

Johnny gazed at Pamela to gauge her reaction. Her face was blank, her mouth unsmiling.

Doesn't she like me at all?

Johnny liked to think of himself as an accomplished and dignified man. He was the youngest capo in Brooklyn and had worked his way up from being the only son of an absentee factory worker in a street youth gang to an employee of one of the most powerful men in New York. Aside from that, he was handsome and well-mannered. What more could Pamela Kelly want in a man?

Johnny tried to ignore the doubt melting his confidence. He marched over to Pamela, pushing her hair back as he pressed his mouth upon hers.

It wasn't an enjoyable kiss, because he knew she didn't reciprocate his feelings of affection.

Unsurprisingly, he felt her resist beneath his grasp, and a surge of guilt stilled the powerful physical desire within him.

"I'm sorry," he whispered into her ear, quiet enough so that no one watching would hear what he was saying. He wished she wanted to kiss him as much as he did her, but he hated the idea of forcing her, or any woman.

When he pulled away, she nodded, but her eyes were cold with anger.

The company left for Mario's Restaurant on Pioneer Street, just a couple of blocks away from the Mancini residence.

The ten sleek automobiles glided through the streets of New York in grand procession, with Johnny and Pamela in the front and the rest of the company and their wives driving behind.

Johnny wished he had more to say to Pamela, but he was silent. He had always flirted with women without significant trouble, but Pamela was different. She wasn't impressed by his car or his smooth talk. She would never be impressed by him, as long as he was a made man.

Johnny had stopped being impressed with himself too. Every time he had held a gun, commissioned a death, tossed a corpse into Hudson's River, or coerced money out of the pockets of decent businesspeople flashed through his mind. He remembered Mr. Murphy's kid that day he had driven out to Levittown. He had done awful things. The power and the money, but mostly the respect had blinded him. He had found men who had given him the one thing he had never found—belonging.

The shine was wearing off.

Regardless, Johnny couldn't just leave. He knew no other way of life, and no sane person would forgive him for his wrongs when they knew what he had done. Not even a girl as good as Pamela Kelly.

As Mario's Restaurant and Bar unearthed itself among the laundromats and the Italian delicatessens, Johnny regained his voice.

"The clams are good here." He remarked.

Pamela didn't seem to hear him.

"You should try 'em." Johnny encouraged, wondering why he was continuing with such a painful lack of response.

The rest of the gang went in ahead of them, the women gossiping with their sharp Brooklyn accents and the men charging ahead, made giddy by illegal Canadian whiskey.

"You don't have to pretend to be nice," Pamela whispered, startling him.

"What?"

Pamela turned. Her eyes were spheres of vulnerability. "I know this is just a job for you. I'll spare you the trouble of having to be courteous when we're alone."

Johnny opened his mouth to respond, but couldn't think of anything. He wanted to claim his innocence.

Pamela could see straight through his irony. He had robbed her of the normal life he imagined she must have had once. She despised him, and he had forced her into this intimate position. How could she ever believe that he truly cared for her?

Before he could defend himself, Pamela had faded into the restaurant bar, her arms clutched around her chest and her head bent.

Johnny leapt over the car door to follow her. Whatever he felt for Pamela, he refused to let it interfere with business. He would feel these things for a million more women, wouldn't he? He wouldn't allow this sentimental attachment to become his one weakness.

Pamela crept inside Mario's Restaurant and Bar. It was decorated in the typical Italian style, with sunny vineyards painted to the walls, candles on every checkered table, and a lengthy bar spanning between two Roman pillars. Velvet red curtains were draped from odd places in the room, some in front of booths, others languishing from the middle of the ceiling. Cigar smoke tangled with ladies' perfume tore through her lungs, making her eyes water and her chest hurt.

There was no one in the restaurant but Johnny and his guests and after they had entered, the bartender had flipped the sign in the window to *closed*, leading Pamela to suspect that it was an exclusive mafia hangout, despite its cheap exterior.

The moment her presence was recognized, women Pamela didn't know fawned over her, grabbing her hand with sharp talon-like nails and stooping low to inspect the enormous diamond on her ring finger. They touched her hair and praised her dress and slim figure, granting advice on what wedding gown she should choose for a day that would never come.

Caterina didn't stray far from her side, ensuring that none of the women asked too many nosy questions that might make Pamela uncomfortable, and shooing them away when they got too close.

After drinks were served and a hired crooner had sung a ballad, Caterina led Pamela to a secluded table, away from the men. Four women were parked there—presumably the wives and girlfriends of wise guys.

Two middle-aged women introduced to Pamela struck her with interest, especially Victoria Palermo and Giovanna Romano.

Giovanna was of average appearance, but extravagantly dressed. Her brown hair was curled close to her head, giving the illusion of a shortcut. Glistening white jewels decorated her ears, and a string of diamonds even larger than the one on Pamela's finger grappled her neck. Of course, her evening gown must have been pure silk and her coat made of authentic fur shorn off the back of some poor animal.

Victoria boasted a more comfortable, self-assured presentation. She was nearing her late forties but still bore a shockingly thin frame, her purple dress desperate to cling to her khaki-coloured skin. Though lines like writing carved through her forehead and the places around her precise lips, her cunning black eyes deflected from any evidence of age. Out of the two women, Victoria had been the beauty in her youth. From the prance in her step and her faultless posture, she knew she had this advantage over Giovanna Romano.

"Caterina De Lorenzo. The last time I saw you, you had been a little girl playing hopscotch with my Francesca!" Victoria stood regally, kissing Caterina on both cheeks. Her laughter peeled through the restaurant, though it sounded flat and bitter.

"Mrs. L. Nice to see you," Caterina said uncharacteristically softly, linking her arm through Pamela's. "This is Pamela Kelly, the future Mrs. Johnny Siciliano."

Pamela cringed at the title.

Then she reminded herself that this was only temporary. When the bargain was concluded, she would return to being Pamela Kelly, the reserved American girl who found excitement only between the pages of a book. For now, she would be the future Pamela Siciliano: an elegant mobster's future wife. A woman who feared nothing and nobody—one who was educated in the ways of the world.

Pamela tilted her chin and extended a hand to Victoria Palermo. "I'm pleased to make your acquaintance."

Victoria smiled tightly, accepting Pamela's hand and patting it. "So this is the doll who stole Johnny's heart. You must be somethin' real special."

"Thank you." Pamela forced a confident smile.

Giovanna slid over, gesturing for Pamela to sit.

When introductions had been formally made, the women insisted on ordering Pamela a cocktail. The server brought it over, and Pamela sipped at it carefully, though it burned her throat. She rarely drank and hated the taste of alcohol. Caterina called her a square because of it, but Pamela found no joy in the social function.

"So, how does an Americana end up getting hitched with a Sicilian?" Victoria's eyes scanned the small table before resting upon Pamela. There was a scintilla of suspicion within the woman's hawkish gaze, one that Pamela knew she had to stamp out before it caught fire.

"I'm no more American than the rest of you." Pamela attempted a friendly tone, idly stirring her cocktail. "That is... my father is Irish."

The admission stilled the table.

Victoria spoke. "I guess that makes us all Americans."

The other women snickered.

"How did you know Johnny was the one?" Giovanna interjected, straightening her decadent necklace.

Tell them the truth as much as you can, Pamela commanded herself.

"He's very charming," Pamela fidgeted with the red and white tablecloth, "and he's quite honest and thoughtful when he wants to be."

The women cackled, their voices scratchy with smoke. They chattered in quick Italian, their smooth hands clapping and gesturing almost as passionately as their speech.

Caterina exchanged a look with Pamela, assuring her she wasn't in on the joke.

"There's nothing wrong with wanting a man for his money." Victoria lowered her voice in English, her eyes roaming to the men shouting and waving their arms at the bar. "If my husband had been a lazy bum, I wouldn't have married him. A man needs to take care of his woman."

The other women nodded in agreement.

They think I'm a gold digger, Pamela realized. *Why else would a sane woman marry a killer?*

"We weren't calling you a gold digger," Giovanna asserted, reading her thoughts. "just a *cercatore d'oro.*"

Everyone except Caterina laughed, her nostrils flaring. Her hands were held into fists.

"Come. Let's go check on the man of the hour." Caterina rose, dragging a confused Pamela away from the commotion.

"Don't pay any mind to those old cows. They're just jealous because of the *gumads* their men keep behind their backs. And Johnny is sweet on you. He's never been this way around anyone before." She giggled. "You shoulda seen the way he gawked at you tonight. Besides, I think old Mrs. L wanted Johnny to marry her sweet Francesca."

At that moment, Pamela wanted to admit the truth to Caterina. She had become a good friend, perhaps the best she had ever had.

"Their husbands are unfaithful?" Pamela whispered, resorting to gossip rather than ingenuity. "How do you know?"

Caterina smirked, her dark lips curling.

"Oh, Cat! You couldn't mean..."

"Oh, what does it matter?" Caterina sighed, tossing her black mane. "It was fun while it lasted. Besides, Lorenzo treated me well. How do you think I got my job?"

Lorenzo, Pamela remembered, had been the man at Copacabana with his arm around the blonde. She had noticed nothing peculiar between him and Caterina, other than him being subjected to Caterina's usual flirtatious antics.

She couldn't imagine Caterina being with a married man, especially when she had so many single ones throwing themselves at her feet.

Besides, the man was older enough to be Caterina's father. Why was she risking so much for someone who cared nothing for her?

"Don't look at me like that." Caterina scolded. "You gotta do what you gotta do. That's the way it is, isn't it?"

"B-but—it's a sin." Pamela clutched her stomach as if she had just been hit. She could only imagine what Lorna would say if she was there.

"Sometimes I wonder why we're friends. You're no fun, Pamela." Caterina sighed, adjusting her hair as if the matter was nothing more than a burnt batch of cookies. "Leave the church talk for the old stuffy people."

Interrupting their talk, Lorenzo Palermo strode across the floor to greet them.

"I don't believe my eyes!" He rasped, grabbing Caterina's fingers to plant a kiss upon them. "Where have you been all night?"

Pamela was dumbfounded by his overt, unabashed flirtation with his wife in such proximity. She whirled around, catching Victoria's scrutinizing glare, searching between clusters of people.

"I was looking for you, *amore mio*." Caterina winked, relishing in the attention.

Pamela wanted to whisk Caterina away from the scandal, but her feet remained rooted to the floor. The lights above her were spinning.

"Hello, Pamela Kelly." Lorenzo chuckled, his fleshy arm still tight around Caterina's back. "We never expected Johnny to fall for an *Americana*."

Pamela couldn't find her voice.

Luckily, Caterina spoke instead, whispering through sultry red lips into Lorenzo's ear. "Love is real unpredictable, isn't it Lorenzo?"

The two shared a knowing look.

Lorenzo seemed to forget where he was, kissing Caterina on the mouth. "Especially with women as intoxicating as you, Miss Caterina. Why don't we head over to the motel? Remember, that one by the side of the highway..."

In a flash of violet, Victoria was charging across the room, the crowd parting for her like the Red Sea.

"Lorenzo Palermo!" She hollered, throwing her fists against Lorenzo's chest. "How dare *you* insult me like this? When I've given you everything I have?"

To Pamela's horror, some men had formed a triangle behind Lorenzo, guns being reached for. Apparently, it was normal to threaten a wife with violence if she made a scene over a husband's infidelity.

"You don't wanna do this." Lorenzo shushed her, arresting her flailing arms with his hands.

"What? You're gonna threaten to kill me if I don't keep my mouth shut? I'm the mother of your children, Lorenzo Angelo Palermo!"

"*Cara*," Lorenzo drawled, "calm down now. You've exhausted yourself. Go home, spend some time with the kids, drink some wine, and I'll be back soon. Okay?"

Victoria stepped back, her arms still raised as if in prayer and hands trembling. Tears flowed down her cheeks.

Pamela felt Johnny beside her, his hand lingering on her shoulder.

"You're right. I'm just tired." Victoria straightened, her tone regaining composure though still shaky.

As if nothing unprecedented had just happened, Victoria kissed Lorenzo on both cheeks twice and then strolled away, though she didn't leave before assaulting Caterina with a furious look. "Don't you ever go thinkin' that he's not still my husband, little Caterina."

Caterina appeared stricken, her dark eyes wide with fright and perhaps a little guilt. "I should go too."

"C'mon, don't let a little disagreement spoil our fun." Lorenzo turned to the crush of people and pounded his fist on a table. "Joey! Get us some more booze!"

With a little music and dance, everyone seemed to forget that there had ever been a problem. But Pamela couldn't shake the feeling that Victoria Palermo was reminiscent of her own mother. Whenever her father had been unfaithful, Caroline had handled the ordeal as if it were only a dinner reservation mix-up. She had never lashed out as Victoria did, and yet Pamela knew that privately, she must have also felt betrayed and humiliated.

When Johnny asked Pamela if she wanted to dance, she declined his offer with the simple excuse her feet hurt.

To her surprise, Johnny had not looked like his usual chipper self. He had sat beside her, sober, and watched as his friends danced and drank themselves into delusion. Even when one girl asked Johnny to a waltz, he declined.

"Lorenzo wasn't always like this," Johnny said after a few minutes of silence.

Pamela followed his gaze to the middle-aged man, now slouched against a booth with another girl.

Pamela didn't prompt him to continue, but he did anyway. "He was the smartest guy I knew. Graduated high school and everything. Victoria was his high school sweetheart, and they got married the moment they could.

"He's the reason I'm here. When I was a kid and my dad wasn't around, I learned how to shoot real good with soda cans and slingshots. I got hired to get rid of hawks on neighbors' roofs so they wouldn't eat the pigeons. The first time was hard. I had never killed something before. Then it got easy." Johnny heaved a sigh and turned to face her. His eyes were sad. "One day, Lorenzo and his best friend, my Boss Roberto, were at the same bar as me and some friends. Lorenzo heard about my little talent and asked if I could show him. I did, and he took me under his wing."

He hadn't taken his eyes off Pamela, not for a second. She got the feeling he was far away.

"I don't know what happened to him." Johnny confided, breaking his stare.

Though she didn't dare say it, Pamela knew what had happened. His immortality had become a habit, as killing hawks had become Johnny's not so long ago. Little by little, his conscience had ebbed, and his heart had become hardened to his crimes.

One day, she feared the same would happen to Johnny.

"You shouldn't tell me these things," Pamela whispered. "I'm not supposed to know any of it."

Pamela knew that when he raised his eyes to her, she had wounded him. He had spoken in earnest, revealing things about himself he had never shared, and she had rebuked him.

Pamela opened her mouth to apologize, but Johnny stood first, combing his hand through his hair. "Forget it."

He strode to the other side of the room and sat at the bar, striking up a conversation with another man.

Pamela rose, too, wanting to find Caterina to bring her home. She wouldn't let her friend stay while Lorenzo Palermo was around, or any of the other slimy wise guys who might try to take advantage of her negligence.

She saw her friend locked in an embrace with a young man, one she had never seen before.

"Cat!" Pamela cried, running over to her friend. "We have to go!"

Caterina ignored Pamela, swaying to the slow song of the crooner. The man bent over to kiss her.

Pamela grabbed Caterina, trying to pull her away from the greasy-looking man. She felt like she was going to vomit. "Please Cat, let's go."

Suddenly, a scream ripped through the restaurant, followed by a shattering of glass.

Lorenzo was darting towards them like a cannonball, his face red and his hand extended. Silver flared in his grasp. There was a loud bang. A stripe of blood gushed across Pamela's gown. She collapsed on the floor, her hands covering her face.

"Get your hands off her!"

Pamela peered through her fingers to see Lorenzo pointing the gun at the young man.

"Do you know who I am? You have no business around her." Lorenzo shouted.

"You shot me!" The young man cursed, pointing to the patch of red blooming on his white blouse.

Caterina was crouched on the floor behind him, her face pressed against the floor and her arms shielding her head.

Lorenzo groaned, still holding the gun, and shook Caterina's arm. "Get up woman."

"What are you doing?" Johnny yelled, putting himself between Lorenzo and the trio. "Why did you fire?"

"He kissed Caterina! This nobody, from who knows where, put his hands on my girl!" Lorenzo fumed. He tried to pace back towards the young man, but Johnny dug a hand into his chest to stop him. "Does he think I'm some kind of *cornuto*? Does he know who I am?"

"She isn't your girl!" the young man hollered, forcing himself to stand. "She's tired of you, old man."

Lorenzo shook Johnny off of him, firing a shot into the air. The restaurant screamed, and people began scuttling towards the door, carving a clear path around Lorenzo.

"Forget about your stupid pride, and leave the damn kid alone!" Johnny tore the gun from the disgruntled man.

Then Johnny knelt beside Pamela. His eyes widened as they grazed the blood on her gown. "Are you hurt?"

Pamela shook her head. It was the truth. The blood had not been her own, but the poor man who had kissed Caterina that night.

Johnny turned his attention to Caterina. She was shaken, but otherwise unharmed.

The man was injured, but only with a wound that needed stitches to heal.

One of Lorenzo's guards begrudgingly sent him to a cousin doctor who he knew wouldn't inform the cops.

Pamela thanked God, knowing that things could have gone differently.

Johnny drove Pamela and Caterina home.

Caterina was exhausted and slept in the backseat like a newborn baby.

Johnny was looking ahead with a stony expression, his forehead creased with worry.

Pamela never wanted to experience such terror again. She needed to escape but knew she wouldn't make it without Johnny's permission. Even if she had to pretend to be Johnny's future wife, she couldn't bear to live in the belly of such evil for the rest of the bargain.

"Let me go back to my family." Pamela pleaded, her request sounding foreign. She had never predicted wanting to return, but now that she was supposedly engaged to Johnny, how would her mother force her into marriage with Timothy Atwell? "Nothing on your part will change. I just can't stand to endure this anymore. But, you'll still get to meet my father, and afterwards, I'll leave for Canada or somewhere you know I'll never speak a word."

Johnny considered this and nodded somewhat. "I guess that'll be okay."

So he changed routes and headed for Pamela's childhood home, where nothing could ever be the same.

CHAPTER 18

Pamela trembled with Johnny's automobile as it lurched to a stop.

Instead of opening the door, Johnny turned towards her, his eyes blackened by the night. The streetlights had come on, though that night they seemed less beautiful than they had before.

"You sure you don't want me to go back to Albright Trimmings for anything?" Johnny asked for the umpteenth time.

Pamela shook her head, not wanting him to say another word. The turmoil within would not subside until Johnny had manipulated her father into a business deal and accomplished whatever else he had in mind.

"What about all your stuff? Your clothes?" Johnny persisted, making Pamela wonder why he cared so much about her belongings. She had little energy left to care about her possessions. She didn't want to think about Albright Trimmings just yet—not until it had faded into the long-ago stretch of time behind her—like an unwinding road in the rearview mirror of an automobile.

"I don't need them," Pamela said. She had enough frocks and cardigans within the sanctuary of her childhood bedroom to rival a princess's wardrobe. Despite failing to provide her with love or affection, her mother had ensured she never wanted anything of the material variety.

"You might wanna wipe that thing off before you go in." Johnny gestured to the fine trickle of blood on the bodice of her gown as if it was just a bothersome dash of ketchup she had gained from eating French fries. "Or I can help you."

He extended a hand to assist her in removing the blemish. But Pamela jerked away at the last moment. "My mother will be asleep. So will my father. I'll go to my room and freshen up before they know I've returned. You should really get going, Johnny. Bring Caterina home and see to it she has something to eat, or she'll feel terrible tomorrow."

The two turned to look at the backseat passenger, who was still comfortably asleep with shallow snores escaping her half-open mouth.

"I guess I'll come back tomorrow morning for brunch. You'll tell your folks about me before then?" Johnny said, his tone a mixture of hopeful and excited. Either he was an excellent actor or he sincerely believed that he was about to meet his future in-laws.

"Sure." Pamela grappled in the dark for the drawstrings of her purse but found Johnny's arm instead. Pulling away in embarrassment, she saw his eyes soften with a wounded look.

Before she could escape, Johnny placed a palm on her shoulder innocently. "Are you swell?"

"How do you expect me to be swell at a time like this, Johnny? You've forced me into an engagement with you to appease your bloodthirsty gang and needle an illegal business deal out of my father. They could have shot me tonight, thanks to you. And yet you *expect* me to be alright?"

Johnny stammered a half-hearted apology, but Pamela couldn't hear it as she made a beeline for the place she had grown up in.

Pamela stood outside of the apartment door for a few minutes, praying for some kind of divine intervention. Maybe her parents were vacationing in the Hamptons, or Havana, as they often did during the winter. Maybe then she could explain to Johnny that they had moved, and he would release her, freeing her to sail to captivating Australia or disappear into the quaint Midwest.

She took a chance and knocked, her knuckles barely grazing the polished wood of the door.

An eternal moment passed.

Pamela was about to turn, but someone undid the chain with a clank and a warm face leaned out at her from the ajar door.

Lorna, her velvet fascinator clipped to her black curls and lines of exhaustion grooved into her face, grasped Pamela's shoulders to prove she wasn't just a vision. "Pamela Anne! I almost thought I saw a ghost. I've been praying and praying for some kind of sign that you were safe, and here you are, right in front of me! Thank God!"

"I've missed you terribly, Lorna." Pamela sniffed, attempting to contain the sobs desperate to rupture through the surface of her chest. Lorna had been more than a fixture in her childhood: she had been a beloved friend and guardian. She had been more of a mother than Caroline Kelly, and not having her kind and enduring presence caused great emotional affliction.

"I've missed you too, honey." Lorna abandoned social formality and enveloped Pamela in a reassuring hug. "But at least you are back here with us now. What happened, my dear? Where were you?"

"I'm sorry for worrying you..." Pamela allowed the tears to stream down her cheeks, no longer caring to compose herself. "Mother wanted me to marry Timothy Atwell, but I couldn't, so I took a job as a salesgirl on Fifth Avenue, and tried to make my own way in the world."

"I understand, dear one. I was on my own at seventeen, younger than you are today. Sometimes a little independence helps us grow. I could only trust the good Lord that you were out of harm's way." Lorna smiled, the scent of dishwashing soap and basil leaping up from her ash-coloured uniform.

Pamela remembered what had happened to Lorna from her mother's gossip circles: she had fallen pregnant with the child of a soldier leaving to fight in the Great War. She had run away from home and her baby had died from the Spanish flu, the soldier never to be seen again.

"You haven't gone off and fallen in love with some boy, have you?" Lorna's dark eyes glinted with mirth.

"I... I do think I've fallen in love with someone." Pamela's admission was startling even to her. She had wanted a confidante so badly that the words had simply bared themselves. "I—I met a man when I was away. I didn't mean to fall in love. It just happened."

"Does he treat you well? Just as the child of God you are?" Lorna asked sternly.

Pamela nodded.

"That matters the most."

A hallway clock ticked softly. Gentle footsteps padded on the floor above them and the whooshing sound of traffic passing by the apartment outside created a sense of calm.

"I hope they've been treating you well here," Pamela whispered, not wanting to disrupt the silence.

A look of painful understanding passed between them.

Her parents, especially her mother, were not always kind to Lorna, despite the many years she had worked tirelessly for them. Though the words were ordinarily left, unsaid—Caroline and Stuart Kelly thought themselves above Lorna—owing to the color of her skin. There was no question that she, along with the other black employees of the Kelly residence, were treated differently from the rest of the help. It wasn't fair. And it was yet another reason Pamela resented the family she had grown up in.

"Don't worry on my behalf. They've been treating me the same as ever." Lorna patted Pamela on the arm. But the statement was no consolation.

"Why don't you leave, as I did?" Pamela insisted, lowering her voice in the quiet of the hallway. "If I could get a job, I'm sure you can too. There are plenty of places hiring, and I could help you find one with good pay."

Lorna's smile faded, and she shook her head with obstinacy. "Places are hiring young white girls like you, Pamela, not me. But I can manage, as I have all these years. And maybe, someday, I can start my fancy restaurant downtown. Remember how we used to talk about that? You'd keep the books, and I'd cook the food?"

Pamela laughed, remembering. But the dismal truth of Lorna's proclamation echoed in the chamber of her mind. She couldn't just up and leave as Pamela had. The world was a cruel and twisted place, in more ways than one.

Before Lorna could continue their conversation, a commanding voice shattered the sentimentality of the reunion. The two women withdrew, standing to attention as if they were soldiers in the American army.

"What is going on here?" Caroline Kelly, her dyed hair wound tightly in curlers and her face wet from an Estee Lauder night mask for aging skin, marched through the doorway.

Her reserve almost deteriorated when she beheld her long-lost daughter, but after a crinkling of her nose and a tightening of her mouth, she resumed her untouchable demeanor.

"Oh my, what a delightful surprise." Caroline Kelly said, her eyebrows arching. "You must be proud of all the commotion you've caused, nearly frightening the better part of the city to death."

Pamela bent her neck, finding it painful to stare directly into the seething gaze of her mother. "I am sorry for my unexplained absence. But you must understand, Timothy and I would have been awful for each other, and I wanted to..."

"Never mind that. You wasted a perfectly good opportunity to chase a girlish dream. And what came of it?" Caroline demanded, waiting for Pamela to speak of her disastrous failure and how she regretted her impulsive nature.

"I'm engaged," Pamela said dryly. She didn't look at Lorna as she said it. She hated lying to Lorna.

Almost instantly, Caroline's nostrils flared and her night mask cracked. She threw her hands to her hips, her hair flopping out of the curlers. She uttered a word crude enough to startle all the mafia in New York State and pinned Pamela with her glare.

"You are *what*?"

"Engaged Mother, to be married," Pamela repeated, marveling at the switch between them. Caroline Kelly had always been the one to make her daughter squirm, not the other way around.

"To whom?" Caroline exclaimed, pacing into the parlor.

Pamela and Lorna followed her in. Caroline perched herself on the edge of the sofa in the living room, rubbing her lean fingers against her temples to soothe herself.

"Johnny Siciliano," Pamela folded her hands into her cardigan pockets, "I met him when I was a salesgirl."

"An *Italian* fellow? Really, Pamela Anne?" Caroline agonized, rocking back and forth like a woman in mourning. "From Sicily, no doubt. Your father and I vacationed there in fifty-two. They were wretched, poor people, begging for crumbs on every street corner and cathedral step."

Pamela wanted to point out to her mother World War II had induced poverty in Italy when the country had been left toiling in economic and social trauma. If she kept up with current events more or studied basic history, she would know better.

"Your parents resented Father for being Irish, yet you married him." Pamela reminded her mother instead.

Caroline rolled her eyes, ignoring her obvious hypocrisy. "This can still be fixed. Timothy has been going steady with a girl from the rotary club named Betsy, but his mother disapproves of the match. She hasn't the connections. Your disappearance will be forgiven, and the wedding can come about this May."

Pamela maintained a safe distance from her mother, Johnny's instructions clear in her mind. "He has money, Mother."

The words were a balm for Caroline's grief, and she rose, waltzing across the room to her daughter. "How much?"

"His income must be at least sixty-thousand a year." Pamela was guessing because she did not know how much Johnny made. She knew her father made around that, or more. But as a salesgirl, she had hardly made five thousand.

"Well, I won't believe it until I see him in the flesh." Caroline sniffed, dabbing the skin beneath her eyes with her manicured fingers. Pamela noticed that her wedding ring was missing, the one with the behemoth of a diamond and the little sapphires.

"He wants to come for brunch tomorrow morning."

"I suppose you'll be staying then," Caroline said, her lips thin and pursed but her blue eyes wide and clear. If Pamela wasn't mistaken, she saw a kind of longing there.

"Yes, Mother," Pamela replied. "I will stay here with you and Father."

"I shall send for your father in the morning." Caroline decided, a fragile smile spreading across her lips.

CHAPTER 19

Boston Massachusetts, January 1955

Mrs. Carlotta Bellucci stared at her husband in their decrepit Boston apartment as he wolfed down his plate of lasagna and defrosted peas, his fork clinking loudly against his plate.

When Tony had insisted that they settle in Boston instead of a small New Hampshire town, Carlotta's dream of suburbia had been painfully extinguished like the flame of a cheap candle. Instead of a picturesque bungalow with a white picket fence, she had gotten a one-bedroom apartment with holes in the floorboards and a broken furnace that keened and groaned like a wild animal.

The malodour of mold and rotting wood from the walls caught in her nose and made her wheeze, making it nearly impossible to sleep at night. She complained to Tony about the smell, begging him to choose another place. But he slept just fine and didn't see the point in moving again as he couldn't stomach the idea of living in the middle of nowhere as a nobody. His ancestors had left country living behind long ago and he was a city boy through and through, he explained.

He had found a poorly paid job as a car mechanic for an old and slightly irritable fellow from Calabria. Every morning, he exchanged his shiny sports coats and polyester pants for oil-stained coveralls, laden with sweat and gasoline.

Carlotta envied him for his freedom, but Tony had convinced her staying home was far preferable to someone finding out Don Roberto Mancini's little girl was working in Boston. With her looks, it was hard to go unnoticed. So instead of working, she spent her time leafing through *Good Housekeeping* magazines, experimenting with recipes and undertaking minor renovations. Sure, the apartment wasn't exactly a *pilazza*, but at least she could make it nice with a few paint jobs and a new set of drapes.

That night, she had tried to recreate her mamma's famed onion and beef lasagna. When Tony scarfed it all down in a few bites, she concluded it was a success.

"How was work?" Carlotta asked Tony as she fixed the buttons on her blouse. She had gotten all dolled up just for him, knowing that he liked the shade of sea green against her olive skin and pale blue eyes. But since he had arrived home all he had done was collapse on the sofa and laugh wildly at the sitcom that was playing on television.

"It was swell. Some guys bought pizza for lunch. It was the best thing I've had in weeks," Tony replied, absently touching the dark growth of hair above his lip. He was intent on wearing a mustache. He wanted to be less recognizable if he crossed paths with anyone from New York. Carlotta thought the facial hair did little to change his appearance, but Tony thought otherwise.

Carlotta stared at her beloved husband and his uncut hair, his dirty blue uniform, his dirt-smattered face. His bedraggled appearance made him look much older than his twenty-six years. Or maybe she saw him differently because of his violent encounter in Hooksett.

She shook her head, willing herself to forget the violence that had shone in her husband's gaze that day. They had not spoken about it since it had happened. Carlotta hoped he wanted to forget it as much as she did. She had tried to kiss him and love him the same way she had before, but the thought the hands that touched her were the same hands that had killed men in cold blood nagged at her.

Tony noticed Carlotta's apprehension and reached over to caress her forearm, his palm rough and calloused from work. "Some fellas are comin' over after work."

"Some fellas? Who?"

"Some Calabres' fellas from the repair shop. I told them they could come over for a drink after work." Tony explained offhandedly. "I owe them for the pizzas they got last week."

"I thought we were gonna spend the evening together. *Alone.*" Carlotta looked down at her unfinished plate of lasagna, which was utterly gray and depilated. She had spent hours making it. That Tony didn't even acknowledge her hard work broke her heart.

Tony gazed at her pleadingly. "C'mon baby, it'll be fun. You always complain about how you never get to meet any Boston folks."

"But you didn't ask me! We're supposed to decide everything *together*, Tony. As married people do." Carlotta's heart sank as her plans for the evening melted away.

"That's a silly notion. Nobody lives like that." Tony chuckled, not noticing the angry flush blooming in her cheeks.

There was a pounding knock at the door, followed by a rambunctious burst of laughter.

Tony pushed his chair back, letting it skid across the floor, then raced over to meet his friends.

Tony's guests made the apartment look even smaller than it was—their large, hulking figures leaving little room for anything but the sofa, television and table.

"Nice place, must've cost you an arm and a leg." One man chortled sarcastically, socking Tony in the arm.

"Real elegant," another insulted. "I thought you were some rich guy from the Big Apple."

Carlotta's face burned with indignation. She took a deep breath, squared her shoulders, and addressed the men bluntly. "You fellas better mind your manners."

Her scolding alerted them of her presence, and their eyes widened in surprise. She felt them stare at her for a long moment. She hated the way they made her feel like a cheap art exhibition in a museum.

"You didn't tell me you got a pretty sister, Tony." One man joked with a Boston lilt, his eyes traversing her frame. He made a crude gesture with his hands to his friend, and Carlotta found herself on the verge of gagging. *Tony hadn't even told his friends about her? Was he ashamed? Or was she just not important enough for him to talk about?*

"Wow, you're a real knockout. Those eyes. You any relation to Elizabeth Taylor?" The other appraised her.

Tony chuckled uncomfortably. But when he noticed Carlotta's scowl, he smartened up and offered a defense. "Take it easy, fellas. I'm circled, Carlotta is my girl."

Carlotta had never witnessed any man disrespect her mother in such a way, or her for that matter. They wouldn't dare. Then again, Tony Bellucci possessed far less power than her padre did. If Roberto Mancini had caught a man trying to smooth talk with his wife, someone would have whacked them within the hour.

"Sorry, Tony," one man offered through a juvenile grin. "Just surprised a pretty dame ended up with a fella like you is all."

"You boys oughta learn some respect." Carlotta glowered, her skirt fanning out as she whirled around.

When Carlotta left the men, she decided to eavesdrop from the bedroom. Perhaps she was being juvenile, but she was bored out of her mind. That and she wanted to know what Tony talked about when she wasn’t there. She didn't think it was invasive; she was just looking out for him.

The Calabres' men spoke softly in another dialect of Italian, but their words were discernible through the thin wall connecting the rest of the apartment and the bedroom.

"A shipment coming in Sunday morning..." someone was explaining, "we need guys to drive down there, unload, and bring the goods to the location in the South end."

"How many soldiers?"

"Ten strong ones. We don't need anymore—if there are too many of us we'll be found out. Tony, you in? Or is the old ball and chain going to keep you home?"

"C'mon, Tony, an opportunity like this doesn't come every day. You gotta think about how much dough you can earn with a single job like this."

"With some extra dough, you can buy somethin' nice for that pretty dame of yours."

Carlotta caught her breath, squeezing her eyes shut and digging her nails into her wrist.

Tony's voice was quiet but distinct. "Yeah, yeah, I'll be there. Just don't tell anyone else about it, okay? I gotta few enemies in New York I wanna avoid."

Carlotta couldn't listen anymore. She buried her head into the cheap cotton bedspread, drenching the floral pillowcase with her tears.

How was Tony doing this to her? The reason they had eloped had been to start a new life—a life free of crime, violence and secrecy. She had given him everything she had, and now he was betraying her. She had left her family, her city and her friends to be with him, believing the promise he was a better man, and that they were going to make it without the help of the mob.

She wanted to scream at the top of her lungs, pummel her fists into the wall, or throw the lasagna she had spent all day making into the garbage.

She sat up abruptly, looking around at their bedroom and thinking about the grand dream she had constructed for them. Maybe Tony hadn't ever wanted to leave New York. But he had—*hadn't* he? In that case, she had built her life upon a lie.

Frantically, Carlotta changed out of her blouse and skirt and into a plain slip: not the pretty one she usually wore when she was with Tony. She yanked her dark curls from her headband, using her fingernails to scrub away the itchiness clinging to her scalp. Then she stood in front of the mirror, splashing her face with cold water to rid her cheeks of their blotchiness. It was no use. The tears kept coming.

She didn't care what Tony thought about her complexion anymore.

Carlotta stalked to the bedroom and pressed herself against the mattress, wanting to wake up in her very own room with her mamma holding a hand to her forehead, telling her she had a terrible fever but she would be fine now. She imagined her mamma's curly bob and molton brown eyes as they embraced and promised to begin the day anew. She felt their joyous tears intermingle and fall upon the pillowcase beneath her.

But the daydream was only that. Soon Tony came whistling and humming into the bedroom. He was in the best mood he had been in since they had moved to Boston, and it only made Carlotta more furious.

"You in bed? I thought you'd wait for me. You said you wanted to spend a romantic evenin' together." Tony plopped down beside her, the mattress flattening with his weight. He pressed himself against her back and traced the side of her cheek with a finger, a whiff of gasoline and tire making her cough.

Carlotta ducked her head close to her rosary, fondling the beads as she attempted to pray some sense into the man.

Tony ignored her act of piety and pulled her into his firm arms, letting his lips travel down her neck and across her collarbone. His hands caressed her breasts and she felt warmth rush through her.

Melting into his touch for a moment, Carlotta let him. How she loved being held in his arms, kissed and touched by him. But when he fiddled with the zipper on her slip, she remembered her contempt.

She twisted away, leaping to her feet and covering herself with a silk night robe.

"*Amore mio*!" Tony pouted like a cat being denied a ball of yarn. "What's the matter?"

"How could you do this to me? You promised me you wouldn't go back because you love me. But you went back. What does that mean? That you don't love me as much as you said?" Carlotta sniffed, covering her trembling mouth with her hand. She marched to the other side of the bedroom, placing her manicured hands on the dresser to steady herself. Her body was quaking with an anger that couldn't be quelled with even the sweetest of words.

Tony trailed behind her, groping her shoulders with his hands. "I don't know what you're saying."

"You going to pick up a shipment? With those greaseballs who came over here?"

"What?"

"Don't play stupid, Tony Angelo Bellucci! I was listening to the whole thing! I'm your *wife*. I deserve the truth, don't I?"

"*Tesoro mio*!" Tony didn't appear shocked, angry, or upset in the slightest. In fact, he was grinning from ear to ear like a puppy dog. "I said I was gonna help. We need the money. I thought I'd leave this as a surprise—like a late Christmas present or somethin', but I guess you found out."

Carlotta tossed a pillow at him as hard as she could. She could hardly believe his reaction. How could he find her anguish amusing?

"I'm sorry *amore*. I've been awful lonely here, and I guess I wanted somethin' to do. I know it was stupid." Tony fell to his knees dramatically and grabbed her wrists with his large gasoline-streaked hands.

She shook her head, resisting his sudden apology. If he had acted so brashly once, surely he could do it again.

Besides, hadn't *she* been lonely?

He wasn't the one without a job, forced to stay at home all day fixing up the apartment and picking up groceries from the supermarket down the block. She hated living like a prisoner, confined to the apartment building for fear of her father finding her. She felt like her life had no purpose except as a wife keeping Tony Bellucci from trouble—and apparently; she had failed at that, too. The only person besides Tony she talked to was Mrs. Janowski from across the hall, who occasionally invited her over for latkes and visits with her tabby cat. She couldn't even call her mamma or any of her old friends on the telephone. She was completely alone.

A deep sadness spread over her like a heavy mantle. She began to shake, silent sobs rocking her frame. Tony pulled her to him, trying to comfort her with his embrace.

"You know that I've been lonely too," Carlotta said, pushing a tendril of hair from her blue eyes. "But just 'cause I'm lonely doesn't mean I can go off and break the law."

Tony's shoulders slumped forward as he seemed to deflate like a broken balloon. "I didn't know you were lonely. I thought this was your dream."

"I didn't know it was gonna be like this."

"I'm sorry." Tony stepped forward, offering her his hands.

"I want us to live like good, God-fearing people. Please promise that you do too." Carlotta pleaded solemnly, mapping his work-hardened hands with her fingers. "And… I don't want my padre to find us. Then I could lose you forever."

"That's never gonna happen, my angel." Tony promised, quieting her worries with his embrace. She surrendered herself to him, loving him too fiercely to continue the quarrel.

A few minutes later, an alarmingly loud knocking on the door disarmed their closeness. Carlotta's first instinct was that it was the landlord, telling them their rent was due. Her second was that it was the police who had found out about Tony's criminal activities.

Tony grabbed his gun from under the dresser and slunk towards the door, simultaneously buttoning his pants. He pushed himself ahead of Carlotta, the veins in his neck showing like crimson cords. The noise got louder.

Carlotta's heart hammered, and blood rushed to her face and her ears. She tied her robe around her waist and followed Tony down the hallway. He noticed. His hand shot up in warning. Shadows fell over him when he turned, and he motioned to the cabinet, where he kept his second gun.

A primal fear consumed her, overriding any moral obligations she might have considered.

She hastened to the cabinet and retrieved the gun, her hands shaking as she tried to remember how to use it. Her father had taught her once when she was in her teenage years. He had done it for defense reasons. Only in case anyone dangerous ever tried to harm her.

The banging continued.

"Who is it?" Tony yelled, his voice strong. "We don't wanna be disturbed."

Carlotta thumbed for his hand in the dark, squeezing it when she found it.

The knocking stopped for a few moments, allowing Carlotta and Tony enough time to collect themselves.

"They're gone?" Carlotta wondered aloud, her voice a strained whisper. She held onto her husband, feeling a collective sigh of relief expand in their lungs.

“Someone probably gave 'em the wrong apartment number." The look of relief on Tony's face dissolved into terror when the door was shoved open. A tsunami of wood and hands moved inwards and thrust him onto the floor.

Carlotta dropped the gun.

"Carlotta Isabella Mancini. What have you done?"

CHAPTER 20

The old grandfather clock with claws and horns chimed eleven, and Johnny Siciliano still hadn't arrived. He was expected at the Kelly residence on Seventh Avenue for an informal brunch and had sent no message to explain his absence.

Caroline Kelly wore a mask of indifference, fanning herself with her napkin in the middle of February. Her hair was piled in voluptuous layers atop her narrow head, tendrils of bleached blonde greased back into acquiescent obedience.

Stuart Kelly glared at his wife, his silvery hair gelled back to reveal a high forehead and stout face.

"Fashionably late," she dragged her spoon along the rim of her soup bowl, producing a discordant sound, "is this the way they act in Italy?"

"He isn't *from* Italy, Mother." Pamela sighed, though she had explained the fact several times already. "He's lived in Brooklyn all his life."

Caroline continued, fixing her hair as she stared at the wall in contemplation. "The way those Italians live in tiny apartments, all crammed together like that with their foreign foods, you'd think they didn't even *know* they were in America. I hope he doesn't force you to live like that when you marry him."

Pamela began to correct her mother's ignorance, but she doubted Caroline Kelly would listen.

Even though months had passed since she had last shared a meal with her family in her parents' Seventh Avenue apartment, it seemed as though nothing had changed.

Pamela had awoken to the soft stirring of Lorna in the hallway just off the bus from Queens, then the gurgling pot of coffee in the kitchen—one that worked so much better than the device on Fifth Avenue. The reluctant morning sun had slid itself beneath the crack left by her bedroom drapes, fragmenting the darkness. Her mother had risen half-past seven as she usually did, and met her with a curt morning greeting in the hallway, her curlers askew in a rare moment of disarray.

"You *must* know that schoolgirl outfit makes you look five years younger." Caroline had chided, referring to Pamela's long, navy skirt, old saddle shoes and flannel blouse. "You are to be a married woman, and I wouldn't want this mysterious fiancé of yours having any second thoughts."

At that moment, Pamela had wanted to hug her mother: bury her face into her bony shoulder, and tell her the truth, and that she had missed her terribly, despite all the quarrels and hurt long dividing them. She had grown up in the past few months, and she realized how quickly life could slip away.

Stuart Kelly was called home for the fateful brunch occasion. He had been staying out in New Jersey for the last couple of weeks, conferring with business partners and potential investors, or else avoiding his wife.

Pamela hoped he wouldn't resent her when he met Johnny Siciliano, or that he would laugh him out of New York. She knew

Stuart to be a rational man, and unintimidated by flash and smooth talk.

When he stepped into the dining room, Pamela had recognized her father. She hadn't seen him since the week before she left, but he was the same bushy-haired man she had known all her life, with his pale freckles and firm jaw.

"Pamela?" He examined her through his square spectacles, tilting a silver eyebrow inquisitively and pushing a leather suitcase into the arms of one of the help.

"Hi, Dad," Pamela sniffed, overcome with emotion, and climbed out of her seat to face him. She had never been close to her father, but seeing him after so long was quite overwhelming.

After her father had kissed her on the cheek, his forehead wrinkled with his confusion. "Your mother told me about your sudden disappearance. I've been concerned. If you wanted a trip, you should've told me. I could have gotten you a vacation to Cuba or somewhere."

Pamela trailed him as he strode to his chair at the head of the table, watching his well-polished shoes march forward with perfect timing as she had done out of wonder as a girl. She had never quite understood how a person's shoes could remain so unblemished, even after trekking through the dusty roads of New York City.

Lorna hurried to pour him a cup of coffee, but he dismissed her with a shake of his head. "No thanks. I had a cup on the train here."

Lorna nodded and rushed back into the kitchen. Whenever her father was around, Pamela had noticed that her dear friend became quite unnerved. Perhaps it was because he possessed standards that were often unattainable—insisting upon having the shiniest of silverware and the strongest of coffee. Whenever Pamela's schoolwork had been less than perfect, her father had become enraged.

Pamela had heard worse rumors, ones that suggested her father had once pressured Lorna into an improper affair. It had supposedly happened when Pamela was still in diapers and Lorna's own children were still at school. Apparently, Lorna had firmly rejected her employer's advances, spurning his ire.

If the stories were true, it made sense why Caroline seemed to hate Lorna so much more than the other servants. It also explained why she had once accused Lorna of stealing a pair of her sapphire earrings—which Pamela had promptly found behind the sofa.

Pamela had never asked Lorna about her father's horrible deeds. She knew if she asked, Lorna would simply pretend it hadn't happened. She was too intent on protecting Pamela, even after all these years.

Pamela glanced back towards her father, feeling a pang of revulsion. In contrast to the mobsters she had met in Brooklyn, he made his money the honest way. But she was beginning to realize he was perhaps just as misguided.

"I'm sorry for worrying you. I got a job as a salesgirl. I suppose I needed to be away for a little while, to try living on my own." Pamela explained, sinking into the leather chair beside him.

"Make your *own* money?" Stuart's laughter bounced against the walls of the dining room. "Is that what I've raised my daughters to do? What happened to the old days when girls let the men take care of the breadwinning?"

"I wanted to do something on my own for a change." Pamela defended. "I'm old enough to do so, aren't I?"

"I suppose this single act of independence is the reason Caroline called me here." Stuart thought aloud, popping a roll of cinnamon bread into his mouth. His voice carried an unmistakable note of resentment.

As if she had been eavesdropping on the conversation, Caroline marched out of the kitchen, ushering Lorna and two kitchen maids along behind her, who transported immense silver platters of danishes and more rolls, fruit, meat and porridge.

Stuart ignored his wife but acknowledged one of the kitchen maids with a salacious smile.

Pamela felt her stomach twist with disgust, and she moved so that the poor woman would be obscured from her father's vision. "*Mother* called you for another reason."

Caroline waited for her husband to take notice of her presence, and when he did not, she cleared her throat loudly. Her eyebrows were sunken and her eyes the color of tears.

A wave of pity rose in Pamela as she remembered Victoria Palermo. Perhaps, Caroline Kelly was not as untouchable as she let on. What would happen if she acted out as Victoria had that night at the engagement party? What would happen if she threatened to leave and never come back and actually did it?

Pamela recalled the ceaseless string of affairs and romantic trysts her father had carried out when she was young. She had witnessed women in cocktail dresses walking arm-in-arm with her father at various formal events and parties, beneath her mother's notice. She had also answered the telephone to women with sultry voices and flirtatious messages when her father was absent.

Her father's shameless betrayals made her sick.

"Well?" Stuart waited for his wife to speak, chewing on a piece of toast.

"Pamela has found a new suitor," Caroline announced hollowly, taking her rightful place across from her husband. "I have requested your presence for this reason. He has asked to marry her, and I am told that he is well established in life, if what she says is true."

"You asked me down here for an engagement party?" Stuart demanded, pinning Caroline with a spiteful look. "You know how busy I am."

Pamela glanced between her parents and felt a punch to the gut at how little her father cared about her life. At least her mother had gone to the effort of arranging an engagement party, even if the whole engagement was a sham.

"Fine." Stuart swallowed his toast, noticing his daughters' pained expression, "but no more. I am not interested in your social gatherings."

By ten o'clock the same morning, the rest of the guests arrived.

Pamela's elder sister Cecelia Adams, and her gregarious contractor husband Clark Adams brought their two young children: Linda and Jimmy.

Linda and Jimmy hugged Pamela politely, but she could tell that they didn't quite recognize her. The last time she had seen Linda was when she had been a sleeping infant in her mother's arms, and Jimmy was still in diapers.

Pamela greeted them warmly, drawing them close and remarking on how tall they'd grown. She loved her niece and nephew, even if she didn't know them as much as she wished she could.

Cecelia was as beautiful as ever in lace gloves, and an organza stole draped across her slender shoulders. Her honey-golden hair was cropped in voluminous curls about her shoulders, in a style reminiscent of the latest fashions in the Harper's Bazaar magazine. A pleasantly restrained smile glided over her high cheekbones, accentuating the faint rouge that had been applied there.

As far as looks went, Clark was neither handsome nor unattractive. He was of average height, with an animated personality and booming voice that could shake the walls of any room.

The couple didn't spend more time than the appropriate amount speaking of Pamela's uncharacteristic behavior of the last months. Cecilia and Caroline both asked Pamela why it had taken her so long to secure an engagement, and neither seemed happy she had chosen an Italian. Clark was more focussed on the Pentagon's groundbreaking decision to develop missiles armed with nuclear weapons and the billiards game he had played the evening before.

After a few minutes, the children galloped into the living room to practice their yo-yo tricks, and the adults settled in the dining room.

It was then that the grandfather clock chimed and Johnny had still not shown up.

Pamela was almost relieved. The extra few moments apart from him were good for her, and she was able to pretend that she was detached from the world of crime and deceit that he represented. She began relaxing with the thought he might not come.

"I'm sure the fellow has a plausible excuse for his absence. Maybe he was up late shining his shoes." Clark chortled. "Anyway, there's no way I'm waiting for him to get here before I eat."

He devoured a generous plate of sausages, ham, and bacon.

Cecelia clucked her tongue in disapproval. But soon, the entire table was eating, except Pamela. Even Caroline Kelly, Socialite and Society Hostess, had abandoned her social principles for a petite cheese croissant.

Because of their preoccupation with the cuisine, the group failed to initially notice a young man attired in a dignified blazer and silk tie.

His clean-shaven olive skin was flushed against the tangerine wallpaper behind him.

Pamela startled when she glimpsed him, her elbow colliding with the rim of her glass, almost causing it to shatter.

The party turned with Pamela, taking in the newest addition to the family.

Cecelia was the first to speak as she dabbed the corners of her mouth with her napkin. "Golly, you must be Johnny Siciliano! Pamela is my kid sister. We've heard all about you."

The last part wasn't true in the slightest—Pamela had not said a word about Johnny other than that she was marrying him. She had also been forced to explain his foreign-sounding surname, subsequently earning some raised eyebrows and concerned looks from her relatives.

"I hope you've heard good things." Johnny didn't wait for an invitation, he simply pulled up a chair and sat next to Pamela, folding an arm across her back. The feel of his hand upon her shoulder made Pamela shiver.

"How charming!" Cecelia giggled, a pleasant flush rising to her cheeks. "This is my husband Clark. He's a contractor down in New Jersey and a regular self-made man just like yourself."

"Nice to see I'm not the only businessman son-in-law." Johnny smiled with manufactured joviality, the Brooklyn in his voice repressed but spontaneously appearing with the pronunciation of vowels.

"How d'you do?" Clark extended a hand to shake Johnny's firmly. "What are you in the business of, anyway?"

Clark asked the question in a friendly manner, but Pamela's stomach dropped.

Johnny barely hesitated a second before offering a firm handshake and a reply. "I guess you could say I'm a jack-of-all-trades. I've got my hand in many areas of business."

After the rest of the introductions had been made, Johnny made himself comfortable, involving everybody in conversation and amusing Clark Adams and Stuart Kelly with a drawn-out story about fishing on the Hudson River. Halfway through brunch, Johnny produced a pack of cigarettes, offering one to even Caroline Kelly, who declined in restrained horror.

Johnny managed to make it through brunch without catastrophically usurping the family order until dessert and coffee were served.

"Say, Mr. Kelly. I met your son Sean." He mentioned, disposing of his cigarette on the ashtray beside him.

The family had migrated to the living room, where the children were happily watching cartoons on the television. A Tide commercial interrupted their giggles, and Linda switched the channel to *The Three Stooges.*

Pamela held her breath.

The topic of Sean Kelly was strictly taboo. She knew she should have been more specific in warning Johnny not to speak of her disowned brother, but until the previous evening, she had never known that she would be forced to introduce him to her family.

"What about him?" Stuart grunted, clenching his immovable jaw.

Johnny bristled at the unspoken hostility, and his eyes flew to Pamela for help.

She tried to ignore him, peering out the window.

Perhaps if Johnny offended her father, he wouldn't be forced into a business deal with him and would be spared from involving himself in any type of illegal activity. After all, Pamela had promised to secure a meeting with Stuart Kelly, but she had not promised that he would agree to comply.

"I'm sorry if I offend, Mr. Kelly." Johnny stammered, wiggling around in his chair uncomfortably.

Before Johnny could continue to explain himself, Stuart interjected.

"There's no need to be sorry. Sean is erratic and disappointed me when he became a writer instead of a key holder in my business. I hope you don't let him taint any ideas you have about our family." His words were so detached and unsympathetic that it sounded like he was talking about a news report instead of his son.

Stuart took a bite of his cinnamon roll. "I am sure that the boy is a commie. And I wouldn't want a communist running my company. You understand, don't you Mr. Siciliano?"

Pamela rolled her eyes.

Sean was not a communist. Perhaps he was more of a freethinker than everyone else in the family—a little eccentric, but he was no communist sympathizer. He had protested at many civil rights rallies with his group of Greenwich Village friends, bringing Pamela along with him once or twice, and often complained about Eisenhower and the nuclear race war. But he had never claimed to be anything more than a social rights activist: a characteristic Pamela found quite admirable.

Johnny could not hide his surprise. "Well yes, of course, I understand Mr. Kelly."

"And you, Johnny, where does a young man like yourself find himself on the political end of things?" Stuart's voice boomed through the air.

The entire table turned to Johnny, waiting for his response.

Pamela caught her breath.

Unlike Sean, she didn't think Johnny was one for politics in the slightest. He had admitted that he didn't keep up much with the news, nor did he read any books. If he didn't answer—or answered incorrectly, her parents' impression of him would be in shambles.

"Let's not pretend here, Mr. Kelly." Johnny grinned, "We both know the answer to that question."

"Ah yes, a Southern Democrat if I've ever seen one." Stuart slapped Johnny on the back as they rose to move to his office. A mere minutes later, they returned with the grand announcement that Johnny Siciliano's alleged trucking company would supply Stuart Kelly & Sons with transportation henceforth.

"I like this fellow," Stuart announced, his cheeks ruddy and his voice a slow rumbling chuckle, "Pamela, my dear, I give you my blessing. May your matrimony be prosperous!"

Johnny cheered, proposing a toast, and Caroline and Cecelia congratulated Pamela.

Everyone except for Pamela was ecstatic about her match with Johnny. Her family had paid her more attention than they had in years.

When Johnny had slipped into his cap and overcoat to leave, he swaggered over to Pamela and kissed her on the forehead while still in the view of her relatives.

He was close enough so that no one could hear him. "I guess this is goodbye. When you tell your dad that you're breaking it off with me, beg him to honor our agreement. Tell him it was all your decision. And, don't tell him we're through until the end of the month. That way he'll have honored the terms of our deal, and we can all go on living in peace."

Pamela nodded, tracing his eyes with her own. "You're finally letting me go then?"

Johnny's smile faded, and he pressed his lips to her forehead.

She tried to convince herself that he was doing it for show.

"You must be glad," Johnny whispered, running his hand along the table beside him. "You've hated my guts since the moment you met me."

Pamela had wondered about that, too. He was a mobster, and he had killed Mr. Friedenberg. He had forced her into an unsettling business deal and now infiltrated her father's company.

The world was more complicated than she could have ever guessed from the safety of her bedroom, or among the pages of a book. Johnny was flawed, but there was still hope for him yet. He was kind, and she found it easiest to separate the good-hearted version of him from the cold killer she had pictured him as.

If she dared to think about it, she had begun to love him.

She placed her hands upon his shoulders, tilting her head up to gaze up at him. His eyes were the color of ground cinnamon, glistening beneath the dark brows she had once found imposing.

Before she could think twice, she kissed him.

He drew her to him softly and slowly, his kiss passionate. His fingers caressed her face, drawing circles on her cheeks. She fit her arms around him, and he responded by doing the same, pulling her into his chest.

When he released her, Pamela drew a breath. She had never been so emboldened in her life, and it ashamed her.

"I'm sorry." She said breathily.

"Why are you sorry? Don't be." Johnny asked, bending his head to direct her gaze back to him.

"I've never hated you, Johnny," Pamela whispered, pulling away. "But I hope you try to reconsider... your ambitions. You could do anything you wanted, but you choose this life of crime."

Johnny sighed in exasperation, but there was laughter fragmenting his serious expression. "You know how to scold a man, don't you? It's a wonder I've hung around you so long."

Pamela laughed at the welcome interlude, but her amusement abated. "Johnny, really."

The beguilement had escaped Johnny too. He swiped a cigarette from his shirt pocket and pulled out a light, indulging in his vice. "I can't do anything about that. I've dug my grave, so to speak, decided my fate. I'm as evil as you think I am, as everyone thinks I am."

Pamela could not believe what he had said. He had admitted the faults of his life, the wrongs he had committed. She wanted to tell him she didn't think he was evil, that she knew he was good. He just needed to reform his life before it killed him.

When he returned to face her, his brown eyes were brimming with tears and his lip trembling.

She wanted to wrap her arms around him, to feel his lips on hers, to console him. But she found herself frozen, unable to reach across to cradle his stubbled cheek in her hand.

"You're an angel, Pamela Kelly. If things were different, you could've been my girl."

CHAPTER 21

Once, Carlotta had watched her father kill a man.

She remembered the day in vivid detail. The Mancini children had been crouched around their new General Electric home television set, one that had red dials and a sleek brass antenna. Roberto Mancini was quite proud of the fancy appliance. The war was close to finishing, and their family was the only one on Pioneer Street to know such a luxury.

Most families were still saddled with archaic radios and receiving sets. As a result, there were often up to a dozen of Roberto's associates who would make excuses to come and visit, keen to baffle themselves with the pristine black-and-white figures emblazoning the little square screen. The novel device didn't hurt Carlotta's popularity either, as many classmates befriended her just to come over and watch a variety show.

"Don't sit too close to that television set, you'll go blind," Isabella warned her children, a little circumspect about the novel invention. "And Carlotta, don't drink so much of that sugary Coca-Cola stuff. Your teeth might rot!"

"Fine, Ma." Carlotta scrunched up her nose in disappointment, putting her glass bottle of Coca-Cola on the table.

"If Carlotta isn't allowed to drink it, I can." Louis Mancini giggled, mimicking the fighter jet flying across the screen and spreading his arms wide, bumping against Carlotta in a pantomimed crash landing.

"Don't be a germ, Louis." Carlotta exasperated as she inched away from him.

She knew that her little brother was still too young to understand the atrocities soldiers endured overseas, but she was still annoyed by his callowness. Teachers at their respective schools taught them about the might of tanks, aircraft, bombers, and homing torpedoes, but Louis Mancini treated warfare as casually as he did his GI Joe action figures.

"Don't be a pest, Carlotta." Louis contended, sticking out his tongue and scrunching up his face, trying his best to further provoke his twelve-year-old sister.

Suddenly, Roberto slammed his fist down on the coffee table, a ribbon of smoke meandering from the mouth of his cigar to the side of his rough cheek. "That is enough. Children, go to your rooms."

Louis heeded his father's warning, skipping up the stairs to his bedroom, his red costume cowboy hat bobbing.

Carlotta left the room only to eavesdrop from the top of the stairs, where there was a meager window of space just big enough to see the television and the back of her father's head without being noticed. She had discovered it recently, considering it a perfect bird's-eye view for secretly observing the happenings of the house.

She pulled her head over her knees, leaning against the iron stair rail. From her angle, she could see the living room, where the men most important to Roberto Mancini gathered. Joey Romano, Sal and Lorenzo Palermo, and John and Marco Mancini were among them, forming a protective semi-circle around their untouchable Boss.

Two less senior members of the syndicate stood dutifully by the doorway, Johnny Siciliano and Tony Bellucci. Carlotta had known the two of them since she was a little kid, but only recently, they had been formally adopted into the Mancini Family as soldiers. They often hung around the bars and pool rooms like other teenage boys hoping to be noticed by the mob and did odd jobs that the more senior associates didn't feel like doing.

If she was being honest, Tony Bellucci was a dream, complete with an easy smile and strong features. All the girls seemed to like Johnny Siciliano for his tall stature and charming character, but Carlotta preferred Tony.

Recently, Tony had become the star of all her romantic daydreams. The first time she had stolen a sample of her mamma's perfume and lipstick had been to attract his notice. She had glided by him in the kitchen when he was retrieving a cup of espresso, her cheeks burning as she felt his eyes caress her walking form. Afterwards, she hurried up the stairs to her bedroom, squealing into her pillow with childlike excitement.

"Who is that *ghiacchieron'*?" Roberto demanded, drawing Carlotta's attention back to him.

His index finger was gestured to the grainy television screen, where a man of about thirty years was giving an interview to the police. He was ordinary looking, with a narrow face and a pair of wiry glasses propped up on the bridge of his nose.

"Some guy who broke the story on some bank robbers who robbed the Henderson bank on Lexington Avenue." Sal Palermo replied succinctly.

"I don't like men who snitch," Roberto grumbled bitterly, reaching for his newspaper. "Tell me, is this fellow's brilliant article in the Times?"

"Near the front." Sal passed the newspaper to Roberto. Sure enough, front and center page, there was an enlarged image of the news reporter standing in front of a bank and words in big, block letters that declared:

BANK ROBBERS BUSTED: A LOCAL REPORTER'S COURAGE.

"They call that courage?" Roberto's sour tone mutated into laughter. "I hate rats—and it seems the world is full of them now. Will someone take care of him for me?"

Carlotta dared not guess what he was implying. She held her breath, hoping he meant something different, her fingernails carving red crescents into her folded palms.

"We can't go about doing that without getting the fuzz on our backs." Lorenzo, the only man willing to challenge Roberto, protested. "He's a well-known fella. His articles are real popular with the elite types."

A rare, menacing grin sliced through Roberto's face. "Give me a break. We don't need any more heroes with bright ideas overturning our city. Get one of your soldiers to whack him."

He catapulted the newspaper to the other side of the room, switching the television program to a sitcom.

Regardless, the image of the reporter wouldn't leave Carlotta's mind. He likely had a family, maybe even children. Even if he didn't, he had done nothing wrong. If anything, he had stopped a couple of unruly bank robbers from stealing from hundreds of innocent people. Why couldn't her father understand that?

The men filed out of the living room, shaking Roberto's hand firmly and uttering their well wishes.

When they had driven off into the afternoon, Roberto lingered at the threshold between the living room and the hallway, exhaling sharply and undoing the top buttons of his shirt. Coincidentally, his hawk-like gaze swept around to fall upon Carlotta, searing her with a look of animosity. Of course, the malice inflaming his pale blue eyes was not meant to be directed at her, it was residue from his fury at the news reporter. When he realized his daughter had been watching him, he visibly softened.

"Sneaky kid," he chuckled, his golden tooth showing, "you've always been too strong-willed for your good. You get that from your old man, don't you?"

"Why Papà?" Carlotta trembled, the remnants of the trusting daughter she had once been rising in her voice hopefully and surely. "Are you really going to kill that poor man?"

Roberto leaned close to the stairwell so that Carlotta was looking down on him from the stair she was perched upon. "Just like your mamma, Carlotta, so sensitive."

"But you won't do it, will you Papà?" Carlotta's heart raced with righteous fury. "Killing is wrong. God says so in the Bible and everything. Don't you believe that too?"

The light in Roberto's eyes faded: a sunset turning to night. He paused for a moment, inhaling a dappled cloud of smoke and cologne pooling around him. "I do it for you, *figlia mia*. You are the apple of my eye, you see? My entire life has been to protect our ways for you and your brothers."

"Not my ways, Papà! Your ways!" Carlotta gripped the railing more tightly, splinters of wood horning her skin.

"Don't be silly Carlotta."

Roberto extended a hand to touch her dark curls, but Carlotta recoiled, sprinting up the stairs without looking back.

Kneeling beside her husband with her frame ensconcing him, Carlotta was reminded of her father's eyes the day he had ordered the death of that newspaper reporter.

He had looked the same way as he did the day that he found her married to Tony Bellucci, living a regular life with him in a Boston apartment. Maybe he hated ordinary people leading ordinary lives.

Carlotta pressed a hand to Tony's forehead. He was unconscious but still breathing, his chest rising and falling like shallow waves and his eyes sealed shut. The assault on the apartment door had knocked him out when Roberto had forced it open, but at least he hadn't been shot.

She bowed her frame over him, a tear trickling down her cheek and staining his shirt.

"Why do this, Carlotta?" Roberto stood over her, a swarm of men filtering into the apartment behind him. Roberto waved them back, and they lapsed back into the hallway. "Why would you lead a scandalous life with a man who cares nothing for you?"

Carlotta refused to meet his gaze. Her lip trembled, but she would not dissolve into tears.

"Tony is my husband." Carlotta spat, raising her pale eyes to her father. "There is no scandal in us living together. We were married in front of a priest and God, with a witness."

Roberto's suit was pristinely ironed and crisp, his tie perfectly in place, and his hair combed neatly above his eyes. He had attempted to dress with unreserved normalcy and composure, despite what he saw as his daughter's betrayal.

"You are nothing but a *child*, Carlotta. And you are my daughter." Roberto laughed bitterly, amused by her anger. "How could you let this *nobody* touch you?"

Carlotta softened her knees as she stood, staring up into her father's ruddy face. "You must understand, I am no longer a child you can control. I am a grown woman and I have married the man I love most in the world, the man I have loved since my teenage hood. There is nothing you can do to part us."

Roberto gaped at her for perhaps the first time in his life.

The moment swelled between them as Carlotta's father attempted to digest what she had just said.

For a second, Carlotta imagined Roberto Mancini's resistance melting, her honest confession stirring some compassion within him. She imagined him apologizing profusely for all he had put her through, and promising that like Tony, he would try his best to abandon *La Cosa Nostra.*

He did no such thing.

Instead, Roberto Mancini struck his daughter across the face.

Her face was numb to the blow at first, but then a terrible stinging inflamed her cheek and she touched her hand to gauge the impact. She had never been hit by her father before. He didn't believe in using violence as a punishment, as ironic as it seemed, and forbade Isabella Mancini from ever laying a hand on the children in anger.

An undesirable deluge of tears obscured Carlotta's view of her father, sharp lines becoming soft curves and solid features becoming vague.

"How… dare you?" Carlotta whispered, her voice shaking.

"Tony Bellucci has broken the rule most important to me. He has violated my daughter." Roberto seethed, his fists bunched. "The punishment for such an act is death."

"If you kill him, you must kill me too." Carlotta threatened. Even though her father had struck her, he would never kill her. He loved her too much to do such a thing. "Because I won't live without him. I... I swear! I'll take my life if you do anything!"

Carlotta's voice had grown loud and frantic, urging Tony from unconsciousness. He groggily opened his eyes and writhed in discomfort on the floor. She sank to her knees to tend to him, nuzzling him awake with her tears, her velvety hand soft and compelling against his rough cheek.

Her father stared down at her with an expressionless face. She *hated* his lack of emotion. Even when he was angry, he allowed no one to know what he was feeling.

Out of spite, Carlotta kissed her husband on the mouth. She kissed him harder than she ever had before, folding herself to him, unwilling to let go.

Roberto grabbed her wrist, prying her away from her injured husband with a sharp twist of the hand. "You will never go near this man again, for as long as I live."

Carlotta cried out as she felt other hands restraining her, men locking their arms under and around her shoulders to keep her from tearing herself free. They moved her away as she struggled and kicked across the length of the hallway, calling for help.

She knew what her father was doing. What he was about to do.

She needed to stop him.

When they got to the top of the staircase, Carlotta prayed for courage. She prayed God would give her the strength she needed to wrestle herself free and bring the Mancini Family to justice. A rush of adrenaline coursed through her, and she jolted back, slamming into the men with such force that the two of them eased their hold on her for a second.

She heard them curse as they recovered, but the moment was enough for Carlotta to hold on to. She bid her feet and her legs to run, rushing down the stairs and through the apartment door.

An unfamiliar woman arched her brows in surprise.

"Ma'am, help me, help me! Please! Give me a phone!" Carlotta breathed, grabbing her by the shoulders as she forced the words out. Her husband was in grave danger, she explained, and so was she. There were callous murderers in the building.

A few minutes later, the cops arrived, encircling and combing through the building, observing every fingerprint and footprint left by the perpetrators.

Their precision was misplaced, for all they found was Roberto Mancini and his men vanished, and a dead Tony Bellucci on the third floor.

CHAPTER 22

New York City, Sixth Avenue, mid-January 1955

Pamela looked like an angel food cake. She was standing in a ritzy bridal shop with her sister Cecelia and high school friend Gladys, positioned in front of a long glass-encased mirror with her pale arms hanging limply at her sides and her face solemn. Yards of white chiffon spilled onto the carpeted ground around her like vanilla frosting, ceasing with a narrow ring of candy floss tulle at the hem. The neckline was far too wide and the sleeves were full of rose-coloured ribbons, making Pamela think of herself as a young girl, clothing herself in her mother's old garments kept in a forgotten attic.

Cecelia had urged Pamela to take the nearest Saturday afternoon and try on some wedding dresses, insisting that while the supposed wedding wouldn't occur for many months, it was still a wise precaution to select a gown well in advance.

Caroline Kelly had agreed. After Johnny Siciliano was introduced as Pamela's wealthy groom, she had gone about ordering everything from roses to musicians to caviar for the dubious occasion. She was smitten with Johnny's fortune and consequently saw Pamela's union as a grand victory. She was already sending out invitations to relatives and rivals she thought ought to know of the success.

In a couple of weeks, however, the entire family would know that Pamela and Johnny would never be married. Pamela would inform them they had quarreled, and they were through. She would relay the somber news come at the end of January, when Johnny had told her to do so. Then, she would have to persuade her father to honor his business commitment to the Mancini Family.

Pamela's forehead furrowed in the mirror, creating deep lines between her trimmed eyebrows.

Though they weren't close, the idea of deceiving her father tormented her and drawing the family business into a world of crime and injustice made her fill with guilt. It went against her faith—against everything she believed in.

She had flirted with the thought of telling her parents the truth, but if she did, she might put them all in danger. She had spent enough time around Johnny's peers to know what they were capable of.

"I preferred the first dress," Gladys said, pushing her glasses up the ridge of her freckled nose. "This one makes you look younger than you are."

Pamela had been prompted by Cecelia to invite her friend along with them for the day, and she appreciated the suggestion.

Gladys was kind-hearted but forthright, caring more for charity than frivolity. Gladys had been a diligent student in secondary school but still found time to escort Pamela to many church events and ball games when neither was brave enough to attend alone. She was much shorter than Pamela, with waist-length, mousy brown hair that she refused to trim, and gentle lilac-gray eyes.

The two had not seen one another since graduation, as Gladys' parents had allowed her to study biology at a women's college in Illinois, despite many young women in their class being dissuaded from pursuing higher education. Pamela had been both jealous and agonized that her beloved friend was leaving the State. The two had always planned on attending college together, with Pamela pursuing the humanities and Gladys the sciences.

Gladys had been shocked at Pamela's announcement she was getting married.

"Who is this Johnny Siciliano, anyway?" Gladys cornered Pamela when they were alone in the fitting room, and an attendant was draping another wedding gown over Pamela's slip. Her gray eyes bugged out behind her glasses.

Pamela panicked.

Gladys knew her well and could discern whether she was telling a lie. But of course, Pamela could never tell her friend that Johnny Siciliano was a mobster from Brooklyn, a man she had secretly and accidentally fallen in love with.

Pamela blushed at the realization.

She was not supposed to think about such things, and yet she couldn't help herself. When she had parted with Johnny, he had confessed his wrongdoing and a desire to change. She remembered his watery brown eyes, a desperate expression softening his face.

He had told her he thought she was an angel. That she could've been his girl.

The words had been sweet music to her, the strumming of stringed instruments at the Copacabana beckoning her to forget her inhibitions and dance.

Then she remembered the kiss. It had been strong and soft and shattering, words she never expected to put together. She longed to be in his embrace again, to feel his heartbeat through his suit jacket. Should she have kissed him? It didn't matter now; she supposed.

No matter how much Johnny liked her or how much she liked him, he couldn't change his ways. He couldn't just leave without consequence. Pamela had heard of mobsters who tried to leave their life of crime behind. Often, they would be pursued and killed for their disloyalty.

Johnny had made his choice an eternity ago, and it was none of her concern. Either she could pine after him pathetically, like a love-sick girl, Pamela decided, or she could forget the wonderful new feelings he had stirred within her and make her own life like Gladys was doing.

"Pamela?" Gladys nudged her with her elbow, confusion burgeoning behind her smudged glasses lenses. "Why do you have that strange look on your face?"

"I'm fine." Pamela twirled around the changing room, her eyes not leaving her feet as she stood in front of the mirror.

"I don't understand. Why get married so suddenly?"

"It seems like the right time, I suppose."

Gladys sighed, marching over to the mirror to stand beside Pamela. "All I'm saying is—you don't seem so happy. Who is Johnny Siciliano? Are you truly smitten with him?"

Pamela steeled herself to respond, pinning her shoulders back. She didn't want to lie to her friend. Sure, she had felt things for Johnny, but she could not pretend to love him. "Johnny is my fiancé, silly. Don't you remember me telling you that on the telephone?"

"Yes, you told me about a fella, but you scarcely mentioned anything other than his name." Gladys shrugged, shuffling her feet against the sand carpet. "I want to know what he looks like. And what your parents think of him."

"He's tall and quite the looker. An Italian, can you imagine that? He is charming, and has an unfathomable fortune." Cecelia interjected coyly, sweeping in behind them and waving her diamond-ringed hands in the air. "Everyone was pleased with him, even Mother."

"An *Italian* pleased the untouchable Mrs. Kelly? Then, I cannot wait to meet him." Gladys raised her eyebrows. Her voice carried an unmistakable note of skepticism.

When Cecelia released Pamela and Gladys from their bridal shopping duties, the two young women enjoyed a banana split at the soda shop across the street. They spent a delightful afternoon reminiscing about past teachers and classmates, inserting countless coins into the jukebox machine to play their favorite songs, and sipping on creamy malted chocolate shakes.

The excitement was enough to distract the girls from Pamela's equivocal engagement. In the soda shop, they were no longer twenty-one and a half and twenty-two years old—they were innocent schoolgirls with no care for marriage or courtship or men.

The distraction helped with Pamela's broken heart somewhat. But when Gladys left, and she waited alone for her way home in the enclave of a bus shelter, she was reminded of Johnny again.

It was strange being apart from him, and worse, knowing that she would never see him again. Whether or not she liked it, she had grown gleeful with his presence.

Wind slapped against her legs, somehow bypassing the meticulously sewn threads of her nylons, and she huddled closer to the inside of the shelter. Even though it was almost spring, the air was still cool and bitter.

Across the street, Coca-Cola and Ritz Crackers billboards were suspended from the slab gray buildings, and people scampered along the long stretch of pavement, their faces partially concealed by newsboy caps and silk scarves. Only two figures remained stationary within the fast-paced crowd: a man getting his shoes shined and a little boy doing the shining.

Amid all the business of the city, Pamela Kelly noticed one specific thing. The police station she had first visited when she wanted to report her suspicions about Mr. Friedenberg's disappearance at Albright Trimmings & Co—the grand Romanesque building with a small fountain out front. Somehow, she had unwittingly returned to this part of the city after what seemed like a thousand years.

Before she knew what she was doing, she was marching across the street, receiving many affronted car honks from the one-way traffic.

"Whaddya think you're doing?" One cab driver yelled out his window.

Pamela wasn't sure.

All she knew was that she needed to speak to Sergeant Marino. She had promised him information, and though he had been impossible to contact, he had guaranteed her safety. Perhaps, after the time that had passed between them, he would have enough evidence to prosecute Johnny's belligerent Boss, saving both Johnny and her father from his criminal activities.

And if Sergeant Marino locked Roberto Mancini away, wouldn't Johnny be thankful? He had declared he was saddled with his past wrongdoings, but if the threat of his Boss' vengeance was eradicated, they would no longer bind him.

Reaching the steps, Pamela climbed up and swung the door open. The sound of chatter and ringing telephones harmonized around her, and a receptionist with wire glasses and a checkered blouse held her gaze.

Pamela didn't wait for her approval. She marched down the hallway, propelled by her determination. She rapped her knuckles against the cool wood of Joseph Marino's office door.

A brief silence was followed by an abrupt answer. "Come in."

Joseph Marino's eyes widened when he identified his unexpected guest. An empty desk sat in front of him as if he had been doing nothing but staring at the blank wall before she came in.

Gaining his composure, Joseph Marino leapt to his feet, smoothing his pants and adjusting his shirt. A handgun caught silver in an inside compartment sewn into his green vest. "Miss Kelly?"

"Sergeant Marino—I have everything you need to send Roberto Mancini to jail." Pamela announced, holding his gaze. She could feel her heart slamming against the fabric of her blouse. "I'll be your witness."

Joseph Marino blinked, his hand grazing his unkempt black hair. "Sit down, Miss Kelly."

Pamela shook her head, an avalanche of long pent-up emotion surging through her. "I've been forced into a pretend engagement with Johnny Siciliano to appease his superiors. We've agreed that if I tell my father to honor their business agreement after I break our engagement, I'll be safe."

"That's wonderful news," Joseph Marino said, but his mouth was as frozen as one of the television dinners Pamela loathed.

Pamela waited for him to elaborate. He owed her an explanation for his silence. He had left her to the wolves for months, without word or warning. Surely he possessed a good reason for keeping her in the dark.

When he didn't, she took a step closer. "Sergeant Marino, I cannot remain silent. There is tremendous evil in this city. Like you, I've been witness to it all. I'd like to continue helping you and the department if the offer still stands."

Sergeant Marino stood then, matching her urgency with an insistent hand on her shoulder.

She flinched, angling herself away from him.

Joseph Marino noticed her discomfort, but only grasped her shoulder more tightly, his nails sharp and uncut, like barbed wire.

He was leaning towards her so that Pamela couldn't see his other hand. She hoped he wasn't reaching for his gun.

"Miss Kelly, you've been a doll in all this. But now isn't really the right time." A whiff of his breath, laced with cheeseburger and coffee, made her lungs burn.

"What can you possibly mean, Sergeant Marino?" Pamela urged desperately, her throat dry. "I've done everything you've told me to do."

"New York City's economy is built on the backbone of the mob. Remove the mob, and you kill all the industries they control. Countless union laborers, tradesmen, drivers, and small businesses will be gone. Just like that." Sergeant Marino snapped his fingers, extracting his hand, which had nimbly traveled from her shoulder to her arm. She shivered, taking a step away from him. "Getting Roberto Mancini means a good quarter of the businesses in the city closing down because of corruption charges. Is that what you want?"

Had Sergeant Joseph Marino experienced a change in allegiance? Had he been paid off?

Pamela moved backwards. "What about justice? What about Mr. Friedenberg?"

"Being a cop means taking a hefty dose of realism, Miss Kelly." Sergeant Marino countered, ignoring her question. "You shouldn't waste your time. Do the kinds of things nice girls your age do. Go to the movies. Get a perm. Marry a nice man and move to the suburbs. Raise some law-abiding kids. It isn't so hard."

Scorching indignation coursed through Pamela, but she tried to contain herself. "That's just it! I want to do something more, now that I know there is such an injustice in the city. I cannot ignore what I've seen. People are dying, for goodness' sake!"

Sergeant Marino laughed cynically. "Of course, you can. Most people do ignore it. They've been doing it for decades."

The secretary craned her neck through the door behind them, her wire glasses sliding down the bridge of her nose. "Sir, Mr. Lorenzo Palermo is here to see you again."

Pamela's heart sank.

A subtle look of guilt swept across Joseph Marino's features, and Pamela had her answer.

Joseph Marino would never help her. Somewhere along the way, his integrity had been purchased, and his greed had overcome him.

"Miss Kelly, don't you go running your mouth about this." Joseph Marino warned, the guilt ebbing away into fear. "You are mistaken if you think we can change the city because we *can't.* And a girl with no experience of the world is the last person to tattletale and get away with it."

Pamela grabbed a scarf out of the pocket of her coat and tied it into her hair so that Lorenzo Palermo would not recognize her when she passed him in the halls.

She had nothing more to say to the jaded police sergeant, and so she left, disappearing into the city inseparable from the crimes she abhorred, and the man she wanted to save.

The Mancini home slept like a great bear in hibernation. All the floral curtains were draped across the windows, still not drawn back to allow the dull wintry sun to banish the night away. There was no yellow glow of lamplight saturating the living room or the upstairs bedrooms, even though it was well past mid-afternoon. There was no sound at all emanating from the Mancini place, except for the staccato drip-drop of melted snow water as it plunked from the rain gutter and into a gardening bucket down below.

Christmas lights still framed the gable roof, despite the holiday having disappeared from all other houses along Pioneer Street. Once vibrant green shrubbery had become wilted brown, barbed arms weary with the added weight of fallen snow.

If Don Roberto hadn't summoned him, Johnny would've thought he was still away on business. His abode usually drew Johnny in with all its liveliness and chatter, but today it was somber.

Johnny tossed his key into his jacket pocket and clambered up the stairs, his boots crushing shards of ice and snow too stubborn to melt. When he rang the doorbell, he expected to hear Isabella's sonorous voice resonating in the silence, calling to him after peeling back the curtains and gazing out the square window in the door.

Instead, Louis Mancini pried open the door with tentative fingers. "Johnny?"

"Hi Louis." Johnny tried to disguise the concern in his voice with a grin. "Is your padre upstairs?"

Louis, still reluctant to fully open the door, nodded mutely. There was a petrified look haunting his usually merry blue eyes. What had startled him so?

"Hey, what gives Lou?" Johnny resumed his playful demeanor with the boy, feigning light curiosity. "Don't ya remember me?"

"My madre is sick." Louis said finally, explaining the sad mood permeating the house. "She's been in bed all morning. Hasn't gotten up at all."

Johnny released a sharp sigh of relief. It wasn't nearly as sinister as he had suspected. Isabella was probably in bed with a terrible cold, and Louis, being the oafish teenager he was, didn't know how to manage without her.

"Don't look so blue. Your mamma will be just fine." Johnny comforted, socking Louis in the arm. "Be a nice kid and make her some pasta or something."

"Don't treat me like a baby, Siciliano." Louis pushed Johnny back. The mischievous glint characteristic of him reignited in his eyes.

The brightest light in the house was radiating from Don Roberto's office, a slab of golden gray extending beneath the slightly ajar door and then across the striped wall in the hallway.

Urgent voices were talking rapidly in Italian, muffled by the soft blaring of opera music.

"Don Mancini?" Johnny called. "You asked for me?"

Johnny heard the movement of paper and the sighing of voices, followed by a low, gruff voice. "Keep it down, Johnny. My wife is sick."

Unnerved by the sharp reprimand, Johnny steeled himself.

Roberto probably wanted to know about Stuart Kelly, and whether the Irishman was going to honor his business deal. So far, he had heard nothing to indicate otherwise from Pamela, despite the fact she was about to inform her father of the breach in their engagement.

Johnny tried to quell the deluge of sadness flooding his chest.

No news was good news, but he wanted more than anything to see Pamela Kelly, if only once more. If that meant he understood the deal was abolished, he wouldn't be opposed. There were many other construction companies the Mancini Family controlled in New York City, and one less wasn't going to make that much of a difference.

He just wanted to see Pamela's sapphire eyes looking up at him again—listen to the flowing honey of her voice, and know she wouldn't resent him forever.

"Come in, Johnny." Roberto turned off the radio.

The scent of smoke and strong liquor curled around him, though Roberto didn't drink. He said it muddled his thoughts, and he needed a clear head for business. Other bosses let their vices torment them into helpless submission, but never Roberto. But today, there was a blur in Roberto's gaze, the whites of his eyes mottled with red.

Lorenzo and Sal Palermo, John and Marco Mancini, Mike, Joey and Luca were present. All of them were sedate, packed into the small room with their thick shoulder blades touching and their hands bunched into fists.

Roberto was enjoying a cigar, thick tendrils of smoke winding around him. He was in an unbuttoned shirt, his stomach bulging through the tight blue fabric. He had gained some weight, the skin around his chin and neck hanging loose.

The men watched Johnny with the insatiable expressions of wild dogs, their eyes hollow and roving.

Johnny tried to relax, telling himself there was nothing to be worried about. He was in the company of men he had known since adolescence, boyhood even. Regardless of familiarity, an invisible string kept him tied to the far end of the room, away from Roberto and the rest of the men.

"Good to see you, Johnny." Don Roberto extended a cup of coffee. "I understand Stuart Kelly has accepted our proposition, and the first crew of drivers arrived last Monday."

Johnny felt an acute twinge of pain twist his gut with the mention of the business deal. He hated knowing he had cheated an honest man. Most of all, he hated knowing he had disappointed Pamela. "Yeah, he was a real gentleman about it."

"And the girl promised that she'll honor our deal, even after you two break off your engagement?"

Johnny nodded again.

"I'm proud of you, son." Roberto approved, a rare grin twisting his lips sideways.

"Now you can go back to seeing the dames you used to. Doesn't that sound nice, Johnny?" Lorenzo waggled a dark eyebrow, smirking facetiously.

Once, Johnny would've offered a mischievous reply or offered an affirmation. He had always been known as a womanizer and used to wear the label with pride. But Johnny had no intention of doing so again. The thought of seeing anyone but Pamela sickened him. There was no girl in the world as good as Pamela Kelly. "Sure, Doc."

Don Roberto disposed of his cigar ashes on a silver tray and drank a long sip of coffee, relieving Johnny of his penetrating blue stare for a moment.

Instead of continuing himself, Roberto shot a look towards Lorenzo, who nodded knowingly.

"You know we've all been worried about Tony." Lorenzo said after clearing his throat. "Any chance you heard from him lately?"

"I haven't heard from him." Johnny said honestly. "I mean—I went to his apartment, but the landlady said she hadn't seen him around in the past month. She said he went to stay with his girl. But, I know Tony. He'd never leave without a good reason. Maybe he's in Jersey, working on his tan."

Johnny expected the men to laugh at his quip, but they did nothing.

He glanced around the room, hoping to at least see their hard expressions softening.

What was going on?

Usually, his jokes and lighthearted remarks were enough to win their favor. When Johnny had first been introduced to Roberto and his associates, one thing they liked about him was his sense of humor.

He wouldn't have to wait long for the answer.

"We found Tony and Carlotta in an apartment in Boston, Johnny." Sal looked down. "They ran off to get married, without the Boss' blessing."

Johnny's mind went blank.

His best friend had gotten hitched to the girl he once pined after, Don Mancini's only daughter. He attempted to imagine the pair, falling in love and going steady beneath everyone else's awareness.

Everything began to make sense. How Tony would never tell them where his girlfriend lived, then disappeared off the face of the earth for a month. How Carlotta had always rebuffed Johnny, yet remained around the men whenever they were meeting, giggling and painting her cheeks with rouge. How young Louis Mancini had alluded to a romance between Carlotta and another mysterious man at the dinner table.

Johnny knew he should feel betrayed, but all he felt was a stilling numbness. When he blinked, all he could see was Pamela, her pained expression when he left her behind and told her they could never be.

Would he ever have the guts to do what Tony did and steal off with the woman he loved?

Maybe Tony and Carlotta running off to get hitched was actually a blessing in disguise. Johnny had thought a lot about Pamela Kelly's suggestion that he should quit the business and find some less sinister work. If he told Roberto that he was going to marry Pamela and move away, surely he would be more inclined, now that Tony and Carlotta had laid the groundwork.

He had been going to church with his mamma a lot, finally appeasing her constant pleas for him to attend alongside her. He had listened to a few sermons about forgiveness from a priest with a lazy eye, but well-meaning. When he heard about the subject, Johnny was reluctant to accept the fact that his many wrongdoings could be forgiven in the eyes of God, since in his life, an eye-for-an-eye had always been law. That God would send His only Son to pay off the debts of the world. That the Son had died and risen again for *him*.

Regardless, Johnny had imagined redemption. And if Pamela Kelly would hear him out, maybe she would forgive him too.

"Johnny?" Sal snapped his fingers impatiently, rudely drawing Johnny from his reverie. "Snap out of it."

Roberto placed a hand on Sal's broad shoulder, shaking his head disapprovingly. "Give the poor kid a minute to think. Have some empathy."

"Where are they then? Is Tony okay? And Carlotta? Are they coming home?" Johnny heard himself ask. Noticing how loudly and desperately the torrent of words surged out of him, he lowered his voice. "How were they when you saw them?"

Roberto laughed, his wan blue eyes grazing the little chandelier attached to his office ceiling. Roberto hated the luminous ornament because he constantly bumped into it whenever he moved about, but

Isabella had awarded it to him as an anniversary present, so he kept it up.

"My daughter was erratic. She made a scene and told me to leave, not even pleased that her papà wanted to congratulate the new couple." Roberto chuckled, but a thread of pain leaked through his amusement. The other men followed him in laughter, but Johnny couldn't bring himself to pretend.

"And Tony?"

Roberto glanced at Lorenzo, who crept up to Johnny and weaved an arm around his shoulders. "He did what he had to do. What any of us would do."

"What do you mean?" Johnny gulped, the back of his neck caked in sweat. "Tony? What did Tony do?"

"I took care of him. He ruined my daughter, and so I gave him a death a lowlife like him deserves." Roberto's voice deepened. His face, despite being round, was angled towards Johnny like a pointed warning. His blue eyes were belligerent, ready to wage war if Johnny dared to challenge his authority.

Shock pulsed through Johnny, rocking him from head to toe. He shook his head and pushed the tears welling up in his eyes back with the calloused palms of his hands. He wouldn't cry. "Tony was my best friend. How could you kill him?"

"Look, Johnny. You still have us, don't you?" Mike grinned toothily.

The rest of the men murmured their agreement, but it wasn't enough.

"I thought Tony was like a son to you," Johnny demanded, breaking the invisible string by slamming his fists on Roberto's desk. "You told me you loved us like sons. You took me and Tony in when our fathers left us, and promised we would protect one another like a family. Has it all been a lie?"

Johnny was a little boy again, sobbing at his padre when he declared he was heading west to find work.

An angry pressure began to expand in the room—strong enough to rival the intensity of an atomic bomb.

Johnny saw Joey and Luca reach for their guns in his periphery.

Roberto was pulling himself out of his chair, like a king descending his bejeweled throne. Blood was rushing to his swollen face, making his cheeks as red as the apples Johnny's Mamma used to make pastries.

"Stop this foolishness for your own good." Roberto growled, stepping around his desk to meet Johnny face-to-face. "My patience has a limit, and I wouldn't want you to end in the same place as your friend."

Johnny's breathing was heavy.

All eyes had turned to him, awaiting his decision. Would he apologize and tell Don Mancini that it wouldn't happen again? Would he say that Tony's punishment was deserved, and that he would have done the same?

"I need some air." Johnny flung around to open the door, watching the carpeted ground become indented beneath his shifting weight. "I'll be back soon. Sorry Boss."

Somehow, after throwing a tantrum in front of the most powerful man in Brooklyn, Johnny still made it out of the Mancini house alive.

Before driving away in his automobile, he stood with his hands shoved into his pockets and looked at the house.

He glanced towards Carlotta's dark bedroom, wondering if she was locked up like a princess in a tower. Though he no longer desired her in the way he once had, he cared about her. They had grown up as childhood friends, stealing ice from the iceman and riding their bicycles up and down the hill at the end of her street.

Johnny had come to the Mancini home as a young teenager. He had been lonely and afraid, with his mamma away at work and his padre having disappeared into oblivion. He had wanted a proper family, and a way to show the world he was more than some lazy greaseball Italian kid with no actual future. What he had found was a twisted type of belonging, one that festered in crime and threats and murder.

Johnny knew he could not go on to normal life and pretend like nothing ever happened, but with age, he was becoming wiser. He knew the God of his mamma had been protecting him all along, regardless of his own doubt. The prayers had not been for nothing, and he would leave the evil behind, becoming someone his mamma could be proud of.

He would leave the Mancini home a man.

CHAPTER 23

Carlotta did not scream when she was escorted away from the Boston apartment: the first and last place she and Tony Bellucci had called home. She did not cry either, and went to great lengths to mask her anguish, shielding her face with her hands and pressing a soiled handkerchief to her mouth to keep from gagging.

She closed her eyes when she heard the voices of men echoing off the walls of the lobby, grasping the person beside her. She did not want to see her husband's lifeless body as they lugged it down the stairs and shrouded it in cloth. They had asked her if she wanted to see him one last time for closure—as if seeing his bloodied corpse and lifeless eyes would soften her grief—but she had refused.

She plunged her fingers into her ears, blocking out the keening of sirens outside.

She knew what the local cops and federal agents were thinking about her. From their disgusted faces, she was certain they thought as little of her as her padre did of them. She was just another mistress of the mob, one who cared little for the man who had perished. She had been wooed and impressed by the decadence and precision that the mafia orchestrated, flattered that she was one of the lucky ones to receive shimmering diamond earrings and regular admission to ritzy parties.

Or perhaps they suspected her of being a conspirator in the crime: a person who willingly helped execute Tony's demise.

She wanted to run. She wanted to flee from the cops and the apartment and the federal agents like she truly was a ruthless criminal. She wanted to feel glacial water gush against her frame and ferry her down the Charles River, where maybe she would find refuge amongst the reeds and bulrushes.

She looked down at her arms—clutched to her waist, convulsing. She glimpsed the jagged red imprints and purple bruises: evidence that the police had assiduously photographed and jotted down in their files like she was the product of a failed science experiment. They hadn't asked where she got them from, assuring her they would discuss her involvement in the safety of the police office.

A wail rose in her throat.

God, where are you? Her voice tried to cry out. But it was locked inside, like the rest of her. *I thought you loved me. Every night, since I was young, I've prayed to you. Every night, since I met Tony, I asked for your protection. I prayed for a life with him. I loved you, and I know you loved me. I thought you were good. But if you were good, you wouldn't have killed Tony.*

Your padre killed Tony.

Her gaze dropped to her crucifix. Out of habit, she clung to it, her fingers ricocheting against glass beads.

She had never felt such doubt, despite her inability to reconcile her father's business and her family's supposed faith. She had always known God with such certainty that considering anything else seemed like foolishness. He had been as clear to her as the breath in her lungs. But now, she was lost in an abyss of pain, and she didn't understand why He had allowed it to happen.

"We'll be taking the car to the police station, Miss," a male voice reached her, his hand patting her shoulder gently.

She slapped it away forcefully, letting hot anger course through her. "*Don't* touch me!"

Opening her eyes, she glimpsed a man in a gray suit, his hands raised in apology. "I'm sorry, Miss."

A burst of guilt exploded in Carlotta's gut, but she forced it down.

Another man, heavy perspiration darkening the armpits of his dress shirt, looped an arm around her shoulder blades and assisted her into the automobile. This time, she didn't resist, but collapsed into the back of the car, her limbs iron weights.

Carlotta buried her face in her lap, sobbing into her skirt. She wouldn't believe Tony was gone. She wanted to feel his arms around her again, yearned for him to wink impishly at her in her family home, when they both knew nobody was looking.

The thought crossed her mind that he would have been alive if she had not persuaded him to elope with her. He could've continued on as a made man, marrying another nice Italian girl who was not the daughter of his boss.

Another deluge of guilt flared up in her chest. She wept silently, her lungs heaving and chest aching as she did so.

When they reached the station, the man beside her urged her out of her grief-induced trance. "They're gonna ask you a lot of questions in there. Maybe it'll be easier if you answer them here with me."

Raising her red-rimmed eyes, Carlotta took in the man for a second time. He was pale, with freckles and wire-rimmed glasses sloping down his narrow nose. His eyes were an inky brown—far too dark against his ghostly complexion. He looked harmless. But then, Carlotta had been wrong about many things.

"I don't wanna talk." Carlotta bit her lip, trying to stifle the loud wails, begging to rupture her rib cage. "Leave me alone."

"Look, I know it must've been awfully scary in there. You want to grieve your boyfriend," the man released fumes of hamburger and red onion when he spoke, "but I have to commend your bravery. You've done a great service to the American people. If you knew how long we've been after those crazy wops—well, now we have a good reason to lock them up, thanks to you."

Does he know that I'm one of those crazy wops? Carlotta felt the gravity of his words hit her chest. Her suspicion had been correct. They didn't know or care who she was. Worse still, her tragedy was simply a tool for them.

"I am Carlotta Bellucci. My father is Don Roberto Mancini, and my husband Tony Bellucci was just murdered in cold blood. How can you expect me to be happy?" Carlotta angled herself away, staring out the window. A curtain of blinding light passed over them as an automobile passed, the driver craning his neck to marvel at the commotion.

When the man didn't reply, Carlotta turned around to look at him. His black eyes loomed wide when he finally spoke. "You're kidding! Gee wiz! You're Carlotta Mancini? The one who eloped with Tony Bellucci? Of the... Mancini Crime Family? So, you knew them? And..."

The man in the gray suit, the one who had patted Carlotta's shoulder earlier, arrested their exchange. "Scram, Frank."

Frank, apparently the more junior agent of the pair, didn't protest the order.

"I'm sorry about the unprofessional nature of that conversation, Mrs. Bellucci," the man pinned her with a somber expression.

He looked like he could be a movie star, or a charismatic young politician, or both. His dark eyes were wide and endearing, offset by skin the shade of dark mahogany. Judging from the delicate laugh marks etched around his eyes and mouth, he was in his early thirties. A golden wedding band gleamed around his ring finger, his skin inscribed with small increments.

Carlotta eschewed his apology. Instead, she pursued the most imperative question nagging her mind. "How did that Frank fella know about me and Tony? About our elopement? Were we being *followed*?"

The possibility made Carlotta shake with ire. If the happiest few weeks of her life had been stalked by the authorities, she would be absolutely devastated. All she wanted was to cling to a few private, happy moments, untainted by her father or the police.

"Before I answer any of your questions, I think I should introduce myself." He leaned forward and extended his hand. "Richard Morrison. Special agent for the Federal Bureau of Investigation."

Carlotta hesitated, her grief momentarily paralyzing her.

Steeling herself, she shook his hand limply, but kept her eyes on the rearview mirror. She didn't want to believe it was happening—she was conferring with a federal agent about the death of her husband.

"I'd also like to express my deepest condolences. Losing a sweetheart is no simple thing to endure." Richard Morrison removed his glasses, unveiling his dark eyes. "I understand you must feel very distraught."

She took offense at the way he lectured, without knowing in the slightest the magnitude of pain she was enduring. Her father, once a kind and good man in her eyes, had murdered the only man she'd ever loved, and ever would love. She didn't need his forced, half-hearted sympathy.

"How could you understand?" Carlotta demanded. "How could anyone understand my pain? My father killed my husband. I am mourning the deaths of two men, not just one. I feel—I feel as though my entire life is in ruins. As though I'm not even alive."

Richard mulled over her question for a moment, a dense mist of agony clouding his cobalt eyes.

"My Lynnette died two years ago, come this summer. We met at a dance hall, right before I was deployed to Europe. I kept a photograph of her here in my pocket, looked at it every chance I got. Second to God, she got me through the war." Richard motioned to his waist pocket, his face painted with the expression of a man who had endured unimaginable pain.

Carlotta's guilt could have imploded. She had never been a callous person, and yet she was acting as one in her desperation.

When she didn't speak, he extracted the portrait from his pocket and extended it to her. It was crumpled: no doubt bent by months of brutal combat overseas. Creases obscured a stylish woman, resting her head upon a delicate hand. A shy smile hugged her pretty ebony face.

"What happened to her?" Carlotta heard herself ask. She thought Richard would take offense at her intrusive question, but his face remained placid.

"She got sick." He said plainly. "Shortly after I got home. Doctors said she had a weak heart, despite how young she was. We had been expecting a baby when she died. She was convinced it would be a little girl. We were planning on naming her Violet."

Richard trailed Carlotta's eyes as they fell to his golden ring. "I wear this to remember her."

"I'm so sorry..." Carlotta choked, ashamed by her senseless question. "She was beautiful."

Carlotta stared at her own wedding ring, utterly ungarnished. She hadn't minded the simplicity of the object—she knew Tony purchased it with his hard-earned wages working as a car mechanic. She had only received it from him after a month of marriage.

Carlotta dug her hands into her skirt, concealing the brass ring within the heavy fabric. "Sometimes I say stupid things. I'm truly sorry about your wife."

He nodded, swallowing the lump that seemed to form in his throat. "Life hasn't been easy without her. I can't promise it'll ever get easier. But her memory has kept me going on. Becoming one of the first Black federal agents has helped me to honor her memory."

When he mentioned his profession, Carlotta's resistance returned. She knew he wanted something out of her. A confession.

"Look, I'm not trying to upset you, Mrs. Bellucci. I just want you to know that I am taking this case seriously." Richard's eyes exhibited no indications of deceit. Still, Carlotta couldn't trust him.

"And about your question. We have been keeping records on your father, tapping phone lines and surveying all the companies he seems to control in New York. But no, we never could figure out where you or Tony went. It was like you disappeared off the face of the earth."

They gave Carlotta an itchy blanket and a glass of water inside the Boston police station, settling into an armchair adjacent from a local officer's work desk.

After allowing her some time to compose herself and down the glass of water, a group of men retrieved an imposing-looking tape recorder from one of their vans and positioned it in front of her. It was a mammoth of a tape recorder, a box with hideous round circles appended to it that looked like the beady eyes of a fish—an agglomeration of mechanical dials.

"I don't wanna look at it." Carlotta heard herself say. She hated how the thing stared, willing her to break a million vows and sever ties with her family for the rest of her life.

"Turn it away." Richard instructed the men without questioning her strange request. They complied with the order, not bothering to disguise the confusion in their expressions.

"Thank you." Carlotta said, hoping her courtesy might help them overlook her strange behavior.

"When we record, Mrs. Bellucci, you must know there is no going back." Richard explained below the din of the agents and the dismal murmur of the tap recorder readying itself for the impending interrogation. "There is little else more powerful than a child of a mobster giving her testimony. I don't think we've ever encountered something like this before, in fact."

Carlotta saw Frank across the room, his eyes fastened to her in amazement. She realized then the tremendous momentum of her decision. Family members and relatives didn't speak out against the mob because to do so branded one as a treacherous traitor.

"If I answer all your questions, does that mean my father will be sent to jail?" Carlotta wanted to be indifferent. She wanted to tell them all she knew, without caring about what would happen to the man who had gifted her with a phonograph on South Beach an eternity ago. But an ache dwelled within her, a persistent ache for Tony and her mamma and brothers.

Sometimes she wished she had been oblivious of her padre's evil, content only to be his daughter and the apple of his eye. Perhaps if she had remained a naïve little girl forever...

He had killed her husband. She could not forget that. Would not forget.

"No one can be sure of what happens to him." Richard said succinctly, perching himself upon a ledge beside her. "But your testimony, combined with one of a woman from New York who wrote a letter to us—could be as good as gold."

Carlotta could only guess who the New York girl was. She was probably one of Lorenzo Palermo's many girlfriends, hoping to avenge herself after being discarded. Her father had always warned him about his myriad of romantic trysts, and Carlotta had pitied his wife Victoria, a dear friend of her mamma.

"And after?" Carlotta held her breath. "After I give my testimony, what happens to me?"

"Don't worry about that, Mrs. Bellucci." Richard consoled gently. "We'll take care of you."

Carlotta's head spun with a prayer. *I don't know where you are, Lord, but I'm going to do this. Please let it be for the best.*

"Do you want to do this Mrs. Bellucci?" Richard asked, kneeling to meet her eyes.

Carlotta felt her chin move in a hesitant nod. *Thy will be done…*

"Ms. Mancini—I mean, Mrs. Bellucci. We're ready to record." Frank sputtered.

Richard shared a look with her, one that assured her he would be next to her for the entire recording. "If you need to stop, just give me a wave."

Carlotta closed her eyes.

She had not chosen her father. She had not chosen to be a daughter of the mob, or to fall in love with Tony Bellucci.

She was determined she would choose justice.

She inhaled, letting the stale office air expand in her lungs. She straightened, staring ahead, and opened her eyes.

She saw the gulf between herself and Roberto Mancini widen, until he became nothing more than a speck of dust in an expanse of light.

She began to talk.

CHAPTER 24

A faint breeze moaned through a grove of oaks on Lafayette and 3rd Avenue, the major intersection across from Sean Kelly's Greenwich Village apartment. Branches bent and flailed like broken arms, their leaves shuddering in the wind.

The balm of city-dwelling wildflowers drifted with the gust. Despite the wind, there was an electric feeling of spring humming through the sinews of the city, in the schoolchildren's games of hopscotch and the businessmen choosing to picnic outdoors with their paper bag lunches.

Since returning to live with her brother, Pamela had understood what jazz musicians, disaffected beatniks, and fervent artists appreciated in the charming enclaves of Greenwich Village.

With taverns, cabarets, theaters, bookshops, and cafés congregating along every boulevard and hidden alleyway, there was enough culture to rival that of Paris or Madrid. She spent countless hours promenading up and down the streets in the afternoon, admiring the lethargic songs of saxophone players and the upbeat melodies of blues singers. She knew it wasn't the wisest idea to be out in the open so much, but Pamela loved immersing herself in the wonders of the Village.

The soothing turquoise of the sky fragmented as Pamela hopped onto the fire escape, the grates slicing against the soles of her saddle shoes. She climbed up the stairs, the sun warm on her limbs and the wind whipping her hair up past her shoulders.

She rapped her pale knuckle across the smeared windowpane of Sean's apartment when she reached the third floor.

Through the glass, she glimpsed her brother's stubby fingers flying over the keys of his Remington Rand typewriter, engraving patterns of black ink upon the crisp white sheet before him like magic.

Strands of greased hair flopped over his pinkish ears as his shoulders hunched over the writing. He hardly seemed to notice her. Or else, he was unwilling to depart from his colorful fictional world like usual.

Pamela knocked again.

"Coming, coming! Can't you see I'm *interviewing my brains* here?" He slammed one last word into the paper, scraping his chair across the hardwood with a frustrated grunt.

Pamela unbound her hair from a sea foam floral scarf, removing the dark sunglasses she had been sporting. Lately, maintaining an air of confidentiality had become a necessity. If *La Cosa Nostra* knew what she and Sean had been orchestrating, the two of them would be finished.

Sean heaved the window ajar and Pamela shimmied through the narrow opening.

"You get anything good from the grocery?" Sean grasped her hand, helping her land safely on the carpeted ground.

"Nothing spectacular. A dozen eggs, milk, flour, and a few apples."

Sean's eyes sparkled with mirth. "No green Jello? Or Ritz? Or Bugles?"

Pamela had grown accustomed to Sean's eccentric quirks during their childhood. It was only recently that she could study his writing strategies, which consisted of him ritualistically devouring a box of

Ritz crackers or a pack of Bugles, along with a bowl or two of green Jello and smoking a cigarette. He claimed the snack food helped spur his imagination.

"I only had five dollars!"

"Five? Thought I gave you seven."

"Even if you had, it wouldn't matter. We're broke, Sean."

Sean groaned, drawing the drapes over the window, darkening the burgundy and coal black of his apartment's Persian carpet.

Even before Pamela came to stay, he had quit his job at the greasy spoon in order to commit himself to the writing of a paperback novel. It was a mystery set in prohibition-era New York City, concentrated around a pair of bootleggers and a spunky elderly widow. Regardless of how groundbreaking Sean considered his work to be, it wasn't yet paying any of the bills. Pamela was still searching for jobs in the city, but as a young unmarried woman—finding work was difficult.

"Sure, but when I'm through with the manuscript, we'll be millionaires skiing in The Poconos and sailing the seven seas. You'll be over Siciliano and I'll be enjoying all the Bugles and Ritz I want." Sean simpered, popping an apple into his mouth and chewing.

"I'm sure you'll be consuming more expensive snacks than that if you become a millionaire writer." Pamela ambled over to the window, drawing open one end of the curtain to peek below.

"*When* I become a millionaire writer." Sean winked.

"You've thought an awful lot about this, haven't you?" Pamela laughed.

"A man's got to have goals and aspirations." Sean countered, amusement flooding his gaze.

Pamela wanted to share in Sean's hope for the future, but the reminder of the past beckoned.

It had been almost one month since she last met with Johnny Siciliano.

In that time, she celebrated her twenty-second birthday and moved into a new apartment. She thought the pain of his absence would've subsided, but it remained perpetual—lingering as poignant as ever. Especially when wondering what would become of him when all was said and done. Would he be killed? Or would he go to jail?

Pamela prayed for the latter if she was forced to choose from the two options.

Sean seemed to detect Pamela's melancholy because he steered her towards his writing desk and put forth a sealed envelope with a flick of his wrist. "Come here, Pam. I have something to cheer you up. I got the letter from the mail carrier while you were out at the grocery."

The long-awaited letter rested in the smooth palms of Pamela's hands.

The day she turned up at Sean's apartment, after discerning Sergeant Marino's corruption, loomed in her memory. Perhaps unwisely, she had told Sean everything, begging him to assist her in sending a letter to the Federal Bureau of Investigation informing them of all she had witnessed at Albright Trimmings & Co. They had penned the condemnation under the pseudonym Cheryl Parsons; a fictional matronly character from Sean's current book.

After a couple of excruciating weeks, the response had finally come.

Pamela's fingers worked as they freed the page from its flimsy shell.

A brief bunch of words ascended into her view.

Sean bent over her shoulder, mouthing the text aloud.

Dear Mrs. Parsons,

Thank you for your letter of February 16 and the abundance of evidence you have provided us with. You should know that we are reviewing your claims, along with others. Though I am bearing in mind that such a situation may not be possible for you, we would greatly appreciate your presence at the Boston Police Department on Beacon Hill at your earliest convenience. I encourage you to arrive within the month.

Please do not inform any non-familial third parties of your plans should you decide to travel. I would like to ensure you are out of harm's way.

Respectfully yours,

Richard Morrison, FBI.

Pamela released the paper with a sharp breath, letting it float onto the mahogany of the writing desk.

"What do you make of it?" Sean queried, looping an arm around her shoulder.

"We need to go to Boston."

The night before departing to Boston, Pamela and Sean celebrated their success with an upside-down pineapple cake and some purple fruit punch. They didn't have the money, but Pamela ceded to Sean's declaration that he deserved some thanks for constructing Cheryl Parsons' letter.

The two of them lounged on the sofa in front of the radio, the lights of the city painting every object in their vicinity in an enchanting shade of yellow. Sean turned up the radio, filling his small apartment with the crooning songs of Frank Sinatra and Sammy Davis Jr.

"Cheers, to my kid sister, for singing on the mob and getting away with it." Sean pretended to clink his plastic cup to hers.

Pamela's skin prickled, but she smoothed down the goosebumps with her hands. There was no way she could escape the mafia that easily, but at least she was safe until they figured out her role in being an informant. No one except Johnny and Sergeant Marino knew she had suspected criminal activity, and she prayed it would remain that way. "Thanks, Sean. I mean it. If you hadn't taken me in like this, I don't know what would've become of me."

Sean sobered, an unexpected pathos settling over his features. "Lorna took me to look after you. She could see you were going to do something special, Pam. And she knew you wouldn't spend the rest of your life cooped up with Mom and Dad on the Ave. So when the time came, she made me promise I'd take care of you for her."

Pamela's own heart squeezed with emotion. Knowing that Lorna still believed in her made everything seem all right. She hoped they would reunite once again when all was said and done.

"You didn't have to listen to her, but you did. And I'm grateful." Pamela reached over to squeeze her brother's ink-smudged hand.

"Hey, no sweat. I'm glad Mrs. Parsons came in handy. The old broad always does." Sean grinned, turning up the radio to the crooning lament of a love ballad—prompting Pamela's thoughts to whorl back to the man she had left behind.

When Sean was asleep in his bedroom and Pamela's frame was curled beneath a quilt on a mattress in the living room, an insistent hammering upon the front door wrenched her fully awake.

She hadn't been able to sleep very well anyway, with scores of anxious thoughts goading at her. She had been dwelling upon the memory of a Chicagoan journalist who inexplicably disappeared after writing a piece on the Chicago faction of the Italian American mafia. It had happened years ago, at the beginning of the war, but the incident still plagued Pamela's memory. Would she become like the journalist? Was she dragging Sean along with her if something as terrible transpired?

A few anxious moments passed, but Pamela did not hear the knock again.

Pamela hoped that the noise had just been a figment of her imagination. Sometimes, in between waking and sleeping, she imagined things she'd seen in her dreams. Or perhaps the clamor had emanated from one of the neighbors' homes. Sean lived in a noisy apartment, with an abundance of loud residents and equally boisterous families and guests.

A muffled voice from outside rushed through the apartment.

Convinced of the ominous presence of an intruder, Pamela crawled up from her mattress and grabbed a pan from the kitchenette, should she require a weapon of defense. Her knees wobbling, she trod towards the front door, cursing the archaic planks of wood as they groaned beneath her shifting weight. Fine beads of perspiration lined her lip and arms.

A garland of moonlight settled upon her features as the flesh on her hand grazed the chilling brass doorknob. "Who is it?"

The speech on the other end of the passage was remarkably telling. "Pamela? You in there?"

Her heart pounding, Pamela swung the door open, unveiling large brown eyes coupled with a familiar grin.

The two stood apart for an eternity.

Johnny was illuminated by the fluorescent headlights of every passing automobile that meandered along the street by Sean's apartment. His restrained smile engaged Pamela with the tentative greeting of a stranger, but his eyes shone with an unbridled warmth that suggested they were far more. The wine-coloured wallpaper in the hallway behind him complimented the swarthy hue of his skin.

"Been a while," he remarked casually, propping his sturdy arm against the equally strong wooden beam of the doorframe.

"How have you been?" Pamela's voice quivered with the question. Her breath was uneven and coarse, and she knew blood was rising to warm her face. Nerves were tangling together in her throat—ridding her of anything intelligible to say.

Pamela had not predicted being so affected by Johnny's reappearance. In all of her dreams, she had emulated the confidence of Jane Russell or Dorothy Dandridge. She imagined she would hold Johnny between her arms—bridging the impenetrable chasm that had grown in the past month as it ruptured fantastically between them. She dreamed she would kiss his lips with an urgent fervor. She fantasized Johnny would poetically relay his love, and bestow her with a bouquet of red roses like he had once before.

But reality and fantasy were disparate concepts.

Pamela did not know what Johnny was doing in Greenwich Village, standing outside of her older brother's apartment. He could very well be there to threaten her, or kill her for ratting on the mob. Whatever the case, he was most definitely *not* there to profess his undying love and affection *or* to present a bouquet of red roses.

"What's with the pan?" Johnny chuckled, glancing down at her trembling hands.

Pamela became conscious of the cool cast iron handle in her hooked fingers. Laughing a little, she parked the object on Sean's hallway table beneath a replicated painting by Kandinsky. Sean possessed an affinity of art and culture from the 1920s, as the painting and his latest novel suggested. "Perhaps I thought you were a criminal."

"Aren't I?"

Pamela sobered, tightening the strings of her housecoat around her slender waist. "Everyone can change. How am I to know you haven't?"

Johnny pondered this, his brow deepening.

The air from the apartment corridor was thick with paprika and kefir—likely billowing from the homes of Sean's Hungarian and Portuguese neighbors down the hall. The smell, along with the quick chattering of people from upstairs, made Johnny aware that any private conversation should take place inside, away from the other residents of the building.

"Can I come in?"

Pamela widened the door for him, then bolted it, and they strolled into the living room together, stepping over her crumpled mattress and quilt on the floor.

Switching on the industrial ceiling lamp invited a comfortable glow to Johnny's features, pleasantly flushing his complexion and casting traces of light brown upon his dark hair. He was garbed in blue jeans, a casual brown camp shirt, and polished saddle shoes, just like her own. He looked more like an ordinary young man than the ruthless *mafioso* she had once thought him to be.

Pamela became aware of her own blotchy skin, mangled blonde hair, and the frumpy housecoat that gathered at her ankles and encased her frilly white slip. But the way Johnny was staring at her suggested he cared little about her bedraggled appearance.

"I quit." Johnny exhaled, the words quietly but pointedly, quickening Pamela's pulse. "I quit 'cause of the things you said."

Am I dreaming? Pamela twirled a lock of blonde hair around her finger, staring up at him like a love-struck schoolgirl. "What did *I* say?"

"You said I could change. I—I had this weird feeling in my chest since the day I joined the mob. Like I wasn't the same as everyone else. Every time I stole or killed or threatened someone, I felt guilt. Even when I knew it was supposed to just be business. My mamma and you were the only people to show me it wasn't. The guilt was normal. The business was evil, Pamela, *evil.*" Johnny took her hand then, staying it to his heart. The simple act elated Pamela, as it had before. "I came to wonder if you could forgive me."

Pamela's reply was instantaneous. "Of course I forgive you. I forgave you a while ago, when I..."

She was about to say *when I began to love you*, but her audacity to say the words dwindled.

Tears welled in her vision as her exhaustion and shock caught up with her. She raised her hands to expunge them, but Johnny acted first by gallantly extending a handkerchief. She gladly accepted, though not without some embarrassment.

"I feel awful, that I brought crime to your father's company. He seemed like a good man." Guilt edged Johnny's voice as he shoved the soiled handkerchief in his pocket. He traced a circle with his shoe in the Persian carpet, withholding his face from her.

"My father is far from perfect." Pamela sighed, remembering the pain his adulterous affairs had caused her mother—the nights she had heard inconsolable weeping from her parents' room while her father slumbered soundly in his study. The repulsion that rose in Pamela's throat whenever she suspected her father was going to visit one of his young mistresses. His indecent glances at the pretty young maids and female visitors.

She also remembered his rejection of Sean, and the heartache it had caused for the family.

"It doesn't matter, it was wrong. Besides, I hurt you. And you matter more than anyone else."

The sentence dangled between them. Pamela didn't know if she was hearing correctly. Had Johnny longed for her as much as she treasured him? Did he love her? Had he meant the words he had spoken to her that day at her parents' house?

"I... I'm in love with you Pamela."

The words encircled Pamela, gently rousing her senses. They sounded like a crystalline lake in July, shimmering against a peach and pink sunrise, or candy floss on the beach at Coney Island, or the taste of hot cocoa after a blustery winter evening in the snow. They were better than any of the words penned in professions of love Sean had written to Karen or Shakespearean sonnets.

Pamela ran her hand along Johnny's arm, refusing to let him go again. "I think I've fallen in love with you too."

Johnny caved to the desire burning in his gaze and kissed her—his lips urgent and strong. Pamela kissed him back, her thoughts becoming clouded by the longing pulsing through her veins.

They held each other for a few moments, basking in the newfound comfort of reciprocated love. Their embrace felt familiar—as though they had held one another many times over many years.

Pamela rested the crown of her head upon his shoulder as they stood, their frames apart yet somehow also together. Resting in Johnny's arms felt as natural as breathing. They didn't move or speak, as if the two of them wanted to preserve that posture forever.

"How did you know I was here?" Pamela tilted up her head to gaze at him, hoping to detract from the powerful emotions stirring within her.

"I worked in the mafia for ten years. I got good at finding people." Johnny's chest undulated with his chuckle.

Pamela smiled, glad to see that Johnny's sense of humor was still intact. She offered him some of the leftover, upside down pineapple cake and fruit punch. Soon they were seated across from each other at Sean's flea market table, like they had been going steady for months. The table was too squat for Johnny's lanky legs, so he sat sideways—his knees tapering peaks.

"That was some cake," Johnny complimented, licking the crumbs from his fingers. The act was a social taboo in Caroline Kelly's social circles, but Pamela didn't mind it.

"The recipe was straight out of one of those silly homemaker magazines." She laughed.

"Is that what you wanna be? When you're through with all of this?" Johnny teased, his dark eyelashes casting shadows upon his cheekbones.

"A homemaker?"

"Yeah, you know, a homemaker in the suburbs with a bunch of ankle-biters to take care of. A husband who comes home from the city and reads the newspaper while she cooks." Johnny's eyes gleamed with manufactured joviality, but his expression was earnest, searching for her answer.

Was he asking because he imagined her running off and marrying another? After all they had been through together?

"I'm going to go back to school. To college." Pamela asserted, gathering up their dishes and carrying them to the kitchenette. She scrubbed frenetically with Sean's half-empty bottle of Joy dishwashing liquid. "I've always wanted to continue with my studies, and now that I'm living with Sean, I'll be able to do so just fine."

Pamela held her breath.

Few people approved of higher female education. According to the homemaker magazines she occasionally flipped through, she was supposed to be most content darning her husband's socks and orchestrating enormous meals for a growing family. She hoped Johnny would at least understand her desire if not support it.

"You'll be the smartest pupil in the class." Johnny assured her, rising from the table and strolling into the kitchenette. He placed a hand on the small of her back, looking over her shoulder.

Pamela's heart raced at his nearness—his muscular hand against her back. His touch made her feel dizzy and untethered, like she was floating on clouds. She had never experienced this kind of physical affection before, and her gaze flew around the apartment for something to comment on—anything.

Pamela's eyes fell on the opened letter left discarded atop the coffee table. She had forgotten the impending trip to Boston, being so engrossed in seeing Johnny again.

"What are you looking at?" Johnny followed the trajectory of her sight and strode over to the coffee table before she could stop him. Unfolding the paper, Johnny bent his head to read silently.

Pamela held her breath, awaiting his reaction. Her hands lingered over the sink.

"So, you're going ahead with this, then?"

Pamela nodded.

Johnny positioned his body towards the window. Greenwich Village unraveled in front of him like a patchwork quilt, taverns and shops and apartments twinkling in the night sky. A pale crescent moon, barely visible against the busy glare of the city, spilled its dull light upon one half of Johnny's profile as he turned to face her again. "I'm comin' with you."

The following morning at dawn, Johnny convened with Pamela and Sean at the Dixie Bus Centre on 42nd Street. After greeting them, Johnny assisted Pamela with the compact bundle of food, clothes, and toiletries she had packed for a weekend in Boston.

Despite the early morning, a knot of people surrounded the trio as they ventured through the hotel that dually served as a bus stop, perhaps eager to enjoy a weekend away. A couple of musicians serenaded them, their sweeping music soothing the anxiety in Pamela's throat. Children threaded through the crowd, one of them colliding with Pamela while they played a carefree game of chase.

Johnny grasped Pamela's hand, squeezing her gloved fingers tightly as they waited in line to board a silver and navy greyhound bus.

"Don't worry," he whispered, "no one knows what we're doing. They haven't caught on yet."

Pamela wanted to believe him, but she wasn't so sure. What would happen if someone recognized Johnny? Would they realize what he was doing? What were they about to do?

"I'm just a little nervous. That's all." Pamela told herself aloud.

The man ahead of them projected a friendly look. "Don't worry Miss. These greyhound buses are terrific—nothing like those noisy airplanes. We'll be in Boston in a jiffy, and soon you'll be enjoying a bowl of chowder by the Charles River."

"See Miss Pamela? We'll be there in a jiffy." Sean grinned, glancing up from the thin paperback novel he had been perusing.

Climbing onto the bus and showing the driver their tickets, Pamela, Johnny, and Sean located a row of three seats. Pamela slid into the window side, and Johnny scooted in beside her, looping his arm around her shoulders.

The bus rolled forward, but an ominous figure standing near the gate caught Pamela's eye—a man with an upturned collar and a shapeless overcoat. His dark eyes seared into them, pursuing even as the bus gained speed.

"Who was that? That man watching us?" Pamela gasped, elbowing Johnny.

Johnny craned his neck to perceive the acrimonious figure, and his jaw hardened. "Ignore him. Probably nobody."

The city slipped out of view and into the rolling indigo of East River. Pamela looked away, clutching Johnny's hand.

CHAPTER 25

Carlotta stared down at the city of Boston from her motel room. With the window ajar, the floral curtains floated with the cool wind—printed yellow daisies and oddly shaped petunias, granting a welcome relief from the sprawling streets below.

It had been two weeks since the FBI and police took her in, two weeks since Tony's death. In that time, Carlotta had little else besides praying, staring out the window, and falling in and out of slumber.

Even eating was hard.

Whenever Richard Morrison coaxed her into consuming a morsel of hamburger or a sip of chocolate milkshake from the drive-in down the block, Carlotta would feel the bitterness of gall ensnare her throat.

Richard was always asking her what kind of food she liked, even suggesting that he pick up one of her mamma's traditional delicacies from an Italian produce market nearby. Once, he brought over a slice of pizza from an American place down the block. I had tasted terrible—especially compared to her mamma's home cooking—but Carlotta had swallowed her dissatisfaction.

Carlotta knew he meant well. He was trying to make her time at the motel more bearable while the agents merged their evidence and reviewed her testimony. But Carlotta was inconsolable. Nothing could make her stay at the gilded prison of the Palm Tree Motel Inn less excruciating. And it certainly was just that: a prison with a gaudy neon sign, a heated swimming pool, and a smoke-filled cocktail lounge.

Carlotta turned, listening to the gentle whir of a vacuum cleaner in the hallway.

The motel room contained a single twin-sized bed with a floral spread, an armchair, and a writing desk with a telephone. However, the agents had disconnected the telephone before she arrived, prohibiting her from contacting anyone without their granted permission. She wasn't allowed to leave her bedroom either, except to take a daily walk down the hall with one agent—usually Richard—escorting her.

Even on their walks, people looked at them with unease, likely because they didn't like the idea of a Black man keeping company with an Italian girl. When she thought about it, Carlotta realized that their association would horrify her own father. Although mob men rarely spoke about it, they shunned outsiders.

But Roberto Mancini and his cronies were hardly the moral examples she wished to follow.

Carlotta rested her knees upon the rug at her bedside and pulled a closed suitcase from underneath the mattress. Her initials were engraved on the wooden outside in curly silver letters, giving the writing a lyrical flare. The trunk had been a gift from her father on her twelfth birthday, right around when he had revealed his true identity to her.

Undoing the brass clasp with great care, Carlotta's fingers slipped over the few items she had brought from Pioneer Street when she eloped with Tony. The federal agents had gone back for it, adding several of Tony's things to the eclectic collection. Items from their life as newlyweds.

Her gaze combed over a prayer book, a diary, a hairbrush, her children's Bible, and the gown she had donned on her wedding day. A photograph of her mamma gleamed in the glow of the coloured glass pendant lights attached to the ceiling, animating her cheerful smile and lightening her dark flapper bob.

Carlotta's hands froze as they found Tony's jacket.

It smelled of him, with the potent musk of his cologne and ivory soap. More recently, a vestige of gasoline had woven its way into the fibers of the fabric, besmirching the coat with painful memories. But Carlotta would not think about the Tony who broke her trust by erring back into his old ways.

She would remember the Tony who loved her.

A tear slid down her cheek, splashing onto the jacket collar.

Embracing the material between her arms, Carlotta carefully returned it to the suitcase, folding the sleeves so that they wouldn't crease.

"Mrs. Bellucci? Can we talk?"

Carlotta slid the luggage beneath her bed again, standing, smoothing the pleats of her plaid dress. "Sure, just come right on in."

She hoped he wouldn't notice how sarcastic she sounded.

Keys jangled and Richard entered, keeping a respectful distance as he stood guard-like by the door. A few agents lingered behind him, more interested in their cigarettes and newspapers than her.

"Ready for our walk?" Richard provided a jovial smile, keeping the door propped open with his foot.

Carlotta nodded, grabbing her cardigan and throwing it about her shoulders.

Richard and Carlotta walked beset by the other men, pacing up and down the floor that contained her room. Richard did his best to make cheerful conversation, commenting on the paintings lining the walls and inquiring about her day. Carlotta had little to say. What intriguing anecdote or pertinent insight could she relay when all her days were spent in the same dreary motel room?

"How are you really, Mrs. Bellucci?" Richard asked, quickening his pace to match her expeditious steps.

"What does it matter?"

"It matters. Of course it does. You've helped us tremendously with this case, Carlotta. It's only right that we ensure your well-being."

His use of her first name exasperated her. He had no right acting as though he knew what was best for her. They had only known each other for two weeks.

Regardless of how much Richard irritated her, Carlotta knew he was a good man. He spoke to her patiently, listening when she had something to say. He realized she was human and treated her as such. The other agents regarded her as though she were nothing more than some rare specimen they were examined through a scientific microscope in a laboratory. A Martian, perhaps.

Carlotta ceased walking. She turned to Richard, straightening to confront his wide brown eyes. "Let me get outta here to get some fresh air, Mr. Morrison. Just for a few minutes. Then I'll feel better."

"Carlotta, Mrs. Bellucci, you know I can't do that."

"If I've given my testimony, done my part in helping the investigation, why can't you let me go?"

"You know why. Your father is a dangerous man, Mrs. Bellucci. We have no idea what he's planning next. We have to keep you under our watch for now."

"My father won't kill me."

The statement was an absolute every daughter ought to be certain of. It was supposed to be an uncontested given—that no father would ever bring harm down upon his child, for whatever reason imaginable. But Carlotta doubted the accuracy of her assertion. If her father could slaughter his own son-in-law, wasn't he capable of doing the same to her?

A shudder pulsed through her. "Please, just lemme take a walk outside, Richard. Just for an hour. A few minutes, even. I can't stand being stuck inside this motel like a... prisoner."

Richard offered a handkerchief. She accepted, using it to dry the dampness on her cheeks.

"I hope to God that your father wouldn't consider committing such an atrocity, but I'm not a betting man, Carlotta. And I won't allow you to wager your life away. The entire American mafia is watching you. They don't take nicely to an insider giving away their precious secrets. And now that you have, making an example of you is all they can do to maintain the natural order of things." Richard's answer was resolute and annoyingly rational.

Carlotta heaved a breath, Richard's features becoming a blur as she turned away. With Richard, thinking of a witty response or argument was impossible, because she knew he was right.

"You aren't just a daughter of the Mancini Family, Carlotta. Now you're a daughter of the mob."

That evening, Carlotta grew restless.

Pacing back and forth in her gilded prison cell granted her no relief from the festering desire to leave the motel.

When she listened to Richard telling the other agents, he was going down to the cocktail lounge for some dinner; Carlotta resolved to leave. She would not stay out for hours—just long enough to stretch her legs and breathe in some fresh nighttime air. She would return before Richard even knew she'd been gone.

Seizing Tony's jacket from her childhood traveling bag, Carlotta stepped into the hallway and smiled disarmingly at the two policemen guarding her room. They exchanged confused glances, their brows marred with bewilderment.

"Hello fellas," Carlotta twirled a plump lock of dark hair around her index finger, "mind if I take an evening walk outside by the swimming pool?"

"Did Morrison allow this?" One man questioned the other, scrutinizing Carlotta with cool caramel eyes.

Before the man could offer a reply, she interjected. "Yeah, he told me I could take a short walk this evenin'. He's awful tired of all the work he's doing. Maybe he forgot to tell the rest of you."

The police officer with caramel eyes shrugged, whispering something to his counterpart.

"Be back here at seven o'clock." He directed. "That gives you a good half an hour to take your evening walk. There's a clock by the pool, so it shouldn't be hard to watch the time."

Carlotta tried to maintain her composure as she turned from them towards the stairwell.

The officer's hand on her shoulder stalled her. "We're just trying to help you, Miss. *You're* the one that the entire New York mob is out looking for."

The evening air against Carlotta's skin was heavenly.

Droplets of cool rainwater streaked her forehead and cheeks as she raised her face to the sky, squeezing her eyelids shut and standing perfectly still for a moment. The rain lamented with her as she succumbed to tears again. The wind flirted with her skirt, sending it into graceful pirouettes about her ankles.

She emerged from the carpark of the motel and rounded a blunted corner, passing a department store and a Chinese food restaurant. It was eerily quiet. She walked for a few blocks; her figure fading into the dark shadows of buildings as they mounted the sky above her like Egyptian pyramids.

When her high heels pinched against her toes, Carlotta ventured back. But her shoes weren't the only reason she wanted to return to the safety of her motel room.

There was building pressure in the pit of her stomach. It was the kind of gut feeling she got when there was something amiss—when she knew there was danger nearby. Perhaps she had inherited the sensitivity from her father. There was a reason Don Roberto Mancini had survived a handful of murder attempts, after all.

Carlotta ran.

Her high heels struck against the pavement, echoing down the street.

What was she thinking, challenging the logical Richard's explicit orders and wandering out into the night alone? What had overcome her—prompting her to act so recklessly?

Carlotta quickened her jog into a sprint, her heart reverberating in her ears.

When the dim neon sign of the motel glistened in her perception, Carlotta felt her lungs heave in relief. Relaxing, she slowed to a walk.

"Carlotta."

Carlotta's pulse returned to full alarm.

Before she could scream, a gloved hand was smothering her mouth, with another pulling her back into a thicket of shadows.

Struggling to break free, Carlotta whirled around, her back slamming against the wall of the alleyway the perpetrator had dragged her into.

Lorenzo Palermo released his hold on her arm, a rifle positioned in his fisted hand. "Nice to see you, *bambina.*"

The use of Carlotta's Italian pet name infuriated her. Once, she had considered the man a beloved uncle. He had spoiled her with candies and trinkets and weekend trips to the cinema. She had trusted him almost as much as she had trusted her padre. But Lorenzo Palermo was her father's most trusted accomplice. No doubt he had played a pivotal role in the murder of her husband. "Get away from me, Lorenzo, you slimy dirtbag!"

"Take it easy, darling." Lorenzo flashed her a devilish smile, loosening his grip on the weapon a little. "I'm only here to check-in. See how you're doing. It must be awful lonely up here with your new pig friends."

"If you're here to stop me from giving my testimony, it's too late. I told them everything, Lorenzo. So do whatever you want. Kill me. I don't care." Carlotta stepped towards him, angling her chin forward like a poised dagger.

Lorenzo balked away.

His mouth drooped and his jaw twitched as if undergoing the effects of anesthesia.

The fastest-talking man Carlotta knew was at a loss for words.

A surge of courage provoked Carlotta into moving closer, bringing her almost chest-to-chest with Lorenzo. The muzzle of the gun was inches from pressing into her. She peered up into his bronzed face, noticing the age that had crept into his cheeks; his forehead.

"Carlotta, what are you doing? Are you crazy?" Lorenzo hissed. "I never said I was gonna shoot you."

"Then what did you come for?"

"I'm here to bring you home. Your father misses you, Carlotta."

The admission did not phase her. "My father killed Tony. My husband—the man I loved."

"Your mamma misses you."

He had found her vulnerability. The mention of her mamma made her chest swell with unimaginable agony.

Carlotta longed to see her mamma again. She wanted to discuss the joys and sorrows of married life together, standing over the kitchen sink and doing the washing as they always had. She wanted to explain herself—that she would've done things differently if she had a different father. She would never have left her mamma behind.

Lorenzo knew he had touched a nerve. He lowered the gun to the side of his waist, offering an outstretched arm. "Come home, little Carlotta. You can't desert your people like this, your own kind."

"You're *not* my people."

"You've got some nerve, *Mrs. Bellucci*." The temper so characteristic of Lorenzo Palermo ignited, reddening his cheeks. "What do you think the feds are gonna do with you when they've taken your testimony? You think they'll treat you real nice, give you some money and send you off far away? No, they'll leave you to fend for yourself. They're not your kind. At least your pops promises he'll look after you."

The angry fervor in Lorenzo's glare sent goosebumps down her arms.

He raised the gun again. All camaraderie disappeared from his demeanor.

"I'm gonna ask you one more time," Lorenzo warned. "Follow me nice and quiet to my automobile. Don't make a fuss."

"I will not." Carlotta raised her voice, the reality of death looming closer with every waking moment. "Kill me, Lorenzo. God will judge you for your evil."

"Get away from her." The voice rang into the dark alley like a church bell.

"I'm going to ask you again, Mr. Palermo. Get out of here, or when you'll be interfering with a federal investigation." Richard Morrison approached them, the streetlight unveiling the solemn resolution carved into his features. His hand was grasping the metallic stock of a gun.

"What is this?" Lorenzo laughed in disbelief, though without removing the gun from Carlotta. From between his bared teeth, Carlotta heard a muffled racial slur. "Now you're going out with *this* fella? What would your father think, Carlotta Mancini?"

The veins in Carlotta's neck stuck out. The insult was familiar, reminding her of when the gas station attendant had derided her and Tony.

Instead of beating the man like Tony had done, Richard calmly stepped forward and brandished his weapon. "No need to swear in front of a young lady. Scram or I'll shoot."

Carlotta felt the gun depart from her person.

"I'm leaving." Lorenzo stalked away, swerving around Richard. "But don't forget, Carlotta. We're not done with you. We'll never forget you, for as long as you're living."

"Why didn't you arrest him?"

Carlotta and Richard were seated in the cocktail lounge of the Palm Tree Motel, facing the imposing vanity mirror in front of them. Richard was draining a glass of whiskey while Carlotta nursed her cocktail, nibbling at the maraschino cherry speared by a straw.

Richard leaned against the back of his orange swivel chair, crossing one leg over the other. "I don't have to do anything of the sort. When this investigation is through, they will deport your father and all his cronies to Sicily or behind bars for years."

Carlotta wanted to share Richard's conviction, but she didn't doubt the savvy of her father. He had gotten himself out of plenty of fixes before, and he could do so again.

"I hope so." Carlotta tried dismissing her cynicism with another sip of her sugary beverage.

She slid back in her own chair, watching the waning light bulbs in the vanity mirror. She had not recognized herself when she perceived her own reflection. Somehow, her posture had become more confident and self-assured. The redness around her eyes was no longer as prominent, and the bruises staining her arms were healing.

She was healing.

The ache for Tony was no less searing, but for the first time since his death—she felt hope. Hope for the future. Hope for justice. Hope that one day, God would show her what it had all been for. She didn't understand the pain, but she knew He hadn't abandoned her in the suffering. And for now, having hope was enough.

Richard sidled his gaze towards her, his strong jaw softening in a smile. "I believe that this is the first time I have ever seen you smile, Mrs. Bellucci."

It was then that Carlotta realized she was, in fact, grinning like a kid. "I guess it is."

She raised her glass and proposed a toast.

"To the future."

CHAPTER 26

The compelling aroma of cinnamon bread, grilled salmon, crisp bacon, poached eggs, and ketchup coiled around Pamela as she indulged in her first meal of the day.

She hadn't eaten anything since dinner the evening before, and the charred toast in her grasp had never proved more appealing. She took a bite as though she hadn't enjoyed the comfort of food in years, feeling the silky warm butter melt on the roof of her mouth.

Despite her generous appetite, she had not been the one to suggest a mid-morning brunch at the Uptown Boston Diner—an old railway car swathed in sheets of steel with an interior clothed in modern Art Deco designs. Sean had insisted on dining before their appointment with Richard Morrison at the station. Apparently, one of the other beatniks in his writer's group had claimed the dive to be especially endearing. Besides, it was only a few blocks away from the station—which they had located prior to their arrival.

If it were up to Johnny and Pamela, they would've gone to the station without making any stops. The man watching them at the bus terminal had been enough to convince them that the mafia—or someone—was very aware of their whereabouts, and perhaps even what they were about to accomplish. But Sean had been adamant, declaring a long day ahead meant they needed food to fill their bellies.

Pamela glanced uneasily across the cherry-red padded booth at her older brother, who was enjoying his egg salad and tomato sandwich between snippets of light conversation with Johnny.

Johnny had his arm looped around her like it belonged there—warm around her shoulders.

Being with Johnny felt remarkable.

The pair had spent the entire bus ride engrossed in lively discussion—speaking on everything from childhood reminiscences to television to the civil rights movement.

It amazed Pamela how versatile Johnny was. He could carry a conversation with an extraordinary amount of ease and intelligence, despite his self-professed lack of schooling. He was charming and interesting. He never tired of things to say, and she never tired of hearing him. Unlike Timothy Atwell, he listened to her in earnest—asking her questions and seeming genuinely interested in her responses. Then again, she supposed as a *mafioso* he had gained an ability to converse with many people on many matters.

Pamela chafed at the reminder of her suitor's past.

She was certain he had changed, but the worn fear of him reverting to his old ways tore at her. She had to believe he was helping them testify to the authorities out of remorse for his wrongdoings and a desire for justice. But what if he hadn't nullified his former alliances with the mob? What if he was leading them straight into a world of danger? What if he was only playing along in some callous charade?

Pamela studied Johnny—her eyes tracing the curve of his lips, the slight slope of his aquiline nose, and the endearing roundness of his amber-brown eyes. She saw gentleness there that she hadn't perceived months ago. A softness which perhaps pulverized the cruelty that had killed Mr. Friedenberg.

Pamela took his hand, feeling the roughness of his skin as if to prove to herself he was real.

He sent her a reassuring smile, drawing her away from her unforgiving fears and back into the current.

Johnny and Sean were debating the film industry and whether the growing popularization of motion pictures and television would bring about the death of books. Sean was arguing in the affirmative, while Johnny claimed the two could coincide.

"You don't even read Johnny. How are you suited to provide an opinion on this topic?" Sean was saying.

"*I* don't read, but some people do. And everyone said books would stop being written when the talkies came out. But we're here, in 1955, and the libraries are as crowded as ever!" Johnny moved his hands as he spoke, finally placing them into Pamela's when he was finished.

"What do you think, Pam?" Sean pressed, wiping a streak of hollandaise sauce from the corner of his mouth.

"I think you're being fatalistic," Pamela told her brother, glad for the diversion, "of course, literature and cinema can coincide. The best motion pictures come after novels, after all. Think of *The Wizard of Oz*, *It's a Wonderful Life*, *The Maltese Falcon,* and *Grapes of Wrath*. All were novels before they went to the movies."

Johnny grinned at her, squeezing her hand gently. "See, Sean? She's the smartest girl on the East Coast. She'll do well in college."

Pamela's chest filled with warmth. It felt good to know that Johnny supported her dream of pursuing higher education.

"She only agrees with you 'cause she's your girl." Sean accused, though his tone was playful. "Anyway, this place is a real bore. All I see is cement for miles. And no people. Does anyone even live here?"

Indeed, Boston was a ghost town compared to the sweeping grandeur of New York. Ever since the trio had set foot at the station, a naked grey skyline had sprawled before them. There weren't as many skyscrapers as in New York. Pamela read in the papers that Boston's economy had stagnated in recent times, in part because of an abundance of companies moving southward—where production costs were cheaper and people worked for less.

Unlike Sean, Pamela didn't lament the lack of activity plaguing their present surroundings. She was far too preoccupied with their mission to care much for sightseeing. And the fewer people around, the less of a chance the mob would find out what they were up to—if they hadn't already.

"Don't be so cynical, Sean." Pamela chided. "It's peaceful here. And we'll be back in New York before the day is through."

"All I'm saying is I need some kind of inspiration to write my novel. How will I ever finish the manuscript when there's none to be had here?" Sean sighed, dropping his fork to his finished plate with a soft *clank*. "Hey, Siciliano! What are you looking at?"

Johnny's intense, dark gaze was trailing something outside.

When Pamela squinted through the fogged windowpane, her breath caught.

A figure was slinking through the parking lot with unsettling resolve. Though he was still quite a distance from them, they could see the man's face—unspectacular, yet disarmingly menacing.

"I *know* that guy." Johnny frowned, his voice low. "He was a soldier for one family in New York that Roberto had connections with."

Pamela gripped the table. "Does he see us? Does he know we're here?"

The answer to her question seemed obvious.

The man was looming closer, approaching the front door of the diner. He disappeared past the boxwood bush out front, being obscured by shrubbery.

"We're not gonna wait to find out." Johnny unfolded a crumpled bill from his pocket and nudged it onto the table—leaving more than enough money to cover the expenses of their luncheon.

Pamela heard the diner door swing open. A bell chimed above the clamor of the jukebox, the sound of frying eggs, and the chatter of the other customers.

"We need to get outta here."

Pamela climbed to her feet, her knees creaking with the sudden movement. Lunging forward, she almost tripped on a loose piece of carpeting, but Johnny caught her arm to keep her from dropping to the floor.

"Run." Johnny's voice was thick in her ears. "Don't look back. Just run."

A scream wailed through the diner, followed by gunshots—firing all around them. Shards of ceiling sprinkled down from above as if confetti.

Without looking back to see what was happening, Pamela sprinted after Sean through the backdoor of the diner, trying her best to block out the chaotic cacophony of noise hastening after them.

The cool slap of air from outside relieved her.

A splinter of sunshine banded across the skin of her arm, and the wind rippled through her skirt, creating little waves.

She wanted to cease running for a moment—to look back and make sure Johnny was still behind them, but she remembered his warning and kept her eyes trained to the unwinding concrete path before her. She thought of the story of Lot's wife in the Old Testament, a woman who had turned into a pillar of salt after looking back at the city she was fleeing from. Pamela had never understood the meaning of the story until that moment.

She ran close behind Sean as he cut through an alleyway, his coat billowing behind him like a tail as they threaded past a few parked automobiles and trash cans.

They continued their sprint until they reached the steps of the station.

Pamela thanked God Johnny had insisted on them mapping out their route to the station earlier that morning. Things could've gone differently if they hadn't known where they were headed.

Pamela stopped then, instinctively pressing her palms to her legs—her breath ragged in her lungs.

She looked back.

Johnny was behind her, his dark hair unruly and tousled with the wind. Runnels of sweat coated the sides of his head.

She had never felt so relieved to see anyone in her entire life. She wanted to throw her arms around his neck—tell him she was so glad to know he was unharmed.

Her eyes widened in terror, however, when she glimpsed a dark trickle of blood blooming through the fabric of his shirt—close to his collarbone.

"Johnny... you're... bleeding." She gasped.

She stepped forward to stop the blood with her hand. When she pried it away, crimson liquid stained her fingers.

He winced at the sight. "It's just a cut. I'll take care of it later. C'mon, we gotta get inside before they figure out where we've gone off to. It won't tell 'em long."

He took her bloodied hand, rushing to her side as they ascended the steps to the station.

A man dressed fashionably in a navy blue suit strode into the office of the station, where Pamela, Sean, and Johnny were sitting in comfortable armchairs beside a window veiled with velvet drapes.

The red-haired receptionist had welcomed them into the station with a curt Bostonian accent and appraising green eyes, leaving them in the four-corner room with a pitcher of ice water and an ashtray.

Johnny had rummaged for a cigarette in his waist pocket and drew it out to smoke. Pamela supposed he was seeking a way to manage the pain of the laceration.

The receptionist hadn't seemed to notice Johnny's wound, and he had said nothing either. Pamela was debating returning to reception and asking for medical care when the man entered the room. She knew Johnny was putting on a brave face, but the blood wasn't stopping. If Johnny didn't get help soon, he could fall ill. Or worse.

"Mrs. Parsons?" The well-dressed man hesitated at the threshold of the office, surveying the three of them with brown eyes. His gaze settled on Pamela, and he walked towards her, offering a polite smile with a faint twist of his lips.

Pamela allowed a few seconds to pass before she answered. She wasn't as trusting as she had been the first time she met with Sergeant Marino and no wonder. "Actually, sir, there is no Mrs. Parsons."

Confusion gathered in the handsome man's features, revealing worried lines on his forehead. "Oh? Then did you three write this letter together?"

He held up a thin slip of paper, and Pamela recognized the fine black letters left by her brother's Remington Rand typewriter.

"Actually, my elder brother, Sean Kelly and I, penned the message under a pseudonym," Pamela explained, her thoughts whirling back to Johnny's wound. She needed to get him help. "I'm Pamela Kelly."

The officer nodded, understanding. "And I'm Richard Morrison."

Then he stared at Johnny, his confusion deepening in his brow.

"Johnny Siciliano," Johnny said, gritting his teeth to persist through the pain. "I'm here to testify with Pamela."

Richard's eyes widened.

Surely, he had heard the name of the youngest capo in Brooklyn and was bewildered by his unexpected presence.

Before Richard could comment on his unexpected witness, a petite raven-haired woman appeared behind Richard Morrison, her hands tied in nervousness at her chest.

She possessed a stunning type of beauty—especially owing to the pair of piercing blue eyes encompassed by bronzed skin. Her mouth was full and her face gorgeous, with no makeup. She reminded Pamela of one of the mythical Greek deities she had studied in her classics courses at school. A willful Atalante or cunning Aphrodite.

A bottomless well of sadness lurked within the woman's sharp gaze and Pamela wondered what had pained her so. She looked like the type of person who had endured a lifetime of suffering, despite her apparent young age.

At Pamela's side, Johnny stumbled up from his chair, dipping his cigarette into the ashtray. "Carlotta?"

"Johnny!" Carlotta dashed forward, her slight frame collapsing in Johnny's arms.

The two clung to each other in a fraternal embrace until Johnny released her, resting a brotherly hand on her shoulder. Pamela wondered if the two were related, and if not, who the woman was. Why was she here at the station with Richard Morrison?

"You heard 'bout Tony," Carlotta stated rather than asked, her voice verging on tears.

"Yeah," Johnny muttered, his brown eyes downcast, "I'm real sorry, Carlotta. I didn't know Don Roberto—your padre, was gonna do it. Otherwise, I woulda stopped him."

Upon learning Carlotta was Don Roberto Mancini's daughter, Pamela felt a tremor of shock jolt through her. Connecting strands of information, Pamela realized that the woman standing before them had been terribly wronged by the mafia. By her own father, perhaps.

Carlotta nodded. "He was your best friend. I know you wouldn't have wished him dead."

"I'm just glad you're here, alive. I thought Roberto woulda kept you locked up or somethin'."

"Yeah, I'm here, thank God." Recalling the others in the room, Carlotta swept around to study the rest of them. Her pale eyes landed on Pamela. "Who are you?"

"Pamela Kelly." Pamela felt disoriented. Carlotta was looking at her acrimoniously—as if they were mortal enemies.

"You one of Lorenzo's women?" Carlotta demanded, pinning her hands to her hips.

"No! Of course not!" Pamela exclaimed, shocked that Carlotta would suspect her of such a thing. Then again, the two didn't know one another, and it was understandable that Carlotta would jump to conclusions.

"Then why are you here?" Carlotta's dark brows gathered and she jutted her chin forward.

Johnny fell back to stand at Pamela's side, encircling her back with his arm. "Pamela is one of the bravest people I know. She worked at Albright Trimmings & co. as a salesgirl and wants justice. She never agreed with anything we did."

Carlotta considered this, her apprehension diminishing, though only marginally. "Well, what I don't understand is why you're helping us when you could just go back to your own life."

Pamela knew her next words would be irrevocable. She had wondered the same thing many times—why she hadn't deserted her desire for justice when Sergeant Marino had warned her to do so. She could've returned to a normal life and forgotten about her time as a sales assistant on Fifth Avenue forever. But somehow, she just couldn't. "I believe one's duty is to speak upon witnessing wrongdoing or evil. I can't ignore what I saw. My conscience won't allow it."

Near silence filled the office. The only noise present was the quiet ticking of a clock on an adjacent wall.

A smile curved Carlotta's lips upwards, brightening her otherwise somber expression. "Okay. We're gonna do this all together, then."

"Mr. Siciliano, I am eager to hear your testimony. And yours as well, Miss Kelly. But I think what we must do first is take care of that gun wound." Richard Morrison gestured to Johnny's injury.

CHAPTER 27

Carlotta vomited into the hospital bathroom toilet bowl.

As another debilitating wave of nausea surged through her, she clutched the base of the pearly white basin—willing herself not to throw up again. When she was sure the spell had passed, she wiped her mouth with a crumpled wad of tissue paper and then rinsed her mouth with tepid water from the sink. She hoped the unappealing taste of bile would dissipate in a few moments.

Leaning her elbows up against the metallic sink, she stared into the mirror.

Her face was slack with exhaustion, and her red-rimmed eyes hooded from a perverse lack of sleep. She wanted to convince herself that the nausea resulted from the past week and a half tending to Johnny at the hospital with Richard and Pamela, but she had been sick for far longer.

Carlotta smothered a disconcerted groan.

She didn't have time to be sick.

Richard had promised them that the case was almost closed—that with her help, Roberto Mancini and his cronies were going to be served as retribution for Tony's untimely death. There was already talk of bringing Roberto's case to federal court, and if they did, they would set a precedent for the rest of the mafia families in America. They only needed to wait until Johnny's gun wound healed to collect his testimony, as they had with Carlotta's and Pamela's.

As the doctors explained—Johnny would be free of his hospital bed and bandages in no time. Miraculously, he had lost little blood, and plenty of rest had contributed to a fairly swift and easy recovery.

The salesgirl from Albright Trimmings Pamela Kelly, had also surprised Carlotta. At first, the girl had appeared to be shy and unaware of the evils of the world, perhaps even slightly pretentious in the way she spoke and her Upper East Side upbringing. However, she wasn't the wide-eyed dolly she appeared to be. She spent hours keeping vigil by Johnny's bedside, reading Psalms from the Bible to him and praying with him. She was fiercer than she appeared.

To Carlotta's immense despair, another barrage of sickness crested in her throat, sending her back to the cold tile ground.

Simmering in severe discomfort, the realization arose in her consciousness as clear as a polished pane of glass.

Instinctively, she dropped her hand to her bodice. She hadn't observed her monthly cycle for at least as long as Tony had been gone. She had been tired and grumpier than usual—though she had attributed those feelings to her mourning.

As she connected the dots, Carlotta stared down at her stomach.

She was *pregnant.*

Carlotta's initial reaction was one of joy. She had always wanted to be a mother. As the oldest child in the family, she had adored fawning over her baby brothers and sprinkling their chubby cheeks with kisses. Even before Louis was born, one of her earliest memories included swaddling her porcelain and cloth dolls in hand-sewn dresses and accessories—admiring their miniature fingers and delicate toes as she lined them up on her windowsill for pantomime wedding processions.

But a baby was not a doll. A baby came with an entire host of responsibilities and duties—ones she had always assumed she would render with a loyal husband at her side.

Without Tony, how would she ever manage? She had no education to speak of, no remaining relatives who would help her, no funds, no home. She would be more vulnerable with a baby. When the mob caught wind of her pregnancy, they might kidnap the child or do far worse.

Lord, why are you doing this to me? First Tony dies, now I have to worry about a baby? Carlotta stayed her hand to her belly, almost imagining some responsive movement.

There was nothing.

She needed to tell Richard. He was the only person in the world who would listen to her concerns—even if he only did so out of professional responsibility.

Climbing unsteadily to her feet, Carlotta rearranged the checkered hem of her skirt and took another drink of water from the tap, cringing at the still-astringent taste of vomit cleaving to her tongue.

Going in search of Richard, she rushed out of the hospital bathroom and down the hallway, threading through groups of pinafore-clad candy stripers, stretchers, and pensive physicians.

She nearly collided with a medical student, who assailed her with a reprimanding scowl, when Carlotta uttered her apologies.

To her relief, she located Richard outside of Johnny's hospital room, his dark eyes skating across the paper in his hand—his tall frame bent like a river reed against the powder blue wall.

As if sensing her presence, he lifted his gaze. "Mrs. Bellucci! I was worrying you had run off again. I have something of the utmost urgency to tell you."

He closed the paper, opening his mouth to relay his news. But Carlotta spoke first—trying her best to assume a tone to match the formality typical in all of his exchanges with her. "I gotta tell you somethin' first, Mr. Morrison. I'm expecting... I mean, I'm having a baby."

Richard hung his head in embarrassment.

It wasn't seen as proper to explicitly discuss one's condition in public, and especially not in the presence of a male audience. Even making the slightest mention of pregnancy was a social taboo. Carlotta's own mother had gone to great lengths in masking her maternal progress—so much that when the babies arrived, Carlotta was convinced the stork had ferried them into the Mancini household. A scandal erupted when Lucille Ball had made her pregnancy common knowledge on her popular television show.

"That's wonderful news." Richard dropped his eyes, awkwardly withdrawing his smudged spectacles from the bridge of his nose to clean them with a handkerchief.

Despite the serious situation, Carlotta concealed a giggle with the back of her hand. For a man who had survived the deadliest war in human history and seen the liberation of Europe, he sure was unusually sheepish.

"What's so funny?" Richard asked, genuinely confused.

"The way you look... it's as if I told you I got the plague or somethin'." Carlotta laughed, the noise sounding good in her ears.

Richard chuckled, allowing the seriousness of the matter to be forgotten for a moment.

The vile taste in her mouth reminded Carlotta of her request. "But Richard—Mr. Morrison, I mean, I don't know what to do. I don't have money or anything. How am I supposed to be a mother when my husband is gone, and my family won't ever speak to me again? Where will I live?"

Richard gently extended a hand to her shoulder, undefiled kindness brimming in his smooth brown eyes. He truly was the most unusual man Carlotta had ever known. "You mustn't fret over those things. After all this is over, I'll find you and the baby a home far away from here with enough money to take care of all your expenses. I'll see that your child grows up in comfort."

Carlotta threw her arms around Richard in a spontaneous embrace, eliciting disapproving looks from two white police officers guarding Johnny's hospital room. They had been positioned there throughout the entirety of Johnny's treatment—placating the unspoken fear that whoever had tried to kill him might do it again.

Feeling the rigid back of Richard's neck and inhaling the musk of his cologne, Carlotta remembered herself and moved away. "I'm sorry. I guess I'm just glad you're my agent instead of someone else. You're the nicest fella I've ever known, Mr. Morrison."

"Thanks for the compliment, Mrs. Bellucci, but there's really no need for it. I'm just doing my job."

"But you didn't have to help me. I'm glad God brought you into my life, Richard." When Carlotta saw the embarrassment still raging across Richard's face, she wondered if she had been wrong to use his first name so casually.

Carlotta had never seen him so frazzled. Throughout the duration of their acquaintance, he had been composed and dignified. To think that a simple kind word could unravel him was awfully surprising.

It was almost as if he was sweet on her.

"You had somethin' to tell me?" She asked, steering their conversation into safer territory and banishing the discomfort between them.

"Oh yes," Richard practically exclaimed, brandishing the folded piece of paper. "I've just received news that your father has gone to Sicily. Rather than staying to face allegations of racketeering in court, he left the country the first chance he got. He knew he was done for, with a trio of viable testimonies."

Gone to Sicily? The words swam in Carlotta's head—eliciting a pounding headache at her temple.

She would not have to witness in court or see her father again, as she had so feared. But the news provided her with little closure. She had expected to watch the once-esteemed Don Roberto Mancini sent to prison for all the lives he had so mercilessly claimed. In a strange way, she had *wanted* to see him again—and have him apologize for his wrongdoing.

"What about all that stuff you said?" Carlotta demanded, trying to curtail her confusion, "About bringing about the end of the mob in all of America? How will anyone stop their crimes when we just let my father get away?"

"That's the magic of it." Richard tucked the paper into his pocket and wrapped an arm around her shoulders. "You've done more than we could've ever done at court. If we had sent your father to jail, he would've gotten a short sentence. Between you and me, there are many flaws in the system, and wealthy men rarely pay their due. But you scared the powerful Don Roberto Mancini away, Carlotta. You and a salesgirl. Your testimonies were enough to show the American mafia that their crimes *can't* go unnoticed. *Won't* go unnoticed."

The passion in Richard's voice increased with every word until Carlotta felt as though she were listening to the speech of a persuasive politician or preacher via radio.

"You truly think we've done our jobs?" Carlotta faltered, gazing up into his glistening eyes.

"I know you've done your jobs." Richard grinned.

Tears obstructed Carlotta's vision. She thought of Tony and what he would want her to do next. Surely, he would've wanted her to leave the mob behind for good, and he'd be proud that she was giving their child a virtuous life free of crime, deceit, and murder.

Wiping her tears away with her sleeve, she whispered a silent prayer of thanks for safety and renewal. It might be years before the monster called *La Cosa Nostra* was finally eradicated, but she had done her part.

"Are you alright?" Richard asked, concern weaved into his voice.

"I'm okay." Carlotta decided, offering him a hesitant but hopeful smile.

And she would be.

There was a garden in the Boston Hospital.

It skirted along the maternity ward and ended next to the ward Johnny had been recovering in for most of his stay. Nurses and nuns tended to the pretty fuchsia rhododendrons and yellow daisies in between caring for their patients, and some wildflowers bloomed between patches of concrete despite the often gray and forlorn Boston skies.

The perfume of spring foliage and pungent flowers wafted on the breeze, wrapping all the hospital guests in a pleasant aroma. Since spring had just begun, there was still much work to be done, and many of the plants were only just blooming.

Pamela supposed the natural sanctuary provided solace and beauty amid terrible suffering. Though Johnny's wound wasn't particularly life-threatening, he asked Pamela and Sean to accompany him there from time to time to get some fresh air.

They often saw other hospital patrons and their families and friends visiting on the benches and marble outdoor tables scattered throughout the vicinity, or a physician taking his work break outside with a cigarette or newspaper in hand. Johnny had passed the time talking with elderly patients and listening enthralled to their stories of the Great War and long ago times. He complimented the elderly nuns on their garden work, making them blush with pride.

On his very last day at the hospital—after Richard had informed them of Roberto's sudden departure to Sicily, Johnny asked if he could take one last walk in the garden with Pamela. Alone. He urged Sean to remain behind—which struck Pamela as peculiar. Johnny enjoyed her brother's company, finding amusement in his candor and eccentric sense of humor.

Regardless, Pamela was glad for the diversion and happy to gain some time alone with the man she adored. She was wondering what would become of her and Johnny when they left the hospital and returned to New York.

Would they continue to act as a courting couple, or would the loss of their shared experience signal the end of them? Would he forget his profession of love and become smitten with someone else when he no longer needed her to care for him?

She often worried about these things in the thick of night, terrified that her beloved would grow tired of her or forget his passion once he had captured her heart. She had heard many men were like that—only desiring a woman until she returned his feelings.

Looping her arm through Johnny's strong one, Pamela tried to ignore her worries about the future.

The sun was flooding through the vines that climbed the glass roof above them—creating mishap shapes and patterns on their faces and arms.

A powdery sprinkling of fallen petals and leaves paved the walkway before them.

Johnny found a blue flower that had drifted from its tree branch to the ground and pinned it to Pamela's blouse like a tiny corsage.

"It matches your eyes." He teased, pecking her on the cheek with his lips.

"Really?" Pamela teased, resting her head on his arm—careful to avoid the sensitive spot on his shoulder left by the bullet. "I don't think my eyes are that color. All these hospital procedures must have altered your eyesight."

The man who had shot Johnny had not been caught, and the worry that someone might try something again had not vanished with Roberto. There would still be an abundance of mobsters who wanted to enact justice for a crime they saw as punishable by death. Johnny was now a rat and a menace to every vengeful *mafioso.*

"Do you think things will change when we go back to New York?" Johnny questioned, his voice warbling. Clearly Pamela hadn't been the only one pondering the future.

"I think nothing will ever be the same after all of this," Pamela admitted. "I... don't think my feelings will change as easily, though."

She felt a pang of hurt when he didn't respond to her admission, instead guiding her forward into the sanctuary of some flowers and plants. They found a bench shaded by a generous lilac shrub. The sweet aroma of lilacs soothed Pamela somewhat, and she assisted Johnny in sitting comfortably on the wooden structure beside her.

"I have somethin' to tell you," Johnny admitted quietly, as though it was a secret.

Pamela felt her former worries thunder in her head again, but she turned to Johnny with a solemn expression. She knew he had the ability to break her heart with a single sentence if he wanted to, so she steeled herself for the worst. "Tell me then."

"I wanted to know..." Johnny cleared his throat, angling his frame towards her and clasping her hands in his, "If you'd like to marry me."

Pamela stared at him, registering his words carefully. Her heart was as light as a feather. All of her previous fears about what he might say, or do, faded as joy rose within her. She had never imagined her life would be like this—with a man who loved her and wanted to love her for the rest of their lives.

"Do you really want to marry me?" She breathed, tracing his cheek with her palm. "We come from such different worlds... and I'm not the same as the girls you've gone with before. Do you truly love me?"

His eyes were wide and earnest, and his fingers trembled within her grip. "I love you, Pamela. You know that. You showed me the difference between right and wrong, and now, you've stayed by my side through the worst. You've made me feel somethin' I've never felt for anyone else."

Pamela studied the distinct contours of his face as the sunlight filtered through the lilac bush and noticed the simple vulnerability of his proclamation. His words were the stuff of romance novels and motion pictures, though not as refined. But she loved him for his frankness.

Again, she felt as though she was in a dream.

"I understand if you have to say no," Johnny said nervously, trepidation cloaking his handsome face. "After all I've done, all I've put you through, I'll understand if you don't want to be my wife. But, I'll love no one else but you."

Ridding him of his agony, Pamela answered by kissing him, then closing her arms around his chest. "Yes, of course, I'll marry you. I love you too, and I forgive you, Johnny Siciliano. There is no man in the world who could make me happier."

He brought her lips to his, stroking her hair with one hand and squeezing her arm with the other like he didn't want to ever let her go. When he released her for air, she noticed tears streaking his face, his deep brown eyes full of innocent love and wonder.

She kissed him again, drawing his head closer to hers. They both laughed, but they didn't know why. At that moment, they promised to love one another for the rest of their lives, knowing whatever they faced couldn't be overcome with faith in God and one another and the thick resilience they had developed during their most trying times together.

Pamela Kelly would become Mrs. Siciliano after all.

CHAPTER 28

Taormina, Sicily, March 1960:

The Sicilian sun shimmered down on the little town of Taormina, bathing the fertile hills in a brilliant morning light. Beneath the blunted mountain ridges and gushing rivers was the turquoise Ionian Sea, heralding in the swift winds of Greece and ancient Byzantine. The humid air was saturated with the scent of lavender. It tasted of fresh citrus.

Four men stole up the side of the mountain, traveling past a stone-walled villa and a battered cathedral. They were not conspicuous as dozens of adventurers and leisure seekers found their way up the unpaved hills of Taormina at that time of year when many unique flowers and songbirds made their long-awaited annual debuts. Others came to watch the vast green-blue ocean as it crashed splendidly against the cliffs below or swim in the cool brooks for refreshment after a hot day.

One of the male travelers, dark-haired and with skin the shade of espresso, paused at the side of an ancient clay-roofed cottage and approached the door.

Before he could knock, however, an elderly woman as old as the mountains behind her appeared from the back garden, hitching up her heavy black skirts as she waded through a flock of rambunctious poultry. She looked as though she was part of the scenery; her furrowed cheeks and archaic dress matched the old age of the building behind her.

"*Buongiorno*," she greeted above the cluck of hens, staying wisps of hair to her disheveled silver braid. "*Posso aiutarla?*"

The dark-haired man replied in fluent Italian, the intonation of his voice rising and then falling again as he asked her a question.

The woman pointed towards the long dirt road, talking rapidly and eyeing the three other men as they hung back. It was not uncommon for mafia men to export their crimes to the mountains, where local authorities rarely dared to venture. Blood feuds between neighboring gangs meant that bombs sometimes erupted in the forlorn mountain villages, and stray bullets often skated through the otherwise quiet air.

The other men smiled with a sheepishness that suggested they could not speak Italian as proficiently as their peer. From the canvas bags slung across their backs and their modern American clothes, the men were in fact tourists and the dark-haired man their guide.

The woman's shoulders slumped as she breathed a sigh of relief.

"*Grazie*," the Italian gestured for the three Americans to follow, and they did so—coasting down the uneven path through a pear-green thicket of trees, towards the endless blue of the sea.

"She said we've got less than half a mile to go." The guide informed them as their knee-length striped shorts and cabana shirts snagged brambles. "Shouldn't take too long."

They continued their journey for minutes more, sharing a flask of sun-warmed water as they jogged downhill. When they came upon a clearing, the Italian stopped in his tracks, holding up a hand. "There it is. By the waterfront."

The three Americans strained their eyes against the glare of the sun. Before them was a castle, sprouting up amidst a canopy of lush greenery—positioned conveniently like a lighthouse atop a bouldered plateau. The water lapped softly against the rocks, carrying an empty wooden fishing boat kept close by a rope.

The men quickened their pace.

Finally, the front door came into view.

From up close, the castle was unkempt. Vines crawled up the stone walls and strangled the unmanned tower. An armed Italian villager was stationed by the entrance, his gaze sweeping lazily across the turquoise waves ahead. Sleep was heavy around his eyes, and from the emptied red wine bottle at his feet—it became apparent the man had been drinking on the job.

With unexpected skill, the Americans and their Italian guide descended upon the villager like wild dogs, ridding him of his weapon and his consciousness as he slumped to the ground.

The troop entered the great hall of the castle with ease, separating at the stairwell and creeping up to the opposite corridors of the second floor in a practiced fashion. Swarming through the area, the men took out two more soldiers as they went—able to dispose of them with the element of surprise on their side.

The Italian was the first to locate their target.

He was napping on the balcony off of the main chamber, the acrid smoke from his half-finished cigarette intermingling with the fresh mountain air. Moving over in his sleep, his watery blue eyes fluttered open at the sound of footsteps. "Isabella? *Che fai*?"

"*Buongiorno,* Roberto. You have a pleasant sleep?"

Roberto Mancini bolted awake.

His fleshy arm slammed against the ashtray beside him, combining with his swearing to form a loud cacophony of noise.

Heaving himself onto his feet, he fished around his pocket for a gun. But it was too late.

The Italian stuck the barrel of his gun into Roberto's pudgy chest, cornering him onto the balcony railing.

"Louis! Isabella!" Roberto yelled, his spittle assaulting the Italian's cheek.

"Forget about them." The Italian sneered. "You have more important things to worry about."

Roberto refused to give into the man's grasp, his muscles tensing and veins bulging through his skin. "Get your filthy hands off of me."

But the Italian wouldn't give up either. "You are under arrest, Roberto Mancini. As a suspect of the murder of Tony Bellucci and a ringleader in domestic crime, we are summoning you back to the United States to await your trial."

Sacramento, California, 1960:

"*My* oh *my*, that little one of yours is getting *so* big!" Mrs. Crawford shrieked in a sing-song voice, tucking her fingers underneath two-year-old Theresa's chubby chin.

Theresa was far from a docile toddler and squirmed away, preferring the company of her raggedy Ann to the affectionate old woman.

By then, it was practically a weekly tradition for the elderly Mrs. Crawford to stop Pamela and her daughter Theresa in the aisles of the Sacramento market between the jars of pickles and the tins of coffee. There, they would spend a few minutes chatting, with Mrs. Crawford often insisting on buying a piece of licorice or bag of old-fashioned hard candies for the little girl, and Pamela politely declining.

Mrs. Crawford was a widow, and never having had children of her own meant she enjoyed spoiling Theresa and the other little ones she knew. She was known around town for her cheerful demeanor and conspicuous fox-fur scarves, which she frequently wore to the distaste of members of the Sacramento Animal Rights Group.

"She certainly is," Pamela smiled, lifting up Theresa to place her back in her stroller, "I'm afraid I'll have to buy her new clothes each week if she keeps growing so quickly."

"And that frock must be new. I daresay I've never seen it before." Mrs. Crawford lowered her eyes to admire the little red-and-yellow plaid dress.

"My friend Lorna sent it in the mail last week as a present. She sewed it herself." Pamela smoothed down Theresa's chestnut brown hair with her palm, aware that her own gingham dress was missing a button and wearing thin around the knees, her Mary Janes varnished with dust.

She and her husband had little money to spend, with him having just recently finished his training to become a detective and her completing her college courses to be a legal assistant.

Lorna's recent hobby of sewing clothes for Theresa helped ease some of the financial stress they had been under. Without Lorna's help, Pamela suspected that Theresa's clothes would be as tattered as her own.

"How lovely," Mrs. Crawford cooed, cradling her paper grocery bag to her chest, canned peas and a carton of eggs spilling over the top. "I hope you and your dear husband have more children. Do you think you will soon? How wonderful that would be, a new baby!"

Pamela wondered if she had noticed the growing bump beneath her bodice. She had only recently told her husband she was expecting, and she wasn't planning on telling anyone else before she wrote to Lorna and her brother Sean.

She also needed to tell Gladys, who had just started a fancy new job as a scientist at a laboratory in Washington, and Caterina, who had married a good man and was working at a department store.

Pamela sensed a blush warm her cheeks, offering another smile in place of a response. Mrs. Crawford was a dear old lady, but she could also be quite the busybody.

The two women parted ways, and Pamela finished gathering garlic cloves, tomatoes, olives, cheese, and pasta for dinner. Paying and then bidding the store manager a good day, Pamela wheeled Theresa's stroller out the door.

When the thick August air wrapped around them, Pamela thought of the beach just a few miles southward, where her husband had taken her swimming once—long before Theresa's arrival. It had felt something like inhabiting a picturesque postcard or idyllic magazine—the turquoise waves towing them out to meet the orange-red horizon.

He had lifted her above the water, his muscular arms wrapping around her bathing costume-appareled frame. They had spent hours kissing beneath their little beach umbrella until the sun turned from yellow into a shade of tangerine.

Perhaps they could venture there tomorrow and dress Theresa in that little swimming costume Lorna had sent the month prior.

"A trip to the beach, Theresa, wouldn't that be sublime?" Pamela cooed to the toddler, who stared blankly at her in return.

She hadn't taken more than a few paces to the parking lot before colliding with someone.

"Oh!" Pamela cried, pulling herself away from the solid figure.

"Papà!" Theresa bounded out of her stroller and stumbled into the man's arms, squealing as he spun her around midair.

Johnny Siciliano, Pamela's husband of five years, gave his daughter a mirthful look when he set her back down into her stroller.

Instead of his usual work clothes, he was dressed in a blue camp shirt and jeans that complimented his tanned skin, and his dark hair was combed back to curl around his ears. His dark eyes creased in worry when he said *hello*.

Pamela felt a twinge of foreboding in her stomach. She had grown used to all of Johnny's expressions and habits. After several years of marriage, she had learned to sense his pain and fear like expert fishermen predicting an oncoming storm.

Something was wrong.

She ran her hand along his arm, feeling the taut muscles beneath his shirt. "What happened Johnny? Why aren't you still at work?"

"I asked to take the rest of the day off." Johnny kissed her with a strength that made her knees weak. She inhaled the familiar cologne and chewing gum and shaving cream lingering around his collar as he placed her grocery bag in the crook of his shivering arm. "I needa tell you somethin'."

"Papà, again!" Theresa hiccupped, throwing her arms up and trying to wiggle out of her seat.

"Not now, Theresa," Johnny said, his voice assuming a stern tone that was not usual for him. Usually, Pamela was a strict parent. She was always scolding Johnny for indulging in little Theresa's every extravagant whim. "Roberto is back from Italy, Pamela."

"*What*?" Pamela's breath caught. The warm summer air no longer seemed so comforting.

"Not here," Johnny whispered. He circled a protective arm around the small of her back, guiding her to their automobile at the end of the parking lot.

A pair of teenyboppers in floral bell bottoms and matching bright pink tank tops raced past them into the bowling alley, giggles resounding in their wake. A fast-food employee exited the glass doors of the McDonald's to take his lunch break outside, slumping against the concrete wall and sinking his teeth into a cheeseburger. An elderly man with a cane tipped his hat to them in passing.

Johnny's frown made Pamela think he suspected every one of them. *No wonder.*

Leaving the mob had been the hardest thing he'd ever done. In their first year of marriage, someone had sent a burnt effigy to their door—the inscription *rat* etched below it like words on a tombstone. A poster of the infamous "Black Hand" had appeared in the mail the next month. That was why they had moved from New York, hoping the Golden Coast might live up to its name.

Despite that, Johnny slept with his gun underneath his pillow. Sometimes, he didn't sleep at all—choosing to keep vigil by the front door with the television at full blast, drinking cup after cup of coffee until he shook. He confessed he had nightmares about Roberto returning to avenge him. The only things that kept him sane, he said, were his faith and his family.

Johnny's terse silence didn't subside until they were inside the car, with Theresa confined to her car seat.

She adjusted her lips into a pout, sensing the tenseness accumulating between her beloved parents.

"He's back," Johnny whispered, even though no one could hear him through the sturdy walls of the automobile. "The cops got him. They're bringing him into federal court."

The news was much better than Pamela had been expecting. "That's good, isn't it?"

Johnny's dark eyes glowed black with terror. "It means it isn't over yet, Pamela. They want *us* to be witnesses. And that gives them all the more reason to kill us."

CHAPTER 29

Bryson City, North Carolina, late August 1960:

“Mamma! Look at me!"

Tony Bellucci Junior raced across the dock, raising his spindly arms above his head as he propelled himself from the perilous edge. He bent his knees into his small belly, then slammed into the water with an impressive force for such a tiny frame—a miniature current peppered by beads of foam cresting in his wake.

Sunbeams made his raven black hair appear almost indigo, and a cluster of freckles fanned across his wide smile like a miniature constellation of stars. He was smaller than the other boys of his age, but that had never stopped him from his habit of risk-taking.

As had become common in most of her experiences with raising the daring little boy, Carlotta Bellucci felt her breath hitch in her throat. Striding forward, she shielded her face with her folded magazine to see through the blinding columns of sunlight filtering through the thicket of trees behind her.

She bit her rose-coloured lip, wishing she had worn her bathing suit in order to accompany Tony into the lake rather than leaving him on his own. But then, she wouldn't hesitate for a second if she needed to wade in after him. "Tony? You okay?"

She breathed a sigh of relief as he bobbed back up to the surface, gasping for air. "Yeah, Mamma! Come swim with us!"

"Not now, *amore mio.*" Carlotta called back to him, her voice practically inaudible against the deafening roar of a motorboat gearing up to start and the other children's giggles.

She stood still for a moment, watching her five-year-old son as he dug up a perfectly formed eggshell white pebble, throwing it as far as he could across the surface of the lake. His eyes reflected the sapphire of the lake, and clumps of dirt clung to his black hair, the groove in the side of his tanned cheek showing off a dimple.

Except for the eyes, he looked just like his namesake.

A burst of sadness swelled in Carlotta's chest, and she blinked away the tears that had pooled within her gaze—reflecting the vast body of water before her.

How was it possible for one person to fill another with so much joy and so much sorrow at the same time? She would never guilt her son for what had happened to his father. It wasn't his fault. It never had been. But she had to admit that his image made her sad sometimes, as it reminded her of everything that had happened. Everything that had been lost.

It hurt even more to know that her son would never meet his father, but she soothed herself with the consolation that one day, they would all be together again.

Tony's cheerful voice echoed and bounced across the waves as he tossed a colorful beach ball up into the air.

Carlotta waved to him, her happiness returning once more in a torrent of pride. It was supposed to be a peaceful day after all, *not* a sad one. She would do her best to enjoy it and not dwell on the past.

She shook out the sand from her sundress, squinting up into the sky.

A mourning dove drifted with the wind above, swooping down to rest upon a gnarled tree branch, its pewter-gray eyes inspecting Carlotta with mild curiosity.

When she had first moved to North Carolina, she had been slightly unnerved by the naked skyline. She had grown up in a concrete jungle, after all. However, she had also grown to adore the way the North Carolinian horizon sprawled uninterrupted by skyscrapers or concrete apartment buildings—the way pine and honeydew perfumed the mountain air and rivers babbled to one another like old friends in the early mornings. She was glad Tony knew such a tranquil place to grow up in, and was determined his childhood would be far better than hers.

Here, he would be safe. He would have a good life. Unaware of death and violence and deceit. Untouched by the memories that lingered like an unpleasant cologne.

"Carlotta dear! Want some lemonade?" Donna Beaumont, Carlotta's friend, chirped, her hazel eyes flashing gold in the sun.

"Yes, come join us." Yvonne Williams, another of Carlotta's friends, coaxed from the shade of the forest's edge.

Donna and Yvonne were good friends, despite them not knowing much of Carlotta's true history. They had been told that she had moved to Bryson City on a whim after her husband had perished from some undiagnosed ailment. They also knew that she was originally a New Yorker with Italian roots.

Even if Carlotta had wanted to tell them the truth, she wouldn't have been able to. Upon sending her into the world with some funds, Richard had made her swear she would never disclose her past to *anyone,* no matter how close they became.

For that reason, Carlotta had determined to imitate the local accent, keep her head down, and attract as little notice as possible. Even the way she dressed had changed drastically. She rarely wore lipstick and draped herself in plain gowns, shawls, and work clothes rather than the bold, fashionable outfits she had once fancied. She had become an entirely new woman.

Sure, it was difficult to blend in when most of Bryson City had never met an Italian girl from Brooklyn before. Carlotta's unusual appearance didn't help matters. Most of the folks around Bryson City were husky rednecks. Fortunately, though, most inhabitants of the township were too polite—or else too stunned, to remark on anything they found unusual. Veiled whispers and darting eyes were the most they dared to show.

As Carlotta sauntered over to her companions and slumped into a striped beach chair, Donna poured her a glass of sweet tea from a yellow Tupperware juice jug.

"How's work been for you ladies?" Donna asked as she took a sip of her own tea.

Out of the three women, Donna was decidedly the wealthiest, although that hadn't stopped her from befriending the two others. Her husband was the owner of a steel company nearby, and they lived with their two little girls in a large Victorian-era mansion at the edge of town. Her blonde hair was perpetually bobbed and curled, and she dressed like a governor's wife. Often, she claimed *her* Ron would have become some kind of statesman or bureaucrat, as her own father had been.

Yvonne was the wife of a salesman. She and Carlotta had met while working together at an office downtown. She was the mother of a boy about Tony's age and possessed an enviably small waist as well as captivating brown eyes.

As one of the few Black women in town, Yvonne had experienced her share of spiteful comments and prying eyes. When she met Carlotta, they had bonded over their struggle of feeling like outsiders in the place they lived and worked—even though Carlotta had been far more fortunate in her encounters with the townsfolk.

"It's been a real whirlwind." Yvonne sighed, fanning out her navy blue shift dress so that it fell evenly about her dark calves.

"It's been crazy. But it's nice to get a break, even just for a day." Carlotta took a sip of her sweet tea, her gaze still fastened to the lake. She never enjoyed taking her eyes off Tony. Even watching him from a distance felt painfully irresponsible.

"Carlotta, do you *want* your son to grow up with an overprotective mother?" Donna chided. "Give the kid a break, for crying out loud! Have some fun, you deserve to enjoy your one day off!"

Carlotta forced a laugh. Being a single mother was something she didn't expect Donna to understand. "He's still little. I gotta keep an eye on him."

"Maybe if you had a husband..." Donna winked mischievously, leaning close to elbow Carlotta in the gut.

"Donna!" Carlotta laughed, genuinely this time. She had thought little about men since leaving New York five years ago. The one man to whom she had found herself drawn had never pursued her in return. Though she knew it wasn't seen as respectable for a woman to raise a child on her own, she had managed for the past five years. Besides, she worried she wouldn't have as much time for Tony if she started seeing someone.

"How about Wayne Howard? People say he's got an eye on you." Yvonne smiled, flipping her ebony-black hair over one shoulder. "He makes a good living too, fixing people's toilets and such."

"Yvonne! Really!" Carlotta thought of the city's resident plumber, his tawny mullet and coral leisure suit branded in her mind.

Wayne Howard was the most outrageous flirt she had ever known. Since the day she had met him in town on an errand at the local supermarket, he had done nothing but chatted about her accent and his love for Italian cuisine. He had asked her out for dinner at the one pleasant restaurant in town several times, but every time she had declined—hoping her refusal would finally quash his relentless pursuit.

"You know we have nothing in common." Carlotta's eyes wandered back to Tony, who had just ambled out of the lake and onto the shore, making his way across the glistening sand toward them. She stood to get his towel ready, not caring much if Donna teased her again for being too doting. "Besides, I know what happens isn't in my hands. If there's a man the Lord wants for me, He'll bring him to me. Otherwise, I'm happy with my Tony."

The next day, after Donna had driven over to pick up Tony, Carlotta readied herself for work.

Two separate outfits were draped across her floral bedspread: a navy blue shift with a drop waist and white cuffs and clear tights, and a lavender contoured sheath dress that ended at the knees.

Opting for the more conservative navy blue shift, Carlotta slipped it on, then tied a matching ribbon around her flipped bob hair. She glimpsed herself in the mirror as she gathered her handbag, and noted the slight bend in her shoulders, the nearly invisible lines etched into her forehead, and the wintry sheen reflected in her cornflower blue eyes. If she tried hard enough, she could almost erase the image of the wide-eyed young woman of six years ago from her mind. But she was still there.

She applied a pale shade of lipstick and powdered her nose, hoping cosmetics would both give her the appearance of complete competence and disguise the exhaustion still hollowed around her eyes.

Then she left the house and drove to work. When a red brick building came into view, she parked her rusting Cadillac by the alleyway and strolled inside.

Bryson City Travel was the smallest business in town. Despite its grandiose name, Bryson City wasn't the most populous area. Only a handful of the people living in the region possessed the means to travel. Carlotta herself had never even been on an airplane. For the past decade, the humble company had stayed afloat, and employed a dozen workers, with Carlotta and her friend Yvonne among them.

Carlotta settled into her desk in a tidy corner of the office when she arrived inside, then typed rigorously, slamming the keys of her typewriter. When Mr. Anderson, the boss of Bryson City Travel, cast her one of his looks, she took care to be gentler with the machine.

The rest of the morning passed quietly. A few people came in and out to inquire about airfare prices and travel destinations, and the cheerful mailman delivered a couple of parcels and envelopes.

It wasn't until after noon, before Carlotta was readying herself for her lunch break, that Yvonne materialized with an enigmatic expression veiling her pretty features.

"What are you doin' over here? I thought you'd finished lunch and were back to work." Carlotta yawned, fumbling around in her handbag for her tuna sandwich.

"You won't *believe* it!" Yvonne lowered herself to whisper into Carlotta's ear. "A man is waiting outside. He asked for you. From the way he talks, I think he knows you from New York!"

A shiver crawled up Carlotta's spine. Nobody from New York had ever visited before. Nobody had called on the telephone or sent any mail. Nobody was even supposed to know where she and Tony *were.*

Trying to compose herself, she gripped the edges of her work desk. "W-who is he? Did he say his name?"

"No, he didn't." Yvonne frowned, confusion replacing her excitement. "Almost looked like he could be a movie star. Maybe he's one of your past sweethearts, here to sweep you off your feet! Wouldn't that be wonderful?"

Carlotta's hands dropped to reach into her handbag, but she wasn't looking for the tuna sandwich anymore. Being reassured by the cool metal beneath her fingers, she rose to her feet.

Without saying another word to Yvonne, she stole across the office and drew back one section of the blinds to peer through the window.

The back of a man she didn't recognize loomed before her. He wore a casual knitted shirt the same color as her gown and brown shorts—the ideal outfit if he desired to attract as little attention as possible.

Praying for safety, she opened the door and stopped the bell with her fingers so as not to be heard. She remained in the doorway, her other hand groping for the handgun.

If her father or some other *mafioso* had sent a hitman after her, she would not be caught by surprise. Though she didn't believe in violence —she had decided that she preferred peace long ago—she possessed a good enough aim that she could target the man's leg or foot, leaving her with enough time to escape and collect Tony Junior. She had considered the situation many times, in the still of the night when she couldn't sleep, or after a bloodcurdling nightmare had shaken her awake.

She gathered a terse breath, her nostrils flaring. "What do you want?"

The stranger whirled around to face her. "Carlotta."

He swirled in Carlotta's vision like one of the swirly soft serve vanilla ice creams Tony Junior liked to have down by the lake.

At first, she thought she had gone crazy, or the heat had gone to her head, or maybe both.

She blinked to see if he would disappear. He didn't.

"Richard?"

A cautious smile lifted the corners of Richard Morrison's lips, bringing attention to the light in his brown eyes—almost exactly the same shade as the tree trunks sprouting up from the earth behind him.

Before she knew what she was doing, Carlotta threw herself into his arms, clinging to his strong shoulders. Tentatively, he reciprocated the action, letting his arms encircle the width of her frame. It felt like the embrace they had shared when he had left her in Bryson City five years earlier when Carlotta had hoped that he would remain for just a little longer.

They pulled apart at the same time.

"How's little Tony Junior?" Richard asked, gazing down at her with the abundant kindness so typical of him.

"Not as little as when you last saw him." Carlotta returned, feeling her heart stretch. "I have to mend his clothes all the time now. Nothing of his fits for long."

The last time Richard had seen Tony was when he was an infant, still in diapers. When she had gone into labor, Richard had driven Carlotta to the hospital and waited for her until the cries of an infant filled the operating room.

Even though the nurses had been visibly scandalized by the idea of a Black man holding a white infant, Richard was the first to hold little

Tony in his arms, buying him a blue teddy bear from the hospital gift shop. After helping her get settled into her place in Bryson City, Richard had vanished, occasionally checking in by telephone before disappearing.

Richard laughed. "Knowing his mother, I'm sure he's grown into a force to be reckoned with."

Heat crawled up Carlotta's neck, warming her cheeks. She was surprised by the way she reacted to his compliment, how her heart sped up and her hands grew clammy. It was the same reaction she had to Tony as a young teenager—a bundle of feelings and nerves she had not expected to endure again as a working woman and single mother.

You aren't supposed to feel this way about him; she urged herself, angered at the sudden torrent of emotions. *He's just doing his job. Nothing more.*

She recalled the night he had left town.

She had just put Tony to sleep in his cradle—one Richard helped her pick out at the local boutique. She had stood bent against the doorway, watching him as his tall figure climbed into his automobile and waved her off. Before he could pull out of the driveway, she had run through the dewy grass without shoes, only wearing her lace chemise, before pressing a palm to the glass to stop him from leaving.

His eyes had bugged behind his glasses as he unrolled the window. "What's the matter, Mrs. Bellucci?"

"Richard..." Carlotta had held her arms close to her waist to warm herself against the frigid night air. "I wanted to... thank you. For all you've done for us. For everything."

He had taken one hand off the steering wheel to place it over hers. "You're welcome. You'll be just fine. Telephone me whenever you need anything."

Carlotta nodded. She wasn't sure what possessed her next. She kissed him. He had gone rigid at first, but then he had molded his mouth to hers, giving in to the desire swelling between them. She had nearly crawled over the automobile door and thrown herself into his arms—forgetting everything but the yearning to be held by him.

After a few moments, he pulled away, breathless. "Carlotta, I mean, Mrs. Bellucci..."

"I'm sorry," Carlotta had rasped softly, his rejection burning her skin. *What had she been thinking?* "I dunno what got into me. I was... stupid. I..."

"It's not that," Richard interrupted her. "I... I must admit I've felt things for you I haven't felt for years. But I cannot subject you to the kind of pain it would cause us both if we were to be together."

Carlotta nodded.

She knew it was impossible. No matter how much she admired Richard, there could never be anything between them more than innocent flirtation. Not only was it nearly illegal for them to marry, but there were also the glares, the threats, and the mistreatment they would endure as a couple. And she would be putting him in further danger. If her father ever found out...

Being summoned back to the present by the sound of an automobile engine, she swiveled her head towards the storefront so that he wouldn't be able to see her blush. "What's brought you into town?"

Richard circled the sidewalk, positioning his solid frame in front of her. "Maybe it should wait. It's big news, Carlotta, and I don't want to spring everything on you at once."

"No, tell me now." The urgency surging through her invited the old Brooklyn accent to rise back up in Carlotta's voice. If Richard was back now, there had to be something of great importance he needed to tell her.

He nodded, drawing a breath and focussing his gaze upon her.

Yvonne had been right.

He was still handsome enough to be a movie star—with his firm jaw, broad shoulders and stormy brown eyes. But like Carlotta, he had changed in appearance. The skin around his eyes was more creased than it had been before, and care was transcribed onto his brow. Somehow, it only seemed to add to the character of his face—making him even more attractive.

"Your father was arrested."

The words slapped Carlotta out of her study. She recoiled in shock. "What..."

"It turns out the Italian government wasn't pleased with his involvement in a Sicilian town which had been free of crime. He had found himself an old castle and was living there with your mother and brothers, as well as a couple of his old accomplices. Anyway, Italian forces notified the American government of your father's whereabouts, and cooperated in his arrest."

Richard pursed his lips in contemplation. "They played the tape recordings that you, Mr. Siciliano, and Ms. Kelly contributed. They talked to some New York policemen who had been paid off, as well as the widow of Mr. Friedenberg. Don Roberto Mancini is awaiting his verdict as we speak."

His explanation was both simple and thorough, as it had been whenever he had informed her of other matters in the past. Despite his calm and measured tone, the news related drove Carlotta into a cold sweat.

Her knees buckled beneath her. She would have collapsed onto the sidewalk, if not for Richard's firm hand reaching out to support her.

"Why did you come here to tell me this?" Carlotta panicked, folding her hands to her sides. "Do I have to go see him? After what he did?"

Richard's handsome face was full of regret. "I'm afraid so. They want you to be there, along with Mr. and Mrs. Siciliano. To prove that you're behind this thing—that there's a voice to match those tape recordings you gave us all those years ago."

CHAPTER 30

New York City, New York, September 1960:

The air in the courtroom was suffocating.

The malodour of human perspiration and cheap floral perfume seemed to strangle all the oxygen from the room, making Pamela wheeze. Adding to the discomfort of the place was the drawling humidity—resistant to dwindling with the swift arrival of autumn.

Pamela noticed that several of the lawyers were equally frustrated by the physical nuisance that the heat presented, using their notebooks, files, and suit jackets as makeshift fans. Dark pools of sweat-stained their faded white undershirts and blouses as they downed endless cups of lemon water.

She could not see their faces—only the backs of their heads; many of them were bald or losing hair. They had been there when Johnny and she entered, each of them reviewing and discussing what had happened in the previous hearings, their voices increasing in volume and intensity, then falling again, in the typical New York fashion.

When one of the heads turned, piercing blue eyes and neatly groomed brows swarmed before her.

The horror of recognition overcame Pamela. She was staring into the face of Timothy Atwell.

His face was reddened with exertion. Like his lawyer counterparts, he had lost some of his hair. He had gained some weight too—the jowls of his face hanging loose around his crimson chin.

When he caught Pamela's gaze, he stiffened, his eyes sweeping across her frame. She supposed he was wondering what she looked like after the seemingly long passage of time that separated their last meeting and their unexpected reunion.

He was at the bench assigned to Roberto Mancini, who had yet to arrive. Pamela had hardly considered the possibility of Timothy acting in defense of the man—she hadn't even imagined seeing him again.

Pamela loosened her gaze from his face, whispering to Richard who sat at her side. "Is that Timothy Atwell?"

"He's notorious. I think he graduated from some Ivy League school. He's been defending mobsters and their friends ever since, and quite successfully. Many of the cases he shouldn't have won." Richard nodded stiffly, a hint of resentment coloring his voice. "Do you know him?"

Pamela watched Timothy as he combed through a collection of files on the desk before him, a wolflike hunger engulfing his features. "I almost married him."

Without elaborating to ease the shock written across Richard's face, Pamela concentrated instead upon Johnny, who was too nervous to inspect the landscape of the courtroom.

Her husband hadn't been able to think of anything but Don Roberto Mancini's impending verdict for the past weeks. The man had ordered his underlings to whack Johnny many times in the past, as well as sent ominous threats in the mail.

What would they do if the verdict was Roberto's innocence rather than his guilt? Pamela had considered that possibility since the day they had been asked to return to New York for the event. Even if Roberto was sent to jail, he still had friends in high places, and seeing his former protégé after speaking out against him in such a humiliating way would push him over the edge.

And if Roberto didn't cause any trouble, someone else would. Since Roberto Mancini's trial had been brought to public notice, the press had brazenly dubbed Johnny as *the man who squealed.*

Some alleged that he had only agreed to break his oaths to escape criminal prosecution, while still reaping the benefits of the wealth he had accumulated as a made man.

Others brazenly asserted that Pamela had only married Johnny for his monetary value. If they knew the couple spent most of their funds on food and children's supplies for Theresa, they would be sorely disappointed.

Pamela stayed her gloved hand on Johnny's wrist, lacing her fingers through his.

Without turning his head away from the front, he gave her hand a firm squeeze.

She felt his nerves running through him, shaking his fingers. He had insisted that he had a duty to come to the verdict today, despite the perpetual stress plaguing him both day and night. He said he felt obligated to choose the side of justice for the sake of his children.

Pamela's eyes flew to the rounded bump peeking through her pale blue brocade dress, praying that her unborn child wouldn't have to know the unparalleled pain that Johnny's decisions had brought him. At least not until they were old enough.

Theresa was still too young to understand the evil of Johnny's past ways and the men who pursued him, and that was the reason they had tried to hide the trial from her. Thankfully, Lorna—now the owner of a successful Southern restaurant in the heart of the Bronx—had offered to watch over Theresa while the verdict was revealed.

Little Theresa had been quite content to stay in Lorna's care for the time being—preoccupied with her miniature dollhouse and slinky dog. She was an agreeable child, which was a great help to Pamela whenever she was forced to coax Johnny through one of his spells.

The courtroom door crashed open, reeling Pamela's thoughts back to the current.

Each head near the booming noise elicited turned, eyes bulging as Carlotta Mancini strode inside.

She was just as beautiful as ever, with her glossy black hair flipped up in the popular style over her shoulders, and her lips coated in a crimson shimmer. Pamela noticed many of the lawyers ogling her like cartoon wolves, so stunned by her beauty that they failed to remember she was the woman they were contending with.

However, an unnatural ghostlike pallor gilded her high cheekbones, rather than the honey-olive shade that was usually there. She fell to the bench, seating herself between Richard Morrison and Pamela Kelly.

On the inside, Carlotta was numb. She had no recollection of arriving at the courthouse, other than she had heard the hounding voices of reporters and journalists and felt the beam of camera lights warm against her skin.

"Are you Carlotta Mancini?" They had demanded. "The daughter of the mob who dared to speak against her father?"

"What will you say when you see him again?" Another had questioned.

"Do you still love your father? After what he did to your husband?"

"Will you ever speak to your parents after what happened?"

Carlotta had pushed through the deafening crowd of people as she ascended the courthouse stairs. Richard had urged her not to entertain any of the reporters or journalists, explaining that it would do more harm than good.

She didn't have an answer to any of the questions they had asked her. She had spent the night before racking her brain for a grand speech to present to her father on the courtroom steps but had come up dry.

A sigh fell over the courtroom as a wave, and heads turned once again towards the entrance.

Feet were marching in procession, keys jangling in someone's pocket.

The hairs along Carlotta's neck sprang up like a jack-in-the-box. She clutched Richard's hand, straightening her spine as she leaned forward. She could almost feel the burning stare of her father's eyes against the back of her head.

"You don't have to look at him," Richard whispered, reassuring her. "Just pretend he isn't here."

But Carlotta knew she had to look at her father. She had promised herself that she would face him, and search her heart for the forgiveness she had beseeched God for.

Slowly, she angled her gaze to the side, glimpsing her father's enormous form as he swaggered down the path to the front bench. His wide gait hadn't changed—it had been that way when they walked the pier together at Coney Island. He had gained some weight from the likely extravagant food consumed while back in Sicily.

Behind him, a young man with an angular face and dark hair trudged like a downtrodden soldier, his eyes rimming the room.

When Carlotta recognized the young man as her kid brother Louis, she suppressed a wail that rose within her. He had grown much taller and lost some of the baby fat he had carried well into adolescence, but his distinctive mannerisms gave him away. The side of his mouth still twisted into a knot and his shoulders bunched when he was perplexed.

The rest of her brothers trailed Louis, and Carlotta's chest hurt when she realized they would go into the family business just as her father had at their age if they hadn't already.

She wished she could leap up out of her seat and rescue them then—tell them they could live with her and continue their schooling for as long as they wanted. She scarcely had enough money to support herself and Tony Junior, but she would do anything she could to save her siblings from her father's trap.

Carlotta felt her heart rupture when her mother faltered past her. The woman in front of her was stooped and transformed by age—her pretty brown eyes hooded with wrinkles and worry. Her hair was no longer dyed and styled, as it had been since Carlotta's childhood, but straight and white down her back.

Lorenzo's wife Victoria had her arm looped through Isabella's, her hair fashioned in a chic beehive, her slender limbs clothed in a flowing paisley dress. After all these years, she was still enduring her husband's philandering, Carlotta marveled. When she passed Carlotta, she visibly steered the frail woman away, toward the front of the courtroom.

"Mamma..." Carlotta whimpered, feeling like a little girl desperate for her mother's affection.

When the ghost of Isabella Mancini raised her gaze, love for her daughter overcame her. "*Vita mia*!"

Carlotta leapt to her feet and the two women flew towards one another. Isabella clutched her daughter like something precious she had lost but finally recovered.

"Mamma... I am sorry..."

"My baby..." Isabella whispered in English, tears veining her cheeks. "You are all grown up."

Carlotta smiled, wiping the tears from her face with a Kleenex. She wanted to remind her mother she had grown up a long time ago. She hadn't been a child since the day she had mistakenly found her father's gun.

"Where is my grandson?" Isabella asked through tears, peering intently into her daughter's face.

Carlotta was surprised by her mother's question. She hadn't been aware that any of her family knew about Tony Junior. But if Isabella Mancini knew, Don Roberto did too. Her gut twisted when she imagined how her father knew, but she was so happy to see her mamma that she couldn't dwell on the thought.

"He's at home. My work friend Yvonne is taking care of him." Carlotta squeezed her mother's hand softly. "I want you to come over sometime to meet him, Ma. He is so kind and learns things real fast. He's asked about you and Brooklyn."

Isabella used her scarf to wipe the tears from her cheeks. "God willing. I want to see him with all of my heart."

"Then you should, Mamma." Carlotta squeezed her mother's hands. "Whenever you can. Come visit us."

"Isabella, come. Your husband is waiting." Victoria's sharp voice interrupted their reunion, and she groped Isabella's thin arm with a fisted hand. Her sneer fell on Carlotta but then skated above her—as if trying to ignore her existence.

Isabella gave Carlotta one last kiss before following Victoria to their handcuffed husbands.

Pamela could scarcely pay attention while the verdict was being read. As the word guilty was announced, a rush of cool air passed over

her. The courtroom became still and deathly quiet as if frozen in time, then a cacophony of noise erupted. Shouts, curses, lamentations, and hollers pierced the air.

Johnny embraced her, folding her to his chest as he wept tears of joy.

Roberto's cronies left their seats, marching up to the judge to plead innocence. One man even swiped a wad of cash through the air to barter for Roberto's release.

Roberto's face remained devoid of expression. His pale blue eyes pressed into them from across the room as he was led away in shackles.

And suddenly, it was quiet again.

Carlotta and Richard returned to his automobile with Isabella Mancini at their side. Johnny whispered he expected an engagement between the daughter of the mob and the federal agent before long. They would have to marry in a state that allowed their union, but Pamela was sure the determined pair could make a good life together.

The flash of cameras illuminated their pleased expressions, but they answered few questions.

Johnny led Pamela out of the stately courthouse and to their own automobile, keeping her hand in his as he sang a love ballad.

They drove until night blackened the sky, and the New York City lights bounced off the Hudson River.

Glossary

In order of appearance:

La Cosa Nostra - Italian for our way or our thing, refers to the Sicilian mafia where each "family" is given sovereignty over a specific area or territory in which they control criminal activities such as overseeing rackets.

Made man - Someone who has been sworn into the mob, usually having participated in an induction ceremony. Made men are supposed to be of Italian descent.

Bog-trotter - Slang or derogatory term for an Irishman.

Da - Irish slang for "Dad"

Beatnik - A person who ascribed to the beat literary movement; rejecting conventional society during the 1950s and 1960s in exchange for freedom of artistic expression.

Jitters - To be nervous or uneasy.

Howdy - Hello

Focus your audio - Listen carefully

Pearl diver - A person who washes dishes (a dishwasher)

Greasy spoon - An inexpensive American diner, sometimes known as being cheap and unsanitary

Wop - A derogatory word used for Italians

Maliocch' - The evil eye

Ganol' - Italian American slang word for cannoli (a type of Italian dessert)

Grazie - Thank you, thanks

Madre - Mother

Padre - Father

Boss - The head of the mafia Family and the person in charge of making the most important decisions

Underboss - The second-in-command of the mafia Family and in charge of commanding units to carry out murders and other crimes

Consigliere - Meaning "counselor," provides a channel of communication between the Boss and Underboss and the capos and soldiers

Capo - A lesser leader within the mafia Family of a crew of soldiers

Caporegime - More significant group leaders

Mamma - Mom

Papà - Dad

Maddiul' - Fool/Rascal

Lascialui - Leave him alone

Big tickle - To laugh at the expense of the victim

Classy chassis - Great body

Jelly roll - A type of greaser hairstyle popular in the 1950s

Baby - Term of endearment for a girl

Dame - A beautiful woman

Mafioso - A member of the mafia

Dough - Money

Phonograph - A record player that uses vibration to play sounds, invented by Thomas Edison in 1877

Bambina - Little girl

Spaghett' - Italian American slang word for spaghetti (pasta)

Figlia mia - My daughter

Famiglia - Italian word for family

Frutta martorana - Traditional marzipan treats usually associated with the states of Palermo and Messina, Sicily

Sesenta fame? - Do you feel hungry?/Are you hungry?

Amore mio - My love

Doll - Term of endearment for a girl

Cast an eyeball - Look (over there)

Aduzipazz! - You're crazy!

Racketeering - Associated with organized crime; obtaining or extorting money illegally through control of a business or enterprise

Loan sharking - Making illegal loans at an extremely high interest rate

Hijacking - Seizing control of something (a vehicle, a place, a shipment) by force

Groovy beat - Good song

Wallflower - Usually refers to a girl standing by the wall at a dance/ A girl not dancing

Fella - Man/Boy

Ballad - Love song

Crooner - A type of male singer, often singing love songs in a sentimental fashion, e.g. Frank Sinatra, Perry Como, and Gene Austin

Scram - Go away/Get out of here

The fuzz - The police

In a jiffy - In a short time/Quickly

Facciabrutt' - Ugly face

Medigan' - non-Italian American/Italian who has lost his roots

I Love Lucy - A sitcom television show massively popular throughout the United States of America starring and focussing upon comedian Lucille Ball, running from 1951-1957

Giamocc' - Idiot

Whack - Kill

Peachy - Fine/Good (as in "I'm just fine")

Disgraziat' - An Italian American insult meaning dirt ball

Gumad - Mistress/Girlfriend

White Christmas - A 1954 American musical movie starring Bing Crosby and filmed in Technicolor

Folks - Parents

Pops - Informal term for a father or dad

Gin mill cowboy - A bar regular (beat slang)

Zonk in the head - A bad thing (beat slang)

Cucciolo - Term of endearment meaning pet (As in "my little pet")

Bambino - Term of endearment for a young male child, like the female version "bambina"

Passerotto - Term of endearment meaning "young sparrow/bird"

Dagos - An insulting term for a person of Spanish or Italian origin, derived from the common Spanish name Diego

Uncle Sam - A common personification for the United States with a patriotic sentiment, often found in war recruitment advertisements

Black dagos - A racist term pertaining to the fact that Italians are presumed to be of partially African descent

Ammonini! - Let's go!

Andosh! - Let's go!

Cercatore d'oro - Italian for gold-digger

Cornuto - Husband whose wife is unfaithful

Pilazza - Palace

Calabres' - Calabrian (Calabrese); can refer to people, objects, customs, etc.

Knockout - Good-looking/Beautiful

Circled - Married

Tesoro mio - My treasure

Golly - Used as a mild exclamation for wonder, amazement, shock, etc.

Ghiacchieron' - Blabbermouth

What gives? - What's happening?/What's going on?

Interviewing my brains - Thinking

Posso aiutarla? - Can I help you?

Buongiorno - A phrase of address meaning good afternoon, good morning or hello

Che fai? - What are you doing?

Vita mia - Literally means my life. A way to address someone very dear to you.

Acknowledgements

I would like to thank my family and friends for their neverending support and encouragement. Their time and kindness has been invaluable.

I would also like to thank the many online readers who have inspired me to keep writing, even when it was difficult. I am especially indebted to those first few readers who left positive comments and constructive criticism when I was beginning my work as a young author.

Additional sources that helped me with the research for *Daughter of the Mob* include:

American Italian, https://americanitalian.net/.

Bisbort, Alan. *Beatniks: A Guide to an American Subculture.* Greenwood Press, 2010.

Dexter, Lucius D. *History of Brooklyn.* Queens County Historical Society, 1996.

Richardson, Martha E. *The Italian-American Mafia: Liquor, Drugs, and Values in an Empire.* 2001.

Skinner, Tina. *Fashionable Clothing from the Sears Catalogs: Mid 1950s.* Schiffer Pub., 2002.

Most importantly, I would like to thank the author of my life, Jesus Christ, who has been my best friend and the crutch I've needed. This book—and so much more—would not have been possible without Him.

About the Author

Writing under a pen name, Ilana holds a Bachelor of Arts in History from the University of British Columbia, where she took numerous English literature and creative writing courses. She enjoys nothing more than imagining and writing the lives of historical women.

You can find more of her work on Wattpad under the username @purplejeans, where she won a 2020 Watty Award for her French-Canadian historical fiction book, *Daughters of the King*. Follow her on Instagram @purplejeanswriter for updates!

Did you enjoy this book? Please leave a review!

As a young self-published author, it can be difficult to promote my books. Please consider supporting me by leaving a review of *Daughter of the Mob* on Amazon or Goodreads. Simply use the QR code here to post your review:

Made in United States
Troutdale, OR
01/02/2024

16633458R00199